I0771442

DAWN OF THE DEMON

THE CROOKED TALES SERIES

In reading order:

The Rising

Night Of The Witch

Children Of The Shadows

Dawn Of The Demon

The Reckoning

(Coming: June 2026)

DAWN OF THE DEMON

CROOKED TALES
BOOK FOUR

CHRIS HARRISON

WICKED INK

PUBLISHING

Dawn Of The Demon (Crooked Tales Series) : Book 4
Copyright © 2025 by Chris Harrison

Published by Wicked Ink Publishing Ltd.
www.wickedinkpublishing.com

Cover and book design © 2025 by Wicked Ink Publishing Ltd.
Editors: Raymond Griffiths & Adam Bamford

First Edition: October 2025
Printed in Canada

Library and Archives Canada Cataloguing in Publication

Title: Dawn of the demon / Chris Harrison.
Names: Harrison, Chris, author.
Description: Series statement: Crooked tales ; book 4
Identifiers: Canadiana (print) 20250259435
Canadiana (ebook) 20250260336
ISBN 9781998278350 (softcover)
ISBN 9781998278367 (EPUB)
Subjects: LCGFT: Horror fiction. | LCGFT: Novels.
Classification: LCC PZ7.1.H377 Daw 2025 | DDC j823/.92—dc23

For Wes and John

Forged from darkness, driven by rage…

DAWN OF THE DEMON

PROLOGUE

THE TANGERINE POP-UP TENT WAS HOT AND STICKY AS the two brothers lay sandwiched together like sardines in its clammy nylon confines.

It was a muggy August evening in Cold Christmas, with neither boy given a chance to cool down from their hike through the forest before being hurriedly shipped off to bed.

Now the hazy yellow glow of their battery-powered nightlight illuminated the condensation collecting on the tent's pitched walls as it gently swayed back and forth from the solitary strut overhead. They were here for a glimpse of the blood moon, among other things, and as the muffled sounds of their parents' tipsy chatter continued to coast along the warm summer breeze outside, Isaac silently schemed.

He was waiting for bedtime all afternoon. A chance to pay his kid brother back for a day of incessant whining and complaining. So what if he was only in first grade. He needed to be taught a lesson. Isaac waited for the wine to kick in, as it always did.

Every Saturday night was exactly the same, his mum

and dad guzzling their way through as many bottles as they could before bedtime, only to both pass out blind drunk on the sofa and sleep through most of Sunday.

Their impromptu family camping trip showed every sign of following the same self-sabotaging ritual. Isaac even helped carry the big bag of booze from the car when they unpacked and set up for the night. Enough alcohol to sink a ship. Another half-hour and it would just be him and his baby brother, alone in the woods.

He heard the story from Derrick Jordan during the last week of school and was saving it up for a moment just like this, to scare the bejesus out of his snivelling excuse for a sibling. With just enough well-timed kicks and nudges spread throughout the evening to keep his cellmate awake, this was his chance. It was finally showtime.

"Did you hear that?" He whispered, sitting up in his sleeping bag to a cacophony of rustling polyester.

"Huh...wh..." His brother was still half-asleep, exhausted from all his whinging, no doubt.

"What if it's the demon?" Isaac gulped in mock fear.

"Demon?"

Another murmur of rumpling polyester rippled through the tent and set Isaac's teeth on edge as his brother sat up with a start. He hated the grating sound. In fact, he hated everything about camping.

From the stink of perspiration clogging his lungs to the flimsy sleeping mat slowly numbing his backside. Camping was for losers and given the choice, he would much rather stayed home to play his shiny new Sega Megadrive in the comfort of his own bedroom.

"What demon?" His brother pressed with a look of worry etched across his pasty little face.

"A long time ago, not far from here, in a place called Crooked House, a boy was born without a soul..."

"What's a soul?" Issac rolled his eyes and sighed. He would need to dumb his story down a little for his halfwit brother.

"Everyone is born with a soul...it's what makes us human. But this boy was different. He was born a monster, pure evil, with eyes black as night and a heart made of stone." As Issac continued recounting the urban myth, he realized what he rehearsed would have made a much bigger impression on someone closer to his own age.

"Shh..." He signalled for his brother to be quiet as he cocked an ear to the tent wall.

"Did you hear that? I think someone is outside...or something..." His brother let out a whimper as he cowered beneath the cover of his sleeping bag, but Isaac could tell he already had him hooked.

"I...I can't hear anything..." His brother whispered, trembling as his bright blue eyes darted from wall to wall in search of the phantom sound.

"Maybe you should just go back to sleep...you're too young to hear the rest of the story anyway...I'll get in trouble." Isaac slowly reeled him in.

"Please...I promise I won't tell on you..." His brother begged. This was all too easy.

"Ok, but we need to be very quiet, otherwise the demon might hear and come for us both...ok?" His brother nodded feverishly, so Isaac carefully unhooked the nightlight and held it under his chin for spooky effect.

"It was the night of a blood moon, just like tonight, and the demon's parents were on the run from the church. A priest who lost his faith and his heart to a woman who worshipped the devil. With the woman heavily pregnant, they stopped at Crooked House for the night to get a good meal and some rest, but the moment they checked in, the woman went into labour...er...I mean, she started having her baby."

"W...why were they running?" His brother's quivering voice leaked through the slender gap in his sleeping bag as he peered out in terror.

"The church knew she was chosen to carry the demon inside her...and they knew the demon's birth would mark the beginning of the end."

"End of what?"

"The end of the world. For you, me, our parents... everyone. All of us condemned to a gruesome and painful death..."

"*Crack!*"

Isaac flinched at the sharp sound of a branch snapping outside and listened for his parents' voices. He was so preoccupied with scaring his brother, he didn't even notice their drunken murmurs get swallowed by the whispering wind gently caressing the edges of their tent.

Perhaps the fresh air helped them on their way to tomorrow's hangover. He paused a moment longer to be sure they weren't eavesdropping and then resumed his story.

"With no hospital nearby, and no-one to call for help, the priest was forced to deliver the baby himself, right there in Crooked House. Room 4 was where it all went down. People say the demon tore his mother in two as he clawed his way out. A wild animal full of fury. She died right there and then, screaming in agony as she bled out over the floor... but the house just soaked it all up. Drinking every last drop through the cracks in its stony ground."

"*Snap!*"

Another noise rang out nearby, and Isaac wondered if he was freaking himself out telling the demon's story so close to where it all happened. Again, he waited, convincing himself it was a nosy animal drawn to the curious orange glow of their tent in the night.

"Wh...why didn't the priest save her?" His brother urged him on, still wriggling on the hook.

"He couldn't...he was too terrified to even try. You see, the baby was so wicked...so evil...that anyone who looked into its eyes, even for a couple of seconds, found themselves compelled to do terrible things. It was as if he could get inside a person's head and fill it with his nasty whispers. Murder...suicide...these were all things the demon could force someone to do with nothing more than a thought...so the priest ran out of Crooked House as fast as his legs would carry him and was never seen again. Some say he was caught by the church and forced to spend the rest of his days locked in a dungeon, like a dirty secret swept under the rug for the crimes he committed against God. Others say he never made it out of these woods, and that the demon wasn't the only monster prowling Cold Christmas that night..."

"Wh...wh...what other monster...and what ha... happened to the demon?" Isaac struggled to contain the smirk worming its way across his lips as his gullible brother stuttered his way right into his hands.

"Didn't you know? This whole place is haunted, and not just by ghosts either, but monsters too. It's like a magnet, attracting every evil force known to man. There are dark and deadly creatures here; the stuff of nightmares...lurking in the shadows. They only ever come out at night, looking to feed on lost hitchhikers and tourists. The monsters found the demon and raised him as their own, turning him into the ultimate killing machine. Didn't mum or dad tell you? The house we passed on our walk, that's Crooked House...that's where the demon was born. That's *his* home and these are *his* woods we're camped in...this is where he butchered all those kids..."

"Wh...what k...ids? St...stop it Isaac...stop it y...you're scaring me..." His brother pleaded, but Issac wasn't about to let him off that easy.

"There were five victims that people know of at least... five children, brutally murdered; their bodies never found. Come to think of it, they were all about your age. It's said their tortured souls still roam these woods at night and if you listen, you can hear their desperate cries for help...Wait! Did you hear that?" Isaac turned his head and whispered out of sight.

"*Help meeeee...help meeeee...*"

"St...stop...please!" His brother begged.

"The police never caught him, you know...they said he was like a ghost, able to drift into children's houses while everyone was sleeping and snatch them from their beds without ever being seen. A real-life boogeyman: 6'5" of solid muscle, with lethal metal fangs, he sharpened himself to take bites out of each of his victims. Now he haunts Crooked House, where his story began. On the night of the blood moon, like tonight, he wanders the woods in search of little boys to murder in their beds. Feeding on their souls to fill his own empty void..."

"*Crack!*"

"That's him now...coming to get you!"

"Argh!" His brother's high-pitched scream was enough to wake the dead, let alone their parents.

Isaac would be in for it now for sure, but it was worth every penny, just to see the little brat's expression riddled with fear; his bottom lip quivering uncontrollably as tears streamed down his miserable face.

"Hahahaha..." Isaac laughed as his brother teetered on the brink of hysteria and bawled his way deeper inside his sleeping bag.

He was bound to wet the bed again after that little episode. Pathetic little pissy pants.

"*Crack.*"

Another sound rang out somewhere beyond the amber afterglow and Isaac glanced up at the tent entrance to find a shadowy figure looming over them.

"Sorry dad..." He yelled out to avoid the inevitable drunken lecture.

To his surprise, the murky silhouette remained silent before wandering back toward his parents' tent. Maybe this time he had too much booze to even bother pretending that he cared. Meanwhile, his brother's steady sobbing continued to suck all the air out of their tawny hellhole.

"Knock it off will you!" Isaac barked, "You're such a baby..."

Not only did he scare his brother shitless, but now, with his parents' sozzled apathy, he also had carte blanche to be as mean as he wanted whilst bullying him back into silence.

"Shut up, you little shit!" He snarled, reaching across and shoving the side of his brother's face. He muted his racket immediately, dialling his cries down to a subdued sniffle.

"*Crack...*"

Another sound echoed in the woods outside, this time behind them, and Isaac stopped his tormenting to listen more closely. If that was an animal, then it had to be as big as a bear.

"*Snap!*"

An ice-cold tremor scuttled its way up Isaac's spine, stealing his breath away, as the strange noise struck again, closer this time.

"Wh...who's there?" His brother whimpered.

"It's just dad...I think..." Isaac snapped, ashamed of the knot of dread tightening in his throat.

"Or mum maybe. They're just drunk, as always. I better check, though. The last thing we want is another fire, especially out here." Isaac grimaced as he clambered out of his sleeping bag.

God, he hated camping. Despite giving himself the creeps, he figured this might be another opportunity to push things further. If he made his brother shit himself, then that would be something he could gloat about forever. That was the holy grail of pranks.

"I'll be right back..." He said, unzipping the tent and venturing out into the dark.

The woods were eerily still as he crept towards his parents' cobalt blue tent, and the air was still thick from the blistering afternoon sun. All Isaac could hear was the dampened crackles of their smouldering campfire as its thin trail of smoke casually snaked its way up into the night sky just ahead of him.

The absence of any flames made it hard to see, but beneath the moonlight, he could just about discern the outline of his parents' fold-up camping chairs on the opposite side of their tent. As his eyes adjusted to the gloom, he saw they both had their backs to him, a parent slumped in each, no doubt tanked-up and comatose.

"Mum? Dad?" He whispered as he approached, but as always, they remained oblivious.

Feeling around in the opening of their tent, Isaac grabbed the pocket torch. They made a point of showing him and his brother where they kept it when they arrived. Its metal handle felt cool to the touch and a welcome relief to the oppressive humidity.

"*Click.*"

He switched it on at its base and released a brilliant shaft of light that bounced off his bare feet as he stood in the dried-out dirt.

"Mum? Dad?" He called out again, not wanting to dazzle them with the beam.

When again he heard no answer, he slowly guided the torch along the ground towards where they were sitting.

The moment Isaac realized something was seriously awry his brain pleaded with him to stop, but his hand refused to listen, shakily following the trail of violence and gore all the way up from the glistening, blood-stained grass to the mutilated corpses slouched lifelessly in their canvas chairs. Both parents brutally murdered, smashed in like paper mâché dolls.

Their viciously crushed skulls cast jagged silhouettes like craggy clifftops under the ambient moon, and although fighting back bile, Isaac felt compelled to ogle their grisly remains.

Forcing his torch higher, what he thought was the moist evening air sticking in the back of his throat turned out to be the coppery stench of death as fragments of bone and cartilage slinked down his parents' hideously crumpled faces.

Swept to shore on streams of viscous blood oozing from their collapsed and busted craniums, the shimmering carnage slowly soaked into the ground, quenching the parched grass beneath them with gloopy claret.

"Yak!...Kaff kaff..."

Unable to keep his dinner down any longer, Isaac puked

his guts up all over his feet, filling the gaps between his toes with slimy chunks of carrot and sweetcorn. Staggering backwards, he tripped over his parents' tent peg and sent his torch skidding under a nearby bush. Its revolving light turned the campsite into a silent disco of death as he frantically clambered back to his feet and ran.

Isaac only made it a couple of yards when he collided with an immovable object in the dark that sent him tumbling back towards the dirt. With barely any time to think or react, he was grabbed by the scruff of his neck and ferociously hoisted up into the air by a herculean hand that felt arctic to the touch. Spun round like a rag-doll, Issac came face to face with his aggressor and his blood immediately turned to ice.

There, just as Derrick Jordan described in his story, stood the demon of Cold Christmas. The towering hulk of a man blocked out the moon with his burly frame. A face barely visible in the shadow of the trees, all Isaac saw was a ghostly aura as his shock of white hair caught the moon's gaze behind him.

Somewhere, deep in the fathomless dark, he thought he glimpsed a twinkle from his serrated steel fangs, but everything beyond that was inky black.

Kicking and screaming, Issac tried in vain to escape his attacker, but it was as if the monster was carved from granite.

"I...Isaac..." Over his shoulder he heard his brother call out above the clamour, and almost in response Isaac was flipped around to face him.

The killer's icy palms slammed against either side of his head like a clamp and lifted him even higher off the ground as his brother watched wide-eyed from below, rooted to the spot like a rabbit in the headlights. Then the demon squeezed.

"Argh!" Isaac's blood-curdling cry echoed through the forsaken forest as he felt the pressure quickly build inside his head.

Ears cupped by the killer's crushing hands, the dying seconds of his life played out like a silent movie, with only the muffled whisper of a distant breeze whirring through the canals of his mind, dancing to the beat of his floundering heart.

A warm trickle of blood snaked its way from his nose onto his lips, followed by an almighty *crack* as his skull splintered beneath the force of the demon's grip. All the while, his brother stared at him, shell-shocked and mesmerized by the sickening brutality.

"*Pop!*"

A sudden release of pressure and Isaac's dwindling vision abruptly narrowed to his left. Somewhere beyond the tingling numbness and excruciating pain now engulfing him, he felt something warm and wet flop onto his squashed cheek.

The evening wind agonizingly whistled its way into his gaping socket as the rest of his head collapsed in on itself, and the last image ever to be seared into Isaac Grady's squelched brain was that of his brother Silas, cradling a glistening, gelatinous eyeball in his hands with a twisted look of satisfaction.

I

The door to St Peter's was a bottleneck of panic as they bundled their way through its narrow archway and spilled out into the tenebrous graveyard.

A bracing gust of ice-cold air slapped Meridia in the face as she made it into the night, but it did nothing to shake the smell of sulphur from her nose. The horseman's malevolent stench still clung to her airways, crawling into the back of her throat, just as it crawled into their temporary refuge. The nefarious harbingers were relentless and inevitable.

Wherever Meridia and her friends ran, their long dark shadow always found them, even here, on hallowed ground.

Outside, the church's celestial stained-glass glow coalesced with the flickering pale-yellow streetlamp, painting the hotchpotch of crumbling headstones and low hanging mist a protean pistachio green. There was no sound from the surrounding neighbourhood, only their own panicked breathing and the creeping silence of dread skulking behind them in their wake.

Once again, they found themselves on the run, but this time, there was nowhere left to go.

"It looks like Return of the Living Dead out here..." JJ remarked, as the eerie setting stopped them all in their tracks.

"We need to get to the cars..." Peter gasped, rekindling the urgency of their ill-prepared exodus.

"If the horsemen know we're here, the Children of the Shadows won't be far behind..." Racing to the end of the winding stone path, he gripped the knotted bars of the rusty iron gate and gave it a shove.

"*Creeeeak!*"

Digging its heals into the ground, the stubborn metal frame scraped against the unyielding slabs of sandstone and soaked up Peter's strength until finally, he forced it open. Just enough for them to squeeze through.

Even the church was conspiring against them, and as Meridia reached the pearly memorial of a guardian angel, the subtle shadows seemed to curl its sombre stare into a smirk.

Following Kane and JJ toward their only exit, Meridia found the marshy ground between each tombstone sodden and spongy, absorbing every laboured trudge and turning her legs to lead.

Lumbering behind her, she heard Zach getting flustered by their slow progress, but beyond him, her mother was now nowhere to be seen. She was right there with them just a second ago, last out the door. As Meridia scoured the murky cemetery, to no avail, her initial pang of worry hardened into fear.

"Wait..." Peter startled her, his voice fracturing as he came to a sudden halt and stooped low between the jaws of the church gate.

"Oh god...no..." He pitched around to face them, punch drunk on shock and cradling a lifeless child in his arms: Izzy.

Scrawny and frail, her limbs dangled limply like wilted spaghetti, and at first glance, Meridia thought she was sleeping. Until she saw her neck.

A flash of crimson rippled beneath the glow of the streetlamp and danced along a grisly gully spanning the width of Izzy's throat. Someone brutally hacked her jugular to the bone, leaving her head hanging by a slender scrap of pasty white skin.

"Nooo!" Meridia screamed and tried to run to her, but couldn't move.

The undergrowth tangled her feet. Glancing down at the shadows gripping her ankles, she found not foliage, but a throng of fetid skeletal hands, clawing at her heels and dragging her down towards their shallow graves.

"*Kaff...gurgle...*"

Struggling to keep her balance, she glanced back up at Peter and found him rigid with shock and his jade eyes bulging in disbelief. A blood-streaked blade jutted from his throat like a grotesque metal tongue, slavering his sweater with lustrous vermillion.

"*Squelch...*"

The knife retracted back through Peter's ruptured Adam's apple, and he succumbed to gravity, slumping face-first onto the stones and burying Izzy's body beneath his.

A hooded disciple emerged from the shadows in Peter's absence, their long, tattered robes billowing in the breeze and their face shrouded in darkness. Wiping the blade clean in their palm, they marched through the open gate towards Kane and JJ, stepping over Peter's crumpled body without even breaking stride.

"Run!"

Meridia's scream trailed off into a whimper as the deadly assassin's knife, sharp as a guillotine, carved a dazzling arc through the air with unstoppable force, slashing both boys' throats in a single strike. Kane and JJ fell to their knees in unison.

A chorus of gurgling gasps bubbling from their mouths as they both clutched their necks. Scarlet rivulets erupted from between their fingers, spraying the church path and filling its trenches with blood as they both finished their descent and flopped to the ground with a sickening thud.

The nauseating sound made Meridia buckle at the knees in sympathy; unable to bear the weight of her crushing loss as both boys bled out. Limbs still twitching beneath the sallow streetlight.

With the persistence of the terminator, the deadly disciple robotically wiped their blade once more and resumed their death-march until they came to a jarring halt in front of her. Even up close, their face remained a mystery, an unfathomable void, cloaked in shadows.

There was something strangely familiar about the way they moved, and their scent as it wafted toward her on the winter wind. Lemon and mint. The disciple's bloodstained fingers curled around the edges of their hood and drew it back in one smooth motion to reveal her treacherous mother, Emily Wilson, appearing less like her older sister and more like an evil doppelgänger from an alternate timeline.

Wearing a wicked sneer on her pale freckled face, she resembled a vampire. Her eyes sparkling like sapphires beneath the flickering glow overhead.

Glaring at her daughter, she cuffed her mouth and smeared a jagged crimson streak across her lips, completing her terrifying transformation from doting mother to blood-sucking monster.

A pathetic rasp rattled from Meridia's lips as the scream she was searching for stuck in her throat. She tried to stumble back towards the church, but despite their brittle bones, the horde of undead hands held firm with unnatural strength.

Chained to a sinking ship, she twisted around in search of Zach, hoping he had the sense to run, then felt the last threads of hope unravel inside her and drift away on the evening breeze. Zach stood trembling in the shadows, his eyes brimming with tears as he sniffed and sobbed, an inaudible garble of anguish and heartbreak at the horrors that unfolded in the bloodstained churchyard. Towering behind him, the Demon of Cold Christmas in all his hulking glory, with a knife pressed firmly to her best friend's throat.

"Let him go!" Meridia pleaded, then she felt her mother's blade at her back.

A spiteful prod, pricking her spine with just enough malice to silence her.

Forged from granite, the infamous child killer was even more terrifying than Meridia imagined: an immovable wall of muscle and menace.

Pale, translucent skin clung to his snarling, raw-boned face as he scowled at her through soulless eyes, black as coal. A shock of white hair crowned his angular head, and his jaws were home to a slash of razor-sharp steel, with each tooth a glinting blade.

"Fate has marked your card, child...and now your time is up." His voice was a guttural rasp from the depths of hell, intertwined with the whispering screams of all his victims.

The ominous words slithered through her thoughts like

toxic déjà vu. Each sneering syllable, revealing the poisonous residue of a recurring dream that tattooed itself on her soul.

As Meridia scrambled to catch up with the grisly fait accompli, the demon beat her to the post, delivering his sickening punchline as a whisper of serrated steel sliced through Zach's throat.

2

Meridia bolted upright in bed with a trembling gasp. Three nights have passed since Izzy's disappearance, and on each one of those nights, she suffered the same ominous vision. No matter how hard she tried to alter the outcome, it always ended in a bloodbath of tragedy.

She missed Izzy beyond words, and although the full ramifications of her sacrifice were yet to reveal themselves, her rumoured death screamed the loudest in a muddled mind jampacked with shock revelations and heartache. Now Meridia spent her waking hours replaying that fateful night over and over in her head, ruminating on all the things she could have done differently to avoid the strangling reality she was now left with.

Izzy was gone and might never come back. What tore her apart the most was the fact she was all alone. Throughout the highs and lows of her belief, Meridia always assumed that win or lose, they would always be together at the very end.

It seemed foolish now, a childish fantasy fuelled by

fairytales and Peter's pep talks. What a curse her gift was. The unfathomable power of a seer rendered completely useless by a bitter old pensioner on her deathbed.

Bleary-eyed, Meridia glanced around the insipid grey walls of the room she now called a home and took in a deep breath of its ventilated air. Her heart sank as the subtle aroma of mildew stuck in her throat and reminded her of where she was.

Hiding underground in a decommissioned bunker with a ragtag bunch of strangers she still wasn't sure she could trust. It still seemed too convenient.

The way Grace was waiting for them all to emerge from St Peter's, engine running and ready to whisk them away to safety. Zach said they should try to stay positive and be grateful they weren't alone anymore, but something about the timing of it all stunk.

She remembered Father Alexander once telling them all he didn't believe in coincidence, and that night was the mother of all coincidences in her view.

The demise of Valerie, Izzy's abduction, the horsemen's return and, to top it all off, the devastating revelation of her mother's duplicity. Her own flesh and blood, a lying and conniving member of the Children of the Shadows.

As the argument spilled into the churchyard, Grace immediately supported Kane's wild and venomous accusation. The remnants of Meridia's past were ripped away, leaving her desperately clutching at straws.

"Grr..." Meridia felt a swell of anger rise in her throat, prickling her skin as she thought about her mum, her supposed best friend, now incarcerated somewhere down here while the adults figured out what to do with her.

How could she lie like that? It was all JJ and Peter could

do to drag Kane off her and who could blame him, given what they knew now?

Of course, she denied it at first, playing innocent. But when Grace wrestled her to the ground and slapped her in zip-ties it didn't take long for the truth to spill out over the frosty grass. To think her whole abduction was just a roose to distance herself from all the other disgraced parents. A ploy to infiltrate the group and win everyone's trust.

No wonder she kept banging on about calling the police. It all made sense now, and as the pieces continued to fall into place, she couldn't help but wonder what role her dad played in all this.

Was he really the monster he was made out to be, or just another victim ensnared by her mum's web of lies?

Riled, Meridia threw the covers back and swung her legs out of bed. So many unanswered questions crowded her sparse boxroom that it now felt suffocating. She needed fresh air, not the poor-quality ventilation system they all endured since arriving. Meridia wanted to feel the winter breeze on her flustered cheeks.

Gasping as she touched down on the chilly concrete floor with bare feet, she soon took comfort in its icy embrace, allowing the sudden shock to unravel her knotted brain and offer a brief respite from the crippling burden she now carried. She wondered what time it was, fumbling under the bed for her phone.

There was no signal down here, another concern, and it was impossible to tell night from day. Her only sign was the occasional chorus of inaudible whispers echoing down the corridor whenever the adults assembled at 9pm to conceive a way out of this nightmare.

Tapping her phone awake, the giant neon clock dazzled

Meridia as it cut through the gloom and screamed 8am. It was time to get up and face the day.

Grace and Peter should have returned from their late-night recon mission by now and, hopefully, they had something positive to share.

God knows they all needed a lift.

3

Kane rolled over in his bunk bed and squinted through the gloom to see if JJ was awake. Wrestling with yet another bout of cabin fever, he needed someone to talk to before his brain turned against him completely.

So far, the days were just fine with plenty of odd jobs and new people to occupy his mind, but the nights were a genuine struggle. The second the lights went out and the chatter subsided, he sensed the drab concrete walls slowly close in on him and suck all the synthesized air from their windowless digs.

On the one occasion he nodded off before the others, he gasped for breath in the early hours, having relived all the gruesome horrors they suffered at the hands of Valerie. He was tired of it now, both mentally and physically, which is why his heart sank the moment he realized JJ was still fast asleep.

Above him, he could hear Zach fidgeting and mumbling in the top bunk, no doubt being terrorized by his own ghastly experiences from the latest in a long line of brushes

23

with death. Even after her demise, Valerie continued to haunt them.

He saw her ghost from time to time, lurking in the shadows of the murky bunker they now called home. She would always glare at him with eyes like frozen flames, cold and relentless, burning through the inky darkness and chilling him to the bone. Not the smug little brat that gleefully reached into their deepest, darkest fears and forged them into weapons.

Instead, the monster he glimpsed now was the withered husk that lay clinging to life in her hospital bed, emaciated and full of malice. Unblinking, she silently bore holes into him with those ungodly white eyes, just long enough to make her presence felt, then evaporate like the early morning mist.

Kane knew it was just his mind playing tricks, or so he hoped, but the long shadow she cast was very real and still felt by everyone in the group.

Sliding out of his shrinking cot, Kane massaged his temples as he tried to distract himself from the monochrome walls, steadily smothering him, but all he thought of was Meridia and the uncomfortable distance between them. His reaction to Izzy's text was rash, to say the least, lunging at Emily in the church the way he did.

However, the fact she was part of this from the very start still made his blood boil. It was a simple yet devastating epiphany that tipped him over the edge, hitting him like a ton of bricks in that awful, angry moment.

Not her web of lies per se, but the sudden realization Emily could have prevented the murder of his parents. He told her as much too, among other things. Truth was, he wasn't sure exactly what he said that night anymore.

It remained a colossal blur of regret. A self-centred rush

of blood to the head that not only blindsided Meridia, but also obliterated whatever was left of her world. It was for that reason he hadn't found the nerve to tell her the other crushing news he received that night. That Retiarius, the man who might have sold Izzy down the river, was none other than her wife-beating father.

If he just kept his cool, things might be different. They might be capable of occupying the same room without one of them feeling compelled to leave. That was why he was finally going to tell Peter everything the first chance he got. It was time to rip the band aid off and come clean.

Kane reached down and glanced at his phone. 8am. Peter and Grace would surely be back from their little fishing trip by now. At the very least, Declan would be up and sipping on his first coffee of the day. Kane liked Declan. Despite his taciturn nature, he often laced his infrequent comments with Irish sarcasm, offering some light relief in the grim situation. Nadia was pleasant enough, too, unlike Grace, who was always serious and regimented like a drill sergeant.

In any other circumstances, they probably wouldn't choose to be together, yet here they were, holed up in Drayton Hollow, having operated as a team for months. Although the timing of their intervention was a little suspect at first, as soon as Declan explained he used Meridia's online post to trace their whereabouts, it all made sense, particularly given his background in cyber security.

What better channel to monitor for the latest buzz about the end of the world than Retiarius, the local authority on all things connected to Cold Christmas?

Kane wondered what part he played in Izzy's disappearance. Her last message said he was untrustworthy, and perhaps her absence proved it. But, if Kane learned anything from their encounters with the cult, it was that nothing was ever quite as it seemed, and with only Emily's word to go on, whatever really went down the day he was arrested was now open to debate.

"Huh!" Zach woke up with a start and nearly toppled from his bunk.

"It's ok spud...it was just a nightmare. I'm still having them, too."

"But it always feels so real..." His kid brother sniffled above him.

"You're not alone." JJ croaked wearily from the shadows of his bed. "Kane's right though...she can't hurt us now. Whatever Izzy did worked. We're safe."

"You guys fancy grabbing some breakfast?" Kane jumped at the chance to steer them clear of any more Valerie talk.

Despite his brave front, she lived rent-free underneath his skin, and he didn't want to add any fuel to the fire.

"Peter and Grace should be back now, and I wanna know what they found out."

"You know me...I never say no to a bowl of Frosties. What do you say, little man?" JJ picked up on Kane's redirection and bolstered it.

"Er...Ok...yeah." Zach's hesitant response was all Kane needed to cajole everyone out of their stuffy dorm and head towards the equally stuffy kitchen.

Perhaps today would be the day they finally got some answers.

4

WHEN MERIDIA SHUFFLED HER WAY INTO THE kitchen, she found Declan sitting alone at the flimsy, grey MDF dining table. He was hugging a steaming mug of black coffee, lost in thought, as he stared gormlessly at his own reflection in the piping hot brew.

Meridia hovered in the doorway and observed him for a moment on the off chance something sinister might reveal itself. On the face of it, Declan seemed an amiable guy, albeit cynical. An ex-cyber analyst in his early forties, he was one of the quietest in the group, but when he contributed to discussions, she could tell he was extremely smart and often talked a lot of sense.

Slumped on his elbows in a black tracksuit he claimed disguised his dad bod, he looked pale beneath the fluorescent lighting and Meridia wondered if he had trouble sleeping too. Patches of dark stubble emerged on his usually clean-shaven head to reveal early signs of male pattern baldness around his hairline, and his typical poker face looked to be harbouring disquiet. It all added up to a dishevelled appearance, and Meridia sensed a seed of dread form in her rumbling tummy.

"Hey." She announced her arrival, fearing her hunger had already given her away.

Declan blinked himself out of his trance and met her scrutiny with vacant hazel eyes.

"Oh, hey...sorry I was miles away there." He rubbed the top of his head to break free of his daze and sat upright in his stackable wooden side chair as Meridia made her way to the breakfast cereal.

Used more like a social hub, the kitchen was the brightest room in the bunker and offered a welcome break from the insipid greys dominating the rest of the building. Decked out with chintzy, pale yellow cupboards and worktops, it was also the most noticeable hark back to its 50s roots.

Built in the height of the cold war to ensure government continuity in the event of a nuclear attack, the bunker housed up to thirty personnel.

Thankfully never activated for its intended use, it was decommissioned in the early nineties and left to rot in the disused wasteland on the edge of town.

Stripped of any sensitive equipment, its entrance was sealed and buried beneath decades' worth of ivy and underbrush, until recently. None of them knew a thing of its existence until Declan brought them there. He came across the place whilst working on a security contract with the MoD.

Now it served as an underground fortress, keeping everyone safely below the cult's radar while they searched for a way to halt their relentless rise to power.

"Do you want anything?" Meridia asked, as she reached for a bowl.

"Nah, thanks, love. I've got all the breakfast I need right here." He gently patted the side of his mug and resumed staring down at the thin film of coffee oils gathering on top.

Somewhere hiding among her hunger pangs, Meridia felt another sharp twinge of worry. If Declan had already caught up with Peter and Grace, then their findings couldn't be as promising as everyone hoped.

"Any more bowls where that came from?" JJ crept up behind her and started rifling through the multitude of cereal boxes. "Sorry...didn't mean to make you jump."

"It's ok...just didn't hear you all come in." She turned to make room and found Zach loitering over her other shoulder wearing a cracked smile.

There were dark rings around his big brown eyes, and she guessed he had another restless night. Behind him was Kane, who quickly averted his gaze to the concrete floor. She hated the friction between them, but remained heavily torn.

Her mum's lies weren't Kane's fault, and she knew that, but the way he handled the whole situation really pulled the rug out from under her. It was so frustrating as they only just repaired the lingering trust issues from learning about JJ and Izzy's parents, and whilst there was nothing to suggest Emily played any part in the murder of Kane's parents, her ongoing charade and fake kidnapping didn't exactly cover her in glory.

Meridia teetered on the brink of spiralling again as she imagined her mum conspiring with a cold-blooded killer like Silas Grady and wondered what other devious schemes they might have cooked up together.

"Have you seen Peter or Grace anywhere?" Zach's voice pulled her back from the edge as he placed a hand on her shoulder and reached across for the box of Frosties.

"Not yet." She whispered. "But judging by the weird look on Declan's face, I don't think they have anything positive in store for us."

JJ and Zach both glanced back at the table, where Declan still appeared deep in thought.

"We can't give up hope, M." JJ tried to swallow his own doubts. "Izzy could still be out there somewhere searching for us."

"JJ's right." Kane piped up behind her and then waltzed over to the dining table.

"Hey Dec...have you seen Peter or Grace this morning?" Meridia watched as Declan answered without looking up.

"They're in with Dr Doo...er Foster. They thought it best not to wake you when they got back, so you might want to wait around here until they're done. They have some news on your missing friend." Meridia's appetite suddenly waned, so she passed the milk to JJ and pushed her bowl to one side.

If they were in with Dr Foster, then their news couldn't be good. From what little she knew about him, he only ever involved himself with the wider group if there was a paranormal aspect to something they uncovered.

Aside from that, he largely kept to himself in the west wing of the bunker where the workshop was located, and her mum was being held prisoner. Occasionally he would resurface for an afternoon snack, or to collect supplies for his makeshift lab, but of all their new hosts, he was the most aloof and out of place.

He always seemed polite enough whenever he showed up, and Peter was quick to vouch for his expertise, having been an admirer of his work in his previous life. But it was the nature of his work that worried Meridia, especially now.

An expert in the occult who specialized in ancient texts and rituals would never fill her with confidence, particularly where Izzy was concerned, but one nicknamed Dr Doom was way more than she could cope with right now.

As Meridia continued to mull over the multitude of bad news that could head their way, a dripping sound interrupted her thoughts, like a leaky faucet.

The idle chatter of her friends faded to a low-frequency drone, humming and purring in the background as if her brain somehow turned the volume down on their mics to home in on the ominous 'drip-drop' more clearly. A sudden chill rattled her bones, causing her to squirm in her seat as she searched for the innocuous but foreboding sound's source.

"Drip...drop..."

Meridia stared at the shiny chrome taps arched over the stainless-steel sink, but it wasn't them. There was nowhere else it would come from, not that she knew at least, and she wondered if the rain somehow wormed its way underground to remind her there was an entire world above them in need of saving.

"Drip...drop..."

A flash of red streaked past the corner of her eye, pulling her gaze towards it like a magnet. Peering over the rim of her cereal bowl, she saw the drip-drop splash of crimson, seeping into her breakfast like a bloody virus, contaminating everything it touched with its sanguine tendrils.

"Drip...drop..."

Meridia cast her eyes up at the ceiling and skated backwards on her chair in dismay. The message 'TOO LATE' was scrawled in blood above them all, seeping into the lacklustre plaster masking their concrete prison.

"M...what's wrong?" She glanced at Zach and found raven eyes staring back at her from beneath his matted fringe.

In each of their centres was a celestial light emanating from within that flickered and shimmered like stars on a clear winter's night, mesmerizing and enticing.

A dusty grey powder soiled his ivory skin, either dried earth or soot. The same grey powder also covered his clothes, and then Meridia noticed his grubby baby blue hoody, instantly transporting her back to the fateful day at Crooked House. This wasn't an unwanted reunion with her best friend's echo. This was something new. Something different.

"What is it?" Zach pressed, oblivious to his ghoulish appearance.

"I...I er..." Meridia stuttered, glancing around the table in the hope someone else might see what she saw. "Gasp!"

She screeched back further into her chair, almost rocking it over as her feet left the floor. A circle of white eyes surrounded her. Dead eyes, framed by grey sinewy veins branching out in search of lost irises.

Kane, JJ and Declan, each dead, yet undead, as they sat around the dining table staring into her soul. Both haunting and terrifying in equal measure, their lifeless gaze turned her to ice in the stuffy confines of the bunker's kitchen.

"Meridia?" JJ's voice sounded normal, although his face was anything but.

An emaciated husk: grey-gilled and decomposing before her eyes as mouldy-green capillaries rose to the surface of his cadaverous skin and furcated across his cheeks, corroding everything they touched.

Craters emerged around his jawline, exposing teeth and

pulling him apart at the seams, as the burden of death became too much for his desiccated flesh to bear.

"Is it the milk? It smelt odd to me at first, but it tastes ok..." A gaping hole formed in his throat, leaking milk as he slurped away at the final dregs of his cereal.

Meridia watched the creamy droplets seep into a crimson stain on his chest that was rapidly expanding as his body bled out.

Beside JJ, Kane sat quiet and still. His cloudy white eyes had sunken deep into his skull and were boring into hers from across the table. A gory stain on his sweatshirt glistened vividly beneath the fluorescent lighting, and poking out from the garnet folds of his ribs was the polished mahogany handle of a pocketknife.

Blood trickled from each corner of his downturned mouth, streaking all the way to his chin and giving him the appearance of a creepy ventriloquist dummy as he sat glaring at her with gaunt accusation, as if she was the one who stabbed him.

Unable to look, Meridia closed her eyes and tried to slow breath her way through the grisly vision.

"Meridia, you look a little pale, love...I can do you some toast if you're not sure about the milk..."

Declan's dulcet Irish twang infiltrated the safety of her eyelids and tempted them open again.

"*Clunk...*"

Meridia took the bait just in time to see his jawbone clatter to the table. Torn off at its hinges, the gruesome chasm of viscous sinew left his tongue languishing in the notch of his neck as he slowly bled out onto the dreary concrete floor.

Stifling the scream clawing its way up her throat, she stared down at the oozing expanse of blood as it stretched across the kitchen and caught the demon's stony reflection staring back at her, as if he was standing in the farthest corner of the room.

Darkness shrouded his inky black scowl as his eyes skulked beneath the weight of his brow. A sneer broke across his brawny face. Sharp and lustrous like the chrome faucet at the sink, it revealed a zigzag of fangs between his reedy lips shimmering in the turbid crimson depths.

She did a quick double take, glancing up at the room, but all she saw was an overused microwave and Declan's old boombox in the demon's absence. When she peered back down at the blossoming pool, he was gone from there, too. Another taunt as he delivered each night since their arrival. Subjecting her to gruesome glimpses of tragedies that were yet to unfold.

As Meridia tried to blink her way free of his deathly grip, she caught another movement from the corner of her cursed eye. Smaller this time, but just as chilling.

Declan's serrated jawbone lay on the table like a rotten conch washed up ashore on a carmine tide, and over the yawing horizon of its rutted teeth she saw two twitching antennas feel their way out of the wreckage of his mouth.

A staccato rhythm of clicks and clacks scampered up her spine as a cockroach reared its ugly head from the shadows and advanced onto the table.

A grotesque herald of decay, its brown bulbus body skittered across the white MDF towards her, leaving the faint pitter-patter of bloody footprints in its wake. And then she screamed, a shrill and terrifying scream that could shatter glass.

She tried to get away, but her chair wouldn't move back any further without tipping; its legs caught in a crack in the concrete. The room was spinning now as the undead faces of her friends continued to stare, wide-eyed and soulless. A harrowing merry-go-round of death, and then...

"*Crunch!*"

Declan's coffee cup came down like a hammer, squashing the bug dead.

"How did that get in here?" He said, his face back as one and his eyes returned to their normal hazel.

"Better not tell Nadia, she hates bugs..." Without leaving his seat, he grabbed a cloth from the worktop behind him and wiped up the slimy cockroach carcass in one smooth motion, sparing Meridia the sight of its sticky debris.

"Phew..." Zach let out a sigh of relief. "I thought you were having another vision for a second..."

She didn't dare tell them the truth. Instead, she considered retreating to her room to regain her composure, but as she made a move to stand, Peter entered the kitchen, followed by Nadia and Dr Foster himself.

"You'd better all take a seat, guys," he said. "I'm afraid we have some bad news..."

5

Peter gazed at the sea of anxious eyes staring back at him from the breakfast cupboard and gently ushered them towards the dining table where Kane and Declan were already waiting.

It never took long for the bunker to overheat and become stuffy whenever a room was congested, which is why people stayed spread around the facility during the day, but this morning would have to be an exception.

"It's Izzy, isn't it..." Meridia mumbled as she followed Zach and JJ like a lost little lamb.

Having spent the last hour debating the news with Dr Foster and Grace, Peter was dreading this moment and felt his mouth go dry the moment Meridia posed her question. What he was about to share would be another huge test to everyone's resolve in what was rapidly feeling like an exercise in futility.

The Children of the Shadows seemed to have every base covered, and despite Dr Foster's knowledge and Grace's sheer tenacity, the truth was nothing either of them attempted to date had even remotely disrupted the impending prophecy.

Peter's only hope was that the coming together of both his group and Dr Foster's might somehow result in a meaningful difference to the world's current trajectory. He took one more look at the exhausted faces gazing up at him expectantly and cleared his throat to answer.

"As you all know, Grace and I paid a visit to the designated dead drop in the early hours this morning and collected a USB drive with new information relating to the cult. With Declan's help, we opened the files securely and have spent the last hour discussing the various implications of what we've learned." Peter pushed his dirty blonde hair to one side and sat backwards on the nearest chair so he could face the group.

"First, I'm relieved to say Izzy is still alive..." Peter's voice broke, forcing him to take a beat as a tidal wave of relief swept its way around the room, reducing everyone to tears. "But...I'm afraid that's as good as the news gets..."

"Where is she?" JJ was first to press as Meridia tried in vain to compose herself. Peter felt the urge to comfort her, but he hadn't finished delivering the bad news yet.

"They have her...she was caught fleeing Chase Side and is now being held somewhere beneath it."

"What was she doing there?" Again, JJ wasted no time pushing Peter to the news he was dreading.

"I don't quite know how to say this, guys, but it was indeed Izzy who saved you all from Valerie's grip...it seems she was somehow manipulated into killing her."

"Good!" Kane blurted without even thinking.

"No, it's not good!" Meridia trembled, her eyes were as red as her cheeks. "Izzy isn't like you...she wouldn't hurt a fly...there must be some kind of mistake...she would never..."

"I'm sorry." Peter interjected, to avoid things escalating.

"It seems she had help...if you want to call it that...but ultimately, Izzy was the one who took Valerie's life. Now I can't pretend to know how she felt in that moment, or what she's dealing with now, but I know, given the situation, I would have done exactly the same for any of you. Make no mistake, we are at war and I'm sure none of you need reminding of what's at stake. There are going to be casualties, on both sides no doubt, but thanks to Izzy, we have landed another significant blow against the cult. Given everything you've told me about Valerie, I would say Izzy not only saved your lives that night, but countless others, and no matter what she is going through right now, I know we will all be there for her when we get her out of that hellhole."

"H...how are we going to get her out of there?" Zach asked hesitantly.

"That we're not sure of...yet. But we must act soon if we're to stand any chance of getting her out of there alive. The article you found Meridia, the one about The Demon of Cold Christmas...it seems there is some validity to Retiarius' cryptic claims and the cult is planning to use Izzy to resurrect him."

"Use her how?" Kane jumped up from his seat and Peter shot a nervous glance toward Dr Foster, who was loitering in the far corner of the room, away from everyone else.

"Sacrifice," he declared, stepping forward to a chorus of gasps. "The Children of the Shadows intend to kill your friend...and they plan on doing it tonight."

6

Dr Marcus Foster was a black, middle-class man in his early sixties who had a PhD in theoretical physics and a deep interest in the occult. Despite the warmth of his broad, beaming smile and the gleam in his eye, he was socially awkward most of the time, unless dealing with a subject he was knowledgeable about.

In the outside world, he had a reputation for being a recluse and was that way ever since Peter first came across his work on astrophysics at the turn of the century. Since their arrival, he was conspicuously absent from any group discussions, preferring instead to consult on a one-to-one basis from the comfort of his makeshift lab. Dressed in relaxed-fitting chinos and plaid shirts, he looked like a retired professor, a stark contrast to the group, both demographically and geographically, hailing from Chicago.

Although Peter was yet to uncover what brought him all the way to Cold Christmas, he could at least vouch for his integrity and expertise, having dipped into his work on numerous occasions over the years when attempting to explain the unexplained. Since he dedicated his early retirement to the exploration of occult rituals, Dr Foster was definitely the best man for the job when conveying Izzy's perilous situation.

"There's a darkness on the horizon, the likes of which none of us have ever seen before. Yes, you may have taken down the witch, and by all accounts your friend has now rid us all of the night walker...but make no mistake, The Demon is even more deadly." As Peter studied the reactions of the children, he wondered how well practiced Dr Foster was at speaking to people of such a young age.

So far, based on the row of panicked expressions staring back at him, he guessed it might be his first time.

"The 50th anniversary of The Demon represents a watershed moment that I've been hoping to prevent for some time now. Er...yes Zach?" Dr Foster acknowledged Zach, who now had his hand raised, and Peter watched Kane roll his eyes in anticipation of what was coming.

"What does watershed mean?" He squeaked.

"It means a time of great change...and I'm afraid if we allow this one change to take place, then it could be the final nail in all our coffins. You see, as a punishment for her crimes against the cult, your friend is in line to be sacrificed on the eve of The Demon's anniversary. One shall die so another can live. The number 50 is significant, you see...has been across most cultures as long as we've been wandering this planet. The cult believe it signifies the start of a new cycle. Regeneration." Dr Foster glanced at his watch and continued. "When the sun sets...about 8 hours from now, the demon will rise...unless we find a way to stop it."

"Who is the demon?" Kane was eager to know more about what they were up against. "I mean, we've all seen his picture, but what do we know about him, other than he's some child murderer from the seventies..."

"Oh, he's much more than a mere child murderer...as if that wasn't bad enough. No, he's an abomination...a bona fide boogeyman...the kind people talk about around campfires to scare little children. Believe me, if even half those stories are true, then his return is the last thing any of us want. Born without a soul, he is the embodiment of evil... a behemoth with an insatiable desire for bloodshed and brutality." For a moment, Peter considered interrupting as he saw the effect Dr Foster's depiction was having on Zach, but deep down, he knew they all needed to hear the truth, no matter how brutal.

"Make no mistake, the demon is unlike anything any of us have come up against to date. Some say he's a phantom that can slip in and out of anywhere just like a ghost...others say just one look at him can put you under an evil spell. Make you do things...terrible things like he's the devil himself..."

"Yeah, and he's got metal fangs too, like someone turned the terminator into a frigging vampire!" JJ blurted.

"I thought he only killed like five kids though..." Zach tried to diffuse the terrifying hype. "I know that's bad, but surely Valerie was worse...right?"

Dr Foster took a beat as if he was holding something back, then let out a deep sigh.

"Have you heard of the lost souls of St Swithun's?"

Peter had a vague recollection of this from his stint at the school, but at the time chalked it up to tragedy. Judging by the blank expressions around the room, it seemed the others hadn't even heard of it.

"Vaguely..." Peter conceded. "What happened?"

"The official line? Well, if you believe the papers, then it was a day trip to Brambleton Beach that ended in the tragic deaths of 23 children and two teachers. On the journey down there, the bus driver cut a corner on the cliff's edge and met an oncoming car. He reacted. Swung back out and took it too close to the other side. Ended up ploughing through the barrier and into the drink. The high tide prevented the recovery of any bodies. It rocked the community. The lost souls of St Swithun's, they called them. Some say it was the cult's doing. That the crash was just a cover for another one of their rituals. Some say it was the demon. Whatever it was, they did a pretty good job of sweeping it all under the carpet. Aside from a few old newspaper clippings Dec found at the local library, folks round here don't like to talk about it all that much, and who could blame them? If I had to put money on it, though, I'd say the demon was behind it. It was around the same time as his reign."

"But why?" Zach was still keen to put the brakes on Dr Foster's history lesson.

"Why is anybody's guess? Maybe they covered it up so as not to attract any outside attention. 5 missing kids is terrible enough, but 28? That's a whole different bag. Scotland Yard would've been crawling all over that. Since then, there have been reports from hikers and the like. Sightings of children wandering the woods at night wearing St Swithun's colours. Wouldn't surprise me if the real reason they didn't find any of those kids down at Brambleton was because they were barking up the wrong tree, if you catch my drift."

"You think they're buried in the woods?" JJ was quick to bite.

"Maybe. Seems an awfully strange coincidence, don't you think? Most ghosts haunt the place they died, don't they?" He raised an eyebrow at Peter as if searching for his endorsement, but Peter didn't have the appetite for scaring Zach any more than he already was.

"What happened to him? In the seventies I mean… someone must have stopped him, otherwise he would have killed even more kids and wouldn't be an echo, right?" Kane was lapping up the doctor's every word and was hungry for more.

"Nobody knows. Some say the house took him back… that the murders were part of some ritual to help him transcend and grant him more power. Others say he was stopped, but if that was the case, then it certainly wasn't the local police…and whoever did it didn't live to tell the tale. Mark my words, though; if the demon finds a way back into our world, for real…then we'll need a miracle to stop him again…either that or the help of a seer…"

"Thank you, Dr Foster…now we've sufficiently scared everyone. Perhaps it might be time to focus on the rest of the intel your contact has gathered?" This time, Peter interrupted.

So far, they kept Meridia's gift a secret, and although Dr Foster already shared his hunch that someone among them might be a seer, Peter wasn't ready to divulge that information to a bunch of relative strangers.

"You're right Peter…the clock is ticking. We know when the ritual is going to take place, and thanks to our contact, we also know where. The birthplace of The Demon…room 4 of Crooked House."

"He was born there?!" JJ's astonishment at Dr Foster's flippant revelation was uncontainable, and another round of gasps followed.

"Sorry, I thought I already mentioned that…he was born in room 4 to a disgraced priest and a disciple of the shadows who was chosen to sacrifice herself to give him life. They are both unimportant, though. Long dead and all but forgotten. To bring us back to Peter's point, in eight hours, they will move your friend Izzy from Chase Side to Crooked House. Until now, I would've said they would use the tunnels, but the Children of the Shadows are getting more brazen by the day, so somehow between us we will need to monitor all routes into Cold Christmas."

"Doesn't your contact know which way they're going to go?" JJ continued to speak up, but Dr Foster shook his head.

"No, they don't. Something has our contact spooked so bad they're looking for a way out. Right now, I'm trying my best to convince them to hang in there, just until we can pin down which way they're gonna take Izzy, but it's getting increasingly risky for them so I wouldn't be surprised if one of you ends up with a new roomie in the next day or so. Either way, this could be the last bit of intel we get for some time while they lie low." Dr Foster held a polished chrome USB aloft to make his point.

"On here we have schematics for the network of tunnels running under Cold Christmas, but with so many access points we just don't have the manpower to cover them all. Besides, the last thing we want to do is challenge the cult on their own turf. On top of that, we hear they have a new weapon, and I don't mean in the same vein as Valerie, or that nut job nurse of theirs. This is something big. Maybe even bigger than the demon, but that's all anybody knows. Whatever it is, they must be thinking about using it if word has gotten out. The cult's inner circle stays pretty tight-lipped when it comes to all the importance stuff."

"We also know Grady is out for blood and becoming increasingly erratic. Trust me, the last thing any of us want is to cross paths with him." Grace interjected from the kitchen sidelines, then wandered over to the sink behind Declan to pour herself a glass of water.

Although no taller than Meridia, she was a force of nature. An ex-PT and climbing instructor, Grace was the only known person to survive an encounter with the psychotic nurse. She stumbled upon him whilst hiking in the Cold Christmas woods and witnessed him butcher an entire group of backpackers within a matter of seconds.

He spotted her instantly, hiding among the hawthorn, and tried to add her to his tally, but she narrowly eluded him. By her own admission, she was lucky that day; falling down a ravine and tumbling out of sight, but that wasn't before he carved a six-inch scar into the small of her back as she fled. Having been warned of his approach to St Peter's, she readily shared the story during their trip to the bunker.

By then, no-one in the group needed much convincing. A horseman breached the church moments earlier, forcing them to evacuate. Although she wore her scar as a badge of honour, it was clear to Peter her brush with Grady still terrified her.

The way Grady systematically dispatched of four adults without so much as breaking a sweat left her questioning if he was even human.

"So, what are we going to do?" Kane was eager to move on from Grady and it was no secret why.

"Ideally, we need more strength in numbers." Dr Foster rubbed his snowy-white buzz cut before continuing.

"Although we know there are others like us scattered around the country, convincing any of them to break cover and venture into the heart of darkness is going to be...er... difficult to say the least, particularly now we're all so close to the edge. With Valerie crossing over to whatever plane of existence the echoes occupy, the cult will pull out all the stops to find that final piece of the puzzle."

Peter watched Zach squirm in his seat at the mere suggestion of room 10, but maintained these were all harsh realities the group needed reminding of.

Based on what they learned, the Children of the Shadows were about to turn the screw once more, which meant their chances of survival were diminishing with every passing second.

<h1 style="text-align:center">7</h1>

Silas Grady rocked back and forth on his heels in the corner of the dank and dismal dungeon as he waited impatiently for his prisoner to stir. A filthy white plastic bucket sat in the centre of the room, silently secreting the vile stench of human excrement as the girl lay sleeping, oblivious to his presence.

She appeared pale and weak beneath the dusty trail of light streaming in through the room's solitary window, and as he watched silently from the shadows, he saw her carotid artery pulsating rhythmically, begging him to slice it open with each mouthwatering beat. Trying to temper his urges, he gripped the handle of his hunting knife, but the familiar curves of its smooth wooden handle offered little respite.

White-knuckled, he closed his eyes and focused on his own breathing, taking in a deep lungful of the rancid clammy air. Fresh from another satisfying double kill, he was still finding it difficult to control himself and supposed the best solution would be to busy himself above ground, but the thought of donning his ridiculous nurse's costume again only made his blood boil. Soon everything would change, and he would never need to pretend again.

Oh, how he wished he could ring that pathetic nurse Grady's neck and choke out every subservient breath from his sycophantic little body. Alas, with no way to vent his years of frustration on his alter ego, he guessed Izzy Di Salvo would have to suffice.

Although if she kept refusing to eat, there wouldn't be much left of her to sacrifice. Perhaps this was her escape plan, to starve herself to the point she could slip through one of the cracks in the stony ground.

"Silly cow..." He scoffed. "You should have stayed in the ambulance with your dad..."

He glanced at the pile of stale sandwiches gathering mould beside her and wondered how long it would be before the roaches found them. Ungrateful bitch.

If she was half as smart as her pathetic parents claimed, then she would be looking to keep her strength up for when her friends undoubtedly try to rescue her, not that it would do her much good.

Grady's mind wandered to their smug teacher and hoped he would be among those who came for her. He was relishing adding his bright green eyes to his collection.

"Huh." Grady smiled as he caught himself looming over the girl, knife in hand, ready to strike. He couldn't even remember leaving the corner, let alone drawing his blade. Perhaps it was his recent ascension, or the demon calling him to kill in his name. Either way, he had enough of waiting, so he kicked the sole of the girl's foot.

"Wakey, wakey, rise and shine..." The girl flinched, then screamed as she scuttled away from him.

"*Chink!*"

Her rusty shackles reached their limit and brought her

to an abrupt halt, almost yanking her scrawny little arm out of its socket. Petrified and quivering, she cowered away, shielding her face with both arms as if she was about to take a beating.

Her mousy brown hair was lank, knocked out of its ponytail from sleeping rough and now matted to her neck and forehead. She appeared grubby with a mix of sweat and dirt from the damp and mucky cobbled floor that was her bed for the last few nights.

Peering through the gap in her guard, Grady glimpsed the big brown eyes he was coveting and smiled when he saw they were wide with terror behind her tortoiseshell glasses. This was his first time calling in on her since bundling her in the back of his van, and he revelled in her reaction. A trembling wreck fraught with fear.

"You should eat, you know..." Grady lowered his hood to reveal an arrogant smile plastered across his pallid, angular face. He fingered a glossy lock of his jet-black hair back into place and then leaned in closer toward his hostage, lowering his voice to a whisper.

"Don't want you flaking out on your big night now do we..."

"W...what big night?" She stuttered, still shielding her face.

"Hasn't anyone told you?" Grady snarled as he held his serrated blade up to the light for her to see.

"Tonight I'm going to take a long, sharp knife...a bit like this one...and drive it straight through your little heart! Then I'm going to watch you bleed out all over the floor of the house you and your friends love so much...just so he can return." Grady slowly dragged the tip of his blade down the side of the girl's ribcage, just enough for her to feel it beneath her dirty grey sweater.

He watched her body tense in response as she winced, too scared to move in case the faintest of motions resulted in the knife being thrust inside her. Grady smiled again as he imagined the feeling of jamming the blade between her ribs, sticking her like a little piggy, just to hear her squeal.

He slowly backed away in case he forgot himself again. Although the blood of pretty much anyone would do for the sacrifice, his master specifically requested the Di Salvo girl as part of her penance for what she'd done.

"M...my parents...th...they won't let you..." Her trembling voice pulled Grady from his dark fantasy and brought about an unhinged smile.

"Oh, I almost forgot...I'm afraid your parents won't be saving you anytime soon. Hahaha..." Reaching into his pocket, he pulled out a small brown leather pouch, then fished around inside it with his thumb and forefinger.

"The buck doesn't entirely stop with you, I'm afraid... and so I stopped in at your house on my way here ..." He tossed a couple of bloody stumps at the girl's feet and waited for her to realize what they were.

"Argh!"

Her scream reverberated around the gloomy chamber as she tried to shuffle away from the severed fingers lying in the dirt. He left their wedding rings on for effect. The diamond encrusted digit of the girl's mother being the easiest to recognize.

"Wh...what have you done?" She sobbed, turning away from the gruesome revelation.

"Ha...you should see what I did with the rest of their bodies." He bragged. "You have your mother's eyes, by the way...and now I do, too."

Grady smirked as the girl emptied her stomach of bile over the pile of mouldy sandwiches, and for a moment he contemplated force-feeding her one. Perhaps later, he thought, reaching for the door.

"The worst is yet to come." He called back over his shoulder as she snivelled and spluttered uncontrollably on the floor.

"It's a shame you won't be around to see what he does to all your friends...there'll be no-one left for poor little Zach to turn to when the demon is done with them. That's if the weavers don't get them first, hahaha...soon Zach will beg to enter room 10, you'll see..." Grady slammed the door behind him and condemned Izzy to darkness once more.

8

KANE WATCHED SURREPTITIOUSLY FROM THE COVER OF his wavy brown fringe as everyone dispersed following their ominous briefing.

As smart as Dr Foster was, he had a lot to learn about rallying the troops and judging by all the glum faces shuffling past him, perhaps it was a good thing their host spent most of his days locked away in his lab.

Even Grace seemed unusually downbeat as she followed Nadia back to the infirmary, and she was usually unflappable. Kane liked Grace, mostly because they both had a score to settle with Grady, but also because she reminded him a little of his mum. Only Grace was far shorter.

He imagined her being a cover model in another life, with her chic cropped blonde hair and piercing blue almond eyes. Before going underground, she spent most of her time climbing and traveling. A lifestyle bought and paid for by a small portfolio of wealthy housewives, she helped stay in shape as their PT.

Like him, she also suffered from cabin fever, jumping at

the first chance to get out of the suffocating bunker. As she disappeared through the charcoal-grey double doors, Kane shifted his attention to Dr Foster and waited for him to follow suit.

Usually distant and detached, he was now talking Peter's ear off, so Kane drifted over to where they were standing to hurry them along. Peter clocked his approach immediately and took the cue.

"Ok Marcus, I'll drop by the lab in a sec to discuss those schematics in a bit more detail and we'll see what we can come up with." Dr Foster nodded and trundled off.

"Is it really too much for us to manage?" Kane asked, stepping into the void left by the good doctor.

"It is, unless we find some way to narrow it down. The cult has been busy building tunnels for centuries, and there's no telling if we've captured everything that exists."

"Do you trust them? Their source, I mean..." Kane was sceptical of anyone connected to the cult, more so since Emily was outed as an active member.

"Outside of the five of you, I'm not sure I'll ever be able to trust anyone again." Emily's betrayal hit Peter hard, as he clearly had a soft spot for her. Kane couldn't be sure if it was platonic or more, but since she was locked away, Peter became even more protective of them all.

"Which reminds me, you need to repair things with Meridia, Kane...we need to be united, now more than ever. I know it's hard, and I'm doing all I can to help build that bridge for you both, but you need to find a way and quickly. You heard how important today is going to be, and we all need to be on the same page."

"I know. I feel like such a prick, flying off the handle like that...but I was in such a dark place at the time...I still am. I'm finding it hard being locked away down here.

Between that and the nightmares, I can't believe the new guys are still sane, having been down here so long. Anyway, it's Meridia that I wanted to talk to you about..." Kane reached into his pocket and pulled his phone out.

"I only relayed part of Izzy's message at the church that night. You'll understand why when you see it." He opened the last message from Izzy and handed the phone to Peter so he could read it.

Kane watched his green eyes widen as they darted back and forth, absorbing yet another revelation.

"Christ! How much can one girl take..." Peter welled up as he handed the phone back to Kane. "You did the right thing holding this back...at least, I think."

"I don't know how it changes anything now...not for us, at least. We know we can't trust him after what he did to Izzy, but what if he didn't give her up? What if Izzy got that wrong and simply got caught? I know it's a long shot, but I can't help but think there's more to the story here, particularly now we know about Emily. What if Retiarius was trying to help us and things just went sideways? It's possible, right?" Kane was spit balling on a topic that was eating him alive for days.

Along with the tremendous wave of relief he felt wash over him the second he handed Peter his phone, he also wanted to make sense of the countless contradictions circling his mind like vultures. Peter rubbed his chin as he pondered Kane's deluge of questions.

"Sorry, I know it's a lot...I've just been dying to talk to you about it, but the timing has never been right since we got here."

"It's my fault." Peter broke his silence. "I've been so caught up in acquiring as much information as I can from our hosts, I fear I've taken my eye off the ball a little, as far as you guys are concerned. It's me who should apologize Kane. I think the best thing to do is get this all out in the open. As much as I know it might break Meridia, the longer we decide to keep it from her, the more harm it will eventually do."

"She's gonna kill me when she finds out..." Although Kane didn't share Peter's confidence, deep down he knew it was the right thing to do.

"Let's round everyone up and do it now. I was going to chat to you all about Izzy, so we may as well throw this little hand grenade into the mix while we're at it. Go tell everyone to meet me in the control room. We have a lot to talk about."

9

Izzy cuffed the vomit from her mouth and forced her shoulders to relax. Her empty stomach ached from all her retching, as did her spine from spending three nights sleeping on a damp and unforgiving floor.

Unsure if it was day or night, her only source of light came from a lamp somewhere beyond the solitary window in her otherwise murky prison cell. She was alone, aside from the occasional visiting psychopath either in the guise of Mrs Hutson delivering food, or now, nurse Grady delivering ominous threats designed to break her.

Little did either of them know Izzy broke the moment she flicked the bank of switches next to Valerie's hospital bed.

Even the sickening news of her parents barely penetrated the profound numbness she felt inside, triggering a physical response more than any emotional one.

Maybe she was still in shock, and the grisly message the ghoulish killer just delivered was yet to sink in. Perhaps it simply trudged to the back of a very long line of gut-wrenching revelations and perturbing verities she lacked the capacity to process right now.

Satisfied she had nothing left inside her to add to her sodden sandwich, she braved a second glance at the gruesome delivery he callously threw at her feet. For all she knew they could've been chopped frankfurters, and this was all one big bluff designed to rattle her. Alas, it was wishful thinking.

The sight of her parents' pale, dismembered fingers made her cough up the tiniest morsels clinging to her stomach lining. She considered crawling towards the bucket but couldn't bear to look at its contents anymore.

For three whole days, she was left to fester in her own filth with no means to clean herself. A slew of imaginary bugs nesting in her hair itched her scalp as the room's stifling humidity soaked her grubby clothes. With blurry eyes, sore from tears and exhaustion, Izzy forced herself to inspect the fingers.

Although her mum's engagement ring was unmistakable with its two-carat emerald cut, she needed to know for certain who the fingers belonged to.

"Kaff...kaff..." Still, she wrestled with her gag reflex, despite her stomach being dry as a bone.

Blinking her eyes clear, she leaned in close enough to smell the coppery tang of malleable blood congealing around the protruding bone at the fingers' gnarled root. She remembered her dad had a small scar on the inside of his ring finger, just below his knuckle, from the one and only time he attempted DIY.

It was all going so well until he dropped his hacksaw and instinctively tried to catch it. Of course, he caught it blade first and took quite a chunk out of his skin, requiring butterfly stitches. Unfortunately, the nurse botched the stitches, leaving him with a slight lump when it healed.

Izzy covered her mouth with a grimy sleeve as she searched for the right angle, and although she couldn't bring herself to touch either digit as they lay half-curled like upturned grubs on the flinty ground, she was sure if it was her dad's finger she would have seen the scar by now. Having studied the finger as best she could under the dungeon's dismal light, Izzy told herself it wasn't her dad's. Sobbing once more, she repeated the lie over and over like a mantra as she yanked at the sleeve of her sweater until the stitching broke and she had something to cover them with.

"This is all your fault..." The rasping voice wormed its way inside Izzy's brain and tugged at her eyes as it begged for her attention.

How could she have forgotten about her other visitor, silently stalking her from the shadows in the furthest corner of the room?

"Look at me child..." The ethereal voice persisted, poking and prodding at her, crumbling Izzy's resolve until she had no choice but to look.

The rotting corpse of Valerie Richards lay propped up in a soiled hospital bed. Her eyes were black as coal, yet twinkled with ethereal beauty like two stars in a cloudless night. In contrast, her face lacked the same allure.

Decay stripped her jaw to the bone, revealing a jumble of crooked teeth clumped together like forgotten tombstones, all held together by desiccated gums. A protruding cheek bone courted the light, perforating the surface of her putrefied flesh, whilst straggles of wispy white hair clung to the loose, shrivelled skin swathed around her crusty scalp.

Deep beneath her soggy, smelly clothes, Izzy sensed the

blood in her veins turn to ice as she locked eyes with the ghoulish spectre that was haunting her every night since her arrival.

"Y...you're not real..." she stammered, trying to pry her eyes away from the gruesome spectacle.

"*Look what you have done...*" Valerie raised a skeletal hand and pointed through the murk.

The accusation stuck Izzy's heart like a dagger as she scrambled back towards the musty wall she was chained to. Even though she knew it was her guilt talking, Izzy couldn't escape the contemptuous gaze of the monstrous woman she murdered in cold blood.

She was right; it was all her fault. Her childish quest to contribute, to feel valued, resulted in even more bloodshed. And for what?

Her friends were no safer than they were before, and yet another monster loomed on the horizon, bigger and badder than those before it. Izzy closed her weary eyes in defeat. Grady was right. She was too weak, both physically and mentally.

There was nothing more she could do but rot until they killed her.

As she tried to cling onto the solitary thread of sanity she had left, Valerie's whining gently subsided and made way for an all-too-familiar hissing noise that turned Izzy's empty stomach. The roaches finally arrived to finish her off.

10

Although each room in the bunker was severely dated, its control room resembled a giant time capsule, fit for a museum.

A row of boxy decommissioned servers, each taller than Peter, decorated the far wall with an enticing array of buttons and dials that wouldn't have looked out of place on an antique radio.

They reminded Kane of old Star Trek re-runs he watched with his dad as a kid. A defunct view of the future which never quite came to fruition. A large, grey, hexagonal meeting table, made of the same material as the flimsy kitchen furniture, stood in the centre of the room. Prioritizing function over form throughout its concrete halls, the bunker's redundant war room was no exception. A handful of bulbous monitors collected dust to their left as the group filtered in and grabbed a seat.

The keyboards and equipment resembled giant Lego pieces rather than anything sophisticated enough to keep tabs on the outside world. The only item of any actual use was a world map pinned to the centre wall, although upon closer inspection Kane noticed even that had a handful of incorrectly named countries.

Despite its obvious shortcomings and unique musty aroma, it made for the perfect meeting room when they needed privacy, with its archaic equipment offering no way for anyone else to listen in.

"Ok guys, we've got about an hour if we need it." Peter closed the door and joined the others at the table. "That's if we can stand being in here that long."

"Why does this room smell so funky?" JJ asked.

"I think it's just the least used...I mean, look around. The equipment in here is at least 50 years old and no use to anyone. I'm guessing all the plastic doesn't help either."

"What are we going to do about Izzy?" Meridia got straight to business.

She was sitting directly opposite Peter and detached from the rest of the group. Kane could tell there was a fire burning behind her steely blue eyes, and her red tinted cheeks assimilated most of her freckles. Kane also sat alone, allowing Zach and JJ to sit next to each other with their backs to the outdated map.

He stared at its wishy-washy hues of green and beige as he waited for someone else to start the ball rolling. All he could think about was the reaction he would get when he shared the news of Meridia's father.

"I'm going to meet with Dr Foster after our catchup, but at the moment we're trying to narrow down how she'll be transported to Crooked House. From what we can tell, there are a dozen tunnels leading into the area and, as we said earlier, there just aren't enough of us to cover all of them. I can't imagine they'll be taking her transport lightly either...they'll expect us to be coming for her, which presents a different problem altogether. Even with the help of everyone in here, we're still drastically outnumbered. M, I hate to ask, but do you have anything to share? Any feelings or visions you think might help us?"

"Nothing...I still haven't made sense of all the visions I had at the church...the strange woman in the graveyard who recognized me...the place where the weavers were...I'm sleeping with Izzy's coat next to me in the hope something might lead me to her, but it's like I'm blind to where she is. All I keep having are the same old nightmares about Valerie and...and..."

"And what?" Peter asked tenderly.

"It's nothing...just nightmares. I'm sorry. I hate this bloody gift. The moment I feel like I'm making progress, it just dries up...it always feels like I'm taking one step forward and two steps back." As Meridia dropped her head into her hands, Kane decided it was time to step up and build some bridges, even if there were about to be burned irrevocably when he came clean about the rest of Izzy's text.

"It's ok M. Nobody is expecting you to have any answers. If the visions...or dreams Valerie gave me are anything to go by, then I can't imagine how difficult it is to make sense of everything."

"Kane's right." JJ added. "We're all in this shitshow together...and we're lucky we all still have each other to lean on. Izzy is on her own right now...stuck in god knows what hellhole, and she put herself there to save us. I don't know how we're gonna do it, but we've gotta get her out of there asap. Forget about the blood moon, monster bullshit. We can't leave it till the last minute like we always do...we need to get ahead of them this time and we need to do it fast."

"I hear you, mate." Kane jumped back in. "We can't sit here thinking we have eight hours to solve this. We need to get her out right now. I've seen enough films about crazy cults to know that they all turn up for a ritual, chanting and prancing around in their cloaks... If we're going to get Izzy out of there, we need to do it quickly. Why is the hospital such a fortress? Do we know that for sure, or are we being fed an excuse?"

"As you all know, Nadia used to work there, and although they never inducted her, she stumbled upon hidden levels and lots of mysterious comings and goings before she eventually fled. When I was there with Izzy, we saw a couple of hoods walking the halls, bold as brass...they must have come from somewhere...and JJ, you said Grady was heading down into some kind of basement needing a special keycard. We must assume the worst here guys. Forewarned is forearmed, remember?"

"What if there's another way in?" Meridia raised her head, and Kane could tell she'd been crying. "Do any of the tunnels lead to the hospital?"

"Yes, there are a couple we know of..."

"So, rather than wait till they try to move her, why can't we sneak into wherever she's being held now and get her out?"

"It's too dangerous M...we don't have the first idea where Izzy's being held, and you all heard what Dr Foster said about his contact wanting out." Peter threw a cold bucket of water over Meridia's proposed suicide mission, but she wasn't about to let it go.

"I could ask my mum...maybe she knows where Izzy's being held?" Kane knew that must've taken a lot for her to offer.

Since their one and only failed attempt to pump Emily for information, Meridia vowed she never wanted to see her mother again. Anyone else who tried was left tangled in knots by her various lies, so it was clear to see she was well versed in manipulation tactics and not to be trifled with.

"Wait." Kane interrupted. It was time to rip the plaster off. "There's someone else we could ask…" He glanced at Peter for a green light to spill the beans, and after a deep contemplative sigh, Peter nodded, allowing Kane to continue.

"Listen guys, I know I've not been myself since…well since our whole lives went to shit…but I've been holding something back…something I didn't know how to share."

"What?" Zach blurted.

His eyes were like saucers and fraught with worry. Kane needed to handle this delicately, as he was all too aware it wasn't just Meridia he let down by keeping secrets.

As he surveyed the row of expectant faces, the right words eluded him. Dry mouthed and floundering, he spewed the truth out onto the table for all to see. A stream of consciousness seasoned with guilt.

"There was more to Izzy's text guys…I'm sorry, I…I just didn't know how to tell you M…it was all such a shock, hearing about your mum…and then losing my shit the way I did…I acted like such a prick, and I know I've said it before, but I'm sorry…I really am. Since then, I just haven't known how to tell you…" Kane felt his eyes welling up and retreated beneath his fringe to hide his discomfort.

"Tell me what?" Meridia sought him out under his refuge, her face awash with angst and confusion.

"Retiarius…" Kane's voice broke the moment he mentioned his name, but he continued, pushing and shoving his shocking confession over the line of his faltering lips.

"Izzy found out who he was…and…and…it's your dad M…Retiarius is your dad…"

II

Kane's words exploded like a flash bang in the crowded control room, leaving everyone reeling in stunned silence.

As the whistling aftermath reverberated in Meridia's shellshocked brain, she tried to make sense of what she heard. It was her turn to speak; she knew that, and the room waited in eager anticipation, but all she could do was replay Kane's last sentence over and over in the hope she heard him wrong.

How could it be?

She glazed over and retreated within, rehashing childhood memories of trips to the beach and family picnics.

Was it all one big charade? Her entire life, the product of two pathological liars, merely keeping up appearances for the sake of an insidious cult?

The more Meridia tugged at the loose threads of her life, the more it all unravelled before her.

Was any of it true? Her parents' love for one another;

for her? The brutal beating leading to her father's arrest, or the months of exile which followed?

The countless tales of a temper she never saw with her own eyes, all stemming from the one person who controlled the narrative from day one: her mum.

"I'm sorry M..." Meridia flinched as Kane rested a hand on her shoulder.

She didn't even notice him get up. Nor did she notice Zach and JJ flock to her side in support. She was overwhelmed, with no idea how long she was lost in thought, staring down at the insipid grey tabletop as it steadily collected her tears.

Meridia raised her heavy head. Thick with a million questions, all clambering over themselves to be heard like a plague of rats, gnawing and nibbling at her composure. Drowning them out was the one question she couldn't answer.

Steeped in self-pity, it raged louder than all the rest, like a violent thunderstorm roaring overhead: why was this happening to her?

"I'm so sorry, dear." Peter met her gaze with one of sorrow. "Please...take as much time as you need."

"Time?" Meridia scoffed. "That's the one thing none of us have..." She sensed the blood rushing to her cheeks, searing her tears as the truth sank in.

"Kane..." she trailed off, wanting to scold him for blowing up what little remained of her life, but deep down she knew it wasn't his fault.

He was just the messenger, and a reluctant one at that. She looked him in the eyes and saw the turmoil he was wrestling with. He lost both parents to the cult, and now she had too. They might not have been butchered by a madman, but she lost them all the same, and for the first time since that harrowing afternoon in the bloodstained wreckage of the Jackson house, she almost knew how Kane and Zach felt.

How all of them felt, JJ and Izzy included. Abandoned, betrayed and robbed.

"It's not your fault..." she mumbled, dazed by the bludgeoning reality that her parents were both mixed up in the impending apocalypse. "Wh...what did she say? Izzy, I mean..."

"She just said he couldn't be trusted..." Kane gave Meridia his phone so she and the others could read it in full.

"But the more I think about it, the less I'm sure. Izzy thought if she got caught, it would be your dad's fault, but maybe she was just unlucky. Maybe he was trying to help. Why else would he take her to the hospital? If we could just access her email, then we'd know more..."

"What about Declan?" JJ suggested. "He found us in the first place. I bet he could hack Izzy's email."

"We don't want to do that." Peter weighed in with the voice of reason.

"We don't know what else might have been said in their email exchange." He looked nervously at the door and lowered his voice. "We don't want anyone knowing about your gift M...it might put you in danger."

"Peter's right..." Kane paced around the table, back toward his chair. "As much as I like these guys, we've only known them a few days. They all seem legit, but then so did all our parents, and look how that worked out. That's why I say we should reach out to Retiarius...er, your dad. We have an email address for him now, so no-one else would need to know."

"But how will we know if he can be trusted?" Zach countered.

"We don't know if we can trust anyone spud, even the people we're locked away down here with. One more isn't gonna hurt. Besides, if we get a bad feeling, we just pull the plug on him. We can set up a new email account and contact him from there so there are no ties to any of us." Kane sat back down and rested on his elbows in contemplation.

"It's M's choice though. Whatever she says goes on this one...I just thought it might be a way for us to track Izzy down." Meridia sensed the mounting desperation in the room as she glanced around at the nervous faces surrounding her.

"Ok, it's worth a try...but Peter, I want you to do it. I need time to figure out how I feel about everything."

"So long as you're sure, M. I know it's a lot to wrap your head around, and for what it's worth, I'm truly sorry. None of you deserve any of this...but we can only play the cards we are dealt. I'll make an excuse to go above ground and reach out then...before I follow up with Dr Foster."

"Do you trust him?" Meridia asked. "I know we haven't been here long, but you've spent more time with him than us. They all seem normal, and nice...but I can't get a read on anything down here. Not Izzy, not anyone. I wish I took something more personal to her than her stupid coat...or maybe it's the fact we're underground...whatever it is, it's driving me nuts. I've gone from being abducted by a zombie in a fridge, to nothing..."

Meridia knew she was bending the truth, but her harrowing visions of their bleak future would only distract them from the task at hand, so she promised herself she would tell them once they rescued Izzy.

"If I'm honest, I don't think I'll ever be able to trust anyone outside of this room again. But, for what it's worth, I don't think there is a secret agenda here. I know Dr Foster has his quirks, but I'm convinced he means well, as does Grace and the others. They still have some way to go before they earn my trust, but if they follow through with their offer to help us save Izzy, then it would certainly get them a lot closer in my book." Peter wearily rose to his feet, and it dawned on Meridia he must be running on empty now.

"On that note, I think it's best I get to it. You guys stay here as long as you need, but I'm keen to get a better look at the maps in Dr Foster's lab."

"Any idea who he's getting all this info from?" Kane voiced everyone's curiosity about who the mole might be.

"Not really, I'm afraid, although I have my suspicions. Beyond this bunker is a modest network of resistance fighters using guerrilla tactics to disrupt the Children of the Shadows whenever possible..."

"Eh?" Kane resisted rolling his eyes as Zach and Meridia glanced at each other, miffed.

"Sorry guys...that means they are avoiding head-on confrontations and simply trying to frustrate and wear down the cult however they can. From what I gather, the network is diverse, but don't all share a common goal as you would expect. Some are more aware of the bigger picture, like we are, whereas others are more focused on their own survival, which makes them unreliable for any larger scale, coordinated effort. That's also why none of them know of our location, in case they try to oust us." Peter gestured to the banal walls surrounding them.

"Declan and Dr Foster have forged a fortress of their own here, and whilst it remains a refuge for strays and survivors, it is off-limits for anyone with more questionable motives."

"Who do you suspect?" Kane pressed.

"It may be a coincidence, but I think their source has a connection to the hospital. The USB drive we collected, although plain, looks the same as one I noticed on the reception desk at Chase Side..." Peter tried to stem the swell of gasps and murmurs rising from the group of gobsmacked teens.

"Now try not to go jumping to any conclusions. As I say, it's just a hunch. But it's as good as any we have right now." Peter sidestepped Kane and made his way toward the door.

"I'll be back soon to share whatever else I learn. We have a long day ahead of us all, and mine started several hours ago." Kane gave Peter a thumbs up and then turned his attention to the others, who were still slack jawed from this morning's news.

JJ returned to his seat and was deep in thought, no doubt wondering if the mole might be someone he knew, whereas Zach stayed next to Meridia and was fumbling in his pocket for something.

"What do we do now?" Meridia asked. Her cheeks returned to their usual colour, but her bright blue eyes still appeared glazed, as if she was under a hypnotist's spell.

"I think we should spend a little more time getting to know our hosts. If we're gonna be relying on their help, then we need to know for sure if we can trust them. It might also help take our minds off things while we wait for Peter." He peered directly at Meridia, but his last comment was meant for all of them.

"Cool. Let's do it then." JJ slowly got to his feet, still distracted by Peter's hunch. "How about Zach and I catch up with Declan, while you and M see what Nadia and Grace are up to?"

"Sound like a plan." Kane spotted JJ's intention to

repair the fractures within the group from a mile away, and assumed Meridia did too, but she didn't protest as she tucked her chair in.

"Here..." Zach placed something in Meridia's palm as he made his way past her.

"So you can always find me." He added, hurrying after JJ, red-faced with embarrassment.

Meridia opened her hand to find a tiny Lego figurine of Wonder Woman staring up at her with oversized cartoon eyes. It was a sweet gesture that wasn't lost on Kane, or Meridia, judging by the tears welling up in her eyes. Zach must have been planning that ever since they left their home.

"C'mon M..." Kane put a hand on her shoulder as she wandered over towards him, transfixed with her new miniature toy.

Leading her out, he was again reminded of the heavy price they all paid for entering Crooked House that fateful day.

A childhood lost, where toys and trinkets were no longer things of wonder or of play, but sombre reminders of the lives they left behind.

12

"You called for me, Grand Master?" Grady entered the secret chamber beneath Crooked House to find it surprisingly bare.

A few days earlier, he summoned a weaver from the dark realm and watched it greedily devour a pile of rotten corpses in the room's centre. Now, all that remained was the residual slop from a broth of putrefied entrails, sloshing around in the canals of a pentagram carved into the stony ground.

Although the rancid carcasses were all scoffed, the stench of death and decay still lingered. Wrestling its way through the thick, damp air and forcing its way into Grady's throat as he surveyed the murky room.

Mould-infested and heavily water-stained, the rocky, windowless walls painted a bleak picture for the dungeon's next hapless victim, with the only light radiating from a smattering of ceremonial candles strewn around the ground, charting each point of the macabre star etched at his feet. Somewhere beyond the flickering gold and amber, a familiar, yet eerily distorted voice sliced through the gloom.

"It is almost time, brother Grady..." The Grand Master emerged from the shadows.

The sacred mask of Baphomet hid his identity. As he approached, the lambent glow brought his twisted metal face to life, as lapping flames shimmered and danced among the elaborate engravings spanning his menacing goat facade.

Towering over Grady, his barbed, razor-sharp horns almost scraped along the dungeon's grimy ceiling as they coiled their way out from beneath his black, silver-encrusted hood.

Staring up at the lavish pentagram engraved in the Grand Master's polished metal forehead, Grady wondered if he would ever learn the true identity of this man behind the mask. In all his time serving the Temple of Shadows, this was the third incarnation of their leader. Each one was a mere host, chosen to harbour a malevolent spirit far older than the rest. Perhaps even as old as time.

"You grow curious..." Grady redirected his gaze to the diabolical black eyes, watching him from behind their shining anonymity.

"The weaver?" Grady asked, shifting topics to avoid further scrutiny.

"Ah, yes, the weaver." The Grand Master's sonorous voice buzzed in Grady's ears like swarming mosquitos as it reverberated around the suffocating crypt. *"It nests in the catacombs, beneath the temple. I sense your eagerness, brother Grady...that is why I called for you. I believe we have a traitor in our midst...one I believe has leaked our plans for the Di Salvo girl."*

"Who is it?" Grady's palms itched at the prospect of killing again so soon.

Whoever it was, he vowed he would take his time and

savour each incision. Unlike the Di Salvo's, who unfortunately fell afoul of his blood-crazed urges. Their slaying was over all-too quickly, and Grady needed to make do with mutilating them after they died, an impulsive act he nearly always regretted.

"Brother Wells."

"The barber? But how...why? He has no knowledge of what we do, nor the brains to find out." Grady was taken aback by the Grand Master's revelation and was expecting someone with more influence.

"He was just a messenger. Which is why we must make an example of him...send a message to whoever he is in league with." The Grand Master stepped into the centre of the giant pentagram as he continued.

"Sister Hutson saw him skulking around the park under the cover of darkness this morning...he tacked an envelope beneath a bench. Within an hour, it was collected by our friend Higginsworth and another outsider I do not recognize...here." The Grand Master handed Grady an envelope of his own.

"Inside you'll find pictures. It seems the writer found himself another ally...a woman. Sister Hutson thought we might use them to our advantage."

"Excellent...I'll be sure to show Wells before I kill him." Grady felt flush with excitement at the prospect of torturing the treacherous barber and knew there would be plenty of him to carve up.

At well over six feet and weighing a shade under twenty stone, he was often used as a heavy to intimidate and deliver threats. He would be a sizeable scalp to add to Grady's growing collection. His mind wandered, recalling his encounters with the man to conjure an image of his eyes.

"It is time to deliver a different message, not just to the

traitors...but to anyone foolish enough to think they can stand against us." Grady was abruptly yanked from his dark fantasy.

"Retiarius?" Grady was desperate to stick his knife in that turncoat too, having somehow evaded capture for the better part of a year now.

Despite serving up the Di Salvo girl on a silver platter, Retiarius remained high on his kill list. Another example, just waiting to have his spleen ripped out. The Grand Master refused to acknowledge the tiny thorn in their side and instead moved straight into his demands.

"You will send the weaver... a demonstration of our power to any other doubters since the fall of the night walker..." The Grand Master's command felt like a knife in Grady's back, as if his one and only pleasure in life was just denied him, but still there was a part of him wanting to witness the weaver take on a live subject. *"Leave the mark on his place of business...the weaver will do the rest."*

"Yes, Grand Master, I'll do it at once. And what about the writer?" Grady tried to salvage a kill of his own.

"Oh, don't worry about him." The Grand Master gestured to the four dingy walls surrounding them. *"I have a feeling he'll come to us soon enough."*

13

PETER CROUCHED BEHIND THE DENSE UNDERGROWTH gathered beside the bunker's entrance and pressed send. His appeal to Retiarius was direct and to the point, simply asking him to share anything he knew about the impending ritual and where the cult might hold Izzy prisoner. The time for beating around the bush was over.

He knew it was a long shot at best, but one Kane was right to suggest. It was crunch time, and they couldn't afford to overlook anything in their quest to rescue Izzy, regardless of the multitude of questions hanging over Meridia's father.

With miles of sprawling underground tunnels and secret passages between Chase Side and Crooked House, they would need all the help they could get if they were to stand any chance of finding her in time.

Peter wondered if mayor Naidu was still a viable option worth exploring. Before Izzy's abduction, they both researched him and were surprised by the lack of obvious ties to the cult. A mayor would have influence worth tapping into, which made him a worthy ally, but for now, Peter had no way to reach him fast enough.

If he was on the right side of all this, why hadn't the cult already recruited him?

The more Peter mulled over everything they needed to overcome, the more insurmountable it all became, so he cleared his mind before venturing back inside. Suffering from tiredness and overwhelm, he needed a second wind before his meeting with Dr Foster.

Taking a lungful of crisp morning air, Peter welcomed the wintery bite as it seared his throat and jarred him from his impending spiral. Somewhere in the depths of its sharp, icy sting, he savoured the subtle notes of morning dew and frosted nettles. A much-needed relief from the banal bunker air-con. The nostalgic bouquet soothed Peter's soul, and he allowed himself to close his eyes for just a moment.

Another deep breath of the floral aroma transported him back to his youth, and a world long before Crooked House. The son of a farmer, he and his brother would often spend similar mornings helping their dad work their family's modest patch of land before catching the bus to school. He could almost hear his dad's voice whispering in his ear, patiently guiding him as they mended fences together, and his brother's infectious laugh as they collected an apple each from their tiny orchard on their way out.

Life was so simple back then, and Peter wondered why he ever wanted to leave his family home. Perhaps if his brother James didn't die, things might be different, and he could've enjoyed the same quiet and content rural life as his father, blissfully unaware of the apocalypse now looming on the horizon.

'*What ifs are phantom thoughts*' JJ's favoured saying burst the bubble of his daydream and Peter opened his eyes to the surrounding wasteland.

Overgrown with weeds and wildflowers, Drayton

Hollow shimmered beneath the opaque sun as it struggled to break free from its cloudy prison. As he admired the rich green hues thriving in such a cold and hostile environment, he felt galvanized by nature's resilience.

What better place to form a rebellion?

It was in that moment Peter caught a glimpse of his true calling. Buoyed by his newfound optimism, he checked his surroundings for any prying eyes, before slipping back inside to reconvene with Dr Foster.

He was so preoccupied with his renewed sense of purpose he didn't even feel his phone vibrate as a response from Retiarius arrived in his inbox.

14

Ginger Chops was one of several barbershops sprinkled along Shawbook's dwindling high street.

Bookended by vacant retail units, its tongue-in-cheek name was a self-deprecating nod to the owner's copper-coloured beard, which made it an instant hit when he opened back in 2017.

In the less affluent end of town, it provided Grady with the perfect opportunity to approach the shopfront without being noticed by any passersby. Dressed in a fitted charcoal jersey tracksuit he donned whenever he was off duty, he blended in perfectly with the concrete graveyard of empty betting shops and pop-up vape dispensaries.

As Grady shrugged his rucksack off his shoulder and opened its zip, a crumpled beer can rattled its way toward him down the narrow cobblestoned footpath, riding the cool morning breeze as it swept through town.

If he hurried, he could make the mark, then get inside and pull the blinds down before any customers arrived. However, part of him wanted another witness to maximise the carnage and put the fear of god in the people of Shawbrook.

Pausing briefly, Grady surveyed the rest of the deserted street, indulging in a moment of pride as he soaked up his bleak surroundings. This was all part of their master plan: the systematic dismantling of society brick by pitiful brick.

Just as the Grand Master prophesied, their carefully crafted cocktail of disillusionment and contempt spread like cancer. Breaking the spirit of the masses as they found themselves subjected to failing economies caused by a sinister coalition of corrupt governments around the globe. It was a glorious symphony of subjugation, softening everyone up for the fast-approaching reign of terror looming on the horizon.

A crooked sneer slivered its way across Grady's pallid face as he envisaged the world's impending demise in all its technicolour cruelty. Then he returned to the task at hand.

Reaching into his bag, his fingertips glanced the handle of his hunting knife and for a second, he contemplated disobeying his orders and hacking the traitor's head clean off.

The imaginary sound of steel tearing through flesh and grating against bone made his hand tremble as it briefly lingered over the hilt. His palm tingled in anticipation of gripping the knife and forcing its serrated blade through the soft pink skin of brother Wells' throat.

"Not now..." Grady whispered through quivering lips, wrestling with his insatiable thirst for blood, before thrusting his hand deeper inside the bag.

It didn't take long to find what he was looking for: a shabby, tan leather pouch that was tied up tight with a coffee-coloured drawstring. Weighing next to nothing, he pinched the hem between his thumb and forefinger, plucking it out of his bag.

The pouch contained the charred phalanges of the witch's index finger, fused together by a centuries-old fire which decimated Crooked House amidst an angry mob's pursuit of vengeance.

Eager now for any kind of violence, Grady loosened the bag's knot and fished around for its contents. The blackened finger was gnarled and twisted, like an old, withered twig, but he wasted no time gawking at it. Steering clear of the barbershop's glass facade, Grady held the grisly digit like a stick of chalk and scraped the root of the bone against the building's red brickwork.

Unsure how hard to press at first, the ease with which it left its smoky black trail after each measured stroke as he meticulously drew an inverted pentagram surprised him.

"Fizz..."

Grady flinched and backed away the moment he connected the last points of the macabre symbol, as the dusty outline scorched the bricks and mortar like corrosive acid, searing itself deep into the fabric of the building like a permanent scar.

Fanning away the fumes of his handiwork, Grady basked in the intense coppery smell as it snaked its way up his nose, akin to a vintage bouquet of blood, the likes of which he never experienced before.

The aroma was intoxicating, like the sum of a hundred kills all at once, and it released a tidal wave of endorphins, leaving his entire body tingling in unbridled ecstasy. As the mist drifted away on the icy wind, it revealed a crimson mark of death, which meant the curse was complete.

Grady summoned the weaver and sealed brother Wells' doom. Heart still racing, he caught his breath and cupped his hands to the shopfront window. The traitor's tools lay on the counter, ready for his first customer of the day, but he was nowhere to be seen.

Picking up his rucksack and zipping it shut, Grady casually slipped in through the front door and flipped the open sign to closed. The loose-lipped barber of Shawbrook was about to have his mouth shut, permanently.

15

Lance Wells gave his face one last splash with cold water, then glanced up at his tired reflection in the washroom mirror as he wheezed on a mouthful of cherry blossom air freshener.

Having failed to sleep a wink during the days leading up to his act of betrayal, he appeared as if he aged ten years overnight. His clear blue eyes were jaded and bloodshot; hemmed in by puffy grey bags that inflated the fullness of his face.

Too tired to style his hair that morning, he turned his black baseball cap backwards and leant on the white ceramic sink to get a better look at himself.

"You look like shit mate..." He muttered, drying his hands on his shorts.

Despite the cold snap, Lance dressed for summer 11 months of every year, with black his go-to colour having been told once by an ex-girlfriend that it was slimming. Warm-blooded and big-boned, comfort was important, particularly as he spent long days on his feet cutting hair. He stroked his scruffy ginger beard and watched the flakes of dandruff float down onto his triple XL black t-shirt like the February snowfall, then wearily shook his head.

"It's done..." He sighed. "Not much you can do about it now, is there..."

On his eighteenth birthday, Lance's father indoctrinated him into the Children of the Shadows. At first, he thought he was being pranked. An early Halloween stunt to bring him down a peg, or too. His father was always jealous of Lance, constantly on the lookout for opportunities to get one over his far more physically imposing and charismatic son. However, on this occasion, he was telling the truth.

Of course, Lance heard all the stories growing up, tales of a secret organization with big plans to create a free world. At least that's how it was sold to him over the years; preparing him for their big reveal. Once he peered behind the veil, he immediately questioned the organisation's motives. Even the name was sinister.

Regardless of their true intentions, it didn't take long for them to get their hooks into him. Insisting the police looked the other way whenever Lance got into trouble, which was pretty often once he reached his late teens. A couple of bar fights turned nasty, and a slew of ignored DUIs.

All the special concessions pandered to his growing ego and made him feel like a local celebrity. In exchange, they asked for the odd threat here and there. Nothing too serious at first, just using his considerable girth to intimidate outsiders and those who refused to cooperate.

When things escalated and Lance almost beat a man to death, they gave him his own barbershop to buy his silence. What a fool he was, falling for their petty bribes and bullshit. Not anymore, though. He was done with all that, and this would be the last week of looking over his shoulder and living in fear.

He couldn't even remember how he got himself into this mess to begin with. The friend of a friend of a customer. Despite the cult's many trappings, even Lance was surprised by how little convincing was required to turn him against them. Just a couple of conversations unearthed the sceptical teen within and reconnected him with his senses.

With his dad recently passed and no longer on hand to brainwash him, it was just Lance and his mum left now, and like countless other residents, her allegiance was nothing more than a tacit agreement.

Obedience born out of fear, just like many lesser people, Lance himself helped enlist. Now, all he needed to do was keep his head down and wait. If he made it to Sunday, the good guys would extract him and his more influential accomplice, or at least that's what he was promised.

Taking a deep breath, Lance forced a smile as he readied himself to brave his first customer of the day and turned the doorknob. As the narrow strip of fluorescent light slowly expanded into the gloomy depths of Ginger Chops, Lance knew something was up.

Certain he opened all the blinds upon his arrival, the studio floor awaiting him now bore a closer resemblance to 8PM than 8AM, and it didn't take long to find the cause.

Sitting on the shabby leather two-seater underneath the blacked-out window was an unexpected visitor. Wearing a dark-coloured tracksuit with the hood up, Lance was certain it wasn't his scheduled 8:15 appointment.

Unphased by his discovery, the wiry looking mystery man remained silent and perfectly still in the middle of the couch. His head was bent low as if he was studying his own upturned palms that were stretched out in front of him.

"What you playing at?" Lance's booming voice bounced around the mirrored studio as he took an aggressive step towards the intruder, but the man didn't even flinch. He just sat there, unmoving, like a jersey shrouded statue in a quasi-meditative pose.

"Oi! I'm talking to you..." Lance clenched his fists and took another thunderous step forward.

Whilst he was busy talking to himself in the washroom, the gate crasher must have closed all the shop's blinds, cutting the morning light down to a criss-cross of murky prison bars deftly dissecting the room.

Dimmed to a formless obscurity, the polished, navy blue décor and swanky leather barber's chairs seemed to cradle the trespasser in their shadowy embrace. As Lance took another step toward him, the man reached up and calmly lowered his hood.

"B...brother Grady...sorry, I didn't recognize you..." The moment he saw the man's deathly pale face in the gloom, Lance's anger soon turned to fear, stopping him in his tracks. His size twelves became heavy like lead and an icy sweat broke out across the back of his considerable neck.

"Brother Wells..." Grady's sardonic voice snaked its way along the black and white tiled floor and slithered into Lance's ears, setting off another icy shiver.

"A little birdy tells me you've been spending your mornings in the park. Taken up jogging, have we?" His unearthly blue eyes twinkled in the shadows, unphased by the darkness enfolding them.

"Can't say it's doing you much good...fatty." Lance felt his temper flare at the childish jibe and squeezed his fists tighter as he jostled with the urge to do something rash.

He saw Grady in action once, and the memory still haunted him to this day. His speed and strength were bordering on superhuman as he cooly dispatched of four rowdy tourists in the alley, backing onto The Rusty Nail, Shawbrook's token bar. Not one of those men landed so much as a finger on the oily little weasel, and although their paths didn't cross very often since, whenever they did, the sight of him made Lance's flesh crawl.

"I've started using it as a cut-through on my way to work some mornings. It ain't gonna shift this any time soon though..." Lance replied, rubbing his stomach. "This is all bought and paid for."

His vague attempt to disarm the psycho with humour fell on deaf ears as Grady stared at him, unblinking. Instead, he began sniffing the surrounding air overly dramatically.

"Can you smell that?" Grady asked. "It smells like..." He held a hand up to stop Lance from answering.

"No, wait...it's on the tip of my tongue...it smells like...a rat!"

Grady jumped to his feet, and Lance's knees buckled in surprise. Suddenly there was a knife in his hand, the one he used to gut those tourists that day, and Lance had no idea how it got there.

"Wh...what are you saying?" Lance dug his heels in, maintaining his ignorance, but inside he was already panicking.

He was built for power, not speed, which left him at a tremendous disadvantage, although if things turned ugly, he was confident he would only have to land one punch to level the playing field. He strained his eyes to see beyond his favoured barber chair and saw his scissors were laid out where he left them.

"I'm saying the game is up, traitor. Consider yourself

caught..." Grady remained standing in front of the sofa, so Lance shuffled back a little to create more distance between them.

"So, I'm going to ask you this once, and I want you to think long and hard about the answer you give me. Who are you working with? Tell me the truth, and I'll make this quick. Lie, and I'll torture you here all day, then I'll pay your mother a visit tonight for good measure...The choice is yours..." Grady started twirling the knife in his hand while he waited for a response.

Its polished steel blade sparkled in the gloom, snatching at the slender strands of light seeping in over the killer's shoulder like he was twining spaghetti. Lance felt torn. Certain death awaited him regardless. Did he go down fighting or roll over?

Beneath his baggy t-shirt, a cold sweat leaked from every pour, clinging to the fabric around his shoulders, and then he made his decision and answered the insufferable little shit.

"Looks like you're going to have to give me your best shot in that case, chief. But I ain't pulling any punches, so if I catch you, I'm gonna break that scrawny neck of yours..." Lance planted his feet and braced himself for a quick response, but Grady remained still, sitting back down on the couch behind him.

"We'll see what the weaver has to say, shall we...we'll let her be the judge." He crossed his legs and cracked a sneer.

"The what?" A strange sound above interrupted Lance's puzzlement.

"*Click-clack...click-clack...*"

"Ah, there she is...right on time." Grady placed both hands behind his head and leaned back into his seat like he was about to unwind with his favourite TV show.

Lance traced the sound across the ceiling and over his shoulder towards the direction of the washroom.

"Wh...what is that?" He mumbled, keeping one eye on Grady.

"*Crash!*"

Lance spun around to the sound of breaking glass and glimpsed the tail-end of an enormous shadow flash across the washroom door, momentarily plunging the room into darkness.

"*Click-clack...click-clack...*"

The sound was louder this time and coming from inside the building. Whatever it was, it was big. With his heart in his mouth, Lance craned his neck to see through the gap in the door, still conscious Grady could pounce from behind him at any moment.

"Wh...who's there?" He stuttered. Then he saw it.

"*Clack!*"

A monstrous black thorny spider leg cracked the slate tile nearest the doorway and sent a shockwave of terror hurtling up Lance's legs. Frozen to the spot, he watched helplessly as the door slowly opened toward him.

"*Creeeak...*"

Two blazing red orbs cut through the shadows like angry car headlights as the colossal mutant arachnid forced its way into the room. Below its searing eyes were row upon row of shark-like teeth, thick with mucus and glistening beneath the flickering flames of its menacing stare.

"What the..." Lance trembled, shuffling back towards Grady as the weaver edged closer, one sinewy leg at a time, until its bulbus body, covered with oily black hair, squeezed all the way through the doorframe.

A nauseating waft of sulphur followed the creature into

the room, causing Lance to gag as it squared up to him, hissing through clenched teeth.

"*Click!*"

The lights suddenly snapped on overhead, dazzling Lance as he stood rooted to the spot like a sitting duck.

"Let's shed some light on the matter, shall we?" Grady gleefully taunted.

He was waving a phone in the air now, filming every second of the imminent showdown between man and beast.

"Last chance fatso...who are you working with?" He jeered, but the pounding of Lance's heart devoured his words.

Face to face with his worst nightmare, any shred of fight Lance thought he had inside him ebbed away the second the hideous abomination was laid bare beneath the fluorescent lights of his violated barbershop.

Black as night, the creature looked even more imposing as it scuttled along the glossy studio floor, casting a long, malevolent shadow in its wake. Staring at its shimmering, razor-sharp teeth, Lance realized any attempt he made to defend himself would be like putting his fist into a wood chipper, which meant his only way out was through Grady.

Backing away a little further, he rediscovered the strength to make a fist, and that was when he felt the blade in his back.

"Nu-uh..." Grady prodded him forward like a lamb to the slaughter as the weaver's hissing turned to a sickening wretch like a giant fly regurgitating its food.

Its furry body rippled back and forth until it eventually brought something vile and revolting up from the depths of its gut.

"*Kaff...splat!*"

16

"Aaaaargh!"

Grady's eyes grew as round as saucers, brimming with morbid fascination as he marvelled at the weaver in action. This was his first time watching the creature tackle a live subject, and he found its wicked restraint perversely exhilarating as it elected to torture and toy with its prey.

A steaming globule of slimy green mucus violently erupted from the weaver's mouth like a bullet from a gun and attached itself to Wells' raised fist as if it were glue. The blow dropped all 6'3" of him to the ground like a sack of spuds, as the venomous discharge eroded his hand to a bloody stump in a matter of seconds. Molten flesh and bone oozed down his forearm, searing whatever remained of his blistering skin as the lethal acid slowly devoured everything it touched, including his wristwatch.

A stomach-turning cocktail of boiled blood and sulphur choked the stuffy studio of all its air and Grady took a step back to avoid the shimmering crimson pool mushrooming at his feet.

Returning to the safety of the couch, he watched in

ghoulish admiration from behind the camera as the weaver waited patiently for its first devastating attack to fizzle out, cocking its gruesome head from side to side and eyeballing its victim with stony contempt.

"Help me..." Wells screamed at Grady, begging for mercy, but in his agonizing throes, a residual drop of corrosive venom streaked across the traitor's thigh.

It set to work immediately, hungrily gnawing its way through the fabric of his shorts, then muscle and tissue like a gooey hacksaw until the bone was completely severed.

Clawing his way along the ground in a last ditched attempt to escape, Wells left his burly leg smouldering behind him like a mutilated magician's assistant, dismembered by a trick gone horribly wrong.

As the dying man sluggishly smeared a gory trail of claret and faeces across the checkered tiles, Grady took his opportunity to zoom in and capture his anguished face, glistening with sweat and tears like a freshly basted hog waiting to be roasted. The similarity brought a twisted smile to Grady's face.

"Poor little piggy...I bet my offer looks much more appealing now, doesn't it?" As he finished his sentence, the weaver heaved again.

The ominous rasp rattled and hummed as the creature prepared to serve up another coagulated dose of death. The stink in the room was rancid now, and not even the breeze wafting in through the washroom's broken window could combat the putrid stench of singed hair and liquified flesh.

"P...please..." Wells, sensing the end was nigh, reached up towards the camera with his bloody stump, but his desperate plea was in vain.

"*Kaff...splat!*"

Another larger dollop of steaming green phlegm struck

the side of his head, knocking his baseball cap clean off as it bonded to the side of his face.

In less than a second, the convulsions started as if he was plugged into the mains. Flailing around like an amateur breakdancer, Grady kept the camera close to the traitor's face in order to capture every grisly detail of his demise.

Unfortunately, the sulphurous blob swiftly dashed all hopes of watching Wells suffer by collapsing the top of his skull and melting his brain to mush. Though the rest was academic, his own enjoyment of watching a man's face wilt like a blood-filled candle surprised Grady.

First Wells' eyes fluttered and rolled back in their sockets, but then the left one unexpectedly popped like a ripe boil and oozed down the side of his drooping face.

As the rest of his skin slopped onto the floor in a steamy pile of glossy red pulp, it left his teeth and jawbone fully exposed for the briefest of moment before they too succumbed to the corrosive power of the weaver's deadly spittle.

From there, gravity took over as Wells flopped to his side and the remains of his face disintegrated to a chorus of sizzles and crackles, covering the floor in a velvety concoction of fat and cartilage like a blood-infused Cadbury's cream egg.

"Click-clack...click-clack..."

The weaver skittered in to gobble up whatever was left, cracking and crunching through bones between slurps. Mesmerized by the beast's vicious brutality and insatiable hunger, Grady watched its globular body swell, then contract with each morsel it ingested. Like a walking meat grinder, it quickly dispatched of the lump formally known as Lance, chomping and grinding his half-melted corpse before licking the tiles clean of any scraps.

Despite its terrifying appearance, when it finished its meal, Grady felt the sudden urge to pet the creature as if it were a loyal and devoted dog. Having fulfilled the curse, Grady waited to see what the weaver would do next. He was assured no harm would come to him, but now, staring into the fiery eyes of the most lethal killing machine he'd ever witnessed, he wasn't so sure.

"Click-clack...click-clack..."

The weaver skuttled forward and sized him up, its breath reeking like a butcher's shop. Slowly slipping the phone back in his pocket, Grady held his nerve as best he could. It was an unsettling feeling, being at the mercy of another, and not one he experienced since early childhood when his older brother used to bully him.

He felt deeper inside his pocket and grazed the handle of his favoured knife then wondered if the weaver could somehow sense his wavering faith so left it there, safe in the knowledge his superior speed would allow him to drive it through the creature's head long before it could ever muster enough acid to vomit in his direction.

The realization of a potential weakness calmed Grady, enabling him to maintain eye contact with a little more verve as he patiently waited for the weaver to return to the catacombs from which it came.

Staring deep into the creature's fiery orbs he noticed for the first time that their blood red flames matched the mark of death he scrawled on the wall outside, and as the standoff drew to a close, they slowly dimmed and returned to their usual amber.

"Click-clack...click-clack..."

The weaver backed away, suddenly subdued, then turned and crawled out through the broken back window. Grady heard its prickly footsteps echo above, just as they did when it arrived, before gradually fading away like the remnants of a distant dream, leaving him alone in the silence of the empty studio.

With his mission almost complete, this would definitely deliver an emphatic message for all those who opposed the Children of the Shadows, and he would make damn sure the infuriating upstart Higginsworth saw it.

Reaching into his bag of tricks once more, Grady pulled out a scuffed and battered black metal water bottle, then unscrewed the plastic cap. It belonged to his brother and was covered in faded *Mortal Kombat* stickers, his favourite game around the time of his death. Grady found it amusing. The miserable little shit had his head crushed like one of the game's gory finishing moves, and so kept the bottle as a souvenir from that momentous night.

Today, however, it offered far more than a shot of sepia-toned nostalgia from his brother's brutal comeuppance.

Having filled it with gasoline on his way into town that morning, he took a lungful of the sweet woody fumes as they mingled with the coppery stench of death, and then doused the wooden counter with its contents.

As Grady fumbled around in his bag for a lighter, he became aware he was about to stray from the Grand Master's instructions, but he figured he deserved at least a little creative license having donated this kill to an eight-legged freak.

"*Click!*"

Grady watched the golden flame dance and sway seductively in his hand for a moment, then tossed it onto the counter.

"*Whoosh...*"

The blaze ravaged the worktop, blistering the paint as it streaked towards the back of the studio, but Grady wasn't hanging around to admire its destructive beauty. He had bigger fish to fry. Making his way out through the front door and into the deserted street outside, he closed his eyes and let the cooling breeze wash over him.

The air streaming in through the broken window would keep the fire burning long enough to reduce Ginger Chops to ash, and with a bit of luck, wipe out some of the other worthless scum. Flipping his hood up to hide his face, Grady slipped away into anonymity, with no one in Shawbrook being any the wiser about what he just did.

17

Peter found Dr Foster hunched over a desk in his lab with his head buried in a large leather-bound book. Without glancing up, he gestured for Peter to enter with a subtle wave of his short, stubby fingers.

Although he dressed like a run-of-the-mill university professor, the doctor's physical appearance was more in keeping with the foreman on a building site.

Stocky with broad shoulders, he had a low centre of gravity, standing somewhere around 5'7", and as Peter stepped inside and closed the door behind him, he half expected to find a high-vis jacket and a hard hat hanging on the back of it.

Large enough to sleep six, the converted workshop resembled every other room in the bunker, with drab grey walls and a matching concrete floor. However, it was also home to a long wooden bench which Dr Foster now used as a makeshift workstation.

Running along the back wall, the repurposed counter was littered with various trinkets and textbooks he acquired over the months since he commandeered the room for his research. From witchcraft and alchemy, to occult history and ancient rituals, he had quite the collection, with the odd physics book thrown in here and there for good measure.

Peter assumed this was how he garnered the affectionate nickname of Dr Doom, having heard he regularly sent Grace and Declan out on scavenger hunts to the local library as he strived to understand the dark forces they were all up against.

Amongst them were also several journals, some old, some new, and amongst those was the directory. A who's who of outsiders like them, who were also fighting against the cult in their own unique way. Foster mentioned the book when they first arrived, stating it was off limits.

It remained that way ever since, and understandably so given its importance.. Peter often wondered how many names were among its ranks, but anytime he asked either Declan or the doctor, they ducked the question. Perhaps there were fewer people on the right side of this than they cared to admit. Perhaps the book was empty and a whimsical aspiration.

In the awkward silence of Dr Foster's studying, Peter tuned into a monotonous hum purring in the distance. Next to the bunker's power room, he heard the generators ticking over, whirring and vibrating against the wall to his right. Declan did a great job resurrecting the place, yet any connection to the outside world remained elusive.

The bunker's construction predated LAN by a couple of decades, and its underground location prevented connection to any nearby Wi-Fi. The only form of modern technology present, aside from their redundant phones, was a secure laptop which they used to access USB's passed between informants and factions. Any real-time monitoring online was carried out by Declan using a burner phone on his many cigarette breaks throughout the day.

"Sorry Peter, I was just revisiting some old notes I made on satanic rituals...although the more I read on the subject, the less I'm convinced we're dealing with conventional satanists." Dr Foster closed the book and rubbed his weary eyes.

"I was hoping I could find something to help us save your friend...but short of tracking down a seer, it looks like there's no other way than a good old-fashioned jailbreak."

"A seer?" Peter played dumb, having deflected Dr Foster's mention of the word once already today. "Why a seer?"

"I'm gonna level with you Peter, because...well, I'm hoping you'll be able to see the bigger picture here." He gestured towards the chair opposite him and Peter took it.

"I've seen the way you are with those kids...and I know you have their best interests at heart. But they're just kids... and we both know there's no way you would've all made it this far without some kind of help..." Peter opened his mouth to protest, but was waved off by Dr Foster.

"Wait, just let me say my piece..." A wry smile snuck across the doctor's face and Peter relented, allowing him to finish.

"We'd been at this for months before you arrived... slowly building a network of people we can trust whilst gathering as much information we could on how to stop all this madness. I know a lot more now than when I first got started, let me tell you. But in all that time, we haven't been able to make even the smallest of dents in the cult's plans... hell, I doubt they even know we exist...and maybe that's why we're all still alive. That nurse of theirs, the crazy one, he's killed more people than smallpox, and don't even get me started on the night walker. Yet here you are, a successful writer, and I like your work by the way...I even have some of your books down here...but here you are with a handful of kids who are barely teenagers and some kind of double agent, yet you've done more damage to the Children of the Shadows than anyone else has in the last 300 years... shit, you've even taken down a witch who, by all accounts, has been around since this whole thing started back in the early 18th century. Now you and I both know, this goes way beyond the realms of luck...so I need to know what it is you're not telling me Peter, cause if it's what I think it is, then it could be a real game changer, for all of us."

Peter took a moment to consider his response. This wasn't how he imagined the meeting going, and whilst he remained determined to protect Meridia, something about the doctor's tone suggested he knew more than Peter did about her gift. He just needed to encourage the doctor to show a little more of his hand.

"We're keen to put an end to all this just as much as you...more so, given everything we've been through. But, as I said before, I don't even know what a seer is, Marcus. Perhaps if you tell me why a seer is so important, then maybe I could help?"

Dr Foster lethargically rose to his feet and wandered over to his workbench. It was clear to see he was burning the candle at both ends and the room reeked of coffee. Perhaps that was partly to blame for the doctor's direct approach this morning.

Peter found him a bit of an odd fish on the whole, highly articulate and forthright, yet spent most of his time in isolation with his books. He wondered if he was always this way, or if his extended time in the bunker played any part. Living in seclusion wasn't easy at the best of times, and even after a few days of being locked down here, Peter experienced the odd bout of cabin fever himself.

Regardless of the doctor's reasons, there was certainly no denying his dedication and desire for answers, although it remained a little unclear what drew him to the cult to begin with.

So far, all Peter knew was he stumbled upon them by chance whilst conducting research for a book, and that each subsequent pull on their insidious thread eventually led him from the other side of the Atlantic to Cold Christmas. Perhaps today's conversation would shed more light on the matter, given the doctor's eagerness to 'level' with him.

"Here..." Dr Foster returned and placed two old, but very different looking, cracked leather journals on the desk between them.

"We're not the only ones to have walked this ill-fated path, it seems. There were others before us over the years. What you see before you are two private journals, Declan managed to 'borrow' from the local museum. They were kept under lock and key, away from the public, which got me wondering why...Why wouldn't they display them with the other artifacts? One dates to the 1700s, and the other a hundred years later. Both are very different in their accounts of Cold Christmas, and both offer different perspectives of what I've come to learn is a seer."

"Who did they belong to?" Peter asked, barely able to stop himself from opening the first book on the pile.

"I suggest you take both books with you and read through them...they may hold some answers that I'm unaware of. In the meantime, I'll give you the whistle-stop tour of what I found, if I may?"

"By all means..." Peter drew the books closer to him as the doctor continued.

"The older book, at the bottom, belonged to a woman named Jane Rowe. She is the wife of the man who built Crooked House, a self-made landlord by the name of Thomas. Have you heard of him?" Peter shook his head, but surmised he might have just learned the identity of the echo residing in room 1.

A mystery until now. The only clue to his identity was tangled up in an urban myth about a man who murdered his wife and her lover in the house.

"I tried to dig a little further when I first got here, but unsurprisingly, there were no public records of anyone associated with the property dating back that far. Rumour has it he murdered Jane and her lover when he discovered them together in bed one night. He is said to have disappeared the same night and has haunted the halls of Crooked House ever since."

"I remember the owner mentioning that story when he showed me around the house, but when he couldn't give me any names or dates, I just figured it was part of his schtick. He had plenty of little anecdotal stories...some true, some clearly manufactured to rustle up business. With hindsight, I probably should've taken more notes, but I had no idea what I was getting myself into back then..."

"There's no smoke without fire as they say...Anyway, for the years after Thomas Rowe went missing, his ghost was said to have lingered, scaring away crooks and robbers who used the abandoned building as a safe house when traveling to and from town. That's actually where the name comes from...Crooked House, as in a house full of crooks." Dr Foster gave another wry smile, alluding to a competitive streak simmering beneath his calm exterior.

"Father Alexander told us the same. He also had a journal dating back to a similar time which referenced the cult and the witch...that's how we discovered her name. I'm certain he had other useful records back at the church, but I never had the time to check and it's just not safe to go back there anymore." Peter sensed an unexpected pang of sorrow grip his throat at the mention of the priest's name.

Although he was only in their lives a short time, there was something about his tenacity that Peter admired and warmed to. His death served up a stark reminder of his own mortality, something he took for granted until then.

"Fascinating..." Peter's flippant retort caught Dr Foster off-guard.

"Er...let's circle back to that as you'll be surprised how good Declan is at sneaking into places...there might still be a way to salvage whatever information the priest had. Now, back to Jane...having read her journal cover to cover, I can't see any evidence she was ever cheating on him, but their marital state wasn't what I was drawn to. It's her account of her husband in the days and weeks leading up to her last entry, which caught my attention. They were childhood sweethearts, according to her journal. Destined to be together in her eyes, although I suspect they had a somewhat rosy tint if you catch my drift...particularly once he made his money. Cold Christmas was already a town in decline back then, rife with petty thieves and violent criminals. Then things got so bad it wasn't safe to walk the streets during the day, let alone at night. So, Thomas built them a house...a haven she called it, somewhere hidden away from all the trouble. Rowe Lodge it was called... although that didn't last. They were only living there a week when the journal stops, and I'm guessing Jane was murdered. What's interesting though, and this brings me back to your question, Peter, is that nightmares plagued Thomas ever since he was an adolescent...but not just any nightmares...these were often the kind that came true. Now aside from Jane, he always kept the full extent of his dreams a secret for fear of being locked up, but throughout these pages, Jane maintains he was telling the truth the entire time, citing many examples of him seeing glimpses of the future."

"Like what?" Now interested, Peter was eager to compare Thomas Rowe's experience with Meridia's.

"Some big, some small. The death of his mother, the rise of crime in Cold Christmas...even a violent incident where a couple of young boys were found mauled by an animal in the woods. Jane often mentions his dreams in her journal... mostly out of concern for her husband's mental state, and then a few days later she chronicles the actual events. I think maybe it was her way of proving to herself that neither of them were going mad...but then his visions took a dark turn, and she worried about his sanity...and her own safety."

"Safety from whom...or what?"

"She was never sure...it was just a feeling she had the longer things went on. You see, Crooked House was a vision that came to him one day whilst hunting in the woods. He stumbled upon the exact spot the house is now built and saw it in every detail. According to Jane, he abandoned his hunt that instant and came back to town, scribbling drawings of what he saw like a man possessed. In a matter of days, his scribbles turned into blueprints, and then the blueprints turned into the house that stands there now. Jane said it was an obsession that changed him... and every time he went to work on the house, his visions would intensify. They got so bad in the end, he couldn't tell the difference between his dreams and reality...and that's when he stopped sharing them with her. He became gaunt and withdrawn...hell his hair even fell out in the final days leading up to their big move. By the time it was finished, Jane had her doubts about everything, including her husband's sanity. She desperately wanted to help him, but what could she do if he refused to open up? Not exactly the behaviour of a woman who was cheating..."

"Is there any clue what happened? To her or to Thomas?" Peter enjoyed a good story as much as the next person, but the clock was ticking, and he was still unsure how this all related to a seer helping Izzy.

"Only her description of his unravelling. She often found him standing in the same spot of the house, staring into space. A look of terror on his face as if he'd just seen a ghost. Other times she heard him talking to someone who wasn't there...like he let the devil in...or at least that's how she described it." A sudden wave of dread washed over Peter, causing him to squirm in his seat.

Having heard of the horrors Meridia endured in her visions, was she heading along the same dark path?

"You ok Peter? You look a little queasy..."

"I'm fine...just conscious of time. We need to come up with a plan to save Izzy, and I still don't understand what help a seer can be. It sounds to me like it might be a seer who caused all this to begin with."

"Well, yes, and no...There is a specific point in Jane's story where Thomas changes...what I believe might have been the perfect storm. According to Jane, he would often find things on his hunting trips...trinkets and such. You see, with the influx of thieves using Cold Christmas as a go-between, they would occasionally drop their spoils along the way. Some in panic, some through choice when they realized they stole some worthless shit nobody would wanna buy. But one man's trash is another man's treasure, as they say, and Thomas would always pick up whatever he found and bring it back with him. The day he found the perfect spot to build a gateway to the underworld, he also found something else...a mirror. According to Jane, it was ugly as hell...a black vanity mirror that had a handle made from bone. Anyway, despite it giving her the creeps, Thomas kept it, and I'm convinced that's what ultimately proved to be his downfall."

"How so?" Peter rubbed his palms down the legs of his jeans to stop their itching. This was all new information, and he was now desperate to read the books for himself.

"I think what he found was no ordinary mirror, Peter. I think Thomas found The Eye of Corvus...or perhaps it found him..."

"The eye of what?!" Peter couldn't mask his confusion as Dr Foster picked up the more recent of the two books and flipped through reams of fluorescent yellow post-its he used to mark its pages. He stopped about a third of the way through and glanced up at Peter. "Which brings me to our second seer, Eliza Wilson."

Peter's blood ran cold at the mention of the name Wilson. There was no way this was just a lucky coincidence. Was Meridia's family entwined with Crooked House from the very beginning?

Regardless of the tiredness gently tugging at his eyelids, and the ticking clock echoing in his mind, Peter was now hooked and needed to know more.

18

MERIDIA'S EARS WERE STILL RINGING FROM KANE'S bombshell as she languidly followed him into the infirmary.

The jarring aroma of antiseptic that greeted them both wasn't enough to break her from her trance, nor was the muffled welcome from Nadia, which was drowned out by the tidal wave of static coursing through her mind.

Once again, her world was upended, like a ship capsized by a vicious, unrelenting storm, and now here she was, desperately clinging to the wreckage of her life to stay afloat.

"Meridia?" Nadia's voice persisted against the tide, finding its way to her as she drifted helplessly at sea.

"Meridia...are you ok? You look a bit peaky..." Meridia snapped to with the help of a gentle nudge from Kane, who circled back beside her.

As the haze of her addled brain subsided, she found Nadia's heart-shaped face in front of her, full of worry.

"S...sorry...I'm ok, just tired." Meridia bluffed, slowing Nadia's approach.

"Still having trouble sleeping?" Nadia asked, her look of

concern softening a little as she opened the nearest cupboard and rifled through its shelves.

The infirmary was little more than a cupboard in size, tacked onto the end of the kitchen and separated by a flimsy stud wall sharing the same creamy yellow as its neighbouring room. As far as colour was concerned, that was the entire gamut of what the bunker offered.

The rest of the room was the standard dreary grey with a black faux-leather seat at its centre resembling a dentist's chair, and a boxy stainless-steel sink behind it on the far wall. A pine-coloured barstool chair was the only other furniture to speak of, which Nadia popped herself down on as she rummaged through a plastic container she plucked from the depths of her medical supplies.

"Here, this might help..." She raised her head and handed Meridia a tiny glass bottle of lavender oil. "A dab of this on your pillow and duvet before bedtime should help you relax."

"Thanks...I'll try it tonight."

A slender dot of a woman in her early thirties, Nadia had a kind face that reminded Meridia of a Disney princess. With huge brown eyes and naturally plump lips, her warm and reassuring smile was framed effortlessly by a loose raven bob that stopped just short of her cleft chin.

A third-generation British Indian, she spent most of her adult life working as a nurse in the midlands, until an opportunity arose to join the emergency ward at Chase Side. Considering her profession a true calling, it was only a matter of days before Nadia found herself knee-deep in deception and malpractice, citing various cases of missing patients. Particularly outsiders and those with no known next of kin. She was about to take her findings to the police when Declan intervened, convincing her she was in grave danger.

He and Dr Foster regularly monitored newcomers in the area as part of their recruitment strategy, and what would be more helpful to their cause than a dedicated nurse?

With a little persuasion, she gave notice at the hospital, claiming she needed to return to the midlands to care for a sick relative, and that was the last anyone at Chase Side saw of her.

The very next day, Declan carried in a bruised and bloodied Grace, fresh from her encounter with Grady. From that moment on, Nadia was convinced that fate brought her to Drayton Hollow, and she remained there ever since, using her extensive training and keen interest in holistic medicine to keep everyone in tip-top shape.

"So, what brings you two here this morning? Anything I can help with?" Nadia placed the makeshift first-aid box down on the floor beside her and crossed her legs, giving the pair her undivided attention.

Her ripped blue jeans and cozy red sweater gave her a 'cool aunt' vibe that drew Meridia in from the moment they met. As she stared deep into her rich espresso gaze, she felt the truth pressing against the inside of her lips, desperate to spill out over the concrete floor.

"We just wanted to chat." Kane stepped up as spokesman and Meridia finally let out the breath she was holding in.

"We thought you might know something about the hospital that could help save our friend...you used to work there, right?" A solitary crease formed on Nadia's brow as she let out a deep sigh of contemplation.

"I was only there a matter of days, so not sure how much help I can be guys, but I'll give it a shot. I really feel for you all, and everything you've been through...I just want you to know, we're gonna do everything we can to help get your friend back, ok? Here, take a seat..." She gestured to the chair and released a side lever, reclining it so they both had room to sit down.

Meridia wasted no time slumping onto its padded cushioning, but Kane remained standing as he waited for Nadia to answer his question.

"Chase Side is a dangerous place, that's for sure. I still can't believe how much danger I put myself in by taking a job there, but I've learned a lot since then. There's a hidden dungeon on the basement level where they experiment on patients that won't be missed...to think I could have been one of them. I came here on my own, a single woman with no ties to the place...it would've been easy for them to make me disappear..."

"How did you even get a job there if you weren't...you know, one of them?" Kane made a good point and had obviously been sitting on that question for some time.

"I got the job like any other. I wanted to step up, but also wanted to get away from the city...enjoy a bit more open space and connect with nature...ha! Look how that worked out." Nadia shook her head at the irony of her circumstances.

"From what I could tell, I wasn't the only outsider working there...I'm just nosier than most, I guess. I asked a lot of questions...Looking back, I suppose I came in hot... like a big-shot city-girl looking to make her mark on a small community hospital...boy did I get that wrong, but I wasn't alone. I think there were some turning a blind eye, working paycheque to paycheque, and some who didn't have a clue what was going on. Janitors, porters...those kinds of roles have limited exposure to the management side of things."

"So how did you first find out something was up there?" Kane pressed.

"I lost a patient...and I don't mean he died. I mean, he actually went missing. They put me on nights for my first week and a victim of a hit and run came in. A John Doe...so no ID, no next of kin...he was unconscious and suffered a severe head injury, so I sent him off to the imaging department to get some scans. The doctor on call was Dr Chapman..."

"I know him!" Kane blurted. "I...I mean I've seen him... He treated...er a friend once, and it didn't turn out too good." Meridia watched Kane clumsily backtrack having almost divulged Peter's possession and swooped in to save him.

"He got a diagnosis wrong, and our friend ended up pretty sick. He's quite old, though, right?" Maths wasn't Meridia's strongest subject, but Kane's reminder jogged a memory she shared with Valerie.

Surely there was no way Dr Chapman could still be alive, given he treated Valerie when she was a child.

"He's in his late fifties...I think his dad was a doctor there back in the day. They even have a ward named after him." Nadia clarified, and Meridia sensed they were in danger of pricking her suspicion, so tried to smooth things over.

"Sorry...you were saying about your missing patient?"

"Yes, so Dr Chapman...junior that is...he was with me when the patient came in and just seemed a little too excited by the fact he was a John Doe...don't ask me how I knew, I just had this gut feeling something was off. He wasn't interested until that point, and then suddenly he couldn't do enough for the poor guy. He even fast-tracked imaging...so Dr Chapman and I watched as the porter wheeled him away for his x-rays, then I got back to dealing with the next patient in line. Anyway, around 1am, things slowed, so I went to check in on the John Doe and see how he was. I imagined somewhere someone must have been worried sick about him not coming home...so I checked the logs and couldn't find him anywhere. It was as if he had vanished. When I tracked down Dr Chapman again, he said he couldn't remember taking the patient in...that it was a long night and perhaps I was confused. He even suggested that someone might have identified and discharged the patient, which would explain the lack of a John Doe in the system. I knew it was bullshit...er sorry, I think I've been hanging around with Declan too long...I knew he was lying...I was sure the man had a fractured skull so there was no way he would've been discharged that fast."

"Sounds like what they did with Father Alexander." Kane interjected on steadier ground this time. "When Peter called, they denied all knowledge of him. So, what did you do?"

"Well, I tried to track down the porter and ask him... after all, he was the last one to have seen him. That was when another nurse took me aside. She politely told me to stop asking questions if I knew what was good for me and to go get some rest. There was something about her tone that spooked me...kinda like it was a threat...Alice Jordan was her name. Do you know her?"

Meridia thrust her shoulders back to trap the icy chill frantically clawing its way up her spine at the mention of JJ's mum.

"No...sorry." Kane somehow clung to his composure and quickly batted away the question. "Didn't she kind of help you, though?" It was a fair observation despite the touch of menace Nadia described.

"I guess...not that I listened. The next night, I started watching things more closely and discovered there was a strange hierarchy in the hospital around access to certain parts...certain levels. Some porters and cleaners had higher clearance than I did, which is pretty unusual to say the least. I had no idea what was going on in that basement though...how could I have? It seemed like any other hospital on the surface, but that little bit of digging opened a whole can of worms. I started spending my days researching the place online, then walking into night shifts, utterly exhausted. I'm not sure if it was the lack of sleep or all the coffee I was drinking, but after a couple of days, I felt everyone's eyes on me...watching me. Chapman, Jordan... and then eventually Grady. He gave me the creeps... watching my every move, smiling that sickly smile that made my flesh crawl..." Nadia shivered.

"Then one morning, when I finished my shift, I found Declan waiting for me in the carpark. He told me everything and now here I am...I knew I couldn't leave it alone...and if I'd stayed there much longer, then I dread to think what might've happened to me. All because a complete stranger came in one night, having been left for dead. What are the chances?" Nadia seemed lost in the memory of her brief stint behind enemy lines, and Meridia could feel her anguish as if it were her own.

Whether it was her gift or the raw emotion in her voice, in that moment, Meridia knew Nadia could be trusted.

"Do you have any idea what they're doing down there? With those patients?" Kane pressed, still trying to fill some gaps in their knowledge of the cult. Nadia shook her head solemnly.

"No one knows...anyone who goes down there is never seen again...much like my John Doe. There are rumours of horrific experiments...some even say there's a monster in the basement feeding on people's souls. Whatever's going on, it isn't good...but we're going to get your friend back...we have to. If they manage to resurrect the demon, then I'm afraid all hope will be lost and there'll be nothing any of us can do to stop them."

<h1 style="text-align:center">19</h1>

PETER MASSAGED HIS EYES BACK TO LIFE AS HE WAITED for Dr Foster to finish skim-reading the page of Eliza Wilson's journal.

"Ah, here it is..." he announced. "For some context, Eliza Wilson was a budding historian who lived in Thundridge during the early 19th century...around the time your king lost his marbles. The youngest of three girls, she set her sights on bucking the family tradition of becoming a seamstress, and instead pursued a slightly morbid fascination with the history of Cold Christmas: namely, its church. If her journal is anything to go by, then she was certainly a feisty one...or at least she started out that way until this place knocked the stuffing out of her..."

"How so?" Although Peter was keen for the doctor to arrive at his point, he was intrigued to learn more about a potential ancestor of Meridia's. Dr Foster peered over the top of the brown marbled leather cover.

"Her whole persona changes over the course of these pages...Eliza goes from a feisty young upstart with lofty ambitions, to a washed up drunk desperate to lose herself in the nearest bottle of gin...I'm not gonna lie, it all makes for a depressing read...but her insight is invaluable. At least it is until she fled to Scotland to escape this place." Peter felt a sudden rush of blood to his cheeks as the doctor more or less confirmed Eliza and Meridia were related.

"Like Thomas, she saw things, but instead of looking to the future, Eliza looked to the past. She called it her gift, to begin with at least, but it didn't take long for that gift to become a curse given some of the horrors she saw. You see, these pages hold the key to how this whole thing started. Eliza saw it all play out in a vision. There are other things she mentions too, which is why it's full of post-its. It all came to her at once to begin with, like a massive data dump, then she spent the rest of her time unravelling it all in her mind. She saw your witch burn for the first time, even though it probably happened 70-years before Eliza was born. She saw the burnt-out carcass of Crooked House that was left behind, and she saw a river of blood flow through the streets of Cold Christmas as a deranged lunatic in a metal mask tightened his grip on its residents and squeezed the life out of them all..."

"The Grand Master..." Peter blurted.

"See, now how the hell do you know about that without a seer? Or did the priest tell you about him, too?" Peter's slip clearly peeved Dr Foster.

"It was in the old priest's journal he showed us all..." Peter lied.

"A priest named Father John who made the move from Cold Christmas to Thundridge in the 1700s. He also mentioned a member of the Children of the Shadows purchasing a grave for Molly, the witch, to conceal her true identity..."

"Ok...I guess that tracks, given what Eliza tells us about

the Grand Master in here." Dr Foster rattled the book to make his point. "We'll definitely need Declan to pay that church of yours a visit, though. The more sources we can pull from, the closer we'll get to unravelling the truth."

"So, I'm guessing the Grand Master is just another glorified lacky for the horsemen?"

"We wish...I'm afraid he may be much more than that. Let me read you this extract so you can hear Eliza in her own words, and we'll see what you make of what she saw the first time at Crooked House. I'm just conscious I might lead you up the garden path with my own interpretations here...can't have you following me down a rabbit hole now can we..." During his time in the bunker, fraternizing with the others, the doctor clearly embraced some of the local dialect, and Peter found it amusing as he wrapped his subtle twang around some of the older, less common expressions.

Dr Foster cleared his throat as he drew the book closer and switched to reading verbatim.

My mind is a flurry with thoughts that are not my own, and I fear for my sanity. I am at a loss where to even begin and my hand is still shaking as I write, but having finished my errands today and with time to spare, I walked the long way home on a whim.

Even though my sisters and I were warned repeatedly about the dangers of the woods, in my daydream, I somehow strayed from the beaten path and stumbled upon a small clearing. Little did I know my dream was about to become a nightmare.

Despite never having set foot there before, I recognized the building at its centre the moment I clapped eyes on it. The old Crooked House is notorious for its violent and tragic history, and it certainly lives up to its baleful reputation. Blackened and agog like an evil face made of stone, its busted old door was hanging from its hinges like a ravenous mouth, craving to swallow me whole.

Abandoned for almost a century now, and said to be cursed, its burnt out, ramshackle carcass casts a long dark shadow, even now, and left me wondering why anyone would want to stay there, criminal or not.

Yet despite the chill it gave me, I now count myself among the unlucky few who have ventured inside its forsaken halls and lived to tell the tale. Oh, how I wish I stayed clear of that wretched place and stuck to the path.

There is an evil in that house, an evil old as time, and today I saw its face. It began with a whisper, seductive and persuasive, enticing me to enter. Not a man, nor a woman, but something else, something not of this world. Yet it felt strangely familiar, as if I heard it once before, in a childhood dream long ago. The voice knew me too, wily and astute, like a devil on my shoulder, or an inner demon nestled in my ear.

It knew the ins and outs of me. Saw way beyond the lowly daughter of a seamstress, but all my dreams and my secrets, too. It even knew of my gift.

'Come seer' it whispered. 'I've been waiting.' Then I saw it, glimmering like a star had fallen from the heavens and now lay tangled in the building's cobbled tongue. An object of some kind, dark and mysterious. It beckoned me as if I were a magpie. 'Come' it said, 'come now my child'. So foolishly, I did.

As I tiptoed towards the jaws of hell, the rest of the world fell silent but for the wind whistling amongst the barren trees, goading me on like a bully at my back. The dark seed of curiosity it planted in my mind bloomed and so I hastened like a moth to the flame. There, on the stony *path, was a morbid looking hand mirror, its glass black as the night sky with a handle made from bone.*

The sight of it made my spine tingle, yet I remained intoxicated, beguiled by its melodious whisper, and so I stooped to pick it up. The moment my fingertips grazed its icy hilt, the mirror's bony handle coiled around my hand like a serpent, and in an instant, everything around me faded to nothingness.

It was as if I was thrust into the mirror's inky abyss, and the enchanting whisper that ensnared me soon gave way to a discord of screams. The deafening cries rattled my bones like the winter wind. Each tormented voice begged to be released from their dark pit of despair, imploring me to gaze within the mirror's lustrous glass while its ever-tightening handle vowed to draw blood.

Hand shaking, I held the haunted mirror aloft, but the reflection I saw was not my own. Staring back at me, licking his lips, was the devil himself. Eyes black like coal, his face was a hideous tapestry of dark purple veins pulsing beneath grey, lucent skin. His tongue looked like a slug as it slithered along his withered mouth, and there was no hair atop his skeletal head...

"Wait..." Peter interrupted. "Aside from the veins, it sounds like she's describing a horseman."

"Mm...interesting." Dr Foster paused a moment in contemplation.

"I have another theory about who she saw in that mirror, and it ain't no horseman, but I'll come to that in a sec. May I?" The doctor raised both eyebrows and glanced down at the pages in front of him.

"Sorry, of course..." Dr Foster continued, relaying Eliza's story.

As I gazed into the monster's eyes, I saw his grisly story unfurl in my mind's eye. Not in a straight line, but all at once.

A tornado of torment, whipping and snapping inside my head, filling my cup with a hundred years of bloodshed. A fallen angel's vengeance that was long overdue.

His death toll: penance for centuries of incarceration, cast out of heaven and trapped in the very mirror fused to my hand like a genie in a lamp. All for the good of God's children.

All that was until a man named Rowe unwittingly set the evil spirit free and unleashed hell on the town of Cold Christmas. It seems Rowe had a gift like mine, and I saw his miserable life play out in my mind, as if he was a traveling player separated from his troupe, forced to re-enact his journey into darkness for my private viewing.

It was Rowe who found the mirror, not I. It was he who provided the vessel, and he who has infected our land like a plague.

The deck was always cruelly stacked against poor Rowe. His love's senseless murder ignited a rage that lay dormant within him, and avenging her death just wasn't enough. Nor was denouncing God.

As he screamed up at the heavens, consumed by hate, he became ripe for the picking, and pick him the evil spirit did. There were two of them from that night on. Rowe the servant, and Rowe the master, hidden behind a terrible mask. A spirit fractured in two, like a reflection in a mirror.

Now all I am left with are their memories. They cling to mine like leeches, sucking on my sanity. There are just too many to share in one sitting, for they would surely fill a thousand books, and my mother is due back at any moment.

When my vision finally released its hold, I found myself standing in the master room of Crooked House. Its walls smeared with blood and no cursed mirror in sight. It was all an echo of the past, yet I still bare the mark of the mirror's grip on my hand, and even now it remains sore to touch.

I ran all the way back to town without looking back, screaming at the top of my lungs for most of it, and have sworn never to return to that wretched place so long as I live.

Instead, over the coming months, I shall use the rest of these pages to unburden myself of the countless horrors I witnessed as I strive to cleanse my soul. God, give me strength.

Dr Foster softly closed the book and glanced up at Peter, who was hanging on his every word.

"So, Peter, tell me what you make of that before I tell you what I think is really going on in Cold Christmas..."

20

Peter's mind was racing to find a home for the new set of puzzle pieces the doctor scattered on the table in front of him.

The extract certainly left him hungry for more, and he was desperate to read the rest of Eliza's journal to find out what else she saw on her visit to Crooked House. Despite the brevity of what he just heard, Peter still made some connections given the knowledge he already held.

"I'm assuming Thomas Rowe started this somehow when he found the mirror, what you called The Eye of Corvus...but you'll appreciate artifacts such as that are not exactly in my wheelhouse. I'm no Ed Warren. If what you call a seer started all this, then is it a fair assumption a seer can also end it somehow? Again, that's a bit of a leap on my part until I know more about the eye. Aside from that, it still sounds as if Eliza described a horseman, and somehow it turned Thomas. Are you suggesting he is...or was the Grand Master? The timings definitely align between his disappearance and the sudden upsurge of the Children of the Shadows...but I still think there's something I'm missing.

Care to fill me in?" Peter knew he was being lined up for another earth-shattering revelation, the way a comedian sets up a punchline.

This one would no doubt come from the doctor's extensive, and superior, research: yet another sign of his ego at play. Dr Foster adjusted his posture and allowed a half-smile, confirming Peter's suspicions.

"You're on the right track, Peter, for sure. I believe the mirror is The Eye of Corvus, and when you Google it, you should find enough information online to piece everything together as I have, but I'll break it down for you to save you the hassle. The eye is an ancient myth said to contain the evil spirit of the angel of death. You see, as I've come to appreciate there is often a grain of truth in every lie, and whilst I'm no religious man, it seems there is, as we both know, a light side to the universe, and a dark. Personally, I'm not keen on the terms good and evil, as those are both just perspectives. Two sides of the same coin, if you will. However, according to my research, the angel of death was named Samael. Now, based on his description, which varies wildly, there's very little to distinguish him from Satan or the devil..."

"The reflection Eliza saw in the mirror..." Peter interjected.

"Exactly. At least that's what I believe, and as I explain more, you'll see how it all fits together. Now Samael was also known as the King of the Demons. What good is a king without his queen, right? Enter Lilith, his wife. Lilith, or Lilitu, as she's sometimes known..."

Peter sensed the colour drain from his cheeks and the room spin at the mention of her name. A wave of clammy sweat leaked from all his pores as he succumbed to the sudden claustrophobia of being couped up in a glorified concrete rabbit warren.

He was certain the witch referred to herself as Lilitu once when she infiltrated his mind, and the unexpected recollection triggered all the old feelings of being powerless under her control.

"Peter? Are you ok...you look like you've seen another ghost." Dr Foster slid a glass of water across the desk and Peter grasped it shakily, then took a sip.

Taking in a mouthful of air, he held his breath for the count of four and slowly let it out. There was no way he was wriggling out of this one and so he took another deep breath and then tried to salvage the situation with another white lie.

"Father Alexander said the witch ...or at least the demon inside her, called herself Lilitu."

"No shit...wow. Ok, that only adds strength to my theory in that case." Dr Foster rose from his seat and paced along the back wall a little whilst he mulled over Peter's admission. "Peter...can I ask you something straight-up? Are you a seer?"

"Ha! God no...I wish." Despite his blush, Peter felt he laughed off the accusation convincingly enough before encouraging Dr Foster to finish explaining his theory.

"Although I see why you're so keen to find one. Why is this all happening here? Surely, an angel of death could've picked a better location. I thought Crooked House was built on some kind of concentration of dark energy...is that not the case?" Dr Foster circled back around behind his desk and sat down before continuing.

"Truth is, I don't quite know the answer to that one, and I'm not even sure it matters anymore. It's a bit like the chicken and the egg. Something, call it fate or whatever you want, really, brought the eye here."

"So how did Samael end up trapped inside it?"

"Well, for that, you have to travel a little further back in time and further afield. Lilith is said to have been Adam's first wife, but was soon banished from the Garden of Eden and replaced by Eve when she refused to do her husband's bidding. That's when Samael swooped in and the two of them united against their common enemy: God and all of humanity. They became the antithesis of Adam and Eve...the yin to their yang. In some places her name translates as 'night monster' and with the help of her new husband, she set about spawning demon children to form an army and reclaim her birthright: Earth. When the other angels got wind of the couple's plans... and just for the record, I don't really believe in angels in a biblical sense...not the kind that grant miracles to everyday folk like us. I've come to think of them more as foot soldiers in a war that's been raging since the dawn of creation. Anyway, the one commonly known as archangel Michael imprisoned Samael in a mirror forged from obsidian, which even now is said to absorb negative energy...again, there's no smoke without fire."

"And the bone handle?" Peter still found that aspect a little macabre for an angel.

"The spine of an infant demon...one of Samael's and Lilith's offspring, if the story is to be believed. The curse needed to be bound using the demon's own bloodline. Now all this was said to have happened in Jerusalem, and the mirror was placed under the protection of a sacred tribe tasked with keeping it safe. I theorize looters found it, or that its discovery followed the death of the tribe's last member. Maybe it happened during the crusades, and from there the eye somehow wound up in the hands of a local thief who didn't know what he possessed. After all, the eye is said to be ugly as sin..."

"I know from my research this area had strong ties to the Knights Templar, so your theory is as good as any, but I guess that doesn't matter so much either..."

"Exactly. The fact is, the eye is here somewhere, and it's the key to this entire shitstorm. I expect it's under lock and key and heavily guarded by the cult. None of our contacts even know it exists, let alone where it might be, but if we had a seer on our side, I believe we could find it and cut off the head of the serpent...but even that comes with risks."

"What risks?" So far, Peter was blown away by the amount of research the doctor conducted and felt more and more like a rank amateur the longer their conversation continued.

If there was ever a reason to let their host in on Meridia's secret, now was that time, but something was still niggling his gut, telling him to hold out a little longer.

"Well, first, we already know what the eye did to Thomas Rowe, and maybe Eliza too...and she only ever experienced its influence second hand, but it's more than that. Legend has it...shit that sounds corny whenever I say it...legend has it. Only a seer can wield the power of The Eye of Corvus, because they are the only ones who can hear its voice. A low whispering sound surrounds the glass. It's said to provide a seer with the same ancient incantation that archangel Michael used to trap Samael in the first place. It's like the eye has its own built-in user manual, telling a seer how to direct all this dark energy back to where it belongs and restore balance. But...and this is a huge but...the sound of the mirror can just as easily seduce a seer and send them mad with terrifying visions until, ultimately, they themselves become an instrument of darkness. Therein lies our dilemma...even if we find a seer, how the hell can we trust them not to lose their mind? Based on all I have read, a seer inherits their gift at the age of thirteen, which means if it's not you, then it can only be Kane or JJ...that's if you're not being straight with me of course..." Dr Foster gave another wry smile and a wink as he pushed the books back towards Peter. "Read them for yourself, but keep in mind time isn't on our side at the moment."

"Just one more loose end. I can't quite tie up...are you saying the Grand Master is the spirit of Samael? Eliza said Rowe gave the devil a vessel in her journal, and from that moment on they were split in two..."

"I was hoping you'd pick up on that...well played, Peter. Yes, the Grand Master is, in fact, the spirit of Samael. Who better to summon the four horsemen of the apocalypse than the angel of death? That makes the Grand Master more dangerous than any other monsters living in that house. He used Rowe as a host to form the Children of Shadows and has been using other hosts to accumulate power ever since. Eliza elaborates on this in her account of what she saw, but if what she says is true, the Grand Master could be any one of us. Her odd remark about 'a spirit fractured in two' is quite literal. Thomas Rowe was a loving husband by day, and the King of the Demons by night without even knowing it himself. From what I gather, it was the rage which made Rowe more susceptible, but that trait isn't limited to a seer, heck who doesn't have an axe to grind these days? Anybody could be the Grand Master now...and I mean absolutely anybody. Even I could, and I would be no more aware of it than you would if it were you. It seems the devil has been hiding in plain sight for centuries..."

Peter's blood turned to ice as the implications of Dr Foster's claims crawled beneath his skin. Every time he glimpsed the top of the mountain they needed to climb, he found it to be another false summit. All thoughts instantly gravitated to Meridia's temper, and then Kane's.

Did that make them both more vulnerable? Was that Emily's plan all along?

Peter needed time to process all he heard. He needed to read those damn books, as there were still things he was withholding from Dr Foster that could help plug the gaps in his knowledge.

Despite the daunting prospect of a monster who could hide out in the body of pretty much anyone he knew, he felt even more optimistic now than when he entered.

For the first time since this nightmare started, he felt closer to knowing what they were truly up against. Meridia's gift would never stay a secret forever, and perhaps now was the time to share it. Little did Peter know that his newfound optimism was about to be shattered into a thousand tiny pieces.

"*BANG!*"

Declan burst into the room, white as a sheet and gasping for breath. In a total state of shock, he brandished his burner phone with a trembling hand and slammed the door shut behind him.

"Y...you've both got to stop what you're doing and look at this now...something terrible...*gasp*...something terrible has happened...it's the cult...*gasp*...they're coming for us..."

<h1 style="text-align:center">21</h1>

Jonny Alman's hands were quivering as the harrowing video reached its gory conclusion and the screen on his iPhone finally timed out.

He traced his scalp with a clammy palm in the hope it might settle his nerves, but all it did was grease the tightly cropped bristles of his dirty blonde buzz cut. Beneath his denim sherpa jacket, he felt his fried breakfast gurgling in the pit of his stomach, ready to erupt like a volcano of vomit.

"Bleurgh...kaff-kaff..." He puked a warm, slimy casserole of mushy baked beans and mangled sausages, splattering it all over his Air Force Ones and the tree he was leaning against.

"Kaff...kaff..." He cuffed the trail of phlegm still attached to the pile of steaming sick at his feet, then felt a throb of pain shoot up his nose, tingling his nostrils and making his eyes water.

He couldn't believe what he just witnessed. He knew Lance for years and went to him every month for a haircut ever since he opened his barbershop.

How could this be? What was that thing in the video? The thought of the huge arachnid slurping up his friend's mutilated remains made his stomach churn again.

"Kaff...kaff..." Jonny coated the remnants of his breakfast with a layer of gloopy bile and then wiped his mouth again, more delicately this time to avoid aggravating his bruised and battered nose. A painful souvenir from his humiliating encounter at Chase Side. He told everyone it was a lucky punch to avoid any further embarrassment, but the truth was he had been out of his depth. Exposed by a teacher of all people. Who knew Higginsworth had such a good right hook?

Jonny slipped his phone back into his pocket, glancing around to see if anyone spotted him throwing up. The vomit was still steaming in the cold winter air, but lucky for him it was a school day and Jubilee Park was empty but for a few pigeons arguing over scraps from a boozy bag of chips that were chucked on the ground the night before.

He watched their tiny grey heads twitch back and forth as they searched wide-eyed for anything they might have missed in the frozen grass. Their offbeat, jerky motion bordered on comical and offered a mild distraction from the horrors he had just been sent by his boss. Shady Grady, he called him, not that he would ever say it to his face. Definitely not now.

Poor Lance's brutal execution was a message intended to flush out traitors, but it also served as a startling reminder of what Jonny got himself into. He was already having serious doubts after his misadventure at the hospital a few days ago, and since his early morning visit to Mrs Huston's cafe, he was wandering aimlessly around Jubilee Park like a lost puppy while contemplating the path he was on.

Now, considering the terrifying creature Grady unleashed, he was seriously thinking about fleeing the country to get away from it all.

Ambling over to the nearest bench, he slumped down in its wooden frame, surprised by how comfortable the smooth teak slats felt beneath his shaky legs. He needed to come up with a plan. A real one, but with a headful of screams, all he could think about was Lance's face melting into a pool of bloody pulp.

The grisly image of his friend's eyeball bursting like a water balloon was now imprinted on his brain forever like a tattoo, and despite his best efforts, Jonny kept circling back to it repeatedly, like a scab he just couldn't stop picking at.

Leaning forward, he watched his nervous breath steam up the air between his knees and popped a mint to rid himself of the bitter aftertaste of sick. It was time for him to disappear. He already pissed Grady off once, and there was no way he was going to risk doing it again in case he ended up as an afternoon snack for his giant, acid-spitting pet spider.

Skipping the country wasn't exactly feasible, with no money and no career prospects. Since being kicked out by his parents, Jonny depended entirely on his newfound family for all of life's staples. It felt good at first, free from his nitpicking parents and their constant jibes about him being the black sheep of the family. But the more the Children of the Shadows gave, the more they asked of him in return, until one wet and miserable afternoon he found himself gearing up to murder a minor celebrity in a hospital forecourt.

Jonny wondered if he should simply return home with his tail between his legs and lie low for a while. At least that way, he could warn his family of what was coming. Perhaps they might even see him as a hero, swooping in to save them all from a fate worse than death.

"Fat chance..." He muttered, shaking his head.

No-one on the outside would ever believe him. Even if they did, he knew damn well his parents would find a way to blame him for it all. They always did. '*Why can't you be more like Jacob?*'

He heard their nagging mantra as if they were sitting right next to him. Laughing at his constant shortcomings and poor life choices. They won't be laughing so hard when their precious Jacob ends up on a missing poster in a shop window like those Jackson boys.

Jonny let out a deep sigh and wearily rose to his feet. He couldn't sit around in the park all day. It would eventually attract suspicion. Mrs Hutson had eyes like a hawk and the last thing he needed was to find himself on her radar, given the current climate.

Things were escalating beyond his control, and he needed a place to gather his thoughts. Somewhere away from the growing paranoia and watchful eyes of his brethren. Then the idea came to him like a thunderbolt from above.

He would simply go underground. The cult's network of tunnels was vast and ran close to his family's home on Woodlands Road. It wouldn't take much effort to evade detection on that side of town, plus it would allow him to keep a close eye on his family.

When the house was empty, he would sneak in and grab some supplies. He knew his mum always kept cash in the house for emergencies.

All he needed was enough for a train ticket to get out of

Shawbrook. From there, he could easily vanish into the crowd and start over.

As Jonny made his way to the park's main gate and hurried out into the street, he didn't notice Alice Jordan watching him from the bus stop on the opposite side of the road.

<h1 style="text-align:center">22</h1>

Peter stared slack-jawed at Declan's phone until the horror show reached its harrowing conclusion, and the screen turned black.

In the glossy veneer that remained, he was confronted by a reflection that felt alien to him. Aghast and skewed by the bloodbath he witnessed, it took him a moment to realize the unfamiliar face was his own.

As his peculiar out-of-body experience loosened its grip, Peter was able to adjust his ungainly expression whilst his mind wrestled to reconcile the terrifying truth: weavers were real.

Sick to his stomach from the grisly atrocities that played out in Grady's snuff movie, he glanced up at Dr Foster to find him wearing an equally uncharacteristic expression. The footage on Declan's phone punched them both in the face, leaving them shellshocked and stupefied as they clung to the desk whilst the room spun around them.

Meanwhile, the nauseating reek of stale coffee permeated the stifling air, snaking its way up Peter's nose and into his brain until all he wanted to do was swipe away the empty mug responsible and send it crashing to the other side of the lab. His fleeting bubble of euphoria was burst and trampled on by Declan's gruesome news and now he was teetering on the brink of a meltdown. Another false summit.

Declan was the first to break the despairing silence, rekindling the same anxious energy he burst in with, as Peter and Dr Foster both remained slumped in their chairs, reeling from shock.

"This is some next-level shit we're up against now. A nut job nurse is one thing, but fucking mutant spiders spitting acid is a whole other ball game completely! You both saw that! The poor bastard in that video has a puddle for a face...well that's not gonna happen to me! No way...I'm getting out of here right fucking now and I suggest you guys do the same."

As Peter watched Declan unravel in front of him, he realized just how green their hosts were. Almost everything they experienced until now was theoretical or second hand, so it was little wonder Grady's video left him visibly rattled.

Peter wondered if the time was right to come clean and tell them both they just saw a weaver in action. Deciding it might only exacerbate matters, he held his tongue and waited a moment to gage Dr Foster's reaction.

"Where will you go Dec?" The doctor attempted to corral his spiralling comrade as he paced back and forth in front of the door. "We're safe here...they don't even know where we are."

"Not yet. But how long do you think it'll take them to find us after that message? You heard what Grady said...he's basically put a bounty on all our heads."

"He doesn't even know who any of us are," Dr Foster

countered calmly to impose some logic on the matter, but all he did was agitate Declan even more.

"He knows who they are!" He pointed at Peter.

"All it takes is for one of them to be seen loitering above ground and we're all done for. We're kidding ourselves Marcus...look at the video. Watch it again. We're not cut out for this...no way. You think reading a few books will help us fight that...that thing? And now we're expected to risk our necks for some kid none of us have even met? It's madness, Marcus, madness. We had a good thing here...but now everything is going to shit. Giant spiders, Marcus...giant fucking spiders! Anything in your books about that?" Peter sensed the growing scrutiny baring down on him as he waited for Dr Foster to respond.

Declan made a fair point, and although none of them had asked to be rescued, their presence there brought a new level of heat, given all the damage they inflicted on the cult's plans to date. He was about to volunteer to leave when the doctor spoke over him.

"Has our girl seen this?" His tone was one of resignation and proved enough to defuse Declan momentarily.

"Of course she has...who do you think sent it to me? This has gone out to everyone in their little murder club. She wanted out before...now she's terrified they're onto her. She's running Marcus. And how long do you think it'll take them to break her if they catch her? That's if they even bother trying...you saw that sick fuck. He wasn't interested in getting information from that poor guy... he just wanted to see him suffer. He burned down half the high street when he was done. He's out of control...he's an animal... After everything she's done for us...everything she's risked... we can't just throw her to the wolves now, Marcus, it ain't right. I don't want her blood on my hands...do you?"

"Can you bring her here? Safely, I mean...without being seen?" Peter watched on silently like an unwanted spectator at a tennis match as the two men rallied towards a resolution which hopefully didn't result in him and the kids being thrown out on their ear.

Whoever the mystery girl was, she seemed important to both of them, which suggested she might be more than an informant.

"I can...but then what?" Declan shot a troubled glance in Peter's direction.

"We both knew it would eventually come to this Dec..." Dr Foster wrestled Declan's attention back to his side of the table.

"Peter and those kids have seen far more than we have being locked away down here. What do you think we were going to do? Sit here and wait it out? We can't wait out the end of the world Dec...we can't hide from it anymore. We need them if we're to stand any chance of stopping this..." Dr Foster got up from behind his desk and circled behind Peter in a pensive show of support.

"I think maybe we've all come together at the right time...No wait, hear me out Dec. You know I'm not a religious man...I'm not talking about divine intervention...or maybe I am in a roundabout way, I dunno. I guess I'm taking about fate. All those tiny decisions...the forks in the road each of us has faced... the coming together of circumstance that led us all to this moment, right here, right now. It can't all be for nothing. The work we've put in...the things Peter and these kids have been through. What if this wasn't an accident? What if this was all designed somehow...for us to come together at exactly the right time? This idea of balance we're all clinging onto in hope...What if that's what we represent? Nature's way of balancing the books..."

Declan stopped his pacing, closed his eyes and let out a deep sigh before leaning against the door in resignation. He rubbed the salt and pepper stubble on his head, then glanced back at Dr Foster through weary eyes.

"When I was a kid growing up, my folks didn't have that much money. I didn't see my dad all that often 'cos he worked long hours to make ends meet, and when my mum wasn't working in the convenience store at the bottom of our street, she was mostly busy tending to the house or in the kitchen cooking for me and my brothers. We ate a lot of sandwiches back then...jam was my favourite...still is, as it happens. Back then, we all lived for the summers. No school for six weeks and left to our own devices. Latchkey kids in the truest sense...a couple of years before gaming took over and turned everyone into couch-dwelling zombies. Anyway, one year, at the end of the summer break, it was time to get my schoolbag ready for another year of torture. I was in 7th grade moving up to 8th..." A smile cracked the thick stubble surrounding Declan's mouth as he basked briefly in the nostalgia of his childhood.

"So, I reach down into my schoolbag, and I feel something soft and squishy...at first, I thought it was my pencil case, but when I pulled it out, it was a jam sandwich wrapped in clingfilm...I was so eager to get out into the wild and play with my mates on the last day of term that I forgot to eat it, so that thing was there nigh-on six weeks turning all kinds of funky colours as it went mouldy in my bag. I remember holding it and it reminding me of the way the world looks from space...all those patches of colour. The idea stuck with me ever since...shaped my outlook on the world, I guess. So, when you talk about fate...and faith...

you're barking up the wrong tree, Marcus. These days all I see when I look around is a rotten sandwich...maybe God left it in his bag too long and we're nothing but mould... spreading like a plague, ruining everything we touch, and just waiting to be found and tossed in the trash where we belong...Don't tell me there's any balance in this shit-hole of a world when you've got lunatics like Grady running amok, killing people willy-nilly, and now giant spiders chewing people's faces off..."

Declan's story offered a bleak glimpse at his state of mind, and in that moment, given the evils they had just seen, who was Peter to blame him.

Maybe it was the isolation down here, slowly infecting them all, or perhaps the world above wasn't worth saving as Declan implied. Either way, it was clear the man was running on empty.

"Go get her Dec...bring her back here." Dr Foster cut through the depressing canvas Declan painted in front of them.

"We'll see what else she knows and figure out our next move. If you still wanna leave after that, then you have my blessing. None of us are being held prisoner down here... well none of us on the right side of this at least. When you get back, we'll pull everyone together, kids included. I have a feeling they've seen more than you or me anyway, so it's high time we gave them a voice in all this."

Declan nodded and skulked away without another word, leaving Peter and Dr Forster alone again.

"The creature in that video..." Peter blurted before the doctor spoke. "It's called a weaver. Don't ask me how I know...just give me half an hour and then I'll tell you everything. It's time you all know the truth..."

23

The faster Jonny walked, the more paranoid he became. He was flustered, cursing under his breath each time he glanced back over his shoulder as he pounded the pavement of Woodlands Road, the street he grew up on.

A cluster of thick, heavy rain clouds gathered in the bright grey sky overhead, casting a foreboding shadow over the town of Shawbrook. On the ground, the temperature plummeted, and the arctic breeze clawed at Jonny's flushed cheeks as it clambered over the top of his upturned collar.

Glimpsing his reflection in a parked car, he realized how shifty he looked, with his hands stuffed in his pockets and his head thrust down as he marched blindly toward his family home. A home he was still in exile from.

"This is stupid..." He muttered angrily, frustrated by his own naivety.

If he was on Grady's radar, then this would be the first place he would look. Any idiot knew that, and yet here he was, a stone's throw from his old front gate. Somewhere in the back of his mind, his subconscious was screaming at him to slow down, telling him he did nothing wrong, but the agonizing screams of Lance took up residence inside his head.

The swirling cacophony of bloodcurdling shrieks drowned out all reason like an echo chamber of terror, whipping up an insidious sequence of what ifs and fanning the flames of fear burning in the pit of his stomach.

He could see his old front door now. It's aubergine paint job stuck out like a sore thumb amongst the monochrome neighbourhood of pensioners and early retirees.

As he sailed past number 144, he glanced at the front window in the faint hope he might spot his mum, dusting and polishing as she often did whilst his dad was at work.

Jonny's pride outweighed his need for asylum, and he didn't linger long. Instead, he continued on beyond the darkened house he once called home and towards the adjoining corner of Buxton Close, where he knew he could gain access to a disused section of the tunnels.

He would be safe there, for a while at least. Just until he plucked up the nerve to approach his old house and search for the spare key without arousing suspicion. Curtain twitchers were rife in this part of town, and he didn't know who he could trust anymore.

As Jonny put his family home firmly in his rearview, he paused at a telegraph pole by the roadside. Someone stapled another missing poster to the wood, and it was rippling in the wind. This one featured an unfamiliar face, a balding middle-aged man smiling at the camera. Clearly cut from a family photo, his arm was up high as if draped over someone's shoulder just out of shot.

He was the latest in a long line of people reported missing in the area. No doubt his body lay mutilated somewhere beneath Crooked House with all the rest. Poor sod. People in this town were dropping like flies, this one leaving behind a son named Tommy who was now appealing to anyone who might have seen him.

"Outsiders..." He mumbled, shaking his head.

He had a good mind to call the boy now and tell him to pack up and go home. The only thing he would find in Cold Christmas was the devil himself, unless Grady found him first.

The Children of the Shadows were more brazen than ever, particularly in these unscrupulous streets they called home. That meant no-one was safe anymore.

The stark reminder catapulted Jonny's mind back to his family, and he hesitated a moment, glancing back towards his old house. In the distance, he heard rubber grinding against loose stones on the tarmac, then the sound of an engine. Someone was coming.

Instinctively, he ducked down behind the nearest car. This was getting ridiculous. He did nothing wrong, yet his every action painted a different picture altogether. A cold sweat broke out on his neck as he cowered behind the blue sedan, instantly recognizing the approaching van.

A flash of gun metal grey shimmered above the other parked cars as Grady pulled up outside number 144 and cooly stepped onto Woodlands Road. Dressed in his hospital scrubs, the psycho was all smiles as he skipped up the garden path and rapped on the door.

"Please be out...please be out..." Jonny whispered.

His hands were shaking as he clutched the car bumper to steady himself. Why was Grady looking for him?

Despite his shifty behaviour, he did nothing to warrant a house call, unless the mere association with Lance was enough to cast suspicion.

Jonny waited for what seemed like an eternity as Grady loitered on his parents' doorstep, even cupping his hands to the glass, before eventually shrugging and bouncing back towards his van. Where to now, he wondered, as the engine started in the distance.

Ducking down even lower, Jonny put his right hand back in his jacket pocket and gripped the knife he was clinging onto since leaving the park. There was every chance if Grady continued this way, he would spot him hiding like a coward in the gutter.

"Can I help you?" Jonny flinched, almost spearing his leg with the knife in his pocket.

An elderly man in the house behind stepped out onto his porch and was staring straight at him. Wrinkles etched with confusion and concern lined his face as he propped open the door with a crooked hip.

Heart in his mouth, Jonny glanced back down the street as Grady's van crawled towards the corner of Buxton. He was a matter of yards away now and would surely see him.

"Well?" The man pressed impatiently.

"Sorry...I...I just dropped my phone..." Jonny murmured, unable to take his eyes off the approaching killer as he reached the junction.

Jonny knew if the van crept any closer to his hiding place, he would be dead.

"Do you need any help?" The old man called down and shuffled forward a step.

"No! No...thank you..." Jonny tried to hold the old man at bay as he waited for Grady to make his next move.

Thoughts of running crossed his mind, but where to? He stupidly walked into a dead-end, with his only chance of escape a series of tunnels Grady knew like the back of his hand.

Trapped between a rock and a hard place, Jonny's legs were now trembling as he squatted down even lower and peered around the wing mirror in time to see Grady's van take a sharp left and wheel spin away from him in the opposite direction. Perhaps he found some other poor sod to terrorize.

"Have you found it?" The dithering pensioner bleated as Jonny let out the breath he was holding and slowly rose to his feet with his head still slumped.

"Yeah...thanks..." He sighed, waving the man off as he hurried on down the cul-de-sac in search of the tunnel's entrance. That was close. Too close.

For whatever reason, Grady was on the warpath and Lance was only the start. Maybe Hutson saw him throwing up in the park? She was always the first to snitch on people, the silly old bat.

As he mentally retraced his steps, he couldn't recall passing anyone on his way here. Whatever the cause, Jonny knew it wouldn't take long for Grady to catch him if he stayed above ground.

Pulling his collar in tight to cover his face, he veered left at the end of Buxton Close and trudged toward a green metal junction box occupying a small plot of communal grass between two houses. There was an array of different access points dotted around town, each coming in various disguises, but this was one of the more straightforward to operate.

Once inside, he would wait for nightfall, then sneak into his family home whilst everyone was sleeping.

His mum kept her cash in a kitchen drawer at the back of the house, so he could be in and out with no one being any wiser. From there, he would use the tunnels to make his way to the train station.

It would be risky, venturing so close to the heart of the cult's network, but less risky than navigating the streets where he would be exposed. Perhaps he would leave a note for his family and warn them to get out of this wretched place? It would be the most humane thing to do, given what was coming.

Checking the coast was clear, Jonny slipped behind the junction box and quickly crouched down out of sight. The rear panel was fake, as was the entire box, and with a firm push, the magnetic door opened with a click.

Slowly peeling it back, Jonny almost toppled backwards as a sudden surge of damp, musty air slapped him in the face.

The stench didn't instil him with much confidence, but he took it as a sign the opening wasn't tampered with in a while. Inside the empty steel cabinet was a four-by-four hatch with a rickety old wooden ladder attached to it.

Peering down, he saw nothing but impenetrable darkness, so he pulled his phone from his pocket and shone the flashlight directly into the chasm. A mix of dirt and grubby limestone was all that awaited some thirty feet below, so, satisfied he was alone, Jonny turned his back on the opening and dropped his legs down behind him.

Feeling his way down, rung by rung, he waited until waist deep before closing the outer door behind him. There was no going back now. With each fumbling step downward, the stench of mould grew stronger, and Jonny counted his blessings that he already had an empty stomach.

It was going to be a long afternoon, down in the dungeons with nothing but rats and roaches for company, but it would be a small price to pay if he was ever going to make it out of town alive.

24

WHEN MERIDIA AND KANE WANDERED BACK INTO THE kitchen, they found JJ and Zach looking baffled at the breakfast bench.

"What's going on?" Kane wasted no time calling out the weird energy they were both emitting.

"Something's up..." Zach squeaked, his elfin face suddenly shrouded beneath a dark cloud of concern.

"Everything was fine until Declan went up top for a quick smoke...then he came bursting back in like a bat out of hell and raced off down the corridor without saying another word."

"He was white as a sheet, guys..." JJ added. "Something spooked him, for sure."

"Any idea what?" Kane asked.

"Whatever it was, he wasn't telling us." JJ shrugged. "Looked like he was heading towards Dr Foster."

"That's where Peter is..." Kane added, taking a seat opposite.

Despite the obvious bewilderment hanging in the air, the atmosphere had lightened since their previous visit to the kitchen and now felt more in tune with its bright and airy decor.

Meridia studied all three boys as they idly slouched in their chairs like it was a sixth form common room and they were waiting to shuffle off to their next lesson. Since integrating with the doctor and his team, the dynamics had shifted, and she sensed everyone was in a state of flux, waiting for their next instruction. She felt they were in danger of slipping back into old habits, assuming the roles of obedient children whilst the adults made all the important decisions behind closed doors. It irked Meridia, although she knew it wasn't all the adults' doing.

An unexpected pang of sorrow tightened its grip around her throat, bringing tears to her eyes as she watched the boys exchange a bit of light-hearted banter. She missed Izzy, and perhaps all her wallowing contributed to their recent lack of impetus. The rift between her and Kane didn't exactly help matters either, but she felt they went some way to repair things today, despite the bombshell about her father.

Listening to Nadia's story gave the reality of their situation time to sink in, and she was seeing things more clearly again now. Although they were in the company of relative strangers, they were all very much in the same boat, and the time for treading water was over.

The clock was ticking, and she was tired of hiding who she was and waiting for everyone else to think for her. Meridia needed to roll her sleeves up and make something happen.

It was time to have it out with her treacherous mother once and for all.

25

Meridia wasted no time slipping out of the kitchen. The boys were engrossed in theorizing what might have Declan so worried, and true to form, Kane and JJ were already rifting on decades of horror movies for inspiration. She saw them wander down that rabbit hole many times now.

Zach was firmly in tow, wide-eyed in admiration as he tagged along for the ride. As much as she would have loved to partake, there was a time and a place for speculation, and this wasn't it. Declan's news would find its way to them soon enough, particularly if Peter became privy.

Now, hellbent on forcing something meaningful to happen, all Meridia thought of was what she would say when she confronted her mother. Since all the commotion the night they discovered her duplicity, Meridia gave her a wide berth, largely because of Peter's counsel.

'*Give things time to settle*' he told her. '*Hard as it is to accept, there are always two sides to every story*'. However, that was before they found out about the demon's impending resurrection and her best friend's sacrifice.

Her mother's makeshift prison cell was located halfway between the kitchen and the bunker's only exit. A tiny boxroom originally intended for storage, it was since cleared out to accommodate their enemy within, and had a thick enough door to keep all sounds to a minimum. The chair propped under the door handle was just a precaution, because inside, Emily was bound to a chair.

Although Meridia knew all this, it still couldn't prepare her for what she found when she plucked up the courage to open the door and step inside.

"Hello dear..." Her mother's voice was all at once familiar, yet alien to Meridia as it snapped through the silence like a whip and sent ice-cold shivers rattling through her bones. "I've been waiting for you."

Emily Wilson appeared to be a madwoman as she flashed an unhinged, toothy smile toward her terrified daughter. Her bright blue eyes, circled by smeared black mascara, were wide as saucers and eagerly drinking everything in around them as Meridia clung to the opposite wall and shuffled her way further inside.

Upon closer inspection, she saw remnants of eye makeup streaked down her freckled cheeks, leftover crusts from the crocodile tears she cried when she was carried in there kicking and screaming. The state of her hair provided the icing on an altogether unsettling cake, as bedraggled auburn curls framed her slender white face, completing the appearance of a deranged witch tied to a fucking stool.

Grace did an excellent job of securing her, putting her extensive knowledge of knots to good use, along with her collection of climbing equipment. Trussed up like a turkey, her mother's ankles and wrists were bound firmly to the chair by a bright orange climbing rope, which also looped around her midriff to stop any wriggling.

Determined not to breakdown and cry, Meridia swallowed her tears and said the first thing that came to mind.

"Why?"

Her mother's demented smile dropped to a sneer as she eyeballed her daughter from the confines of the dingy grey storage cupboard. The overhead light exaggerated her cheekbones, adding to her ghoulish appearance, as she lowered her head to her chest and scoffed.

"Why? You know why...you of all people know what's coming...there's no stopping us. Not now, not ever."

Emily smiled again, a patronizing smile laced with arrogance. Who was this woman? Where was the kind and loving mother that nurtured and raised her for the last 12 years?

Meridia questioned if she had the stomach to continue, then images of Izzy flooded her mind, petrified and alone. Through gritted teeth, Meridia hissed back at the unflinching stranger and stared her down.

"Tell me where Izzy is... I know you know!"

"Hahahahaha...oh...ok, I'll tell you everything...pft!" Emily raised her head again and they both locked eyes.

"*BANG*"

She rattled her chair on the concrete in a show of contempt for her daughter and then took a deep breath. Meridia watched as the tangerine ropes expanded under the strain of her mother's lungs and wondered if they might snap, before she let out a long, rasping sigh and regained her composure.

"You...you are a pain in our arse just like your father, young lady...let me tell you. Do you really think I'm going to help you? You! Ha...I've been a part of this long before I met your father. Do you think it was fate I walked into his showroom that day looking for a car? Do you think it was fate brother and sister Saunders took him under their wing? Silly girl. It took us years to track your father down through the adoption system...years. I was picked because I look like her...the perfect match for your father after his shiny new parents groomed him."

"Wh...what are you talking about?" Meridia stuttered. "Looked like who?"

"His mother, of course...his real one, the junky." Emily smirked as she continued.

"Don't you see...this is all centuries in the making. Your great, great grandmother had the gift...though not as powerful as yours, it seems. We tried to recruit her, but she couldn't handle it...little goody two shoes...it sent her mad in the end. She ran all the way to Scotland and hid in a bottle. Do you know how hard it is to dilute an addiction like that? We were nearly too late when we found your father...if it wasn't for his insufferable temper, he would have gone the same way. Then, in the last century, it was that fucking Cooper woman and her irritating detective friend. They ruined everything before I was born...but it gave us the idea to restore the Wilson bloodline." Emily's wild blue eyes broke away as her mind drifted into the past.

"It was always a risk that it wouldn't work, of course. That it wouldn't be you. Every century there has been a seer...but the others never got the gift until they turned thirteen...unlucky for some, I suppose ha...but not you. You got yours early...caught us all by surprise, even the master. We had it all planned out once we took care of your father... his cold feet gave us the perfect opportunity to bring you and I even closer. He had no idea of our plans...why he was chosen. We kept his past from him...bought him off with his own business and sold him a dream of white picket fences and a loving family...all those things he secretly longed for as a child. Then he got too attached to it all and wanted out...wanted to take you away from me...from your real family. What better motivation to side with your mother than a beating from a drunken lunatic...it was all going so well until you got involved with those Jackson boys...and now here we are. I've been on the back foot ever since...playing the victim until your father outed me. Bastard! He'll get his...just you wait."

Her mother had lost it. Whether it was the burden of guilt she carried, or the effects of solitary confinement, something snapped whatever thread of sanity she was clinging onto and caused her mask of normalcy to irrevocably slip.

Now all that remained was the evil lurking underneath, and in that moment, Meridia knew the mother she idolized all those years was gone and never coming back. Her whole life was nothing more than a lie, concocted by a malevolent force hell-bent on ending a world she cherished.

The more Meridia mulled over her mother's betrayal, the more it stung. Like a giant snowball of anger, it rolled away from her, out of control. All the time getting bigger and bigger until eventually it was she who snapped.

"How could you?!" she raged. "How dare you! Tell me where Izzy is now, you disgusting, vile woman! If there's even a shred of good left in you...a sliver of the mother I thought I knew...loved...then you'll tell me right now where she is and help me stop this madness!"

Meridia charged at Emily in a fit of temper and grabbed both her wrists. She wanted so badly to hit her, to do anything to inflict some modicum of pain and get her to break, but all she did was squeeze as she battled with her own inner demons and tried not to succumb to her anger.

Digging her nails deeper into her mother's flesh, Meridia sensed the room shudder and shake, like she was in the throes of an earthquake. Emily felt it too, and her once steely eyes were now suddenly dripping with fear.

"*CLATTER...CRACK!*"

The concrete cubicle splintered as cracks rained down around them like thunderbolts, but beneath each jagged crevasse was a blistering white light. Its searing rays were hot and blinding, like the rage Meridia felt coursing through her blood.

The sudden rush of heat they carried into the room was unbearable, drenching Meridia's hands with sweat, but still she clung onto Emily, determined to see this latest supernatural phenomenon through to the end with her, despite the fracturing reality crumbling around them.

This was how she felt tackling Valerie, the same furious surge of power, only now she wasn't dreaming, and the light blinding her was far more intense. Trembling, she closed her eyes as she battled the urge to faint under the bludgeoning heat.

A whistling hum joined the fray, pounding at her ears as it tried to break down the door to her mind, and her mother's screams soon accompanied it, until eventually they merged into one almighty, ear-splitting sonic assault on her senses.

Then, just as she felt her eardrums were about to burst, there was a sudden pop of silence, and all was calm. The room stopped its violent shaking, and the dazzling light subsided. Still glued to her mother's wrists, Meridia opened her eyes and found they were no longer in the makeshift prison cell. In fact, they were no longer in the bunker at all.

A thick band of black smoke drifted between mother and daughter, interrupting their mutual disdain with its acrid fumes and leading their attention elsewhere, down the smouldering ruins of the desolate street they were now shipwrecked on.

The air was warm, sticky with the stench of death and destruction as the sanguine sky raged overhead like an angry inferno.

Whatever hellish vision Meridia's gift yanked her to, this time it took her mother, too.

26

As Peter walked past Emily's cell, he didn't even notice her door was ajar. He was too busy reading the response he received from Retiarius.

Screeching to a halt a few yards short of the kitchen, a sliver of bile snaked its way up his throat and tainted the back of his tongue like warm battery acid. A cold sweat ensued, erupting from his hairline, as he frantically read the message again in disbelief.

Dear Peter, at least I assume this is you.

I hope my team is making you comfortable at chateau Drayton and you're not all going stir crazy in its concrete halls. You'll forgive the secrecy, but given the circumstances, there was no way you would have agreed to join them if you knew of my involvement upfront. Now, before you throw any toys out of your pram, let me explain. By now, I'm sure you know who I am.

Izzy is a smart cookie, and I know she alerted at least one of you to my little secret. So why betray her, I hear you say?

First, I'd like to say, with complete sincerity, it was never my intention for Izzy to be in her current predicament, but I must add that she's one brave little bookworm and really stepped up to the plate for you and your fan club. I coerced her into it, of course, but I really had no other choice. Everything was going to plan until a nosey parker alerted the police to a break-in at St Peter's.

It seems your impromptu night vigil didn't go unnoticed, and the neighbourhood watch grassed you up. That put me in a really tight spot. With such limited boots on the ground, I needed to choose who to save: Izzy or my daughter. I'm sure even a man like you can understand why things played out the way they did.

Anyway, we are where we are, and for now, both girls are alive, which I consider a win.

Don't be too hard on Marcus and the others, by the way, they aren't fully aware of my history or my relationship with Meridia. It's still too dangerous for me to show my face at the moment, so the last thing I want to do is blow your cover.

I do, however, know where Izzy is being kept and I have a plan to get her out, but I'm going to need your help. I'll give you some time to process. No doubt you have steam coming out of those perfectly shaped ears of yours right now, but please remember, the clock is ticking.

The last thing any of us want is another monster on the loose, and trust me, the demon is like no other monster you've encountered.

I look forward to your response. Oh, and please tell Emily I said hi.

Tick Tock Peter...

Yours, Retiarius

"Fuck!" Peter's uncharacteristic outburst drew the attention of Zach, who was now staring at him from the kitchen doorway.

His brown puppy dog eyes widened in surprise at the profanity, then sharpened again as he returned to his original agenda.

"Er...have you seen Meridia?" Peter only half heard him through the ruckus in his mind.

How could he have been so stupid, so trusting, after everything they went through? Jumping in a van with a total stranger and dragging the kids with him.

He was so surprised by the revelation of Emily's true nature and Kane's violent outburst, he forgot the very basic principles of guardianship.

Was he really that keen for an easy way out? He would have it out with Dr Foster immediately. And to think, he was about to suggest they let them all in on Meridia's secret.

"Peter? Are you ok?" Zach pressed, snapping him out of his inner turmoil.

Peter stuffed his phone back into his pocket and tried to recall the original question.

"Um...sorry Zach, yes...Meridia...no, I haven't seen her. Have you checked her room? She was looking a bit peaky when I last saw her."

"I've checked. One minute she was standing in the kitchen, and the next she was gone...without saying a word. I'm worried she might have...you know..." Zach flicked all his fingers out at once like a magician demonstrating a trick, and Peter knew exactly what he was implying.

"The only place I haven't looked yet is this end of the bunker, but I don't think she'd go above ground without telling anyone, so that just leaves..." Peter anxiously glanced over his shoulder.

The chair Grace propped against Emily's cell was now pushed to one side and the door was agape.

"Meridia!" Peter blurted, rushing to the open door.

The panic in his voice wrenched Zach away from the kitchen doorway and swept its way toward Kane and JJ, who were on their way to join him. A chorus of frantic footsteps pounded the concrete corridor as they all clambered to see inside the bunker's improvised prison.

"Gone...they're both gone..." Peter filled the narrow opening and felt Zach clawing at his waist to see beyond.

"Her chair's gone too..." He mumbled, stepping inside the empty storage cupboard and crouching in the middle of the room.

"She was tied up right here...so where is the chair...and where are the ropes?" All three boys filtered in behind him, studying every corner in denial as if there was some way Meridia and her mother were still in there, hiding.

"Not again..." Zach whined.

His fists were both clenched as he hid beneath his wavy brown mop in defeat.

"*Click! Clang clang clang...*"

Outside, in the corridor, they heard the bunker's main door close, and an echo of footsteps thunder down the ladder leading in.

"Meridia? Is that you?" Peter called out, rushing past the boys to greet whoever was on their way down.

"Whoa!" Peter clattered into Declan, almost knocking him to the ground.

"Easy there, big fella..." Behind him, a woman was waiting in the shadows, just out of sight.

Peter's heart sank the moment he realized the short, middle-aged blonde standing over Declan's shoulder wasn't Meridia.

"Mum?!" JJ cried, pushing past everyone as the mystery guest stepped forward into the light.

Dressed in a light beige raincoat with her hair tied up in a tight bun, Alice Jordan stretched out both arms and burst into tears.

"James! Thank God you're ok..." She sobbed. "I've been searching everywhere for you..."

27

MERIDIA'S EARS WERE STILL RINGING AS SHE PULLED away from her mother to take stock of where they were. Bound tightly to her chair, Emily was slumped forward with her chin resting on her chest. The strain of teleporting through time and space must have knocked her out cold.

Satisfied her mother was still breathing, Meridia continued scanning her surroundings and found themselves stranded in the ruins of a concrete graveyard. The shattered remains of what was once a thriving town now resembled a bombsite, reduced to nothing but carbonized rubble.

Smouldering carcasses of burnt-out cars lay strewn across fragments of obliterated buildings, upturned and pulverized as if trampled by a monster stampede. Occasional billows of black smoke followed the trail of devastation like a ghostly procession of mourners, hitching a ride on the warm, gentle breeze as it passed through town.

As Meridia watched them snake their way into the distance, she could see the lingering heat still radiating from the scorched tarmac underfoot, wilting everything as far as her eyes could see, like tall grass swaying in the wind.

Meanwhile, overhead, the turbulent sky remained ablaze, painting the ravaged streets below red and amber as it glared down on them with blistering contempt. Meridia saw the same bloodshot sky once before, in a devastating vision of the end.

"Wha..." Emily stirred behind her, punch-drunk and disoriented from her excruciating journey. This was a first. In all her travels, Meridia never once took anyone else with her.

"Wh...where am I?" she slurred. "What have you done?"

"You wanted a seer...and that's what you've got," Meridia fumed.

The mere sound of Emily's voice rekindled the fire in her blood.

"Look around mother...this is what you wanted, isn't it? You and those hooded maniacs you're so devoted to..." The word mother stuck in her throat as she goaded the woman she once worshiped but now despised.

"Take a good look while you can...who knows how long you'll survive out here in the open?" Meridia turned and stormed away.

"Wait! Where do you think you're going, young lady? You can't just leave me..."

"Don't you dare 'young lady' me!" Meridia raged, without looking back.

"Not after everything you've done, you two-faced bitch. I hope the weavers get you..." Tears were streaming down her face as she marched down the broken street, but Meridia refused to give Emily the satisfaction of seeing her cry.

Even though she crossed several lines in calling her mother a bitch, it paled compared to all the evil things

Emily did. Still, it took every ounce of strength for Meridia to put one foot in front of the other and walk away from the poisonous wretch.

She only made it a few yards when she noticed a splintered road sign lying in the gutter to her right. Although half the wording was missing, Meridia recognized it as belonging to Logan Road. She was still in Shawbrook, or what was left of it. She and Izzy walked past that sign every day on their way to school, before both their lives imploded.

She could almost hear Izzy giggling as they traded the latest celeb gossip whilst lugging their heavy schoolbags along in the rain. The bittersweet memory made Meridia wince as it gouged her heart and triggered another torrent of tears. She needed to get back to the others.

Cuffing her bleary eyes, she traced the jagged outline of the road ahead and finally got her bearings. St Swithun's was only a stone's throw from where she now stood, and not far beyond it was a place she once called home. Something inside told her to keep moving, that whatever message her gift had in store lay somewhere ahead, in the wreckage of her past.

As Meridia continued, she heard her mother's ranting in the distance and shook her head. Idiot, she thought. If there was one thing she learned from her visions, it was that most of them were hostile, which meant it was usually best to keep a low profile, not sit in the middle of the road screaming at the top of your lungs.

When she reached the intersection of Logan Road and St Swithun's, Emily was reduced to a murky blob in the distance. A spasm of guilt turned Meridia's fluttering stomach into a fist as she contemplated stepping beyond the imaginary umbilical cord, tying them together.

As evil and insane as she was, Emily was still her mother, and Meridia was under no illusion she could reconcile what she learned in the time it took to creep along an obliterated backstreet in Shawbrook. Still, her intuition told her she needed to press on, and there was no way she would risk setting her mother free, not after what she heard in the bunker.

"C'mon M, Izzy needs you..." She gritted her teeth and reluctantly turned the corner, condemning Emily to whatever monsters might lurk amongst the shadows of this godforsaken place.

The second Meridia entered St Swithun's Lane, she instantly regretted it. The serrated remains of her beloved school cut a chilling silhouette against the searing crimson skyline. A sacred barbican, built to safeguard and cultivate the town's future generations, was ruthlessly scythed down by an evil force hellbent on the world's destruction. The wire fence marking the perimeter of the playground was savagely ripped apart to reveal St Swithun's brittle, charcoal husk inside.

Its burnt tarmac, that used to be filled with so much laughter and cheer, was now littered with the charred remains of Meridia's peers. Their blackened bodies, hardened in their moment of death, lay twisted in perpetual torment like a thorny garden of pain.

As Meridia surveyed the sea of outstretched arms, she felt the weight of her gift tighten around her neck like a noose. So many souls hideously fused together, each one crying out to be saved. A gentle breeze brushed against her cheeks, reminding her of the sulphurous smell of death and decay as she stood transfixed by the grisly boneyard before her. Was this the message she was meant to receive?

Slowing to a shuffle, she hesitated, aware of how

exposed she was in the flattened remains of her ruined childhood. Between Meridia and the melted school gates was the wreckage of old Mrs Brewster's bungalow. Once resembling a magical cottage, fit for a fairy godmother, its dreamy vanilla rendering and caramel thatched roof were now reduced to a scorched pile of broken bricks and plaster.

Laying on the ground, close to where the bungalow's front door once stood, was a perfectly preserved slab of creamy white cladding and the sight of it made Meridia buckle at the knees.

There, in its centre, was the macabre symbol of the cult: an inverted pentagram, painted in dusty red, just like the markings she saw in a harrowing vision once before.

Her mother was with her too that day, buried under a mound of rubble, with only a broken hand to mark her stony grave as it reached up towards the heavens. This couldn't be a coincidence.

Meridia's stomach did a frontward flip, almost dragging her to her knees, as her brain tried to follow the breadcrumbs her gift left for her.

Then she heard it. Somewhere deep inside the wreckage of her school, a bone chilling sound erupted, turning Meridia to stone.

"Click-clack...click-clack..."

28

Meridia turned and ran as a swarm of weavers poured out of the shadows of St Swithun's and scuttled across the corpse-laden playground in hot pursuit. Trembling in fear, she stumbled and tripped along the ragged terrain as she wrestled to regain control of her balance.

"*Click-clack...click-clack...*"

The plague of mutant arachnids skittered effortlessly across the deluge of loose rubble behind her, hissing and screeching as they jostled for position like a pack of ravenous wolves.

Glancing back at the oncoming tide of oily black hair and razor-sharp teeth, Meridia saw they were smaller than the creature she encountered before, but it didn't make them any less terrifying. A flurry of powerful prickly legs, each capped with lethal looking tusks, rattled the streets as they rapidly devoured the distance between Meridia and certain death.

"*Click-clack...click-clack...*"

She felt the ground trembling underfoot from the

fervour of their ferocious onslaught, whilst up ahead Emily sat helplessly tied to her chair in the middle of the road like a ready-made banquet.

Staying close to the gutter where she had more cover, Meridia puffed and panted her way towards her helpless mother, all the while trying to keep one eye on the potholed ground underfoot.

"Argh!"

The last thing Meridia saw before she fell was Emily's petrified face, wide-eyed and staring down the barrel of a hundred hungry mouths, each baying for her blood. Then everything went dark. Down Meridia tumbled, into a ditch or a hole of some kind until she landed with a dull thud on soft, muddy ground.

"*Clang!*"

The sound of metal on metal echoed from above, setting her teeth on edge, then a warm clammy hand clamped her mouth shut from behind.

"Shh...you'll get us both killed." She felt the man's breath tickle her lobe as he whispered into her ear, carrying with it the aroma of coffee and cigarettes.

His voice was soft and unthreatening with a slight northern twang.

"There's nothing you can do Meridia...there's too many..." Overhead, a metal grate was closed, sealing her in with the mysterious stranger who somehow knew her name.

"*Click-clack...click-clack...*"

The thundering stampede of weavers charged overhead, drowning out Emily's blood-curdling screams, as they scratched and clattered their way across the only thing keeping Meridia safe: a rusty iron hatch violently jangling at its hinges. Meridia wriggled and squirmed in the man's arms, desperate to break free and do something, anything, to save her mother, but he held onto her.

"Ow!" Meridia stamped down hard on the man's foot to break free from his grip, but he was unrelenting.

Pivoting, she felt his hip against the small of her back and realized there was no getting away.

"She's gone Meridia..." He whispered. "I'm sorry, but she's gone..."

Meridia scrunched her eyes shut and braced herself for what was sure to follow, as the spine-chilling rampage subsided and made way for a moment of excruciating silence. She wriggled again, half-heartedly, resigned to the cruel inevitability of it all. A stomach-turning outcome she knew would haunt her for the rest of her days.

"Click-clack...click-clack..."

The metrical march of countless weavers resumed above her, this time more deliberate, as they menacingly closed in on their prey.

Meridia served her mother up on a plate. All because of her stupid, uncontrollable gift. Until now, she always found a way to save those she loved, but today, her anger took over. She should've untied her. Then, at least, she would've stood a fighting chance.

Or was this what Meridia was craving all along? To see Emily punished for all the pain and misery she caused.

"Argh!" Meridia flinched in the cramped confines of her unwanted embrace as Emily's terrified screams shattered her morbid ruminations.

Soaring high above the hissing arachnids, her piercing cries reverberated through the desolate streets, but there was no-one left alive to save her.

"Meridia...help...me...Meridia!" Emily's voice was fraught, but all Meridia could do now was pray the lethal killing machines showed her mother mercy for being one of their own. However, as was often the case, Meridia's prayers went unanswered.

"*Click-clack...click-clack...*"

The creatures marched on, unperturbed by Emily's final pleas for help, and then the screams intensified. Ear-splitting and shrill, the agonizing sound of her mother's slow and painful death was punctuated by a sickening cacophony of snapping and slurping as she was voraciously eaten alive.

"Cover your ears..." came the voice at her side, and although Meridia tried, it was far too late for that. Just as it was far too late for Emily.

The hideous tirade of terrible sounds already found a way in, searing Meridia's brain with images of her mother writhing in agony and drenched in blood as the swarm of hungry weavers crunched through bone and gnawed at flesh. Twelve years of loving memories unravelled like a ball of string, as for the umpteenth time, Meridia's world violently imploded.

A surge of memories set upon her like a swarm of angry locusts, nipping at her eyelids, forcing her to look. From lazy Sunday mornings and mugs of hot chocolate, to get well hugs and Friday night pizza.

The shattered fragments of what it meant to be loved, to feel safe, swirled around her like a tornado or torment, clawing at her conscience. Unable to escape the torturous merry-go-round tearing through her mind, Meridia renewed her struggle as her stomach churned, dizzy with self-loathing and guilt.

A warm fountain of puke gushed up her gullet and forced its way out through the gaps in her captor's grip, speckling the dirty ground with slimy remnants of mushy cereal and curdled milk.

"Kaff...kaff..."

The man loosened his grip, giving Meridia room to breathe as she doubled over to cough up the rest of her breakfast. Tainting the tiny crawlspace with the stench of vomit, Meridia had no choice but to open her eyes and let her tears out as she heaved and retched until her lungs burned.

As the stranger tried his best to comfort her in her moment of capitulation, the aural assault overhead faded into a distant hum as the screaming stopped and all that remained was her own coughing and spluttering. The feeding frenzy was over.

How could this be happening? After everything she endured.

"*Bratatatat...*"

Meridia recoiled as the sound of gunfire ricocheted above her, followed by the screeching of tires.

"*Bratatat...bratatat...*"

Each sudden burst of rapid fire sent tremors rippling through her body as she froze like a rabbit in headlights beneath the streaks of vermillion bleeding in through the hatch overhead. Her would-be-kidnapper darted between her and the ramshackle ladder bolted to the wall.

As he stepped out from the shadows in front of her, Meridia saw he wasn't much more than a kid himself.

Dressed in a grubby denim jacket, he was similar to JJ in height, but with Kane's wiry frame. His hair was dark and unkempt in what looked like a loose mullet, and although his face was as dirty as his coat, she saw beneath all the grime he was youthful and fresh-faced.

Upon closer inspection, Meridia figured he might be as

old as twenty, but definitely no older, and as he silently pressed a finger to his lips, she saw his blue eyes sparkle as they latched onto a shaft of light.

"*Screeeech...*"

The car above them sped off into the distance, and the stranger lowered his finger, then flashed Meridia a dirty palm to assure her he meant no harm.

"It's not safe here...we have to go," he mumbled softly.

His voice sounded older than his years, and for whatever reason, Meridia instinctively knew she could trust him. He wore a familiar expression as he turned his palm skyward and beckoned her toward him. It was one Meridia saw countless times in the mirror since this nightmare began: an expression forged by the weight of the world.

"Who are you?" She sobbed, casting her eyes down at the sodden earth as she wiped her mouth of bile.

Overcome with grief and remorse, she tried to make sense of the chaos engulfing her. Was her mother dead, or was this all another warning of horrors yet to come?

"G...go where?" She stuttered, glancing back up at the boy in denim.

"We don't have much time..." He beckoned her with his hand again. "You need to go back. The weavers...they are already nesting underneath Cold Christmas. You must stop them from breeding. You can still stop all this from happening..."

"M...my mum..." Meridia blurted, shuffling forward under the spell of shock as she tried to make sense of what she was hearing.

"There was nothing you could do, Meridia...there were too many. She chose this path...and now the others need you...they're your family now. You need to get back and warn them. We must hurry." He turned and carefully opened the hatch, then peered through the gap.

Red and amber hues flooded the crawl space as he pushed the grate all the way back onto the ground above, and Meridia saw she was standing in nothing more than an underground panic room. The boy hastily clambered up the makeshift ladder and then reached down for her. His eyes sparkled with grit and tenacity as he pleaded for her to take his hand, and, instinctively, Meridia did.

Once again, she found his grip was firm, safe this time, with a strength that belied his slender frame as he hoisted her up onto the scorched tarmac.

"The vultures will be back soon...they never stray far. We're lucky they were babies, otherwise we might have been stuck down there all night. Even the vultures aren't stupid enough to take on a pack of fully grown weavers..."

"Wh...what? Who are you? How do you know all this? How do you know my name?"

"I'm sorry Meridia, I didn't get it at the time and almost gave up waiting...I'm Tommy. You don't know me, but you will...soon."

His cryptic answer sent a thousand other questions clattering against the inside of Meridia's gritted teeth as, all at once, they tried to find a way out. Regardless of whatever lied in wait for her above ground, she knew she needed to go back with as many answers as she could, otherwise it would all have been for nothing. As she shakily got to her feet, Tommy abruptly stepped into the gap between them and startled her.

"Don't look..." He whispered, shielding her from the bloodbath behind him. "Nothing good is gonna come from seeing that..." But this time Meridia wasn't about to let anyone dictate what she could or couldn't see, so she feinted to her left, then darted right, ducking below Tommy's outstretched arm and leaving him in her wake.

"Nooooo!" Before he had the chance to recover, Meridia's deafening scream was already howling through the forsaken streets of Shawbrook like a runaway train, threatening to stir up anything and everything in its path.

In a panic, he fumbled to quieten her again with his hand, but once more she slipped through his fingers and by the time he caught up with her, it was already too late. Try as he might, he couldn't tear her away from the harrowing spectacle smeared across the blood-stained concrete.

Eyes bulging with disgust, Meridia tearfully soaked up every speck of carnage and added them to the gruesome scrapbook of horrors she kept stowed away in the depths of her mind. The rancid stench of sulphur interlaced with the coppery smell of blood and hit the back of her throat as she gasped for breath, causing her stomach to grumble in protest.

A slew of steaming black carcasses lay scattered across the ground like bashed-in pinatas. Their barbed legs were now limp and lifeless beneath their bullet-ridden bodies. Globules of glistening green mucus oozed from their gaping wounds and dripped onto the roadside. Each slimy bead of blood sizzled and perforated the asphalt below.

Whatever coursed through the weaver's veins was like corrosive acid, disintegrating everything it touched as they slowly bled out under the blistering sky.

"Mum!" As Meridia stumbled closer to the smouldering debris, she spotted splinters of wood and crimson-dyed tatters of an orange climbing rope sprinkled like confetti. Then her body finally revolted.

"Kaff...kaff..." Coughing up whatever she had left in her stomach, she dropped to her knees in despair.

There, in the centre of all the murder and mayhem, was her mother's outstretched hand, just as it was in her previous vision. Only this time, it wasn't buried beneath a pile of rubble. It was gnawed at the wrist and completely severed from the rest of her body. A body that was not yet cold in the bellies of the hideous arachnid corpses littered around her.

"Meridia..." Tommy dragged her back to her feet. "We don't have time for this...You can't stay here...it's too dangerous."

"No!" she barked back at him, drunk on regret, as she staggered over to Emily's gnarled, half-eaten limb and slumped down beside it.

Trembling, Meridia reached out with her own quivering hand. She needed to feel her one last time. Sobbing uncontrollably, she hovered her fingertips over her mother's, not knowing what to expect, while Tommy stood stranded on the sidelines, unsure what else he could do to keep them both safe. As Meridia took her mother's hand, the softness and warmth of her skin shocked her.

Clenching her eyes closed, she imagined it was all a dream, and she had never even left her bed. Not the rigid, musty one in the soulless bunker, but in her actual bed. She imagined she was snug under her marshmallow duvet, protected by the warm amber glow of her luna nightlight. The more detail she painted on the canvas of her mind, the tighter she gripped her mother's hand until eventually it vibrated.

She visualized pulling Emily out from beneath a pile of rubble, that her body was still in one piece and in need of rescuing.

"Meridia..." She heard Tommy gasp somewhere in the background. "You're doing it..."

Oh, how she wanted to believe him, that she was resurrecting her mother from the grave and saving her from all the wicked decisions she made behind closed doors. But Meridia knew this feeling all too well. Dazzling light permeated through her clenched eyelids, as if the sun broke free from its bloodshot restraints, and she felt its warm embrace.

However, it wasn't the sun she felt, it was her wretched curse, dragging her back to her miserable life, far away from the daydream denial she conjured up in the throes of her remorse. She clung onto her mother's hand all the same, squeezing her lifeless palm as the tremors kicked in and the world around her crumbled.

"December 12th..." Tommy called out to her again, his voice drifting in and out of her awareness like an untuned radio.

"You need to tell me when to be here..." He pressed. "...Or else this will never happen..." She strained to hear him through the static buzzing in her ears. "December 12th...this year."

Meridia opened her eyes in shock just in time to see everything around her fade to white. If what Tommy said was true, then they only had a matter of days to stop the end of the world.

29

"WHAT DO YOU MEAN, THEY'RE BOTH GONE?!" DECLAN
fumed. "Gone where?"

The raised voices in the entrance hall brought everyone
else running to see what the commotion was as Peter lost his
cool.

"I don't know...maybe your boss Retiarius took them?"

JJ dropped his mum's hands and turned to look at Kane
and Zach. Peter's shocking accusation left both brothers
slack-jawed and stunned in the crowded corridor.

"Wh...what are you talking about?" Declan stuttered,
clearly surprised by Peter's jibe. Before Peter enlightened
everyone, Dr Foster chimed in.

"Now hold on Peter..."

"No, you hold on Marcus..." he fizzed back. "I thought
we were levelling with each other here...isn't that what you
said? So how come I just found out the person responsible
for getting Izzy into all this mess is the same bloody person
pulling the strings here?"

JJ shot his mum a sceptical glance and backed away as

Peter's sudden outburst cast doubt over her true intentions for showing up unannounced.

"I assure you, it's not like that Peter...just hear me out... please." Dr Foster had both palms up to calm Peter down.

In the narrow confines of the corridor, it suddenly struck JJ how imposing Peter was as he filled the doorway with his 6'4" frame. He never seen him like this before, but if anything, it endeared him even more as he watched the mild-mannered writer stand tall and fight in their corner.

What the hell was this lot doing tangled up with Meridia's dad, he thought, as Peter stormed past everyone towards the kitchen.

"C'mon then...let's all hear it shall we..." His voice echoed behind him as he disappeared down the gloomy concrete passageway.

JJ felt his mother's hand on his shoulder, but he was quick to shrug off any attempt to slow him down as he briskly set off with Zach and Kane, leaving her alone in the shadows.

As everyone fanned out into the kitchen, the buttery yellow room took on the shape of a boxing ring, with Dr Foster and his team in one corner, then Peter and his in the other. Although a physical fight seemed unlikely, Peter remained incensed by his discovery.

"What the hell's going on?" JJ whispered to Kane, as all three boys huddled close behind their irate mentor.

"I know as much as you, mate...but if any of what Peter's saying is true, then I think we might be looking for a new home by lunchtime." Kane's comment, although flippant, hit a nerve in JJ.

He was paddling hard to stay afloat in the sea of shifting dynamics surrounding his surrogate family. Now, with the unexpected arrival of his estranged mother, and the mere mention of Meridia's deceitful father, he sensed yet another tsunami of uncertainty looming on the horizon.

"We should be looking for Meridia..." Zach bleated. "She could be in real trouble."

"I hear you spud." Kane threw an arm around his brother's shoulder.

"But if word gets out about her gift, then we could all be in deep shit...particularly if her dad is mixed up in this. We already know what that prick did to Izzy..."

The room was abuzz with the murmurs and mutterings of both camps, like rumbling storm clouds rolling in as tensions continued to mount between both corners. Declan appeared flustered, his eyes darting back and forth around the room, as he whispered into the doctor's ear.

Behind him, Grace and Nadia maintained a little more distance as they both leant against the kitchen worktop, embroiled in their own private conversation.

"Do you think they knew?" JJ nudged Kane and nodded towards both women.

"They're both covering their mouths when they speak, so what do you think? Whatever's going on, we're about to find out..."

"Everyone settle down...please." Dr Foster stepped into the centre of the room like a ring announcer as Alice slipped inside.

She removed her raincoat to reveal her navy-blue nurse's uniform. JJ waited, eagle-eyed, for his mum to choose a side, then frowned as she chose instead to hover in the doorway while the doctor shushed everyone.

"It seems there may have been some kind of misunderstanding here..." Again, he showed Peter both palms as a gesture of amity.

"We've made no secret of the fact we are part of a larger

network who all share a common enemy. Disparate at times, yes...but, united by our desire to...well, stay alive. Now, I can't vouch for every single one of those other folks...hell I haven't even met half of them...but one thing I can say, is that everyone who's part of what I call our inner circle, I trust with my life. Take our girl, Alice, for example." Everyone followed the doctor's gaze to the neutral side of the room.

"She's been out there risking her neck for months. Working behind enemy lines, gathering intel on what the Children of the Shadows have planned...now I had no idea you guys were related...and I'm not looking to get in the middle of any family feuds, but JJ, whatever terrible things you think your mum has done, let me tell you now, she had her reasons, so I suggest you try hearing her out before you go jumping to any more conclusions..."

"With all due respect..." Peter interrupted, also stepping into the square circle. "...we can discuss JJ's mum later. This is about Retiarius...and more to the point, Meridia. Now where is she?"

"But this is precisely the point I'm trying to make, Peter...this is all relevant. I thought you understood that. Everyone in this room is hiding something. We all have secrets...things we're ashamed to admit, or things that can harm the ones we love if they come to light. Retiarius...or Gregor, as I prefer to call him, is no different from you or me. No different to Alice there...we're all just doing the best we can with the cards we've been dealt, don't you see? Gregor was stuck between a rock and a hard place when you guys reached out to him. The man has been in exile for almost two whole years since his wife threw him under the bus. Back then, he just wanted out of all this... to take his family and get away from it all, but for whatever reason, his wife had other ideas, and so here we are."

"No, he threw Izzy under the bus...and now she's paying the price for his cowardice." The doctor's attempt to spin Gregor's actions riled Peter.

"Trust me, Gregor may be a lot of things, and yes, he can be a total arsehole at times...but he's no coward." Grace piped up from the sideline.

"At one point or another, he's saved the lives of everyone in this room. You included Peter. Who do you think tipped us off to where you were? If you stayed in that church a moment longer, you would all be dead. Do you really think Declan sits there monitoring every crackpot conspiracy nut ranting about Cold Christmas? Has anyone seen him do that since you've been here? We have no internet to speak of, remember? Trust me, if Gregor wanted any of you hurt, he would have hung you out to dry that night." Grace's voice splintered as her emotions got the better of her.

"Who do you think found me in the woods that day? It may have been Declan who carried me inside, but it was Gregor who found me. Do you honestly think he would have risked crossing paths with that homicidal freak show if he was a coward?"

Grace batted JJ's attention back to Peter like it was a tennis ball and he found him fumbling for something in his pocket. He pulled out his phone and thumbed through his apps.

"He says here that I shouldn't be too hard on you all... that you didn't know about Meridia...is that true?"

"What about Meridia?" Dr Foster asked, confused.

"She's his daughter." Alice finally spoke up, having watched silently from the wings.

"Wait...what?" Dr Foster looked genuinely stunned, as did everyone else on his side of the quarrel, and a blanket of hush floated down, smothering the room. "So...that means Emily is..."

"His wife, yes."

Dr Foster slumped down on the edge of the dining table in surprise as Alice continued.

"Like Marcus said, we all have secrets." Alice's eyes were brimming with tears as she stepped out of the shadow of the doorframe so she could be seen.

"Isn't that right, Peter?" She raised a knowing eyebrow, then pivoted to avoid adding any more fuel to the fire.

"Peter...I cannot thank you enough for looking after my son...and his friends. I'm forever in your debt for everything you've done, and I have no idea what you've all been through to make it this far. I've heard murmurs through the grapevine that you've remained a thorn in the side of the Grand Master ever since you all wandered into that godforsaken place. But you must understand, the world is not black and white. The Children of the Shadows have made damn sure of that, corrupting anyone and everyone they could get their claws into. You see it's always been this way for us...maybe not for you Peter, and god knows I've tried to shield James from all that I've done...but for us...for those who were practically born into this shitstorm...those of us who've had to fight tooth and nail just to make ends meet and for those who've had everything they held dear snatched away by some cruel twist of fate...for us it didn't take much to blur the lines of what's right and wrong, and that's what those evil bastards are just so damn good at. It starts off small...just enough to tempt you across that line, that one little thing that makes such a huge difference...then before you know it, they own you, and that line you swore you would never cross is so far in your rear view you can't even see it anymore." JJ wrestled with the impulse to run to his mum as she poured her heart out in front of everyone.

"So that's all we're trying to do now...all I'm trying to do...is find my way back to that line...so I can get back on the right side of it again. I'm not gonna lie, it's not easy...and even now I still don't get everything right, but who does? Do you? God, do you know how many times I reached out to my son, trying to explain...and every time I did, it was wrong of me. I was putting my needs over his. I was putting him in even more danger. Truth is, he's far safer with you, Peter. Far safer than he would ever be with me, even now. I can see that now. But unless you've been there...at rock bottom...like I was...like Gregor was...then I'm sorry, you don't really know what you're talking about..."

"What about dad?" JJ blurted.

He couldn't hold the question in any longer. It was eating away at him since she arrived, but Alice simply shook her head and stared at her feet.

"If I thought I could trust him, then he would be here now, but he's too far gone. I'm sorry James...we should've both walked away when the Jacksons did, but we were in too deep by then...and things have just been spiralling ever since..." She pulled a tissue from her pocket and dabbed her eyes so as not to smudge her makeup.

JJ felt his entire body lean to one side, as if gravity were pulling him towards her, but he held fast. He'd already seen enough crocodile tears from Emily to know he couldn't take his mum at face value, no matter how convincing she was beneath the fluorescent spotlights of her makeshift stage.

"Thank you, Alice. I don't think any of us can imagine what it's like to be in your shoes. How scared you must've been." Dr Foster's acknowledgement sounded heartfelt and sincere, then he promptly resumed his petition for everyone else in the room to see sense.

"Peter...putting all this other bullshit aside for the moment, you must believe me when I say that if Gregor was here, I would know about it. So, that just begs the question: where the hell did Meridia and Emily go?"

Before anyone else spoke, JJ felt his ears pop as the air pressure shifted in the room. Shooting a sideways glance towards Kane, he found him looking puzzled with his mouth wide open as if he was forcing a yawn. Whatever it was, he felt it, too.

"*Buzzzzzz...*"

The strip lighting flickered over everyone's heads like a nightclub strobe as all the electrical equipment suddenly came to life. In the farthest corner of the room, Declan's old CD player belted out a crackled garble of inaudible melodies as if it was tuning into a phantom frequency, while beneath it, the clapped-out microwave illuminated amber, even though its plug was nowhere near a power socket.

JJ felt his pocket vibrate, as all the phones in the room gate-crashed the creepy light show, flashing and beeping like a swarm of paparazzi desperate to capture the latest scoop. The disturbing lambent display was enough to trigger a fit as it continued to stutter, painting eerie shadows on the walls with its erratic beats. Then, suddenly, a loud and abrupt '*click*' plunged the room into total darkness.

A chorus of gasps rippled around JJ as the entire kitchen teetered on the brink of hysteria. Before anyone had a chance to react, the lights beamed back on, blinding everyone and dazzling the room as if the bulbs were about to burst.

"Meridia!"

Zach's eyes were the first to adapt, and as JJ fixed his

gaze, he saw her too, standing in the middle of the room. Her hair was wild, and her eyes were red-raw, teeming with tears. She just stood there, silently quivering, her face frozen in fear as the lights above her returned to a more tolerable glare.

"Flop"

Something flaccid hit the floor, and a splash of crimson streaked across the concrete. JJ gasped in horror the second he traced the spillage back to its source.

At Meridia's feet lay a severed hand, its fingers limp and loosely curled up toward the ceiling like the shrivelled legs of a squished spider. Jagged chunks of mangled flesh dangled from its serrated stump, while shards of gnawed bone and gristle glistened beneath the fluorescent glow overhead.

Time stopped momentarily as the crowd stared in shocked silence at the coagulated blood seeping onto the cold kitchen floor. Along with her gruesome souvenir, Meridia carried the stink of bonfires and burnt rubber on her clothes, and a sudden waft of its sulphurous stench tickled JJ's nose, making him balk.

Then he finally recognized the grisly appendage, and his heart sank like a stone into the bottom of his churning stomach. Emerald nail varnish sparkled under the unforgiving lights, and at once he knew the hand belonged to Emily.

What the hell did Meridia do?

30

"I don't know where she is...I swear!"

Grady watched the man twitch and tremble beneath the ragged brown sack covering his face and contemplated sticking him with his knife just for the hell of it.

Dressed for the office in a pair of grey tweed trousers and a crisp white shirt, Grady intercepted him on his way to work and bundled him in the back of his van. Now, instead of casually slurping coffee at his desk, he found himself tied to a chair in a dungeon beneath Chase Side Hospital, begging for his life.

Since being held captive, the prisoner gave Grady little reason to doubt his innocence, which meant he should really let him go. Upon noticing the veins pop on the man's sweaty hands as he blindly wrestled his restraints, all Grady thought of was slicing one open to see how runny his blood was.

Tightening his grasp on his hunting knife in grim anticipation, Grady remained silent. The familiar handle felt warm and soothing as he squeezed its leather grip like a stress ball in his palm. Usually, he would relish the sound of it creaking in his hand, but in the clammy dungeon, all he heard was the worthless snivelling of his captive as he struggled to control his breathing.

Watching the man's chest rapidly rise and fall beneath his shirt, Grady's thoughts graduated to cutting his heart out and holding it in his bare hands. He never attempted it before and was now curious if he would be fast enough to feel its final beat.

Since deviating from his regular kill ritual with the priest, and more recently brother Wells, he had a burning desire to experiment more and experience new things. His excursion with the weaver unexpectedly opened up a world of possibilities which felt quite liberating, as if the shackles were finally removed and he was free to explore his darkest fantasies.

"Please...just let me go and I'll help you find her...she trusts me...she'll reach out to me. I know she will..." The man's whining was grating, so Grady stepped to him abruptly, intentionally scuffing the stony ground with the sole of his shoe. He snickered as a wet patch appeared in the crotch of the man's trousers and then slowly expanded down his inseam.

"Please..." the man begged, dejected and squirming uncomfortably in his seat. "I don't know anything...I swear."

The tangy stench of sweat and piss stuck in Grady's throat, so he decided he was done wasting time. He skulked towards the only door in the damp and dingy torture chamber, then turned the latch. Locking it from the inside.

The last thing he wanted was anyone interrupting his little science experiment. Turning to face his prey, Grady lunged at him full of menace, rattling him in his chair as he gripped him by the shoulders.

"Look at you…" He hissed at the quivering wreck in front of him. "You're pathetic!"

Violently ripping the man's shirt open down to his navel, Grady showered the room with the staccato clatter of buttons ricocheting off the ground like hailstones in a storm.

Grady ogled his hairless, caramel brown chest and traced the man's ribs with the tip of his blade. He was lean for a man in his fifties, despite being a slave to his desk, and Grady figured he would have no trouble carving his way inside.

Stopping around halfway up his sternum, he tickled and teased the man's skin with his knife whilst deciding where best to start.

The allure of the unknown was exhilarating, giving Grady butterflies as he loomed over his helpless prey, grinning from ear to ear like a demented cheshire cat. For years, he rigidly followed the same meticulous process when claiming his victims, aside from those impromptu encounters with random tourists lost in the woods where he roamed at night.

"The master told me to rattle some cages…" Grady whispered into the crumpled mass of sacking material swamping his prisoner's head as he finally picked his spot.

"Ow…" The man winced as Grady pricked him in his side. Not enough to break the skin, but enough to let him know where the knife was.

"So, I thought what better place to start than your rib cage brother Jordan…" Grady beamed as he found the gap between his victim's ribs and slowly pushed the serrated blade deep inside JJ's father.

"Argh!" His bloodcurdling screams were like music to Grady's ears as they echoed around the dingy dungeon.

Making his crude incision just below Jordan's armpit,

he ruthlessly hacked his way towards the centre of his chest, tearing through muscle and cartilage, as he traced the trench of his upper left rib with his knife until he carved enough space to slip his fingertips inside.

"Argh..." The agonizing cries soon dissipated as Jordan's head fell limp, overcome with pain.

A waterfall of viscous blood cascaded over Grady's hand and down Jordan's torso, seeping into his trousers and shirt tail, as Grady foraged to find his grip.

"There you are..." He boasted, pulling on the rib like a wishbone and snapping it outward to create a gruesome crevice big enough to accommodate the rest of his hand.

"Crack!"

Jordan sprung to life at the grisly intrusion, a frenzy of flailing legs and thrashing limbs as he writhed and groaned in his seat like he was being fried by an electric chair. And then, with one final twitch of his ankle, JJ's father drew his last breath, and his body wilted permanently.

"Squelch...squish..."

Realizing his prisoner was dead, Grady hurriedly rummaged between liver and lung, squishing and squelching his way in search of Jordan's heart, whilst his sleeve steadily soaked up the deluge of blood pouring from his mutilated body.

"Dammit..." he fumed, lost in the warm slippery maze of gelatinous organs.

"Dammit!" Grady already knew too much time elapsed, and when his fingertips finally reached the dense, meaty nub of the organ he was fumbling for, it was as lifeless as the blood-spattered corpse slumped beside him.

He was about to concede when another grisly idea suddenly dawned on him and, in a show of brute strength and spite, Grady made a fist and forced his hand further.

Higher and higher, he drove his knuckles up towards Jordan's throat as entrails spattered and slopped to the ground.

Up the trachea, through the larynx, and into the pharynx where he then opened his hand and felt around for something to hold on to, all the while sniggering like a giddy schoolboy as his eyes soaked up the glistening puddle of gore swelling around his feet.

The dead man's gullet felt like thick, sticky elastic, tugging against the hairs on his forearm as he felt around inside the cavity of his jaw, and the smell was unlike anything he previously experienced. A fetid blend of blood and human excrement swamped the room, tingling his nostrils and making his eyes water as he continued to rummage. Then the discord of disgusting sloshing sounds subsided as Grady rested his arm.

"What's that?" Grady asked, still grinning maniacally as he cocked an ear towards Jordan's heavily shrouded face.

"You'll have to speak up...I can't hear you under that bag..." With the arm that wasn't buried up to the elbow in Jordan's slouching corpse, Grady reached over and yanked the sack off his victim's head. The once bright and bubbly furniture salesman was now slack jawed and lost for words. Still gleaming with sweat beneath the creamy opaque bulb overhead, his eyes were wide open, frozen in his final moments of despair at Grady's savage violation.

The empty black voids of his dilated pupils devoured all the colour they could find from his haunting gaze and were now reflecting the oozing pile of intestines unravelling towards his outstretched feet.

Thick crimson streaks seeped from each corner of his mouth, giving him the appearance of a grotesque ventriloquist dummy. That's exactly what he was with Grady's hand lodged in his mouth.

Operating Jordan's malleable carcass from the inside, he pulled the dead man's lips close to his ear as if he was about to divulge a secret from beyond the grave.

"Clack...clack..."

The chilling sound of Jordan's teeth clumsily clunking together echoed around the room like sadistic castanets, and then Grady spoke again.

"What do you mean, you've got a sore throat? Well, whose fault is that, eh? I gave you every opportunity to come clean, didn't I? Speaking of clean, it looks like you might have shat your pants. I guess you've reached the age where you just can't trust a fart anymore." Grady lowered Jordan's head as if he was assessing the mess in his trousers.

"No need to be embarrassed..." he continued, tenderly stroking his dummy's head with his free hand. "Time catches up with us all, eventually. Now, tell me brother... where is that treacherous wife of yours?"

"Clack...clack..."

This time, a more sickening squelching accompanied the hollow clunking sound as Grady twisted his arm deeper inside his cadaverous dummy to tighten his grip. As he forced his thumb further into the squishy depths beneath Jordan's bottom teeth, he sent his flaccid tongue flopping out the side of his mouth like a dead dog.

"The little girl next door might know? I think you may be onto something there, brother. Now put your tongue away will you and show some decorum..." Grady quipped, and with a sharp flick of his wrist and a crack of Jordan's spine, he snapped the dead man's tongue back inside his ghoulish head. "But what should I do if she doesn't spill the beans? The master is saving her for the demon..."

"Clack...clack..."

"You think I should kill her, anyway? Well, I suppose we don't *have* to use her for the sacrifice do we...In fact we can use just about anybody for that little ritual, and the master did tell me to do whatever it takes to find your two-faced wife...so I suppose I'd just be following orders wouldn't I..."

"Clack...clack..."

"Mm...good point. I guess it's settled then. I'll make the girl talk...like I've made you..." Grady pulled his blood-soaked hand from the dead man's trunk with one last satisfying squelch, and then shook the remnants of his innards onto the stony ground with a loud splat.

Giddy on adrenalin, he paused for a moment to admire the sticky morsels of clotted blood still clinging to his hand and breathed in their coppery aroma like he was appreciating a fine wine. After taking one last look at Derrick Jordan's mutilated remains smeared all over the floor, Grady turned his back and vowed to return for his eyes later.

He was relishing this newfound freedom, and although this brief foray into his darker side didn't go exactly to plan, his sick and twisted improvisation taught him to think even bigger next time.

Who better to experiment on next than the pathetic little Di Salvo girl?

"Click!"

Unlocking the door to the dungeon, Grady stepped boldly into the corridor, smothered in blood and knife in hand. It was Izzy's turn to spill her guts.

31

Izzy lay curled into the fetal position with her hands firmly pressed to her ears as she tried to block out the blood-curdling screams coming from the room next door.

There was something truly awful about hearing a grown man scream like that, and as his continuous pleas for mercy penetrated her addled brain like a pneumatic drill, she couldn't help but wonder who the man might be.

When her cynical imagination collected all her thoughts and frogmarched them to Peter's door, she pressed down even harder to suppress the sounds of torture, but her arms were heavy, weakened by severe hunger and sleep deprivation. On the stony ground, a few yards from her face, a handful of roaches chirped and hissed as they foraged beneath the grubby rag covering her parents' severed fingers.

The vile, musty smelling creatures were feverishly scuttling around beneath its cover for at least half an hour now, no doubt feasting on whatever flesh they could sink their slimy mandibles into. As much as the harrowing thought of them stuffing their disgusting little faces turned her blood to ice, Izzy simply lacked the strength and the stomach to shoo them away. She felt a wintry chill in her bones now, despite the dungeon's oppressive humidity, and her throat was so parched that each time she swallowed it felt like she had a hundred needles lodged in her gullet.

The prospect of going any longer without replenishing the much-needed fluid in her dog-tired body filled her full of dread and if she continued on this path, she would most likely pass out never to wake up.

However, the filthy, dirt-encrusted glass of water given to her since her abduction remained untouched beside the plastic bucket serving as her toilet. The only living thing to go anywhere near it was an enormous black horsefly that got too curious and now floated around aimlessly in a watery grave.

A clean freak, fixated with personal hygiene, this was Izzy's worst nightmare. She knew if she didn't overcome her debilitating fear of germs, she would surely die before her sacrifice.

As she pondered the pros and cons of such a bleak proposition in her sluggish mind, she realized the man's screams had subsided and all was silent. She let her weary arms flop back down, listening intently, and thought she heard someone whispering on the other side of the wall to which she was chained.

How she wished someone would rescue her from this stinking hellhole, but she had no idea where she was aside from perhaps being underground, which meant the chances of her friends finding her in time were getting slimmer by the second. Not that she deserved saving, anyway.

"*Click...*"

The sound of metal on metal reverberated outside,

jolting Izzy from her daydream, and then she heard footsteps in the corridor.

"*Click!*"

Her door slowly opened, and a narrow beam of light crept into the gloomy prison cell, animating thousands of dust particles that were secretly dancing around her under the cover of darkness.

Although dim, the sudden surge in brightness stung Izzy's corneas, and as she averted her gaze, she again locked eyes with the rippling cotton waves of her tattered sweater sleeve as the small party of cockroaches carried on enjoying their meal unperturbed.

"Ms Di Salvo..." Grady's smarmy voice sent an icy shiver scampering up Izzy's spine, and for a moment, she panicked and squirmed, thinking a roach somehow scurried underneath her jumper.

"C'mon...sit up. We haven't got all day..." He kicked her between the shoulder blades when she refused to look at him, knocking the breath from her lungs.

"*Kaff...kaff...*" The coughing rattled her aching ribs as she fought to catch her breath.

"I said get up..." Izzy screamed as Grady grabbed her by the ponytail and yanked her upright. She was crying now.

The perpetual torment of her hopeless existence crushed whatever remained of her spirit and all she wanted to do now was curl up into a ball and die.

As she was violently thrust down onto her backside, the cold hard ground sent a lightning bolt of pain shooting up through her tailbone, jolting the air from her lungs once more. Choking on tears, a tangy metallic stench struck the back of her throat, triggering another coughing fit. It reeked like rusty nails left out in the rain, and pretty soon it was all she tasted.

When she found the courage to glance up at her aggressor, the sight of him looming over her kick-started her gag reflex. Grady's outstretched hand, the same hand he grabbed her with, was smothered in blood and gore. Congealed chunks of gristle and cartilage, like a grisly melange of mashed-up raspberry jelly and raw mincemeat, slithered down his crimson-glazed skin.

Izzy's eyes anxiously followed the stomach-churning trail of carnage all the way up his arm until she reached the unhinged expression etched on his face. Try as she might, she was unable to tear her eyes away. Grady's slick black hair hung limp over his ruffled forehead, like a dozen greasy spider legs dangling from their nest.

Beneath his spiny mop, his piercing sapphire stare was wide and wild, sparkling with malice as it bore down into Izzy's soul. She sensed her body seizing up beneath their penetrating glare, as if all the blood in her trembling body was turning to ice, one vein at a time.

Grinning like a deranged lunatic, his reedy lips stretched from ear to ear, revealing an array of dimples and strained creases on his blood-speckled jawline. Whatever unspeakable thing he did to the poor soul next door, it was way more brutal than Izzy could ever fathom, as he looked and smelled like an evil butcher fresh from a human slaughterhouse.

"I've had enough of your silly little games Izzy..." He hissed through clenched teeth.

"You think you can take me for a fool? Well, I've been chatting to a friend of yours next door and we had quite the conversation about you..."

Izzy's broken heart sank in defeat as another monsoon of tears streamed down her cheeks.

"Wh...who...wh...what have...you done?" She sobbed,

her words sticking to the roof of her mouth like treacle as she battled to breathe through snot-filled airways.

"Your chubby little friend James...or is it JJ..." Grady paused a moment, allowing Izzy's shattered cries of despair to lay siege on the room as she descended into hysterics. Then, just as her lungs threatened to burst from the pain, he raised his voice to clarify.

"...well, I've been speaking to his dear old dad, and he says you've been holding out on me."

Izzy's mind galloped away from her as she tried to reconcile what she was hearing. In the short space of time since he burst into her cell, she already felt like she did ten laps on a terrifying rollercoaster as she struggled to stay abreast of her tormentor's unpredictable nature.

Was it all mind games, or had she listened to JJ's dad being murdered? Before she collected her thoughts, Grady came at her again, hacking and slashing at her heartstrings.

"You do know JJ wouldn't even be here if it wasn't for us? That's right...his parents did a deal with the devil. Their undying loyalty in exchange for a child..." Even Grady's voice was erratic. One moment it was patronizing, and the next laced with anger.

"Wh...what?" Izzy mumbled, desperate to keep him talking so she could recover her composure.

"They couldn't conceive, you see...that's why they're so much older than all the other mummies and daddies. Ha, he's not even related to them...not by blood, anyway. Poor little JJ never knew his real parents, but I did..." Lost in thought, Grady pressed a crimson finger to his lips and then smeared a trail of blood all the way around his mouth.

The vivid contrast of cerise against his anaemic skin left him looking like a sinister circus clown and sent another ice-cold chill scampering up Izzy's spine.

"Their blood smelled different..." he mused, before his eyes narrowed again and returned to Izzy's, full of scorn.

"I took baby JJ and delivered him like a stork...they were one of my first kills. I must've been around your age at the time...it seems so long ago now...I remember watching them in the park, strolling around with their newborn boy like their shit didn't stink...lapping up all the attention. It didn't take much for me to trick them into thinking I needed help...after all, who would've suspected someone so young could be capable of something so..."

A slimy smile snaked across Grady's painted lips as he reminisced. It was enough to make Izzy's flesh crawl.

"Oh, what a mess I made...I had no control back then. No code...I just slashed and stabbed anything I could reach until they stopped struggling. I was almost feral...but now look at me...ha...look how far I've come..." He opened his arms out as if he was about to take a bow, and that was when Izzy noticed the hunting knife in his hand.

Streaked in blood, it shimmered hypnotically under the naked bulb as he continued with his twisted monologue.

"So, I guess that means so far, I've murdered three of JJ's parents...ha...what a funny statistic...anyway, I digress." His eyes sharpened again like a knife.

"I need to make it four, and you're going to help me. Either that or I'll cut your miserable head off here and now!" The blade creaked in his hand as he towered over Izzy.

There was no escape from this madman. Whatever shred of sanity Grady was clinging onto when posing as a nurse had finally snapped, and all she saw now was a vicious, untamed animal thirsty for blood.

"I...I don't know what you're talking about..." She stammered. "We thought she was with you..."

The shameful realization she may have been wrong about her own parents lodged itself in Izzy's throat and another battalion of tears readied themselves to charge. She glanced down at the quivering piece of cloth covering their remains and, in that moment, realized she would never get to hear their side of the story.

The black and white town of Shawbrook, the place she called home, revealed itself to be a murky underworld that all its inhabitants were forced to traverse, cognizant or not.

Could it be her ideals of good and bad were exactly that: just ideals?

She thought about all the times she lied to her parents since becoming entangled with Crooked House. All the time she spent skulking around in the shadows. The life she took at Chase Side Hospital.

Was there really anything separating her from them?

The blurring of lines proved a watershed moment for Izzy, and for a split-second she found a sliver of peace, knowing she was no better or worse than anyone else. Unfortunately, her little lightbulb moment was about to be snuffed out by the serrated steel blade headed straight towards her jugular.

Grady's patience snapped.

32

Meridia stared glassy eyed at the sea of shocked and angry faces surrounding her. Although their lips were moving, all she heard was ringing in her ears.

She murdered her own mother, or at least condemned her to a grisly end. Either way, Emily was dead, and all that remained of her was the half-eaten hand laying limp and bloody at Meridia's feet.

"*She chose her path...*" Tommy's words battled to be heard above the raging storm in her mind, but it offered zero consolation. Her mum was gone.

"Meridia...M...can you hear me? Are you hurt?" Peter's voice penetrated the murk, bursting her tempestuous bubble like a child's balloon, and then suddenly she was fully present and in the room.

A dizzying discord of irate voices swirled around her as she surveyed the kitchen, only to find each side of the bunker's soft-yellow dining area seemingly at war with the other. To her left, Dr Foster and Declan were both outraged as they hurled inaudible accusations in Peter's direction, all the while wagging their fingers in contempt. Behind them, leant against the grey speckled worktop, Nadia and Grace were more restrained, erring on the side of discretion as they covered their mouths with their hands.

Meanwhile, to her right, Peter and Zach were now up in her face, their expressions riddled with worry as they waited anxiously for her to speak, while Kane and JJ remained slack-jawed on the sidelines. Halfway between them, in the neutral zone, was JJ's mum. Wearing her navy-blue work uniform, her red-raw eyes suggested crying, but Meridia sensed fear beneath her melancholy exterior.

Of the entire room, perhaps her response was the most natural given the entrance Meridia just made, and although Alice served as another stark reminder that her own mum was never coming back, she felt a fleeting smile take the wheel of her emotions.

Whatever chaos was unfolding around her, JJ's mum was here, so for him at least, maybe things weren't as bad as when Meridia left.

"M...please...just say something...anything." Zach's teary plea snatched Meridia out of her poignant exchange.

"Muh...my mum..." she mumbled, glancing down at her feet.

Feeling cold and clammy beneath her clothes, she tried to say more, but the words remained locked inside her head. Her lips were too heavy to move. Although she now heard everyone around her, Meridia still had one foot firmly in whatever desolate battleground she left the rest of her mother, and the other was now in an entirely different war zone.

"I knew one of you was a seer!" Dr Foster's accusation jarred her out of her daze as the swarm of buzzing voices continued to drift in and out of her awareness.

"But I thought you said she was twelve...no seer I know

of has ever got their gift before the age of thirteen...” It was an odd remark, implying knowledge and understanding of her condition, something Meridia lacked.

Latching onto his voice alone in the unruly racket, she wearily climbed the ladder of his conversation.

“And you said I wasn’t on the level...psh, that’s rich. You’ve kept her secret from us this whole damn time...don’t you see? This changes everything.”

Peter remained with his back to Dr Foster, oblivious to his complaining as he continued to examine Meridia.

“M...I think we need to get you out of here...I don’t know if this place is safe anymore.” Peter glanced at Zach. “Tell the others to get their things. I think it’s time we leave.”

Meridia was still none the wiser about what was happening. Yes, her entrance was quite a spectacle, and she realized she exposed herself to a group of relative strangers. However, she was certain whatever turmoil she found herself in the middle of had already escalated before she arrived.

She looked again at Alice, who didn’t move from her middle ground. She had to be partly to blame. If only everyone would shut up for a second, then perhaps she could hear herself think.

Still, her mouth remained firmly glued shut. This was more than fatigue.

Was it a side effect of her traveling? Was she doing herself damage each time she was snatched from this world and hurled into the next?

Suddenly, another hand grabbed her shoulder and spun her around. It was Declan, and his usual affable demeanour made way for an altogether angry one. His rounded face and soft malleable features were now sharp and pointed, as if he was sucking on a lemon. Before he even opened his mouth, Peter shoved him across the kitchen with an outstretched palm.

Meridia lackadaisically followed his trajectory as he bounced off the dining table and wound up on all fours at the feet of Nadia. His sour-looking expression shifted through the gears of shock and disbelief, before settling on one of surrender when he realized he overstepped the mark.

As expected, Peter's actions only added more fuel to the fire and things quickly heated between the factions. Caught in the middle of a mini-riot, Meridia was soon being jostled amid the crowd as they pushed and shoved their way around her.

It was like being in the mosh pit of a heavy metal concert, and as the room continued to rock and sway, she felt her legs go limp until it was only the bumping and butting of the angry mob that was keeping her upright.

As Meridia's vision faded from white through black, she heard Nadia take the words out of her super glued mouth and shout.

"Everybody stop! She's going into shock…"

33

WHEN MERIDIA CAME TO, SHE WAS LYING FLAT ON HER back in the middle of a much quieter kitchen. Blinded by the fluorescent bulb overhead, she squinted her eyes and glanced down at her feet. She found them propped up on a chair, knees locked, as if she fell asleep doing sit-ups.

Wrapped in Declan's black hoodie, she no longer felt cold or clammy, although the stench of stale cigarette smoke woven into its fabric was making her nauseous. Stifling a tickly cough, Meridia felt a light crackling at the base of her skull and froze in panic, gripping the floor at either side for fear of being yanked away by another nightmare vision.

"Phew..." she let out a muted sigh of relief when she realized it was the sensation of Alice's rolled up nylon raincoat crumpling beneath her head.

"She's awake..." Nadia whispered, peering down at her with anxious eyes that were wide enough for Meridia to make out her own reflection.

"Kaff...kaff..." Another lungful of Declan's signature scent opened the floodgates to her cough, so Meridia lowered both her legs and sat upright to clear it from her throat. Her back creaked from the cold, hard floor, but there was no lingering pain.

"Steady..." Nadia placed a hand on her knee. "You might still be a little woozy."

Nadia wasn't wrong, and Meridia felt a light throb in the centre of her forehead as her surroundings softly shuddered like a laggy video game struggling to keep up.

"How long was I out?" She muttered, relieved to find she regained control of her lips.

"Do you mean this time, or the time before?" Nadia's snarky response was out of character, but soon retracted.

"Sorry...it's been a bit of a day so far. You've been unconscious for the last seven or eight minutes. Wherever you were before that, I'm not sure. Your heart rate and your breathing are both normal. It looks like you've suffered a nasty shock, and this was your body's way of protecting you..."

"Where is everyone?" Meridia asked with a sudden snap of urgency.

"I kicked them out. All but this one, who refused to leave your side..."

Meridia felt Zach's hand on her shoulder and his touch instantly eased the tension she was carrying in her ribs.

"What happened M?" He asked softly.

"I...I don't know...my mum!" Meridia tried to stand too quickly and flopped back down on her backside with a bump.

Her dizzy blue eyes darted around the room in search of her mother's grisly remains, only to find they were crudely covered with a red and white checkered tea towel. The mere sight of the pitiful, hand-sized bump lying on the floor crushed her broken heart, shattering any sliver of hope that

Emily's violent death was all part of another terrible premonition.

Meridia's eyes glazed over like a zombie's as the walls of her daydream denial came crashing down around her. All she heard was her mother's voice echoing in her mind, scolding her for leaving her alone to die. Then, the weavers' vile click-clacking rattled her bones as she relived every harrowing moment of being trapped underground while her mother, the center of her world, was savagely eaten alive.

Drowning in an infinite ocean of remorse, she pulled the shutters down on her torment, clenching her eyes as the haunting image of her mother's severed hand dragged her under with its icy, vice-like grip.

"M...M?"

The sound of Zach's concern was only a muffled drone, as Meridia surrendered to the depths of her despair. A sinking ship with a titanic hole in her heart.

All she wanted to do was turn back time and undo all the pain and suffering she caused. Despite her cursed gift, she knew deep down there was no going back.

There were no do-overs in this waking nightmare, and even if there were, how far back would she need to go? A hundred years? A thousand? It was all so hopeless.

Emily was just a tiny cog in a ticking time bomb that was primed to detonate long before she was even born. A sacrificial pawn in a sadistic game of chess between gods and monsters. An invisible war, just as Zach's echo prophesied when they first crossed paths with Crooked House. It was his voice she heard once more, a last-ditched lifeline, cast into her swirling sea of sadness and self-pity, begging her to come back from the dead.

"M...please...we can't do this without you...Izzy needs you...I need you...please M...just wake up..."

His words served up a sobering reminder that there were still loved one's left to fight for, and it was that thought alone which stirred her back to life, rekindling the fire within and urging her to battle back to the surface. The more vehemently she kicked and clawed her way free from her self-induced coma, the more her sorrow shifted towards anger.

There was only one way to avert the desolate future Tommy had shown her, and it wasn't to sit here feeling sorry for herself. They needed to eradicate the Children of the Shadows right here and now, in this timeline. It started with the dreaded demon of Cold Christmas and ended with whichever coward was hiding behind the Grand Master's sinister façade. Cut off the head of the snake, and the body will die. With that, Meridia finally got to her feet.

"Easy..." Nadia intervened, cradling her elbow in case she collapsed again. "You need to rest...whatever you've been through has taken a toll and..."

"No..." Meridia shut her down. "We don't have time. You need to get the others...we need to save Izzy...and find Tommy..."

"Tommy? Who's Tommy? I think you're still a bit confused..." Nadia tried to placate her, but Meridia dug her heels in.

"Go get them now! We don't have time for this...Zach, go get them. I need to tell you all what I saw...what happened..." Once more, she sensed a river of tears rising behind her eyes, but forced herself to batten down the hatches, remembering what Peter said about there being time to grieve later.

Only now Meridia knew there might not be a later if they didn't thwart the demon's return. He was the next domino set to topple, and whichever way the domino fell would surely determine if they all lived or died.

"B...but I don't know if we're allowed to tell them everything, M..." Zach muttered as he dithered by her side.

"It's a bit late for that, isn't it? I just teleported in front of them all...go get them now. All of them...please. We don't have much time!"

34

Izzy felt a short, sharp, coppery breeze as Grady's knife stopped a hair's breadth from her throat.

Her eyelids fluttered wildly behind her glasses as if they were trying to airlift her away from the clown-faced lunatic she was now nose-to-nose with. There was no escape, no room to manoeuvre. All she could do was brace herself in petrified silence, too scared to move a muscle for fear of losing her head.

Eyes boring into hers, unblinking, Grady's warm breath carried with it the rancid stench of fresh blood smeared around his lips as he screeched.

"Tell me where Alice Jordan is! I know you know... Derrick told me just after I killed him...and everyone knows dead men don't lie. Oh, and while you're at it, you can tell me where the pathetic Alman boy is too...not the jumped-up little shit you go to school with. He's gonna get what's coming to him soon enough. I mean the other one. His useless brother. He's another one who's suddenly gone missing since you and your friends started messing everything up..." Grady sounded exasperated as he ranted and raved like a petulant child.

"This should all be over by now, and I should be free from all this shit..." He pulled at his clothes in protest with his free hand, never once allowing the blade to stray more than a millimetre from beneath Izzy's chin.

"All these silly costumes and masks...all these shackles... well no more! I'm sick of it. Tell me what I need to know, or so help me god I am going to hack your pretty little head off and scoop your brains out with a rusty spoon. Then we'll see what you know..."

Izzy winced as the jagged teeth of Grady's knife pricked her skin and told her this wasn't an idle threat. It was clear to see the psychotic nurse was unraveling, which made him all the more dangerous and unpredictable. Izzy had to say something. Even though her will to live had all but evaporated since being captured, the thought of Grady ripping her throat wide open with his hunting knife ignited a spark in her sluggish mind, bringing her fight-or-flight response online.

Unable to match him physically, she would have to use her wits to buy herself more time. If she couldn't give him JJ's mum, she would need to offer him something else.

"I...I don't know anything about Alice...or Alman's brother...I don't even know him, but..."

Grady cut her off mid-sentence, lowering his blade and hoisting her up in the air by her neck with his free hand. Until now, Izzy assumed Grady was human, but having witnessed firsthand his speed and strength, now she wasn't so sure. Wincing and gasping for breath, she felt her metal shackles scuff the underside of her wrists and break the skin as their chains reached full stretch.

"But what?" Grady hissed as he shook her in the air with unsettling ease.

"But nothing...do I look stupid to you? Do you think I was born yesterday? Poor Derrick said he didn't know anything either...but look at how much he had to say once I stuck my hand up his throat...maybe I need to do the same to you...loosen those lips of yours with my fist..." Rapidly running out of oxygen, Izzy kicked and flapped at the air in search of a foothold, but there was nothing within reach.

She was completely at Grady's mercy.

"*Crack!*"

Her coccyx clattered against the unforgiving ground as he suddenly let go. Coughing and spluttering, she instinctively rolled onto her side to ease the searing pain in her tailbone.

Izzy's whole body ached now as she writhed around, looking for relief. Her wrists were sore, her eyes were sore, and she was completely out of breath, but still her brain kept ticking, searching for a way through the thick red mist surrounding her tormentor.

"But what then..." He jeered, looming over her with his knife in hand. "C'mon...out with it ...I don't have all day..."

"Kaff...kaff..." Izzy nursed her aching throat as she tried to scramble back onto all fours.

Another surge of intense pain radiated up from the base of her spine, snatching away what little breath she could muster, and leaving her wondering if Grady broke her back.

"I...*gasp*...I can...tell you...*gasp*...who will know..."

Grady crouched down and thrust his ghoulish face in hers. Suddenly he looked more monster than man. Bathed in the naked bulb overhead, his sharp, bony features twisted into a chilling mask, revealing deep-set eyes that glimmered greedily as he willed her on.

"Retiarius..." she blurted, trying her best to gage his reaction.

"He's back...he's back in Shawbrook. This is all his fault..." Izzy flinched as Grady sprung to his feet and paced the dungeon in thought.

"He's the one you want..." she added.

"Not me...I know who he is..." It was a gamble on Izzy's part, but if there was even an ounce of truth in what Gregor told her, then he might prove the perfect prey for a bloodthirsty lunatic. A trophy kill like that would surely be worth more to Grady's master than a 12-year-old wallflower.

"Retiarius, eh...he's a clever one...sly, like a fox. But let's not forget he's also the coward who gave you up..." Izzy held her breath as she waited nervously for Grady to take the bait.

"Despite his yellow streak, he's proven to be yet another thorn in our side of late...stirring up trouble with the local papers...throwing wild accusations around to scare away tourists..." Grady circled back to where she sat chained to the floor, and an unhinged sneer swept across his face.

"It's all true, obviously...but that's beside the point. Accusations like that are bad for business...we make a killing from the tourist trade here, if you know what I mean...particularly those foolish enough to go wandering in the woods..." His sneer curled into an equally disturbing smile, caked in shimmering red war paint.

"I've been wanting to stick my knife in him for a long time now...but he covers his tracks well, the traitor. Once one of us, but now nothing more than a worthless troll hiding behind a computer screen..." Grady playfully twirled the knife in his hand as he crouched down in front of her again.

"What makes you think he would be any more interesting to hack into pieces than you? After all, I have you here, and we all know what they say about a bird in the hand don't we..." Once again, the creepy contours of his face seemed to shift under the jarring light, morphing into a malevolent court jester, and Izzy pinched her shoulder blades together to steady her trembling spine.

"I suppose another traitor off the streets is something, though, given the current climate. And who knows, maybe Retiarius knows where your little friends are hiding..." Izzy gulped as Grady made a connection she had missed.

In the blink of an eye, the tip of his blade was back at her throat, and she could feel its point like a tiny pin pricking against the taut flesh beneath her chin.

"Ok, I'm listening..." He concluded, his hand unwavering and poised to lance her head at the first slip up.

"Err..." Izzy mumbled robotically, like one half of a ventriloquist act as she tried to speak without moving her lips.

Although her desperate roll of the dice appeared to have paid off, she now found herself at another crossroads as she contemplated the ramifications of serving up Meridia's estranged father to save her own skin.

Forcing herself to look at the crazed killer eyeball to eyeball, there was little doubt in Izzy's mind she was on the brink of committing the ultimate act of betrayal. Regardless of how anyone felt about Gregor, he was still her best friend's dad, and giving him up now would condemn him to a gruesome and painful death.

The last 72 hours were revealing, to say the least, and Izzy was repulsed by what she found hiding beneath her own mild-mannered façade. Her first foray into morally grey waters was in the name of those she loved, but this was something altogether different. There was no way she could merely chalk this up to survival instincts. This was much more devious and conniving.

She knowingly manipulated Grady to this juncture, a knife-wielding psycho who had hacked and slashed his way to the status of a monster. Although she could plead ignorance to the consequences of her actions, Izzy knew it would be another lie.

Was this the legacy of her parents?

A callous character flaw stitched in from birth that had patiently waited until this moment before rearing its ugly head?

"Ow..." Izzy winced as Grady poked her with his knife and she felt the blade puncture her skin.

Enough to draw blood and remind her who was in control. A warm trickle snaked down her neck and settled in her jugular notch. She was out of time.

"Gregor..." Pushed to her limit, Izzy couldn't stop the name escaping her lips, as if Grady had found a truth button hiding beneath her chin with the tip of his knife. "Re...Retiarius is Gregor Wilson..."

The final damnation of Meridia's father unleashed a tepid river of tears that burst the weir inside Izzy's mind. And as she wept for her best friend's endless suffering, she also mourned the loss of her own morality.

Through the misty haze of regret, Izzy saw the corner of Grady's eye twitch in acknowledgement of her revelation, but his blade held firm.

"S...so...wh...what now?" She sniffled, her sinuses loaded with sorrow and shame.

Cocking his head like a wolf about to bite, Grady's terse response was chillingly sincere.

"Now I'm going to kill you..."

35

Kane watched Peter angrily pace back and forth in front of him and JJ like an overprotective guard dog. He was as furious as Kane had ever seen him, and justifiably so.

They were all lied to from the get-go, and although both sides were guilty of keeping secrets, there was a vast difference between trying to protect Meridia and blatantly hiding who was really in charge at Drayton Hollow. The fact that turned out to be non-other than Meridia's double-crossing father, the same person who handed Izzy over to the cult in the first place, only fuelled everyone's paranoia. The last twenty minutes were a whirlwind of revelations that left all their heads in a spin.

Having been ordered out of the kitchen by Nadia so she could tend to Meridia, the squabbling factions reconvened in Dr Foster's lab. All that was, except Declan. Still licking his wounds from a heated encounter with Peter, he stormed straight past the lab and upstairs to the surface to cool down.

This was Kane and JJ's first time in the lab, and once he got past the stench of stale coffee on the way in, he was then bowled over by the number of books the doctor was squirreling away.

Row upon row of reference books and shabby looking journals decorated the room, offering welcome relief from the rest of the drab grey concrete that dominated life underground.

Izzy would have been in her element here, and Kane imagined without the collection of half-empty coffee mugs scattered around the room like scented candles, the lab would have smelled exactly like their old school library. He remembered Izzy telling them all once that she found the vanilla and almond musk of old books strangely soothing, and the sight of so many here, spanning centuries, underscored exactly what was at stake.

As Dr Foster continued to fill the room with the hot air of his excuses, Kane found it hard to focus with so many other questions running amok in his head.

Were Zach and Meridia really safe alone with Nadia? Despite the growing mistrust, Nadia was the first to react when Meridia fainted and was the only trained person to look after her. On top of that, it made sense to kick everyone out once she knew Meridia's vitals were all ok.

There was no sense in moving her once she was comfortable, and Kane knew first hand Zach could scream with the best of them. If there was any sign of trouble, they would definitely hear him from in here, even considering the other voices steaming up the room.

Besides, with the door to the lab wide open, there was no way anyone could come or go without being seen, so that offered further comfort. That brought him to the sudden arrival of Alice, who was leaning next to the door and still keeping her allegiance close to her chest as she hovered between both groups.

Somewhere in the melange of musty java, Kane smelt traces of her floral perfume as it radiated from her pulse points. Even though she was largely absent from her son's home, the same aroma was always present on the rare occasion they both went there after school instead of Kane's. What he wouldn't have given for it to have been his parents who followed Declan down into this gloomy prison.

To smell his mother's perfume one last time, or his dad's aftershave. The sudden sense of longing was so intense, Kane felt his heart shatter all over again, yet he knew he needed to stay strong for everyone else and so he swallowed his tears back down and grit his teeth.

He couldn't even imagine how JJ must be feeling right now as he stood silently by his side. No doubt he was busy trying to process his own multitude of questions, but there was barely any time to breathe, let alone think between his mother's reemergence and Meridia's.

It brought him nicely to one half of the massive bone of contention now being fought over in the middle of the lab. Where the hell had Meridia been?

"Parking the whole Gregor issue for a moment, I simply don't understand how Meridia did whatever it was she just did..." Dr Foster was perched on the edge of his desk with a perplexed look etched on his face when his low, rumbling voice weaved its way through the tangled knot of concerns constricting Kane's mind.

"Nowhere in these books is there any talk of teleportation. Not one seer, even Thomas Rowe, ever left this realm. The visions were simply that...images which came to them, not the other way around. And all this before her thirteenth birthday. Don't you see...how big this could be for all of us? We have the one person in the world who's able to end all this..." He gestured at the drab concrete walls of their soulless confines.

"That little girl who's currently passed out in our kitchen could actually wield The Eye of Corvus and send those fuckers back to wherever they came from."

"Eye of what?" Kane blurted as he added yet another unsolved mystery to his mind-boggling collection.

For a moment he thought he missed the conversation straying onto the subject of Game of Thrones as he glanced at Peter for an explanation.

"It's an ancient relic Dr Foster thinks is at the heart of all this..." Peter turned his gaze back toward the doctor as he continued, "...but we don't even know where it is."

"When does Meridia turn thirteen?" Dr Foster aimed his question at Kane and JJ as he quickly leapfrogged topics.

"I dunno...soon, I guess. Zach would know." Kane shrugged, still reeling from Peter's blasé remark about the eye. Was everyone in this infernal place keeping secrets now?

"Can't you see Peter? Like him or loathe him, Gregor has somehow brought us all together, right when the world needs us the most. Now call it fate or blind luck, I truly believe we have all the ingredients in this bunker to stop the Children of Shadows permanently, but in order to do that we've all gotta put our egos to one side for a minute and get our heads together. Surely, right now, that's more important than whatever stupid shit we think Gregor might have done to get us here? Now, from what I can gather, it sounds like he's even found a way to get Izzy back. So, based on everything you guys have already been through...based on Alice finding us in the middle of all this madness...is it really so hard to consider the possibility you might be wrong about Gregor?"

The doctor made a compelling case, and Kane sensed the energy in the room shift ever so slightly towards clemency. Even Peter stopped his pacing and mulled over the proposition as Dr Foster doubled down on his sentiment.

"Look, you're all here now, so what have we got to lose by at least hearing him out? If we don't like what he suggests, then we'll do it your way and go our separate ways. I don't wanna see Izzy harmed any more than you do, and I sure as hell don't want no demon to contend with. So, what d'ya say?"

Peter was about to open his mouth when Nadia entered the room and cut him off.

"Meridia's awake and wants us all in the kitchen, now... she said we all need to hear what she has to say together, and we have much less time than we think." Nadia scanned the room with a puzzled look on her face. "Where's Dec?"

"He went upstairs for some air..." Dr Foster was quick to answer. "Kane, can you go get him? My knees aren't what they used to be, so I try to avoid the ladder like the plague."

Kane glanced up at Peter for approval and was greeted by a subtle nod so he quickly set off while Nadia shepherded everyone else in the opposite direction, back towards the kitchen. A cacophony of murmurs and whispers rustled away behind Kane as he jogged down the cramped corridor towards the bunker's only exit.

When he arrived at the foot of the rusty iron ladder, he latched onto the highest rung he could reach and hoisted himself up. Barely wide enough to accommodate an average-sized adult, the gloomy access shaft was damp and suffocating, with only the occasional dingy bulb to guide the way.

The rugged metal chafed his clammy palms as he made

his ascent, and as each clang of the ladder's narrow tread echoed underfoot, he sensed the gritty concrete walls around him steadily closing in.

When he reached the halfway mark, he was confronted by a once vibrant yellow triangular sign which said, 'MIND YOUR HEAD AND BACK!'

The irony of having it so far into the climb wasn't lost on Kane, and although he saw it a few times since his arrival, he tucked his chin in all the same. He hated heights, but his desire to see daylight far outweighed his fear, and so he wasted no time scrambling beyond the sign, all the while doing his best to ignore the nagging temptation to look down.

Each rung grew a little cooler to the touch as he clambered closer to the summit, and the bunker's signature stale air gave way to the fragrant aroma of vegetation and shrubbery camouflaging the entrance above. When Kane reached the top, there was a 10ft long, moss-infested concrete tunnel which led to the outer door.

At the end of the walkway, he found the rusted green metal hatch closed, so he gingerly pushed it ajar to peek outside. It took a second for his eyes to adjust as an ethereal band of sunless daylight seeped inside and painted everything a brighter shade of grey. This was arguably the riskiest part of his mission.

Heart in his mouth, he scanned the densely populated trees and thickets from his narrow viewpoint. For all he knew, Declan was strung up in a nearby tree with his throat slit, whilst Grady waited around the blind-corner, scalpel in hand, ready to pounce.

Listening for any sign of an intruder, all he heard was the occasional chirp of birds up high and the breeze rustling in the undergrowth. As satisfied as he could be that the coast was clear, Kane held his breath and pushed the door further beyond the initial tug of creepers clinging to its joints, and then silently slipped through the gap.

Drayton Hollow was a patchwork quilt of winter greens and parched dusty browns as far as the eye could see, full of overgrown weeds with a smattering of barren trees. Once earmarked for a retail development in the late nineties, it was since abandoned and now long forgotten.

Declan mentioned rumours of contaminated soil and protective covenants during his whistle-stop tour upon arrival. As Kane surveyed the cracked and frozen ground beyond the convenient cluster of evergreen shrubs covering their underground hideout, it wasn't hard to see why any developer in their right mind would avoid it like the plague.

Staying low, Kane shuffled around behind the bushes, concealing the bunker's entrance in search of Declan.

The wind, although gentle, carried with it a bitter chill, but Kane didn't mind as it nipped at his cheeks. He was grateful to be above ground. Taking in a massive lungful of nature's aroma, his throat and lungs tightened, unaccustomed to the cold, as he reached the communal smoking spot and stopped in his tracks.

"Declan?" he whispered, his head on a swivel and heart suddenly thumping.

"Declan?" He called again, a little louder this time, but again there was no reply.

There, cast on the ground at Kane's feet, was a smouldering, half-smoked Marlboro Gold, the freshly opened pack of twenty it was plucked from, and the burner phone they all relied on to stay in touch with the outside world.

Declan, however, was nowhere to be found.

36

Grady closed his eyes for a moment and listened to the bookworm's whimpering whilst her head teetered precariously on the tip of his blade.

Two kills in quick succession were always a treat, but this one held particular significance. This was more than just another notch on his hunting knife. Murdering the Di Salvo girl represented a major milestone in his prophesied metamorphosis. He was sure of it.

Now all he needed to do was settle on a suitably gruesome manner to execute her. Cutting her head off, whilst having its time advantages, was perhaps a little too predictable now, although he could always hollow out the contents of her skull and keep it as a memento, along with her eyes, of course.

"P...please..." Her snivelling plea broke his train of thought, so he pushed his blade a little deeper into her flesh.

"Argh..." Grady felt the satisfying rupture of taut skin vibrate all the way down to the knife's handle and then he opened his eyes with a snap.

"Shh...I'm thinking..." He bleated, as Izzy howled. Too terrified to detach herself from the razor-sharp tip that skewered her chin.

The steady flow of glittering crimson was mesmerizing as it streaked down the blade. As Grady stared deeply at its gory trail, he noticed his own chilling reflection in the smooth, polished steel.

Warped by the knife's subtle curves, his misshapen face writhed and twisted inside the glossy silver sheen, and sent an exhilarating shiver of elation rippling up his spine.

Piercing blue eyes glistened eerily from the dark hollows of Grady's deep-sunken sockets, and a wicked smirk, thick with blood, stretched beyond to confines of his emaciated jaw. It was as if the blade mirrored the darkness of his soul and revealed the despicable monster lurking within. He was about to thrust his knife further up through Izzy's jawbone when a shadow crept over him from behind and put an end to his fun.

"What are you doing?!" The Grand Master's sonorous voice boomed over his shoulder and Grady pulled the knife from his hapless prey, then turned to face him.

Unabashed, he watched his nefarious reflection dance and swirl within the intricate contours of the Grand Master's mask, making no effort to disguise his grim satisfaction.

"It's just a nick..." He snickered, like a petulant child caught with his hand in the cookie jar.

"She'll live."

Over his shoulder, Izzy writhed on the grimy floor, clutching her neck as she tried to stem the bleeding with the one remaining sleeve of her sweater.

Outraged by Grady's tone, the Grand Master stepped

towards him belligerently, his raven eyes fizzing with fury from beneath his fearsome mask. But Grady didn't budge. In fact, Grady didn't even care. After all, he was the one holding the knife. For a second, he even contemplated going toe-to-toe with his master, still caught up in the moment and hankering for the kill that he just lost.

Such was the insatiable nature of Grady's bloodlust. He imagined prising his master's perverse mask off with his blade and plucking his eyes out one by one. He knew he was more than capable. Besides, his master was nothing but a husk anyway, and a dithering one at that.

An evil spirit trapped in a pantomime horse, who was taking far too long to put the final nail in the coffin of a civilization all but conquered. Well, enough was enough. Surely it was Grady's time now?

After all the years he endured, jumping through hoops like a loyal little lapdog. All the worthless lives he was forced to spare. Surely the time for controlling his sadistic urges was over. And what better way to mark the momentous occasion than by slaying their overly cautious leader and becoming the monster he was born to be?

"Steady your rage, brother..." Grady felt his master's breath on his lips, warm and laced with stale cigarette smoke. "...or must I remind you who you're speaking to?"

He flicked his hand out, as if to summon someone behind him, but all Grady saw over the Grand Master's shoulder were their own long dark shadows cast onto the dank and mouldy dungeon wall. Still, the idea of chopping his master up into tiny pieces gathered momentum in his demented mind, like a spiteful snowball rolling away from him down a steep and slippery slope. Then he saw movement from the corner of his eye, the one thing that would convince him to stand down.

It was subtle at first, nothing more than the faintest of flickers, as if the silhouette of his master's cloak somehow tangled itself in a phantom breeze. Then it continued, a wispy apparition winding its way across the wall like a vaporous snake made of shadows.

One, two, and then finally three slithering strands separated from their host and slowly expanded on the jagged limestone like insidious ink spots, tainting the wall with their invasive presence. Then came the eyes, haunting and hypnotic, like twinkling stars on a clear winter's night. Grady knew he shouldn't stare, but he couldn't resist.

Their ethereal beauty was magnetic, drawing him in and soothing his scheming mind. As he drifted away on a cloud of indifference, he didn't even register the rows of razor-sharp teeth emerging beneath the horsemen's shimmering orbs. Nor did he notice them claw their way out from the murky two-dimensional confines of their stony prison and skulk into the room, growling like a pack of ravenous wolves.

Still crumpled in a heap behind him, Izzy eluded their spellbinding gaze, and her bloodcurdling screams soon shook Grady from his trance. Blinking himself awake, he remained captivated by their cadaverous faces as they scowled at him from the shadows, begging him to lock eyes once more.

Long thorny talons scraped against the shingly ground as all three horsemen slinked their way behind the Grand Master in a malevolent show of strength. A private army teeming with serrated teeth and barbarous claws, swathed in tattered and translucent robes which ebbed and flowed around them like poisonous ribbons, polluting the room with the rancid stench of decay.

"You forget yourself brother..." The Grand Master

snarled, cutting through Izzy's desperate cries of terror. "You must be patient...your time will come...unless, of course, you'd prefer to die?"

Grady studied the shadowy creatures snarling at his master's side and discretely tucked his knife back into his pocket.

Long ago, on the night of his family's murder, he had a previous encounter with the horsemen. He was just a child back then and didn't know what they were, but their wraithlike appearance left an indelible mark on his blackened heart, largely because, for the first time in Grady's miserable existence, he felt like he belonged somewhere.

Of course, they could have killed him, snuffed him out like they had so many others, but for reasons still unknown to him, he was spared.

Covered in his brother's blood and still gleefully clinging onto his slimy little eyeball like it was a prized conker, it was as if they stared directly into his soul and glimpsed his wicked nature. The evil within.

Now, as they loomed in the dingy depths of Chase Side's dungeon, all he sensed was hostility as they showed their allegiance to the fallen angel standing before him: a nefarious body-swapping spirit, old as time.

Despite their emaciated appearance, he knew their grip on the world was indeed getting stronger, as was their power. It had to be for them to have strayed so far from Crooked House during daylight. How would he ever wriggle out from beneath the gigantic thumb that stifled and suppressed his every desire?

It was in that moment, as they tried to intimidate him into submission, Grady realized as long as the Grand Master was calling the shots, he would never be truly free, reckoning or not. Perhaps his master's promise was nothing more than a lie, carefully crafted to trap him; to control him. Well, enough was enough.

"That's what I thought..." The Grand Master concluded as Grady stood down. "Now, pray tell me, what has your curious little outburst uncovered that might be of use to us?"

Grady felt a familiar swell of rage rise within at his master's dismissive tone, but instead of allowing it to consume him, as he often did, this time he garnered strength from it, allowing his fiery contempt to course through his veins. It was another first, and one that proved he was on the right path to fulfill his destiny.

A destiny that would no longer benefit the Children of the Shadows, or the deadly creatures gathered in front of him, but one that would serve only Silas Grady.

"Gregor Wilson is back..." He replied assuredly. "...and I know exactly where he'll be hiding."

The reflection of Grady's macabre grin widened across the Grand Master's silvery mask, corrupting it with his own brand of unhinged terror, like a contemptuous court jester.

"Find him in that case...bring him here..." His master barked, clearly rattled by the traitor's unexpected return.

"We will take care of the girl..." With another subtle flick of his wrist, all three horsemen whistled past Grady to the clatter of claws scratching at shingles and charged towards Izzy, leaving a trail of sulphurous smoke in their wake.

"Argh..." the shadowy stampede swallowed Izzy's screams as they circled around her like a swarm of angry locusts.

Swirling faster and faster, the growling, snarling whirlwind of black vaporous mist blurred into one frenetic haze as the creatures smothered her. Squinting through the murk, Grady saw their lashing robes in the storm's eye, like a cyclone of vicious snakes, coiling around her, suffocating her beneath a swell of tattered tendrils. Forcing their way into every airway and ferociously mummifying their defenceless prey, Grady felt the ground tremble underfoot.

Still unsure what he was witnessing, he shuffled back as a series of cracks zig-zagged their way toward him along the floor as if the horsemen fractured the fabric of reality with their relentless revolving.

Around and around, they continued to spin, like a spider cocooning its lunch, sucking all the air out of the stuffy dungeon as their feral growls soared to a high-pitched hiss. Bound from head to toe, Izzy remained static in the centre of the screaming vortex, until suddenly a mysterious portal, black as the midnight sky, bled out across the stony floor and devoured her whole.

Grady watched, full of wonder, as the girl's swathed silhouette melted into the liquid darkness and vanished out of sight.

"What is this?" He muttered, half thinking aloud, as the horsemen corkscrewed after her, down into the inky abyss, sealing the ghostly gateway shut behind them.

"She will remain under their watch now until the sacrifice..." The Grand Master's terse response barely registered as Grady surveyed the empty corner of the room. Now all that remained of Izzy Di Salvo were her rusty shackles and a grubby sweater sleeve.

"You will take sister Hutson with you this time...I want Gregor alive. Are we clear, brother?" Grady nodded.

He was seeing things more clearly now, and a plan was steadily congealing in his malignant mind.

"Yessss master..." He scoffed, ignoring what he witnessed.

Sure, he would toe the line and continue to play the game, for now at least. But one way or another, Grady would soon be free, and anyone who dared stand in his way would be sure to pay with their life.

37

"HE's GONE!"

Kane burst into the kitchen to find everyone sitting around on tenterhooks, waiting to discover where Meridia had been.

Even though he was only above ground for a matter of seconds, the much-needed dose of fresh air cleansed his palette, and he could now smell the coppery reek of blood coming from underneath the tea towel in the centre of the room.

"What do you mean, gone?" Peter was the first to respond, his guard still raised from the earlier fracas.

"There's no sign of him anywhere, and he left this behind..." Kane held the burner phone out so everyone could see.

"His cigarettes were up there too. Something's wrong...I just know it..." He felt his eyes being drawn to Alice who was loitering in the kitchen corner next to the microwave.

Could she really be trusted, or did she just deliver the wolf to their door?

"D...did anyone see you? Did you lock the door behind you?" Nadia stuttered.

Her look of concern spread around the room like wildfire, causing Grace to spring to her feet from the worktop she was perched on.

"It's locked..." Kane reassured.

"There was no-one else up there. It's like...it's like he just vanished..." He glanced over at Meridia to find her staring back at him, steely eyed.

She was standing in the middle of everyone on the far side of the room with her back pressed against the wall.

"Let me see the phone." To Meridia's left and seated at the dining table, Dr Foster reached up without leaving his chair, and once more Kane instinctively glanced at Peter for permission.

The paranoia was at fever pitch now, forcing him to question each micro-decision, and he hated every bit.

"It's ok...I know the pin." The doctor flapped his stubby fingers to coax Kane out of his inertia. "It might give us a clue to where he's gone..."

Kane handed the phone over and watched the doctor hurriedly tap in the pin.

"*Click.*"

The phone's screen coloured the doctor's face with shades of purple and then white as he navigated his way around Declan's apps.

"Mmm..." His eyes darted back and forth, weaving worry lines across his brow as he squirmed in his seat.

"What is it?" Peter pushed.

"Well, in the spirit of being honest, it seems Dec received another distress signal whilst he was up top, and he responded by saying he would go get them..." The chair creaked as Dr Foster shifted all his weight onto the other buttock before continuing.

"Now I'm pretty sure you're not gonna like what I'm about to say, but I'm hoping we all might've learned that keeping secrets only bites us on the ass in the long run... so..."

"It's my dad, isn't it..." Meridia interrupted, sparing him the pain of inciting another riot. Doctor Foster nodded apprehensively.

"It's ok..." she continued. "He's part of all this whether we like it or not...and something tells me he wants the same thing we do...to stop the cult. I've read his posts, and he was trying to help people...warn them. I don't know what happened to Izzy, but maybe Kane's right, and something just went wrong...either way, I think we should hear him out. We all deserve to know the truth..."

It was the first coherent sentence Kane heard pass her lips since her return from god knew where, but there was something about her tone, about the determination in her eyes, that exuded poise and self-assurance. It reminded him of when they first learnt of her gift, and she somehow found the courage to turn her back on the horseman outside Crooked House. She knew exactly what to do that day, saving the world and all their lives in the process.

Ever since then, she let her temper take the wheel in times of trouble. Now, in the overcrowded confines of the creamy yellow kitchen, she seemed different, like she was back in control. In the moments it took the rest of the room to catch up with him, something told Kane it was time they all put their faith in Meridia once more.

"I'm with M..." he blurted, his words surfing the wave of belief as it swelled from the pit of his stomach to his mouth.

"Me too." Zach was quick to second his brother.

"Same..." JJ piped up beside him, which left all eyes on Peter, who remained leant against the corner of the old fifties dining table.

It's added height more suited to the length of his legs. An edgy silence descended on the room and, for the briefest of moments, time stood still while they waited for his seal of approval.

"M...I..." Peter's voice splintered and his eyes glazed over as he wrestled with his composure.

"Ahem...actually this goes for all of you..." He rolled onto the balls of his feet and rose to address the entire group.

"You have all gone through so much...too much. I lack the words to do any of you the justice you deserve. I look around and I don't see children anymore...I see family. Just think of what we've achieved...what we've been through...it makes my blood boil to think of how much you've all lost... how much each of you has suffered. But, whatever's yet to come, good or bad...I want you to know I'm on your side. No matter what. Everything I do has one sole aim, and that is to end this...this nightmare...and get you all safely out the other side of it. I'm not anyone's father...I think that ship has well and truly sailed for me...but I am here for you...all of you...however you need me. So, M, if you say you want to hear what your dad has to say, then I will support you one hundred percent. The truth is, I'd like to hear what he has to say too. We're running out of time and options if we're to have any hope of saving Izzy and stopping the demon, and my shenanigans haven't exactly helped matters today...so for that, I'm sorry." Peter sat back down on the edge of the dining table and frowned as he gave the floor to Meridia.

His jade-green eyes were brimming with tears now and

Kane suspected that was owing as much to exhaustion as anything else.

"Your dad claims to know where Izzy is being held and how to get her out, but he needs our help. So, let's hear him out. If we don't like what he has to say...for any reason...then we find another way like we always do..." Peter's words were raw and unpolished compared to the pep talks of old. Another sign of his growing fatigue, but with only a matter of hours to turn things around, they no longer had the luxury of rest.

"Thank you, Peter..." Dr Foster acknowledged his counterpart's candour with a slow nod of contemplation.

"I think it's safe to say things have gotten a little out of hand today, and we've all had a part to play in that. All I can do now is assure you that you all have a roof over your head here at Drayton Hollow for as long as you want it...even after we rescue your friend Izzy. Like Peter, I guess I've been a bit of a father figure to some of you these last few months...or maybe more a grandfather figure. Who knows? Anyhow, my point being, I've built up a lot of trust in that time...we all have. Whilst we might not have been thrust into battle like you kids, we've been fighting this in our own way ever since we got here. Sure, we've kept secrets from each other, and looking at what's happened here today it's clear we all have, but I like to think that's been with the very best intentions, on both sides of the table..." Dr Foster nodded again at Peter then turned his attention to Meridia.

"We can iron out the other kinks when we have more time, but first we all have to earn that time...and the only way we can do that, in my mind, is together. Now I for one have waited a very long time to find you Meridia...so I think it's high time for us grownups to shut our traps and listen to what you have to say..."

Kane almost felt the tension dissipate as the doctor's melodic voice reverberated around the room and everyone took stock of what mattered most at that moment.

Despite the cynical climate, it appeared his message made its way through the remnants of red mist that lingered in the kitchen, and combined with Peter's unexpected vulnerability, may have gone a long way to repair the fractious energy that was dominating proceedings.

Now it was time to discover what horrors Meridia witnessed on her latest travels, and also what grisly fate became of Emily.

38

Saunders Select Automobiles was a thriving car dealership in its heyday. Once boasting a highly coveted partnership with Mitsubishi, it was the go-to business in the area for used cars, services and repairs. All for the better part of three decades.

On the outskirts of Thundridge, it built itself a solid reputation for providing locals with friendly customer service and quality cars they could count on. And, for most of its tenure, it did exactly that. Until that was, its owner, Richard Saunders, wound up being diagnosed with pancreatic cancer at the age of 60.

Increasingly sick from the side effects of an aggressive treatment plan, Richard eventually had no choice but to hand over the day-to-day running of the business to his adopted son, Gregor. What started out as a cruel twist of fate soon became a more sinister catalyst for Gregor's spectacular fall from grace.

A self-made salesman instantly out of his depth. It happened by chance. Nothing more than unfortunate timing when Gregor's sudden promotion coincided with a global economic downturn, the likes of which his generation had ever seen. Of course, there was nothing accidental about the latter part of that equation.

The Children of the Shadows worked relentlessly behind the scenes, undermining incumbent governments around the world to shoehorn their own people in at the very top.

Pretty soon, a raft of questionable leaders sweeping to power dominated the news, with no morals or scruples. Each taking office in a worldwide revolt against the tired old guard.

Although widely believed, countless accusations of corruption and rigged results never quite stuck, as a carefully curated program of distractions–from mystery viruses crippling health care to protests and riots over cultural tensions–followed. A nefarious cauldron of disillusionment and injustice kept simmering until a malevolent rhetoric rose from its broth.

Divisive and corrosive, this new wave of egotistical leadership leveraged the dissatisfaction of the masses and turned it into a battle cry. A call to arms for extremists and nationalists alike to unite for one common cause: divide and conquer. It didn't stop with politics.

Media, tech and multinational corporations jumped on the bandwagon too, polarizing nations as they monopolized and brainwashed billions in their quest to control the world.

Whilst pockets of outliers with half a brain and a loyal following did their best to draw attention to this unholy matrimony, they were ultimately smeared and discredited within the mainstream media, painted as a collective of disloyal crackpot conspiracy theorists.

So, whilst all the talk of global unrest and the imminent threat of war was being used to disguise the Children of the

Shadow's rise to power, Gregor inexplicably chose the same moment to wander away from his flock. Groomed for their ranks since the age of 16 by his adoptive parents, he found the strain of balancing the books and his conscience unbearable, and suddenly wanted out.

However, unbeknownst to Gregor, by then, he already served his purpose by continuing the Wilson bloodline and bringing a child into the current century. Underestimating his wife's loyalty to the Temple of Shadows, when his brethren got wind of his plans to skip town and run, Saunders Select Automobiles was swiftly bankrupted, and Gregor was promptly framed for beating his wife half to death in a drunken fury. Forced to flee with nothing but the shirt on his back, he had not been seen, nor heard from ever since. Until now.

'Your journey starts with Saunders.'

Grady snickered at the irony of the sun-bleached banner taped to the derelict showroom window.

A simple, aluminium-plated construction with wall-to-wall windows. The lot remained vacant since the day it went bust. Its basic, boxy shape resembled a defunct Lego set, someone obligingly built and then abandoned for a newfangled video game. Its dusty white paintwork was tired and jaded, seamlessly blending in with the oppressive grey skies overhead and the cracked, weed-ridden tarmac of its modest forecourt.

The only contrast came courtesy of a grubby, red plastic sign, peppered in bird poo, which was mounted over the building's customer entrance. A bloodshot reminder of its former glory.

The rain was falling, speckling the windscreen of Grady's van as he watched the neglected building from the corner of Bury Street. Having cleaned himself up since leaving the dungeon, he ditched his robes in favour of his charcoal grey tracksuit for this outing. The soft jersey material was more comfortable when carrying out surveillance, and he had no idea how long it would be before Gregor and his mysterious chubby little friend would re-emerge from inside.

To his left, sister Hutson sat silently in the passenger seat, which was a blessed relief. From the moment he collected her outside Jubilee Park, she did nothing but berate him for his erratic behaviour and blatant disrespect of their master. What a party pooper, always nagging and moaning. Since his outburst, she was giving him the silent treatment, as she often did when they failed to see eye to eye.

Grady inhaled his favourite air freshener as it dangled from the rear-view mirror between them and savoured its synthetic tart notes. The vanilla and almond aroma of black cherry reminded him of the last camping trip he went on with his parents as a kid.

His dad bought one in a petrol station en route to mask the stink of stale booze, but over time Grady discovered it did a pretty good job covering a variety of unpleasant hums. It also helped keep him calm whenever his patience was being tested, like it was now.

"Ha! See...there he is sister..." Grady crowed. "There's the angry little garden gnome..."

Slumping down in his seat to keep out of sight, he watched as Gregor slipped through the glass doors and gestured for his accomplice to follow.

Dressed in a knee-length black parka and matching jeans, the diminutive shit-stirrer resembled a wannabe rockstar with his rugged beard and greasy raven man bun. He was sporting a pair of mirrored aviators, despite the inclement weather, which, along with his beard, covered most of his rectangular face. He looked well for a man on the run and in good shape, unlike his podgy friend trotting after him across the car lot. He was new to Grady. Bald and wearing a dark baggy tracksuit, he looked nervy as he waved a key fob at the row of parked cars ahead of them.

"He's new...have you seen him before?" Grady quickly retracted the invitation for Hutson to speak as he turned the ignition. "Never mind, we've got to go..."

Both men climbed inside a midnight blue Peugeot SUV and pulled away from the curb. Grady took another lungful of cinnamon infused goodness and put his foot down.

At the end of Bury Street was a slip road, leading to the dual carriageway. From there, they could either head right, back towards Shawbrook, or left on to Cold Christmas.

"How much do you want to bet they're going to lead us straight to those snivelling little shits?" Grady beamed.

"Actually, no, don't spoil it...let me concentrate. I don't want to lose them..." He flicked the radio on to avoid any further grief from the old bat beside him and cranked the volume up to ten.

He wasn't exactly a fan of the Spice Girls but couldn't resist smiling as they belted out 'Spice up Your Life' while he cautiously tailed the car in front.

The rain was lashing down now, bouncing off the deserted road and flooding the gutters as both cars stopped for a red light. While they waited for the light to turn green, there was an increased risk of being seen, but Grady didn't mind as he bopped and sang along behind the wheel like an overzealous groupie.

"Slam it to the left if you're havin' a good time...shake it to the right if ya know you feel fine..." He no longer cared what the disapproving battleaxe Hutson had to say either.

Besides, what could she do to stop him?

"Feel free to join in on the chorus..." he chirped, spoiling for a fight, as Gregor and his friend continued to the end of Bury Street and veered right.

"Ooh, they're going back towards home...I knew he'd lead us to the others." Grady turned the volume up to fifteen as he merged onto the dual carriageway.

"What's that sister? Sorry I can't hear you hahaha..." As Gregor accelerated towards the speed limit, Grady slowed down, allowing another car between them and their target to avoid being detected. He might well have lost his mind, but he wasn't stupid.

For ten minutes they trundled along the soulless highway, watching the wipers dance their stilted dance to songs from the nineties, until eventually they reached the sign for Shawbrook.

As expected, the Peugeot signalled to turn off and Grady followed suit. His mind was racing ahead, imagining the look of horror on Gregor's face as he drove his knife down through the top of his skull.

"Don't be silly Silas..." he mumbled, white knuckled and anxiously rocking back and forth against the steering wheel. "We need him alive..."

On they went, weaving their way through the meandering backstreets while Grady did his utmost to maintain a reasonable distance. He felt his impulsiveness bucking inside his chest like a wild bull, impossible to corral.

Past the school and past the hospital, they continued through the concrete maze of Shawbrook, all the way to the opposite end of town, where nothing but backwoods and wasteland awaited.

"Drayton Hollow..." Grady announced their arrival and switched the radio off as he pulled up at the side of the road.

Fifty yards ahead, Gregor and his friend had already parked and were nervously looking around them as they crossed the street. That was one of the many benefits of Grady's van. It was almost invisible. Just another tradesman out trying to earn an honest living, and the fact it was painted grey meant it easily melded with the dreary landscape. He leaned back in his seat and took another lungful of black cherry.

Grady knew exactly where they were heading as both men scurried through a hole in the wire fencing and disappeared into the overgrowth beyond. He heard all the stories about the old bunker growing up.

It was the only place they could be hiding, and what a perfect place it was for his plan. The ultimate kill room, trapped underground with only one exit. It would be like shooting fish in a barrel. However, there would be time to have his fun with them all later. First, he needed to let things play out just a little longer.

"C'mon then...are you not going to congratulate me on my show or restraint?" He turned to face his passenger and smirked.

Meredith Hutson lounged in her seat as if she nodded off somewhere along their journey, lulled to sleep by the gentle swaying and purring of the van. In her left eye socket, Grady's hunting knife was thrust all the way to its hilt, clean through the back of her skull where its blade pinned her to the headrest.

The rapid stream of blood that initially gushed from her savage wound had disappointingly ground to a halt since her heart gave out and was now slowly congealing down the side of her pale, lifeless face. Meanwhile, a rogue crimson trickle that snaked out of her right ear had also regrettably stopped, bleeding out into the soft creamy ruffles of her beige knitted scarf.

It was an impulsive kill, designed to put an abrupt end to her non-stop nagging. It even came at the cost of one of her eyes; not that Grady was fussed about that stuff anymore. He was moving onto bigger and better things. Perhaps another ashtray from her skull, or even a set of breakfast bowls, if this current pattern continued. He imagined slurping his cornflakes out of Hutson's hollowed cranium on a lazy Sunday morning.

"Seriously? Nothing..." Grady pressed the corpse for an answer and then shook his head.

Lopsided and agape, the onset of death slackened her mouth, and she looked like a skewered stroke victim as she stared blankly out the windscreen with her one remaining eye.

"Ok, have it your way sister...but don't expect me to stop for coffee and cake on our way back... I've never really liked your shitty little café, anyway. In fact, I think I'll round your useless husband up when this is all over and burn it down to the ground with you both in it."

Grady glimpsed his reflection in the mirror as he turned his attention back to the wheel. He was still missing something. Although he now felt every bit the monster on the inside, his image was in dire need of attention.

Shooting a sideways glance at Hutson's bloody carcass, another smile crept across his pencil-thin lips. The 'before and after' parody of her mutilated face reminded him of Two Face from the Batman comics he used to collect as a kid, and it sparked an idea in his warped mind. But there would be time for that later.

The trap was already set and now the only question

remaining was did he wait for the dummies in Drayton Hollow to take the bait, or did he storm their underground castle now and slaughter them all?

He felt his palms itching again as he contemplated yanking his knife out of Hutson's skull and splattering the bunker's walls with blood. Staring into the rearview mirror, he watched his smile contort into a sneer as he made his decision and announced it to his fiendish reflection.

"Fish in a barrel..."

39

Somehow, with the help of speed-talking and a surprisingly muted audience, Meridia condensed the last six months of her life into a 30-minute monologue.

Whilst she may have skimped on the grisly details of what hell smells like, or how it feels to have a dagger plunged straight through your heart by a lunatic in a metal goat mask, she was confident she covered every vision in chronological order, right up to her latest and most terrifying leap forward in time. The moment she finished telling her harrowing story, Zach, Kane and JJ buried her beneath a group hug that was jam-packed with squeezes and sniffles.

"I'm so sorry dear..." Peter joined their show of support, draping his arms over the shoulders of Kane and JJ with his back to the rest of the room.

As he locked eyes with her at the centre of their huddle, his taller frame doubled as a protective shield from any judgement, and for a split second, the united front surrounding her melted away Meridia's resolve.

"I know I killed her...one way or another...it was my fault she was there." She sniffed.

"You can't think like that..." Kane was quick to shut her down.

"Your mum signed her own death warrant when she chose the cult over you. She knew the risks, and she made her choice. Like all our parents did. They could've found another way...but they didn't. So no, this is not your fault M...none of it is."

"That's what Tommy told me...but..." She sensed her emotions galloping back to the surface to greet theirs and so quickly wriggled free.

"There'll be time to grieve later," she whispered, rekindling her composure as she glanced back at Kane. Like her, he was teary-eyed, but behind his watery facade was an inner resilience that somewhere along the line hardened into valour.

He nodded knowingly, as if they were kindred spirits, and then backed away with the others, laying her bare to the rest of the room. Shrouded in stunned silence, Meridia watched as each of their hosts grappled internally with what they heard. When all the newbies to her cursed gift rediscovered their voices, she was bombarded by an avalanche of all the obvious questions she asked herself a thousand times.

Is the future set in stone? Can you travel back and change something? Who's Tommy? Who are the vultures? Where did the weavers come from?

Alas, there were no answers she could offer them, not right now at least. The only thing she could do was to emphasize the bone-chilling imminency of the apocalypse if they remained on their current trajectory.

"I know you have a million other questions, and

believe me, so do I. The truth is, I don't know much more about my gift than any of you guys, and it ain't for the lack of trying. All I know is it gets triggered whenever something bad is about to happen. I don't know why...I only know that every vision seems to come just at the right time, and every vision I have is always much worse than the one before. But even that doesn't matter right now...the only thing that matters is saving Izzy and stopping the demon. If we don't, then the world is gonna be over before we know it. I mean...you should've seen it... there were burnt bodies and torched buildings everywhere. I don't even know where the rest of you were...the only other person I saw was Tommy, and I still don't know who the hell he is...I mean...why weren't you all there?" Meridia felt the temperature rising in her cheeks as the gravity of their situation socked her in the face again.

They still didn't even know where Izzy was being held. Only where she was going to be taken when it all became too late.

"Er...may I?" Dr Foster politely raised his hand for a chance to speak.

He didn't move a muscle since Meridia started spilling the beans, and every time she glanced in his direction, she found him staring at her, hanging on her every word.

"I know this isn't my place because I haven't lived it like you guys have, but from what you've just told us, I'd say it's fairly obvious nothing in this screwed up world is set in stone. I mean, just think about it for a moment. Back when this all started, you witnessed the end of the world. Not a vision of it...but the actual end. You didn't know it at the time, but you went there...just like you did again today. You saw the horsemen kill young Zach here and summon death...and then you went back and stopped it. You must have because he's here today...you follow?"

Meridia never thought about her first vision in that way before. At the time, she didn't know she physically travelled anywhere. She always considered that divination to be more of a daydream, like the one she had in detention. Regardless of whether she went there or not, she changed things, but somehow, she lost sight of that fact.

Maybe the horseman's claim that her gift changed nothing burrowed its way inside her brain, or perhaps seeing Zach's echo again shortly after blinded her to the fact she changed things. Lots of things.

"Now I can't profess to know the secrets of time," the doctor continued. "But I do believe time is fluid. I think we absolutely have the power to change things, and we do it incrementally all the time. I don't believe in fate per se, but by the same token, I don't believe in coincidence either. I think maybe there's a middle ground we haven't discovered yet, and perhaps it's that middle ground you go to in your visions, Meridia. The embryonic realm of possibility that hasn't fully formed yet. I've also heard Peter's theory about the multiverse, where each decision we make triggers a new world of possibilities and outcomes, and I sort of agree with that. Science is increasingly leaning in that direction too as we discover more about our universe. Now what I can't decide on is if that liquid of time is sloshing around in a goldfish bowl and we're all just swimming in circles or treading water...delaying the inevitable, like the horsemen say. Or if we really have the power to turn things around beyond the limits of the bowl. I know what I'd sooner believe, and that's what keeps me going. If we think we're only treading water, then what's the point, right?" He gestured at their concrete surroundings.

"You think I enjoy being trapped down here in a fifties time capsule? No sir, not me. What I think you're seeing, or travelling to, are potential or likely outcomes that will come to fruition unless we make a change. When was the last time you saw Zach's echo, for example?"

"In the woods, right after we stopped the witch..."

"Now the fact you haven't seen him since might be a sign things aren't gonna go down that way anymore. Maybe the future you saw this time is what happens if the cult doesn't get their hands on Zach. We know their influence is stronger than ever...maybe they don't even need him anymore. Maybe the demon gives them another route, or maybe the weavers do, and that's why they're here." The doctor shrugged as Meridia allowed what he said to sink in. Had they already saved Zach, or was something else due to happen to him and that's why he wasn't there to greet her with Tommy?

"*BANG!*"

The entire room jumped in unison as the bunker's hatch slammed shut and a series of heavy footsteps clattered their way down its ladder.

Drayton Hollow had a visitor.

40

Grace handed Peter the wooden rolling pin, and he stood poised with his back to the wall beside the kitchen door as if he was readying himself to hit a home-run.

Since calling out twice to Declan, they were yet to hear an answer, so panic set in. Noise always travelled unhindered through the bunker when all its doors were open, so there was no way whoever was approaching didn't hear them. The thunderous interruption of footsteps quickly petered out, and now all was eerily quiet.

Peter wasn't big on baseball, or rounders for that matter, but he would have no problem braining the first person to step through the door if he needed to. His palms creaked against the fine grain of the wood as he tightened his grip in preparation while Grace hugged the wall to his right, having grabbed the heaviest saucepan she could find.

With only one way in or out of the room, Peter sent the rest of the group to the farthest corner of the kitchen, where they were now huddled nervously in front of the microwave.

Kane and JJ both raided the knife drawer for added

protection, whilst Meridia stood defiantly in front of them. Her bright blue eyes sparkling like sapphires beneath the fluorescent bulb as she stared at the darkened doorway.

"*Squeak...*"

Peter's heart leapt into his mouth at the sudden noise just beyond the door. Whoever it was, crept the entire length of the corridor without making a sound. Convinced it wasn't Declan, he tensed up and readied himself to swing at the first person who entered the room.

If the nagging feeling in his gut was right, and it was Grady who found his way in, then their only chance of overpowering him would be to strike first and ask questions later. Peter heard enough stories about the deranged killer's lethal speed to know he wasn't to be taken lightly.

"*Squeak...*"

The sound of rubber scuffing against the concrete echoed louder as the intruder reached the kitchen's entrance. Peter made one last adjustment to his stance, lowering his swing to where he thought Grady's head might be. It was literally do or die time and he felt the warm, stickiness of melted deodorant under both arms as he compacted his upper body and braced himself for impact.

"Marcus?" Gregor Wilson tiptoed into the kitchen as Grace stopped Peter from clobbering him.

"Whoa!" He nimbly leapt through the doorway out of harm's way. "You're much taller than I thought..."

Peter relaxed his shoulders and glanced down at the man staring up at him. 5'5" at a push, the rolling pin would've comfortably cleared the top of Gregor's head anyway, so he was glad Grace spared him the embarrassment. As Gregor took another step forward, the entire room let out a collective sigh of relief.

"Why didn't you answer?!" Grace snapped.

"Sorry, love. You don't avoid those bastards for as long as I have without being vigilant." Aside from the hint of his Scottish roots, Peter was surprised by his tone.

A far cry from the callous and conniving persona of Retiarius. He sounded almost pleasant for a man who nearly had his head bashed in. He didn't even notice Meridia as he continued to explain his shifty entrance.

"Dec thought he noticed a van on the roadside after we slipped through the fence. He just went to check it out and then look for his phone...I bet he wishes he could lose weight as easy as he loses that phone of his..." As Gregor chuckled to himself a cold sweat broke out on the back of Peter's neck.

"What van?" He mumbled, remembering both Meridia and Zach saw a van outside the Jackson's house on the day Grady butchered them.

"Anyway, after I started tearing down the ladder, it occurred to me something might be up so I..."

"What kind of van?!" Peter barked again, this time shaking Gregor by the shoulders.

"You need to calm down pal...I let the whole rolling pin thing slide, but you're getting on my tits now...It was just a grey van...like a tv repair man or something..."

"Or an internet repair man..." Zach's timorous remark wormed its way in between Gregor and Peter's heated exchange, sending a chill through the air that clung to everyone in the room like frost.

"Grady..."

41

Having waited for Gregor to disappear inside the bunker, Declan cautiously crept back through the prickly bramble bushes towards the break in the fence.

With only his hoody to keep him dry, he was shivering from a wintry one-two punch as the lashing rain soaked him to the bone, and the bitter wind nipped at his skin. The grey transit van hadn't moved since he first noticed it, but all he saw from his vantage point was the silvery reflection of the dreary sky above as it clouded up the windscreen.

Tracing the perimeter to get a better view, he studied the surrounding estate for any sign of life. The run-down row of terraced council houses remained a mystery since taking up residence in Drayton Hollow, and Declan eventually reached the conclusion they were derelict or condemned. This end of Shawbrook was slowly dying, a rot that was spreading throughout town as businesses perished and investment dried up.

The interchangeable cars parked along the road were merely vultures from neighbouring estates, swooping in to feast on the free parking spaces that were left behind by the cult's collateral damage. The van, however, caught his attention.

It was a fresh addition to the familiar shiny faces he saw every time he ventured beyond the boundaries of their concrete prison. And whilst there was every chance he was overreacting, he needed to be sure.

No matter how far Declan slinked behind the cover of the bristly undergrowth, he couldn't get a clear view behind the wheel. Conscious his shivering was only getting worse the longer he braved the elements, he eventually conceded and circled back to the bunker.

Instead of going back the way he came, he figured he would cut through the dense woodland at his back to save time. The trees, although bare, would at least offer some shelter from the howling wind and bucketing rain. Once he reached the clearing, he would be able to get his bearings and find his way back to the others.

Relentlessly crunching and squelching through the thick petrichor pong of sodden branches and waterlogged soil, Declan sensed an ominous silence creeping up on him. Too cold and numb to notice the rain stopped, he turned to look over his shoulder, convinced he was being followed. Nothing. All he saw was a suffocating maze of twisted branches and gnarled roots he left in his wake.

A knot formed at the centre of his chest and then slowly tightened, squeezing the air from his lungs as he stared deep into the claustrophobic cage. He half-expected a hooded maniac to jump out from its shadows, but thankfully no-one came.

Still, he couldn't shake the feeling he was being watched, but the longer he remained locked in a staring contest with mother nature, the more he sensed her jagged barbs closing in on him.

Maybe it was his mind playing tricks, or perhaps Gregor came back to rescue him from the rain. He contemplated calling out, but thought better of it. Declan was no hero, and if he didn't feel the constant need to prove otherwise to Gregor, he might have sent him off to investigate the van instead.

"G...get...t...it...t...together...Dec..." he trembled, realizing he was a sitting duck the longer he lingered.

"Crack..."

He spun around in search of the branch that snapped but again found nothing. It all appeared the same now. The same, yet unfamiliar, as his head continued to spin. A catacomb of thorny branches and wooden spikes surrounded him, too hostile and congested for Declan to see a way through. Somehow, he was lost.

Perhaps the cold seeped into this brain, fogging his judgement as he tried to retrace his steps. Just pick a direction and move, he thought. Something familiar will come.

"Crack..."

He whirled around again, punch drunk on paranoia, this time certain someone was behind him, but all he found was another tangle of thickets. There was something peculiar about their stance, hunched and hooked, as if he turned and caught them all laughing behind his back. Declan was losing it.

"Enough man..." he fumed, rubbing his frozen face back to life.

That's when he saw it. A gnarled stump gathering mushrooms, he remembered stepping over on his way though. He was sure it had been on his left before, but now it was on his right, which meant all he needed to do was turn around and walk in a straight line.

"Phew...panic over," he sighed, spinning around for the last time.

"Uaah!" Something flashed in front of his eyes, sailing close enough to his face that he felt the pull of its slipstream.

Flapping and panicking, Declan stumbled backwards and landed on his tailbone with a dull thud.

"Haha...idiot!" He snickered when he saw the huge pinecone lying on the ground and then wearily scrambled to his feet. His backside was soaked through now and tingling from the fall.

"If Greg could see me now..." He mumbled, brushing the twigs and muck from his joggers.

"I see you muffin top..."

"Wha..." Declan flinched at the stranger's voice and then staggered backwards from the deranged lunatic, who appeared out of nowhere in front of him.

Dressed in a dark jersey tracksuit with the hood up, his pale ghoulish face was painted like a vampire clown. Thick, glistening crimson was smeared around his deep-sunken eyes and steadily oozed down his bony cheeks. His mouth was a scarlet stain, stretching messily from ear to ear to form a malevolent smile trickling down his chin, as if he was fresh from gorging on a feast of human flesh.

A vibrant vision of pure evil. Panic wasted no time seizing control of Declan's frozen limbs and rooted him to the spot. Although he never saw him in the flesh, he knew it was Grady, the cult's psycho assassin, only now he looked even more terrifying, covered in what had to be the blood of his last victim.

"Tell you what, fatty..." Grady snorted, "I'm not even going to use my knife for this..."

Quick as a flash, he grabbed Declan by the shoulders,

pinning his arms by his side, and hoisted him out of the boggy mire.

"Grr..." Declan wriggled and wrestled against the ominous show of superhuman strength, but found himself completely overwhelmed as Grady marched forward unperturbed.

Dangling in the air as if he weighed nothing, Declan kicked and screamed for help as he twisted his neck around to see where he was being carried, but nothing he did seemed to slow his attacker. The desolate woodland and all its unseen occupants watched on, indifferent, as he approached the barbed wall of thorny branches behind him.

"Have you ever played pin the tail on the donkey?" Grady sneered, stretching his spine-chilling smile even further across his sinister face.

"Well now, I'm going to play pin the porker on the oak tree..." His icy blue eyes sparkled beneath his hood with a glittering menace, like shards of broken glass laced with poison.

"G...get off me, you fuckin' weirdo!" Declan fumed as his frantic kicks continued to bounce feebly off Grady's shins.

In a matter of seconds, his struggling stopped all at once as the spikey tip of a splintered bough pierced the nape of his neck.

"Argh..."

Declan's tortured cry was cut short, silenced by the unyielding branch as it bore a hole at the base of his skull, severing his spinal cord, and rendering his bloated body a flaccid mass of twitchy nerve endings. A tingly numbness engulfed him from the neck down and his eyes dilated with terror as the jagged bark shaved his taste buds from the back of his throat and gouged his lips further apart.

"Crack!"

Somewhere beyond death's icy anaesthesia, Declan felt his jaw fracture and a handful of teeth ricochet off his chin on their way down to the dirty ground.

"Gag...kaff..." A slurred garble of pewter infused gurgles seeped from the sides of his mouth, carried to the surface on a crest of salty blood-bubbles.

All the while, Grady's twisted grin widened with glee as he gripped Declan by the chin and impaled his head even further. Pushing it back as far as the gore-soaked branch would allow. Another bone-chilling 'crack' echoed through Declan's head, punctuated by a sickening chorus of flesh being ripped apart.

The sound of something wet and heavy landing at his feet followed the stomach-turning sensation with an ominous thud. Choking on the bitter bark, he felt his tongue go limp, prickled by the perishing wind as it dangled beneath the bough where his jaw used to be.

Still, he clung on to the dying embers of life, coughing and spluttering over a mouthful of oak. All the memories he wished he made came rushing to the aid of his dwindling brain, distracting him from the disappointing reality of a miserable, risk-averse existence spent watching and criticizing from the sidelines.

The girl he never met, the job he never found, and all the other building blocks of a life made meaningful that somehow eluded him, until all he was left with was a deep-rooted cynicism masterfully disguised as wit.

With the devil staring him down, Declan's remaining senses succumbed to his wounds as the dreary afterglow of winter shapes seeping through the trees bled into one, and he closed his weary eyes for the very last time.

42

"What do you mean, you don't have any weapons down here? It's a military bunker, for Christ's sake!"

Meridia watched her dad's temper boil over, and the sight instantly reminded her of her most loathed trait.

"You mean to tell me in all the months you've been down here you've not thought to stock up on anything more than a couple of kitchen knives and a rolling pin? He'll fucking kill us all..." Gregor continued to rant, dousing the bunker's sunshine yellow kitchen with a heavy downpour of dread.

This wasn't exactly the reunion Meridia had in mind when she'd heard her dad was on his way.

"He can't take us all on, surely?" Kane chimed in. He was clutching a carving knife and, along with JJ, was acting as a human shield for Zach.

"You've not seen what he's capable of...he's not human... he can't be..." Gregor fumed.

There was a fear in his eyes that Meridia had never seen before, and as she watched him rifle through the remaining kitchen drawers, she struggled to reconcile the man in front of her with the one she called dad for so many years. Perhaps it was her memory that was at fault, bent out of shape by her mother's endless brainwashing as she painted him out to be the monster. Or maybe they were both different people now.

He was smaller than she remembered, and less scary, but beneath the outgrown hair and ragged beard, he looked more like a long-lost uncle than her dad. The disconnect she felt was only amplified by the fact he avoided all eye contact with her since arriving.

She guessed it was understandable given the imminent threat, but as she watched Kane and JJ protect Zach, she couldn't help but feel her father's hunt for a weapon was driven by self-preservation over anything else.

"We can't stay either way..." Gregor continued. "Not if we want to stop them resurrecting the demon."

"What do you mean?" Peter finally spoke up. He was still holding the rolling pin and scrutinizing Gregor's every move from the kitchen doorway.

"That's why I came here in the first place..." Gregor turned to face everyone. "They've already moved her to Crooked House. If we don't go now, while it's daylight, we'll never be able to stop them..."

"How do you know that?" Peter probed, making no attempt to mask the suspicion in his tone.

"I found out from one of my sources...I trust them if that's what you're getting at pal...I reached out to Dec the moment I heard."

"You don't think it was a trap to lure you out of hiding? To drive you here?" Peter wasn't about to let Gregor off the hook. "I mean, it's a bit of a coincidence that Grady finds us the second you show up?"

"It could've been me too..." Alice interjected from the sidelines.

She edged a little closer to JJ, but it was obvious from her body language she was still trying to fathom where she stood with her estranged son.

"Declan drove, and we were careful, I swear, but there are eyes and ears everywhere in town. All it would've taken was one nosy neighbour and..."

Alice sighed, "Does it even matter anymore whose fault it is...if I was followed or Gregor...it doesn't change anything. We all need to get out of here."

"I say us men go up first and clear the path." Gregor was holding a small utility knife he found in one of the drawers.

"Er, speak for yourself..." Grace took offence. "I've got a score to settle with that prick, so if you go, I go..."

"Ok love, I didn't mean to offend." He wandered over to Kane and compared knives. "When I said men, I meant adults..."

Gregor swapped his puny weapon for Kane's carving knife and then plucked up the courage to throw his arm around Meridia.

"That means you too, I'm afraid." His voice softened as he gave her a squeeze, but his clothes reeked of sweat and cigarette smoke, triggering a coughing fit as Meridia found her nose suddenly pressed against his armpit.

"Now you know why I didn't hug you when I got here..." he winked. "I was hoping for a shower first."

The flippant nature of his hollow gesture irked her even more, and as he wandered over to join Peter, she saw Kane swap weapons with JJ from the corner of her eye before staking his claim to go with them.

"Grady killed our parents..." Now clutching a meat cleaver in his trembling hand, he teetered on the brink of tears as he tried to keep his voice from breaking. "If he's up there, then I'm coming too..."

"I think we all need to go." Peter declared, nodding at Kane.

"I'll speak for my daughter, thanks..." Gregor snapped, plunging the room into chaos as everyone battled to make themselves heard at once.

A cacophony of conflicting opinions reverberated around the room as they all pressed their case to run or hide.

Meanwhile, Meridia held her tongue. Silently seething, she sensed her cheeks getting redder by the second as she thought about all the hurtful things she was dying to throw at her egotistical, self-absorbed father.

Even if there wasn't any truth in her mother's account of his violent streak, there was no getting around the fact he still abandoned her that day. How dare he turn up now, after all she went through without him, and expect to tell her what she could and couldn't do?

"*Bang!*"

Peter slammed the dining table with his rolling pin and brought the bickering to an abrupt end.

"I'm sorry, but we don't have time for this shit..." he bellowed. "Grady could be halfway inside here by now and once again we're squabbling like children. We all need to get out of here together. Nobody gets left behind. If Grady is up there, and he's as dangerous as you all claim, then the best we can hope for is to buy Nadia and the others enough time to get away. Just think about it...Last time I counted, there's only one way in or out of this place, so how can we expect anyone else to escape if they wait down here while we're up there getting killed?" As always, Peter's rationale was sound.

"Our best play is for a few of us go out swinging with the view to take him down, or at least keep him busy, while Nadia gets the rest of you to the car...you included Kane, and that's not up for discussion. Zach needs you, now more than ever. Nadia, as soon as you get to the car, you drive as fast as you can, and you don't look back. Drive all the way back to Birmingham if you have to. Just get them as far away from here as you can..."

"But..."

"No buts Kane. You can take the meat cleaver with you in case you need it, but that's as much as I'm willing to offer." Peter held firm, and Meridia knew there would be no arguing with him.

Unlike her dad, he earned the right to put his foot down, and deep down, they all knew that, even Kane.

"We need to hurry if we're to stop him before he gets inside. Marcus, you can either come with us or go with Nadia...same goes for you, Alice. The choice is yours..."

"Here, take my car. It's closer." Grace tossed Nadia the keys to her Nissan as Dr Foster stood up.

"I'm not sure how much good I'll do, but I'm with you, Peter." He walked across to the cupboard and pulled the last saucepan down from its shelf.

"I've spent far too long hiding down here with my nose buried in a book...it's about time I roll my sleeves up with the rest of you. But before I go, there's something I need to fetch Meridia." He marched out of the kitchen and headed for his lab.

"Wait, we'll need supplies too...I'll be back in a sec." Nadia rushed off towards the infirmary, hot on the heels of Dr Foster, and returned in under a minute with a first aid bag slung over her shoulder.

"I'll go with JJ..." Alice finally plucked up the courage to close the distance between her and her estranged son. "I've only just got him back...I can't risk losing him again."

"I understand." Peter nodded solemnly as Gregor wandered back to where Meridia was standing.

"I'm sorry, love...for everything. Maybe if we get through this, you'll give me a chance to explain..." Meridia felt numb as she listened to her dad's half-hearted attempt to ask for forgiveness.

It all seemed so surreal. In a matter of days, her entire understanding of the world, of her life, was shattered irrevocably, and right now she wasn't sure if she wanted to piece it all back together, or simply sweep it under the carpet and walk away.

Somewhere beneath all the grime and greasy hair was her father. The man who once helped raise her and wanted to save her from all this chaos. But, by the same token, he was also the man who left her in the care of a conniving sociopath. How could she ever let him back in, given everything she'd been through since?

As she left his olive branch dangling in the air, she wondered why every facet of her life had to be so damn complicated, so gruelling. Then, deciding to spurn her dad's offer of a hug, Meridia stepped back into the protective cocoon of her real family, the ones who would never let her down, no matter what.

"Maybe..." she mumbled grudgingly, as she skulked away completely.

She wished she could spare everyone the peril of facing Grady, her dad included. If only she knew how to control her gift, she would have zapped the psycho nurse away to a distant future and left him there to rot. But after all this time, she still didn't have the foggiest idea where to even begin.

"Here, take these..." Dr Foster jogged her from her daydream and thrust a backpack under her nose.

"In there, you'll find a few books which should help you understand your gift a little better. I think they'll help you realize just how important you are..." She took the bag and noticed the doctor's eyes had teared up.

"I think I've been looking for you longer than I care to admit...perhaps even longer than I can remember. You are living, breathing proof of my life's work...Your gift...even though it feels like a curse, is the one thing that can save us, Meridia. All of us. I'm just sorry I might not be around long enough to see it..."

"It's time everyone..." Peter rested his hand on the doctor's shoulder, and Meridia realized fate had caught up with them once again.

Whatever happened in the moments to come would determine not just their future and Izzy's, but that of the entire world. How could any of them possibly cope with such a burden? Was it really any wonder her dad fled when he did? He was just a man, after all. An outcast, like her.

Behind Peter, they edged their way along the corridor, hopefully safe, in the knowledge that even someone of Grady's prowess wouldn't be able to stop the bunker door from clattering upon entry.

One by one, they warily scaled the rusty iron ladder for what would undoubtedly be the last time and crammed into the shallow clammy walkway leading to its exit. The narrow passage was made all the more suffocating by the flustered throng of everyday people wrestling to come to terms with the fact they were about to stare death in the face.

Squeezing Zach's elbow, Meridia broke from his side and pushed her way through the sea of worried faces to give Peter a huge bearhug.

"Woah..." She startled him as he was eyeing up the lock, readying himself to lead their charge to freedom.

"I...I..." She couldn't find the words to thank him or explain how she felt.

In the last few months, he was her constant rock of support, shielding her from harm however he could. He even battled his way through a witch's curse for her, and yet there, over his shoulder, was a man who called himself her father, who in all that time couldn't even manage a simple phone call.

"It's ok dear..." Peter did his best to reassure her, but she could feel him quivering beneath his sweater.

"You're all going to make it through this, I promise...I haven't come this far just to roll over...no matter what's on the other side of that door." He broke away and reached for the latch.

The long, heavy-duty metal handle connected to a six-point locking system designed to make the bunker gasproof. The only way to open it from the outside was a nine-digit key code, which was perhaps the only reason Grady hadn't made his way inside yet. Peter turned to Grace and Dr Foster as he gripped the latch.

"Ready?" His voice was resolute, papering over the cracks Meridia had felt in him just seconds ago.

That one word sent a million butterflies flapping and fluttering in the stomachs of those around her, and she wondered if this was how all soldiers felt when thrust into battle.

Peter's question was quickly met by a pack of nodding

dogs, each tacitly agreeing to kill or be killed. Run or get caught.

"*Click!*"

He slowly turned the latch as everyone planted their feet and prepared to bolt.

It was go time.

43

"Stay behind me…" Peter whispered as he tiptoed beyond the shadows of the bunker with his rolling pin primed to strike.

The piercing wind was quick to pounce, howling in his ears and clawing at his cheeks as he crept into its path, whilst overhead a thick band of heavy rain clouds strangled the midday sun. He noticed the ground was soft and slushy underfoot as he made space for Gregor to join him. It was raining, which meant things might get slippery if they were to make a sudden run for it.

There was no sign of Grady or Declan beyond the bushes covering the bunker's entrance, but that sliver of hope did nothing to ease the sinking feeling deep in the pit of Peter's stomach. All too aware that each tentative step forward was another step closer to being seen. He tried to stoop lower, but his height stood firmly against him.

Beside him, Gregor stayed well below eyeline as he nimbly sidestepped his way around the undergrowth, knife in hand and ready for a scrap. Powerfully built and with a low centre of gravity, Peter took a modicum of comfort from seeing him in action as they conducted their initial sweep of the surrounding area.

Perhaps they were wrong about Gregor after all, as now he showed no signs of reservation in risking his life to protect the others.

"You go left, and I'll go right..." he whispered, gesturing to Peter to stay low. "If the coast is clear, we'll circle back to the others and get them on the move."

Peter nodded, safe in the knowledge Grace and Marcus were waiting in the wings as a secondary line of defence should they need it.

Once it was safe for everyone to exit the bunker, the plan was to form a convoy and give Nadia and the kids safe passage to Elmcroft Avenue. Whoever made it that far would have a couple of cars to choose from to make their escape.

Above ground, the bunker looked like any other disused utility shed, but its muck-encrusted brickwork belied the bulletproof fortress hiding beneath the surface. Approximately ten feet long and six feet tall, it did a remarkable job of blending in with the rural surroundings thanks to the mountain of overgrowth, camouflaging the bulk of its structure.

As he watched Gregor disappear out of sight, Peter felt the breeze at his back, nudging and goading him onward. But the truth was he didn't need any coaxing or cajoling.

All he thought of was wiping the smarmy grin off Grady's face with a well-timed blow to his bony little head. If he could just get that one shot in, then maybe, just maybe, some of them stood a chance of making it out of Drayton Hollow alive.

The whistling wind amplified every whisper and rustle of the surrounding woodland as Peter vigilantly traced the outer shell of the bunker's entrance. Stopping and stuttering, he sensed his nerves getting closer to the edge with each false alarm that assaulted his senses, until the unmistakable crack of a branch rang out ahead and brought him to a complete standstill.

"Gregor?" He whispered, tightening his grip on the rolling pin by his ear, but the only answer he heard came from a bitter blast of air as it rattled past his knuckles and raced along the stretch of bushes he was shadowing.

Shuffling forward, he called out again, but this time not even the wind dared reply, and Peter realized both he and Gregor were fools to separate so quickly. Recognizing their rookie mistake, he paused again and scrutinized his surroundings in more depth.

To his right was a small clearing of marshland left waterlogged by rainfall, whilst all that lay beyond it was a dense gathering of oak and elm trees. There was a host of places Grady could hide, including the blind corner directly ahead, but from Peter's vantage point there was no way anyone could get the drop on him, unless they were lying flat on the roof of the bunker this entire time.

"*Gulp...*" The terrifying epiphany turned Peter's legs to lead and catapulted his heart into his mouth. Stepping away from the bunker wall, he braced himself and glanced up.

"Phew..." He exhaled the lungful of dread he was holding inside, then jumped out of his skin as Gregor staggered out from behind the corner ahead of him.

Standing tall with his knife relaxed by his side, Gregor's deathly pale face was awash with terror and trauma as he tottered shellshocked towards him.

"What is it?" Peter tried to see over Gregor's shoulder, fearing an attack or a trap.

"I...it's Dec...he...he's dead..." Peter hurried over to the corner without lowering his weapon and stopped just short of the wall's edge.

"Grady's long gone...he must be or we would both be dead already..." Gregor mumbled. "W...we need to get the others and get out of here now...while we still can..."

"Oh god..." Peering around the corner, Peter gasped in horror at the gruesome spectacle of Declan's mutilated remains.

Slapping a hand over his mouth to stifle his disgust, he gave the body a wide berth and wobbled around the bend on jelly legs to get a better look.

Gregor was right. Grady had clearly moved on, but not before leaving them with a sickening message which chilled Peter to the bone.

Stripped down to his waist, Declan's body was slumped against the wall with his legs stretched out in front of him and his torso on full display. His head was lolled to one side, and his jaw brutally ripped from his face, leaving his wilted, blood-stained tongue to languish in the dark curls covering his saggy chest.

Below that, carved into his flabby white belly, were the ominous words '*IZZY'S NEXT*', followed by a crudely cut crimson smiley. His lifeless body was wiped clean of any excess blood to ensure the message hit its mark, and as Peter struggled to tear his eyes away from the grisly display, he felt Gregor grab his elbow.

"We need to go, pal...we can't stay here..." Slipping out of his coat, Gregor covered Declan's bloodied corpse with his parka and gave Peter a nudge toward the bunker's entrance.

"We can't speak of this...not in front of the kids. When this is over, I'll come back and take care of the body...but right now we need to go...we're running out of time."

Gregor's words floated in one ear and out the other, as Peter stared vacantly at the black makeshift blanket covering Grady's sadistic calling card.

In his mind's eye, he still saw the jagged mess of bone and cartilage where Declan's mouth once was. As the hissing wind coiled its way around him, Peter tasted the metallic stench of death in the back of his throat.

Could any human commit such an atrocity as this? Or was Grady another monster in masquerade?

Whatever he was, Gregor was right. It was time to get as far away from Drayton Hollow as they could.

44

"Uaah!" Izzy sat bolt upright with a start and then promptly coughed her empty guts up onto the cold, stony floor.

With no idea where she was or how she got there, the only thing she knew for sure was the room wasn't staying still long enough for her to find out.

Retching and heaving, she clenched her eyes to stop it spinning, but even beneath the inky blanket of her eyelids there was no escaping the kaleidoscope sensation stirring her brain like a hot cup of coffee. She turned onto her side in the hope the debilitating dizziness would abate. It did a little, but not enough, to prevent her from spewing some more.

Izzy's ribs screamed in pain with each hollow heave, but all she could do was curl up into the fetal position in the hope it would pass.

Tucked into a ball, she tried to slow her breathing as the giddy nausea showed signs of subsiding, but she remained too afraid to open her eyes.

"In for four, out for four…"

Izzy slurred the mantra in her muddled mind as she tried to make sense of what happened. The last thing she remembered was Grady looming over her, his face smeared with blood. After that, everything else was a blur.

"In for four, out for four..."

Eventually finding her rhythm, Izzy noticed the air had a strangely familiar musty smell she couldn't quite put her finger on. She wasn't in the dungeon anymore, that was for sure.

Wherever she found herself now was far cooler, and as she instinctively grabbed her wrist, she winced at the tender lesion where her shackles once were.

With her hand on the floor, she plucked up enough courage to risk one eye and was greeted by the thick pile of a dusty red rug a few inches short of her face. It appeared old and matted, but she could tell it was once a thing of luxury. Beyond it was a shabby slate-tiled floor, and beyond that was a dark mahogany chest of drawers, too high for Izzy to see on top of from where she was laying.

There wasn't an abundance of light in the room, but there was a smattering of cracks seeping in from above. Hazy slivers of sunshine permeating the gloom. The luminous rays diffused enough for her to see without squinting.

As the rest of the room's dismal décor came into focus, her blood ran cold and a jolt of raw terror crackled up her spine. She was back inside Crooked House.

Dragging herself up to her knees, she winced in pain from a stabbing sensation under her chin, and then it all came flooding back to her. Grady's knife, the mysterious figure in a macabre silver mask. Then the horsemen, whirling and swirling around her like a suffocating cyclone of pure evil, choking her with their sulphurous stench.

The thought of being swathed in their putrid robes made her flesh crawl and sent another icy shudder scampering up the back of her neck. The involuntary twitch made her chin throb again, and, dabbing her wound, she found the blood already hardened into a scab.

How long was she out? A cold sweat of panic washed over her as she tried and failed to scramble to her feet.

"Come on, Izzy...think..." she grumbled, hoping to shoo away the remnants of brain fog and formulate some kind of plan.

Deciding she was still too woozy to stand, she shuffled around to take in more of her surroundings. The rest of the room looked as if it was recently emptied, with perfectly preserved rectangles of grey tile and cream wallpaper where a bed and a wardrobe once stood. Behind her were two wooden doors, which Izzy surmised led to a bathroom and the main corridor.

Listening intently, all she discerned was the occasional breeze rustling the trees outside, while inside, the rest of the house seemed dead. On the plus side, as best she could tell, she was alone. Although she was under no illusion, this was just another prison cell like her last.

At least she was safe from the clutches of that psycho Grady. Given the choice between him or Crooked House, she would have settled for this place every time. He was an altogether different breed of monster to the horsemen and seemed hellbent on killing just for the thrill.

Izzy knew if she languished on the floor much longer, her self-loathing and shame would slip in through the backdoor of her mind. So, summoning all her strength, she pushed herself up onto her rickety legs. Staggering forward, she leaned against the chest of drawers to steady herself.

"Agh!" She baulked at the spine-tingling face staring

back at her on top of the unit, and even after she realized it was just a sculpture, its harrowing expression refused to release her from its baleful grip.

Cast in iron, its androgynous face was the embodiment of unbearable suffering. Frozen in perpetual torment, its eyes and mouth were both clenched in agony, throttled by a thorny veil of barbed wire which was coiled around its head like a bloodthirsty boa constrictor. Fixed to the base of the terrifying bust was a small brass plaque with an inscription so tiny Izzy needed to lean in to read it.

"Welcome to room 4..."

The second she blurted it aloud, the sculpture's eyes snapped open to reveal obsidian orbs that sparkled beneath the room's ethereal light. Paralyzed by fear, Izzy couldn't tear her gaze away from its hypnotic stare as a sneer slithered across its shrivelled lips and it opened its mouth to speak.

"Your time is almost up, child..."

A legion of insidious voices poured out all at once, worming their way inside Izzy's brain and infecting her thoughts with their poisonous tongues.

"Your friends cannot save you now...no more than your parents could."

Izzy watched in horror as the cast iron veneer melted like mercury and seamlessly transformed from one horrifying visage to the next. A cornucopia of disparate identities revealing themselves one after another.

Each rising and sinking into its rippling surface, until eventually settling on a face she recognized.

"Mum?" she muttered, choking on grief.

"This is all your fault..." The bitter discord of voices contracted until all that remained was her mother's; her

choice of words cutting deeper than Grady's knife. *"...our blood is on your hands..."*

"B...but...I..." Izzy fumbled over her words, cut off at the knees by her mother's accusation.

It was the truth, though, and it stung like a red-hot poker, piercing her broken heart as she stood sobbing in front of the vindictive statuette. Unsure if this was another nightmare or a window into hell, Izzy tried to blink free of her tears as her mother's black beady eyes narrowed, and her voice became shrill.

"You will burn in hell for what you've done...you and your friends...the demon is coming Izzy...and he's gonna rip your soul to shreds..."

The ghoulish mirage altered itself once more. Rippling like reflections on the water disturbed by a breeze, before adopting a façade far closer to home.

"We did this Izzy..." The face staring back at her from inside its thorny prison was now her own.

A black mirror laced with spite, angling to crush whatever fragments remained of her shattered spirit.

"Our mum's a filthy liar...no one's coming to save us. We don't have any friends. They just felt sorry for us that one time we wet ourselves in class...pissy knickers...pissy knickers...We're so sad and pathetic, clinging onto them all like a needy little loser... Now look at us. Coward! Parent killer! We're going to die in here Izzy...we're going to die alone, just like we deserve...just like all the others..."

"*Chink!*"

Izzy flinched as the barbed wire coiling around her iron doppelgänger constricted, scraping against the metal of its spiteful face.

"*Argh!...*"

A bloodcurdling scream erupted from the statuette's

mouth that shook the walls of room 4 and rattled Izzy to her bones. Transfixed by the glittering razor-sharp barbs, she watched with bated breath as galvanized-steel tore through iron like cheese wire and slavered its cheeks with viscous blood.

"*Argh!...*"

Winding tighter and tighter, the wire continued to cut deeper, carving crimson canals from ear to ear, until eventually, with one last chilling '*chink*', the grisly garrotting screeched to a halt and the screaming finally stopped.

In the eerie silence of room 4, Izzy stared at her own mutilated likeness through blood spattered glasses. She spent enough time with Kane to know there was always one more jump-scare left in the chamber, and so she waited, and waited, for something to happen.

"*Drip...drop...*"

Scarlet snakes zig-zagged their way down the grooves in the chest of draws and dripped onto the stony floor, but everything else remained calm and still. Refusing to play the room's vindictive game, Izzy didn't budge, but the longer she waited, the more the hideous ticking time bomb bullied her towards submission.

"*Drip...drop...*"

She cursed her impatience as she shuffled forward and leant in to get a better look. Whether this was a trick or not, she was running out of time. Mangled and twisted in pain, the sight of her own face frozen in such a violent display made her feel queasy. Was this the fate awaiting her when the demon rose from the dead?

"*Drip...drop...*"

The silence between drips was deafening now, filling her head with a cotton-wool haze and muffling all her thoughts.

"Think Izzy...think..." She glanced up at the boarded window leaking light behind the disfigured ornament and surmised it was her only means of escape.

There was no way the horsemen would allow her to waltz out the front door of Crooked House. If she could just summon enough strength to prise one of the boards off, then she might stand a chance of making it out alive.

"*Drip...drop...*"

Izzy took another step forward, keeping one eye on the mauled statuette. The chest of drawers was in her way, but if she got close enough, she could reach the corner of the bottom board. Slowly, oh so slowly, she raised a trembling arm toward the window. Her shoulder ached instantly, weary from days of inactivity and malnutrition, but she needed to try.

"*Drip...drop...*"

Reaching up on her tiptoes, all she needed was a firm enough grip to see if they might give. Her fingertips grazed the rough edge of the wood, then slipped off, so she pressed her body closer to the chest of drawers and tried again.

"*Argh!*"

Izzy stumbled backwards in fright as the sculpture screamed at her again, but this time its mouth stretched high and low, beyond its natural limits, elongating to form a monstrous chasm of unfathomable darkness, as if it was about to swallow Izzy whole.

Without warning, from its tenebrous depths, a geyser of viscid blood erupted, drenching everything in its path. The gushing torrent knocked Izzy off her spindly legs, dousing her in its warm clotted wares, coating her glasses and clinging to the back of her throat with its chewy metalline tang.

Weighed down by the deluge of gore, Izzy thrashed and

flailed helplessly, her feet slipping out from under her as she slowly drowned in the shallows of a gloppy crimson sea.

"*Kaff...gag...kaff...*"

Choked by the relentless onslaught, she craned her neck to breathe. Desperate gurgling coughs replaced her cries as she was slowly devoured, inch by inch, like quicksand, the tepid chunder filling her airways and dragging her under.

"Argh..."

Her shrill scream punctured the subaqueous hums and bass-heavy echoes of her inner workings as she sat bolt upright and gasped for air.

Bone dry and alone, Izzy scoured her bastille, quivering uncontrollably as she found room 4 returned to its original foreboding guise. The repugnant statuette mocking her from its mahogany tower. Its suppressed scream now looking more like a laugh.

Hysterical and hoarse, Izzy screamed on its behalf, convinced she crossed the final threshold into madness.

45

Squashed together like sardines, the group waited anxiously for Peter and Gregor to return. There was no word from either of them since they left, and with every passing minute, the odds of their survival were looking increasingly bleak.

With his back wedged against the clammy concrete wall, Zach pressed his face to the gap between Kane and JJ in search of Meridia. All he found was Dr Foster and Grace, debating how long they should wait before venturing outside.

The air was getting stickier by the second in the stuffy corridor, and amongst the shuffling of feet and biting of nails, he heard everyone's nerves jangling inside them, cranking up the tension as they transmitted their fear to each other like a virus. Although anxiety was at an all-time high, Zach took comfort that this time he wasn't alone in being scared.

He kept imagining a battlefield beyond the bunker's door, where not just Grady, but an entire army of hooded psychos, were waiting to pounce the second they made a break for it.

"We need to stick together..." he whispered to his brother. "No matter what happens, no-one gets left behind...ok?"

It was a phrase he heard in a Marvel movie forever ago, but for whatever reason, it stuck with him. Perhaps today he would find out why.

"Of course, spud..." Kane breathed back. "Where did that come from?"

"Just a feeling..." he muttered, resuming his search for Meridia.

As his cheek brushed against his brother's sleeve, he caught a delicate trace of apple blossom fabric softener, his mum's favourite, and although its nostalgic notes rekindled his grief, it proved the perfect tonic for his separation anxiety.

"It's gonna be ok. Peter's coming back..." He felt a hand on his arm, and there she was, suddenly beside him.

Her bright blue eyes twinkling beneath the flickering bulb overhead. Zach felt an instant wave of relief wash over him, melting away all the tension he was carrying in his joints. Then, almost right on cue, the bunker door creaked open, and a hazy band of light swept its way across the gloomy corridor. It was Peter, just as Meridia predicted, or prophesied.

Zach still wasn't sure how much of what she said came from her gift and how much was just her trying to imbue some hope in a dire situation. Either way, judging by the expression on Peter's face, everything was far from ok.

"Grady was here..." he warned, fraught with worry. "It looks like he's gone for now, but we need to get out of here. There's no knowing when he might be back..."

The crowd didn't need telling twice and wasted no time bundled past him in pursuit of fresh air and daylight. As they jostled their way to freedom, Zach clocked Meridia craning her neck to see where her dad was.

Regardless of the signals she was sending, it was obvious she still cared about him, and Zach's suspicions were confirmed the moment she spotted Gregor loitering behind Peter and let out a deep sigh.

Like Peter, he appeared rattled, scared even. As Zach continued to stare out beyond Meridia's dad, his heart sank at the realization Declan wasn't with him. Still waiting for his turn to step outside, he heard a muffled exchange between Peter and Dr Foster.

"Nooo…" Grace's voice, fractured with despair, spread her heartbreak like wildfire through the group as Peter confirmed Declan's death with a solemn nod.

Zach gasped for air as he stumbled out into the cold wasteland, overwhelmed by the medley of earthy smells and dazzling grey. This was his first time above ground since they arrived and the winter chill pricked his lungs, buckling him at the knees as he fought to catch his breath.

"Breathe Zach…just breathe…" He felt Nadia's hand on his back as he hunched over, staring down at the squelchy, sopping wet mud.

Her voice was laced with the same sorrow sweeping through the crowd, and although he barely knew Declan, the shock revelation of his demise knocked him sideways. The last few days below ground were insular and surreal, diluting his perception of the outside world and demoting him back down to the baby of the group.

Maybe it was the sudden influx of adults taking charge, or perhaps it was just a coping mechanism after all he'd been through. Until now, Grady felt more like a cartoon villain, larger than life, but one who would ultimately fail, like all villains did.

Now, as he surveyed the grieving faces around him and the boundless strength Meridia exuded, it dawned on him how naïve he was.

"C'mon..." Meridia swooped in to rescue him, as she always did. "We need to find out what's going on..."

Barging their way to the front of the crowd, they were met with a forced smile from Peter as he ushered them into the clearing.

"Our cover's blown now, so we need to get to the cars as quick as we can." Once he corralled them all together, he pointed toward the break in the fence. "The cars are parked over there, but I want you all to stay close and stay vigilant."

Zach resisted the urge to ask what the word vigilant meant and instead locked arms with Meridia. If Grady showed up again, then he was determined to protect her for a change.

Gregor jogged past them both to join Peter at the front of the convoy and established a quicker pace as they led everyone to salvation. He was missing his coat and clearly freezing as the howling wind buffeted them all back, as if it was trying to prevent them escaping.

"We need to get to the old church..." He bellowed so everyone could hear.

"St Peter's?" Peter questioned as they all trudged forward.

"No...the original church tower in Cold Christmas...the tunnels there will take us straight to Crooked House without being seen. It's the last thing those fuckers will expect."

Zach almost tripped over his own feet upon learning of Gregor's plan. The prospect of returning to Crooked House filled him with dread, and he almost felt the horseman's icy fingertips tickling the back of his neck.

"That? That's your grand plan?" Peter scoffed. "That's suicide! Have you seen what's under Crooked House? Last time we were there, it was crawling with disciples..."

"Yee of little faith...trust me, pal. Unlike you, I know what I'm doing."

Zach sensed the growing tension between both men as they stomped through the muddy marshland like a herd of angry elephants. Over his shoulder, he noticed Nadia and Alice were lagging further and further behind, hampered by Dr Foster, who was complaining about his osteoarthritis, whatever that was. The emerging gap made him cling to Meridia even tighter as they switched from jogging to a light run to keep up with the longer legs of Kane and JJ.

"And what about the kids? We need a place for them to lie low while we get Izzy..." Zach's attention was pulled back to Peter and Gregor as they resumed their bickering.

"Well, originally, I was thinking they stay here, but it looks like that idea's shot to shit. There's the old car lot, but I'm guessing Grady knows about that place too now...They can always stay in the car, I suppose? That way if anything goes wrong Nadia can get them away quickly...either that or she keeps them on the move while we're inside. I'd say she probably has the lowest profile out of those of us old enough to drive..."

There was a brief pause as Peter arrived at the fence alongside Gregor and pulled its wire mesh back for everyone to squeeze through. Zach knew if Peter had another safe house tucked up his sleeve they would already be there, but the fact was, at one point or another, all their homes were corrupted or desecrated by the cult.

"Maybe that's our only option after all that's happened..." Peter conceded.

"We'll still need to come up with a longer-term solution now the bunker's compromised. The kids need food and shelter...but for the moment, let's concentrate on getting Izzy out of that hellhole and stop the demon."

Gregor chuckled to himself as he held the weight of the fence and allowed Peter to duck through.

"I hate to piss on your little self-righteous parade, pal, but if we don't stop the resurrection, we won't need another place to stay because we'll all be dead by dawn..."

Gregor's brutal honesty slammed the door shut on the sliver of hope Zach was clinging to. The demon wasn't an urban legend, whispered around campfires to scare children. He was a cold-blooded killer, bearing down on them all from beyond the grave.

As they made their way towards the row of parked cars, Zach took a long hard look at the faces of those he loved, searching for a sign they would survive their impending showdown, but all he found were shadows of doubt.

46

As Gregor started the SUV's engine, Peter clicked his seatbelt into place and took a deep breath to calm his mind.

There were far too many unanswered questions buzzing around in his brain to think straight. Questions he was determined to get answers to once they eventually hit the road. With Grace's Nissan only seating five, and Peter insisting his half of the group stick together, they had no choice but to squeeze into Declan's seven-seater.

He still wasn't exactly sure how Gregor ended up with Declan's car keys in the first place, and the only explanation that made sense was that he rifled through the dead man's pockets when he first found his body.

Was that yet another nail in the coffin of Gregor's character, or the ruthless edge they needed to rescue Izzy?

Peter couldn't be sure anymore, but whichever it was, they were now strapped into the car with Gregor at the wheel.

"I'll take the back roads as much as I can, just to be on the safe side." He declared, pulling away.

"I don't think this car is on anyone's radar yet, otherwise Dec would have been pulled over by the police ages ago."

Peter craned his neck to see out the back, and as agreed, Grace's white Nissan was almost bumper to bumper with them. He saw it didn't sit well with Alice, being separated from her son, but there were still huge question marks hanging over her in everyone's mind, regardless of her rousing speech back at the bunker.

"Make sure you stay low and avoid looking out any of the windows." Peter gestured to Kane and JJ, who were directly behind him, and then watched Meridia and Zach slouch down in the two smaller seats at the back of the car.

Turning to face the road ahead, he caught a mouthful of Gregor's body odour. It tasted like onions, so he cracked the passenger window open to cleanse his palate. The sudden surge of ice-cold air tingled his nose as Gregor put his foot down and sped away, but it was a welcome relief to the eye-watering pong inside.

As they made their way through the empty streets of Shawbrook, Peter was reminded of the old cliched cowboy movies he and his brother used to watch as kids. It was as if everyone in town pulled the shutters down on their saloons in readiness for the big gunfight finale.

"Where is everyone?" Kane was quick to notice the eeriness of it all.

"They'll be busy getting ready for the sacrifice..." Gregor overhead the remark.

"I still don't think you guys quite understand how many people are caught up in all this...there's more to the Children of the Shadows than people running around in hoods. Some of your neighbours are members without even knowing it...dressed up as local community initiatives and volunteer groups...they have their hooks in everyone..."

"But how?" JJ chimed in, still trying to rationalize his parents' involvement.

"Media...pharma...corporations...you name it, they own it. Their lackies are everywhere...from boots on the ground to the very top, and if anything gets out of hand, they own the fucking police and the military, too." Peter felt the car accelerating as Gregor got more and more worked up.

"That's why I've been on the run so long darling...I didn't leave you...I had no choice. I know now isn't the time, but those fuckers took everything that mattered from me... including you and your mum. I just figured I'd lost you to them, like I did her..." He cleared his throat to continue.

"Dec told me what happened...to your mum. Whatever's going on inside that head of yours, all you need to remember is that none of this is your fault. She made her bed a long time ago and now she's lying in it... she never cared about either of us. She left us M...she left us both."

Meridia refused to be drawn by her father's outburst and remained silent in the back of the car until Peter guided the subject back towards the task in hand.

"What do you know about the demon...I mean, we've heard the stories from the seventies...how he was an enigma and suddenly vanished after a year...but there must be more to him. What is he, really?"

Gregor squirmed in his seat before answering.

"The demon tips the scales in their favour once and for all. He's the ultimate killing machine, like a supernatural terminator...controlled by whoever summons him. If we allow him to make it out of Crooked House, then I'm afraid young Zach here will be done for and there won't be a damn thing any of us can do about it."

"But how?" Kane leapt to Zach's defence. "I mean,

someone must've stopped him in the seventies...he can't be indestructible."

"Listen lad, whatever you think you've been through so far...the witch, the nightwalker...even that nut job Grady... the demon is a different monster altogether. Not to be dramatic, but he is evil incarnated, and the most sadistic bastard of the lot. They say he can control people's minds... make them do unspeakable things...He'll compel you to hand over your little brother just by looking at you, and that's just what we know from the last time he was here. God knows what he'll be capable of this time around..."

Peter heard the quiver in Gregor's throat as he spoke. The fear in his voice was palpable.

"Kane's right, though. Someone beat him before...he wouldn't need resurrecting if they hadn't."

"That may be, but I'm afraid whoever stopped him, and however they did it, remains one of life's great mysteries. Trust me, no-one on the inside even knows what happened back then. Old man Richards probably would have, but he croaked the same night Izzy switched his wife off at the mains. The only other person who might know something is their snivelling shit of a son..."

"DI Richards..." JJ interrupted. "He was handling the search for Helen Ashfield when she went missing...fat lot of good he is."

"He's a pencil pusher and brings fuck all to the table as far as the cult is concerned. Seems he didn't inherit his mother's gift, or his dad's work ethic, so it'll be interesting to see how long he lasts now his dear old mum is out of the picture. Anyone else who was involved in the original case died years ago...I know because I looked them all up. I heard a rumour it attracted the attention of an outsider, something to do with a similar case in the city, but I couldn't find any trace of him. My guess is, whoever stopped him back then didn't live to tell the tale, and if by some miracle they did, they probably fled the country first chance they got. Trust me when I say, stopping the demon before he's resurrected is our only chance..."

"I think you're underestimating us." Kane was pissed at Gregor's flippant tone. "We've done more damage to the cult in the last few months than you and your guys have in well over a year."

"Wow...listen to you all. Sorry to burst your little bubble, but have you ever considered the only reason you've made it this far might be dumb luck and my daughter? I mean, I get how you might be feeling indestructible right now, but trust me, you're not. If it wasn't for Izzy reaching out to me, you would never have survived the nightwalker."

"Yeah, and we all know how that went, don't we?!" Meridia fizzed from the backseat. "You ditched her at the first sign of trouble."

"Like I already explained to your babysitter here, I had a tough choice to make that night...that's why I'm here now. Look, we're on a hiding to nothing, even without the demon. Surely you can all see what's happening...just look out your window. Shawbrook is terminal...it didn't get that way overnight. It took time...a long time, and that cancer has now spread far and wide...not just around the country, but around the world. Even if we somehow stop the demon and lop the head of the Children of the Shadows, do you have any idea how much weeding and rebuilding will be needed? They have completely fucked society, almost to the point their poison is one of the building blocks of our DNA...even everyone in this car has been infected. The books you read, the shit you watch on tv, or on those phones you're plugged into 24/7...who do you think is behind all that? It's all designed to soften you up...figure out your weaknesses and then exploit them when you come of age. I mean, do you have any idea how much damage mobile phones have done alone? It's like crack for kids...it's insane! Every ridiculous craze, every fad, is designed to dumb you all down like one insidious algorithm so you don't even realize what's going on right under your noses."

Gregor's rant left everyone shellshocked as he swerved onto the dual carriageway and put his foot down again. Peter never considered an influence of that magnitude.

Yes, conspiracy theorists have become ten-a-penny these days, bemoaning the levels of corruption in corporates and politicians, but not one of them pieced things together on a global scale. It was a concept too vast even for Peter to comprehend, and left him wondering how many others slipped through the cracks of the cult's malevolent methods.

"So, what exactly is the plan?" Peter asked, dry-mouthed.

They were within touching distance of Cold Christmas now, and none of what Gregor shared so far offered any definitive answers.

"I'm glad you asked, Peter. Let me give the famous history teacher a brief lesson in that case..." Gregor loved the sound of his own voice, a quality which was grating on Peter.

"Originally, when St Peter's moved to Thundridge, the cult insisted on keeping one of its tower for their own place of worship. At the time, the church didn't see the point of arguing. They were just keen to up sticks before anymore locals died at the hands of criminals. But that was all a ploy, you see, to run all the meddlers out of town and gain full control of the tower."

"Why I hear you ask? Because the tower was home to a

secret passage which granted access to an entire network of tunnels dating back centuries. The church forgot it even existed, but the cult didn't, and it became a vital part of their operations. They couldn't wait to get their grubby little mitts on the place and pretty soon they ruled the underworld entirely, steeling from the rich and the poor to fund their expansion. Since then, the tower was rendered obsolete owing to various renovations to the hospital dating back half a century. They have a bigger and better tunnel system now. Not the old run-down dungeons you guys tripped over underneath Crooked House...these days they have power, transport...turning Chase Side into a veritable fortress and their new base of operations."

"I guess in sales terms, Cold Christmas was a loss leader. A sacrifice they made to gain a smaller slice of a bigger pie. That's why hardly anyone lives there now...it's a literal ghost town. What better place to plot the end of the world from, eh? People think all that stuff goes on in the ivory towers of the rich, or the underground bunkers of mad dictators...it's all clever misdirection. Years of building and reinforcing stereotypes to keep people looking in all the wrong directions. The real centre of evil is right where it's always been."

"And there I was, hoping we're all trapped in the matrix..." Kane muttered over Peter's shoulder.

"Well, in a lot of ways, we are. It's definitely one big construct designed to screw us all over, only there's no 'control-alt-delete' or reboot button. For that, we have to kill an ancient demon...not the one we're looking to stop today. I mean..."

"The Grand Master..." Peter finished Gregor's sentence.

"Exactly. But we're not going to do that today. He'll be

too protected there. Our best hope is to get in and out before anyone realizes what's happened. Live to fight another day."

"But even if...I mean, when we get Izzy out of there, what's stopping them sacrificing someone else?" JJ made a valid point.

"You're right, young James...there's nothing stopping them from doing that. Our best hope is to steal the ceremonial knife. That's the only thing that can complete the ritual, so without it, there's no resurrection."

The car went quiet again, and the engine's humming took over while everyone processed Gregor's impromptu history lesson. It still begged the question of how they would get in undetected and find the ceremonial knife. Surely such an important artifact would be kept under lock and key.

"That's all great, but you've still not told us how we're getting Izzy?" Kane's temper was getting the better of him, and Peter couldn't blame him.

Much like his online persona, Gregor was slippery, to say the least, and would have made an excellent politician, given the way he continued to skirt around the nitty gritty of what they were about to attempt.

"Zach..." Gregor called out to the back of the car. "Because my darling daughter is still pissed at me. Can you reach behind your seat? You should find a duffel bag... I want you to open it and tell everyone what's inside..."

Peter heard the rustling of nylon followed by a zip being opened.

"It...it's a bunch hoods...like the ones they wear..."

"Bingo!" Gregor bragged. "We're going to put those bad boys on and then waltz right in there without any of them even noticing us."

"We're what?!" Peter couldn't believe the stupidity of what he heard.

"Are you insane? They'll spot us a mile off. Even if we get inside, what then? How will we get the knife? Or Izzy, for that matter? You had the gall to say we're naïve when all the while you're acting like we're stuck in an episode of Scooby-Doo...Oh and by the way, you're about to miss the turnoff for Cold Christmas..."

"Wind ya neck in pal..." Gregor snapped back. "First off, the old church is at the opposite end of Cold Christmas, so we're going the right way. Second, did it occur to you I might be easing you in gently to the plan? Zach, can you look under the hoods and tell me what else is in there?"

All eyes were on Zach as he rummaged around in the bottom of the bag like it was a lucky dip at a school fete. Within seconds, he pulled out a long ceremonial dagger to a chorus of gasps. Closer to a sword, the serrated steel blade shimmered to reveal a myriad of cryptic glyphs covering its shiny surface from tip to hilt.

At the base of its handle, below Zach's trembling hand, Peter saw the beginnings of an ornate and rather solemn looking angel. Its wings tucked tightly behind its back.

Upon closer scrutiny, the hand guard formed part of the same intricately crafted figurine and depicted a woman laid bare at the angel's feet. Zach quickly let go of the dagger as all the colour drained from his face. Beside him, Meridia seemed spooked, as did Kane, who was first to shed light on their peculiar reaction.

"I've seen that before...in a dream."

"Me too..." Meridia added. "The Grand Master had it when I disappeared at the church...that's what he used to kill me...I mean Elizabeth...Elizabeth Cooper, the other seer."

"I saw it too..." Zach closed the bag, unable to look at it anymore.

"It was...it was when I dreamt of the horseman in our house...they used it to...to stab you..." He glanced up in Kane's direction and was brimming with tears beneath his fringe.

"Relax guys..." Gregor bellowed without looking up from the road.

"Don't get your knickers in a twist. It's a fake. I'm going to switch out the real one. By the time they realize what I've done, we'll be long gone." He signalled to leave the dual carriageway and allowed each *'tick-tock'* of the car's indicator to crank up the tension before continuing.

"Once we get inside, all you have to worry about is getting Izzy out of there. I'll take care of the rest."

Gregor took a sharp left and swung the car into a narrow layby, bringing it to a stop beside a small plot of overgrown grassland with a smattering of spindly birch trees on either side.

A thick band of rain clouds were rolling in over the horizon, and in keeping with the rest of their journey, there wasn't another soul in sight. Within a matter of seconds, Grace pulled up alongside and Gregor clambered out of the car to greet them. Meanwhile, Peter remained glued to his seat in silence, still wondering what he got everyone into.

It was little wonder Izzy was hung out to dry given Gregor's sketchy rescue plan, but now, in the middle of nowhere and with no means of transport, he had a decision to make.

Did they take a leap of faith and trust there was more substance to the smoke and mirrors act, Gregor was putting on, or did they go their own way and try to save Izzy alone?

Caught between a rock and a hard place, with time

stacked against them, he turned, expecting to find a bunch of anxious faces looking for guidance, but found them all pressed against the window on the driver's side. There was some sort of commotion outside.

A moment later, Gregor poked his head back into the car, unable to mask the apprehension in his voice as he addressed the group.

"Grace spotted a motorbike parked up amongst the trees. Pass me the dagger, Zach. It looks we've got company..."

47

GRADY CROUCHED LOW AMONGST THE DENSE CLUSTER of silver birch as both cars pulled up outside the entrance ahead.

The icy wind played cat and mouse with the leaves as it whipped in and out of their withered trunks. Whilst high above, the brooding clouds were busy stifling and smothering the dying embers of daylight to make way for the blood moon. Everything was going exactly to plan.

He was waiting impatiently for his guests to arrive since leaving the bunker, and was hungry for blood again. Butchering the chubby little Irishman, whilst fun, didn't come close to satisfying his craving and instead only wet his appetite.

Now, the scrumptious main course had arrived, and it had Grady greedily licking his lips in anticipation. Knelt only a few yards to the rear of where they were parked. He was confident he could slaughter them all in a matter of minutes. And that was exactly what he intended to do. He experimented enough for one day, and now it was time to exercise some deadly efficiency.

The thought of cramming so many kills into a single strike made his palms tingle and so he reached inside his cloak and pulled out his knife. Squeezing its handle as tight as he could, Grady listened for the satisfying creak above the bustling breeze, taking a deep breath to savour the sensation.

Pressed for time on his way here, he was forced to crudely dispose of Hutson's corpse, and his van, but not before donning his robes and giving his war paint a little refresh with the Irishman's blood.

He almost tasted the coppery crimson smeared around his lips. Although never one to get wrapped up in vanity, Grady liked his new image. More to the point, he liked the way it struck terror in the Irishman's eyes. He couldn't wait to see the faces of his latest prey when he slit their worthless throats in quick succession.

The thought of all that fear and blood stoked his zeal. What was taking them so long?

The first car emptied upon arrival, but the second remained dormant. If they didn't come out soon, he would have to go over and huff and puff and blow their house down.

"Click"

Grady heard the remaining car door finally open and smiled.

It was showtime.

48

Meridia bundled her way out of the back of the SUV to find out what all the fuss was about.

The sun was only headed in one direction now and they already wasted enough time listening to her dad prattle on in the car.

"It's just a bike..." she grumbled. "Grady drives a van, so it's obviously not him."

"We can't take anything for granted, Meridia." Dr Foster countered. "He could have ditched his van now he knows we're onto him..."

"Now we're onto him?" Meridia's tone betrayed her annoyance. "He was at the bunker and could've killed us all, but he didn't. Does anyone know why?"

"It could be anything..." Gregor grabbed the opportunity to speak to his daughter with both hands.

"He's kept on a short leash from what I can tell...word is he struggles with impulse control and even goes out with a handler sometimes to keep him in check. Maybe he went rogue back at the bunker and his handler stepped in... maybe he didn't realize you guys were even down there."

"Or maybe this is a trap..." Dr Foster rubbed his chin and wandered closer to where the bike was resting.

"It's an old Triumph..." Peter announced, having clambered out of the passenger seat to join them. "It looks like something a kid might ride..."

"Or a hipster..." Kane threw in his tuppence worth.

"Cars are more my thing, so I couldn't say..." Gregor was still on edge as he clutched the dagger. He was looking increasingly shifty as he scoured the trees for anything else that looked out of place.

"The only reason anyone would be here is the tower. It's literally all there is down this road...just look around. See any shops or houses? Something doesn't feel right..."

"There's only one way to find out, isn't there?" Peter declared, parting the sea of worried faces and stepping onto the grassland.

"It doesn't matter who's out there...we still need to get to the tower, don't we? We're too far down the line for a plan B, so let's find out who it is and get on with it. We only have about two hours of daylight left, tops..." With that, he took a couple of long strides towards the direction of the trees.

"Ha...sorry pal, but you're going the wrong way." Gregor's sarky jibe stopped him in his tracks.

"The tower's this way..." He pointed towards the rear of the SUV. "It's a short walk through those trees."

"Fine. Lead on in that case..." Peter shooed Gregor along, and Meridia wondered how much more bickering they could take before coming to blows.

As much as some part of her still loved her dad, there was no doubt in her mind who's side she would take if things went that far, and it wasn't Gregor's.

"Where do you think you're going, young lady?" Gregor paused and glared at her.

"You and your friends are staying with Nadia, remember?" Meridia didn't even hear her dad.

His gruff voice wilted into white noise, swallowed by the wind and the trees. She didn't hear Zach either, asking her what was wrong. She was preoccupied with the shadowy figure which emerged from behind the trees and was now heading straight towards them. All she could do was point, as she scrambled to speak.

"It...it's him!"

49

Grady broke cover and sprinted towards the crowd of unsuspecting victims. Already knowing he was vastly outnumbered, it suddenly dawned on him there were even more in the group than he first thought. Not that it mattered much, it would all be over soon.

Caught stone cold, he watched the fear light up in each of their eyes, as one by one they realized what was coming. Knees buckled and legs turned to jelly as Grady gobbled up the distance between them and moved within striking distance.

Making a beeline for the biggest of the bunch, he switched his knife to a reversed grip and dropped him with a single slash to the throat. Grady felt the razor-sharp edge of his blade scrape against the bone as he ripped through artery and cartilage with a satisfying '*swish*'.

As he swiftly moved on to the next in line, Grady heard victim number one cough and splutter in his wake and knew he would be dead before he even hit the ground.

Riding the momentum of his first swing, Grady took

another lunging stride forward, stooping low as he changed his grip again.

"*Argh!*"

Springing back to his feet with a vicious uppercut, he thrust the knife up through the shorter man's jaw, impaling his head and spearing his brain. Grady took a moment to watch the lights go out in his eyes before withdrawing his blade in one fluid motion. He felt the knife's subtle vibration as its jagged edge snagged and tore through tongue and soft palate on the exit, dragging victim number two face down into the blood-spattered dirt.

Now the real fun was about to begin, as the remaining survivors' fight-or-flight responses kicked in and sent them scattering in every direction like a bunch of headless chickens. This was Grady's favourite part, seeing their terror take the wheel.

Leaping over the bonnet of the nearest car, he drove his knife down hard through the temple of victim number three and sent her crashing to the ground. A solitary spurt of crimson erupted from her lips on impact as her eyes rolled back into their sockets and her body fell limp.

Stamping down on her blood-smeared face, he yanked the blade out and flipped it in his hand before thrusting it blindly behind him like a trained samurai into the chest of victim number four.

"*Oof!*"

Six inches of stainless steel clattered against her rib cage, lancing her heart. Before her body collapsed, Grady was already onto the next.

"Ooh, a runner..." He caught another of the group from the corner of his eye and vowed to leave him till last.

Right now, he needed to deal with one of the youngest

in the group who, instead of fleeing, was rushing towards him, screaming.

There was always one in a party this size, and Grady smirked as he blocked his feeble attempt at a right-hook and unleashed a ferocious barrage of blows to the young upstart's torso. Savagely sticking and stabbing him to the hilt, he marched him back towards the nearest tree, leaving a trail of gore on the marshy ground.

Each satisfying squelch of his blade gave Grady goosebumps, and he could have spent hours knifing him to a bloody pulp, but he still had a runner to catch.

On he went, hacking and slashing his way through the rest of the pack like a cyclone of serrated steel, until all that remained was one. Dashing after him through the trees, he was disappointed how little distance the man put between them both.

Grady considered playing up to the stalker trope and slowing down to a walk, but like it or not, he was still on the clock. He caught up with the last man standing in a matter of seconds, finding him drunk on fear and bouncing from bark to bark.

Spinning him around to face him with his left hand, he deftly thrust the knife deep into the side of his neck, severing the carotid artery. Grady paused a moment to look his victim in the eyes, all the while allowing the pressure to build beneath his blade.

"I always knew you were a coward..." Grady scoffed, as Detective Inspector Richards' stared back at him, wide-eyed and gurgling on his own blood.

"Guess you and your police buddies won't make it to the party now...such a shame you'll miss my big surprise."

Grady felt the detective's legs wilt and so he held him

upright by the scruff of his jacket and the knife still lodged in his neck.

"*Squelch!*"

He twisted the blade and felt a warm surge of shimmering claret splash against his knuckles.

"Oops..." he snorted, "I think we have a gusher..."

Grady yanked the knife all the way out of the detective's neck to unleash a fountain of blood. Releasing his grip, he dropped the man to his knees and watched him bleed out like a burst fire hydrant until he eventually flopped face down in the dirt where he belonged.

He took in a lungful of his little rampage, basking in the bloodshed, as its metallic aroma wafted through the woods. The smell was intoxicating, and as he waded through the slew of police officers swimming in blood, he felt an unexpected surge of excitement tingle his skin.

Grady had gone way beyond the point of no return, and now it was time to face the music.

50

"It's him...it's Tommy..." Meridia babbled as she rushed over to greet him. "He told me we'd meet soon..."

"Wait!" Peter called out after her. "We don't know the first thing about him..."

"Is this your land?" Tommy asked, as he slowed to a jog. "I heard the cars pull in and wasn't sure if I was trespassing...plus I was worried you might try to take a shine to my bike..." Dressed in denim, he looked exactly as he did the first time they met, minus the grease and dirt.

Before Meridia opened her mouth to answer, Gregor stepped between them like a guard dog.

"What you doing here kid?" He demanded.

As her dad breezed past her, Meridia saw he was hiding the dagger behind his back, and a twinge of panic pricked her spine. Gregor's hostility stopped Tommy in his tracks, but he tackled the question with aplomb.

"I'm looking for my dad...he's missing." Tommy reached into his back pocket and pulled out a flyer with a man's picture on it.

The white A4 snapped and cracked in the bitter wind, as it threatened to whip up into a gale.

"See..." He pressed, waving the piece of paper around so all could see.

"He's been missing for days now, so I've been riding around town putting these up in the hope someone recognizes him...have any of you seen him?"

Once again, Meridia was about to speak when she felt Peter lean in next to her.

"Remember what I told you about Archie and the girl?" he whispered.

"She was looking for her dad, too. I know you feel you can trust him, but let's find out a little more before we go jumping in feet-first, shall we..." Peter walked ahead of Gregor and inspected Tommy's flyer.

"Sorry, can't say I've seen him. I'm Peter, by the way..." He extended his hand to the boy. "What makes you think he's around here?"

"Hi..." The two shook hands and Tommy tucked the flyer back into his pocket, refusing to give up his name just yet.

"You're the first person who's asked me anything since I got here...until now, all I've had is shifty looks and shakes of the head. Even the police didn't seem all that bothered. I was thinking I'd wandered into the town of Hawkins or something..." Kane and JJ snickered behind her, but Meridia didn't get what they found so funny.

"He's a writer...my dad...for a local newspaper in Leeds. He was down here following a story...it was kind of off the books, so to speak. It was a big one, though. About something that happened here back in the seventies. Something his dad...my grandad...was involved in."

Tommy's comment knocked the wind out of everyone,

and Meridia felt the hairs stand up on the back of her neck. It couldn't be a coincidence their paths crossed at the same time the demon was due to return to Cold Christmas.

"What thing in the seventies?" Peter wasted no time beating about the bush, but any idiot could tell Tommy's remark struck a nerve.

"Er...wait...what's going on? Why are you all looking at me like that?" Tommy's ocean-blue eyes narrowed as he studied the congregation of nervy faces slowly closing in on him.

"You know something, don't you..." He shuffled backwards and readied himself to make a run for it. Meridia silently cursed her father and his brash tone; he was about to scare Tommy away.

"Easy kid...we don't want any trouble..." Gregor showed both his hands, and Meridia couldn't tell if he forgot he was still holding a gigantic sacrificial knife, or he was trying to intimidate Tommy into staying put.

"What the fuck is going on here?" As expected, he went from about a five to a ten on the defensive scale.

"Where's my dad? What have you done to him?" His knuckles were white now, and he seemed ready for a fight.

"Stop! All of you!" Meridia took her chance to speak. "Dad, put the knife away now...you're freaking everyone out."

She stepped into the space between them and lured Tommy's gaze away from the rest of the group. "You're Tommy, right?"

"Wait, what...do I know you?" Tommy relaxed his fists and shuffled a fraction closer to Meridia.

"You look familiar...I've seen you before somewhere." His response took Meridia by surprise. If Dr Foster's theory was right and she met Tommy in an emergent future, then it made no sense that he recognized her now.

"It can't be..." He mumbled, shaking his head.

"Can't be what?" Meridia pressed.

"Nothing...you just remind me of someone, that's all..." His eyes narrowed again as he wriggled free of his confusion.

In the natural light of day, he appeared far more clean-cut than she remembered. His cheeks were rosy from the wind, but beneath that, he was pale like her. A complexion that was made more pasty by the harsh contrast of his jet-black hair. He wore a mullet, as she suspected, though it was now ruffled and styled with product. He was trendy-looking and if he was taller, probably wouldn't look out of place on a catwalk with his chiselled jawline.

"How do you know my name?" He asked.

"It's written on your flyer," Meridia bluffed. "I saw it when you showed everyone. Cool bike, by the way...What are you doing all the way out here?"

The rest of the group remained quiet, but she sensed her dad's eyes boring a hole into the back of her head, waiting for an excuse to jump back in again.

"Like I said, I was looking for my dad...there's the ruins of an old church behind those trees...I remember him mentioning it, so thought he might have come out this way... I wasn't here long when I heard you guys...now here we are."

Meridia calmed the situation and wondered if she opened up a little, Tommy might tell them what he was really doing here. She knew he wasn't a spy. Otherwise, why would he have saved her from the weavers in her vision? He must be involved in all of this. She needed to find out how.

"We're out here searching for someone too..." Over her shoulder, the rest of the group broke into a chorus of unease as twigs crackled beneath nervous feet, but Meridia ignored it and continued.

"She was taken...by a gang of dangerous people..." She tiptoed around the truth so as not to scare him whilst reaching for her phone.

Shuffling through her camera roll, she showed Tommy a picture of Izzy. It was one Zach took of the two of them one sunny afternoon in his backyard, back when things were normal.

"Her name's Izzy, and she's in trouble. That's why we're all here...to find her and bring her home."

Tommy looked at the picture of Izzy and then glanced up at the slate-coloured curtain slowly being drawn overhead. A torn expression crept across his face as he took a deep breath and then let it go.

"It's gonna be getting dark soon...which means we don't have much time." He scanned the rest of the group once more, lingering on the dagger in Gregor's hand, before circling back to Meridia.

"Are you one of them?" He asked bluntly. "I mean, you show up mob-handed, on this of all days, with a knife that looks like it's been nicked from an Indiana Jones movie... and you're asking me why I'm here...I mean you have to admit it looks a bit suss right? But then you show me a picture of your friend and in a weird way it all kind of makes sense, especially given the last few days I've had." Tommy raised his hand as Gregor opened his mouth.

"Wait, let me finish. You'll get your turn in a sec. Like I said, we don't have much time. So here you all are, looking as anxious as me...that means you're scared too. But it isn't of me, because there's only one of me and there's like a dozen of you. Now as far as I can tell none of you are wearing any rings...which leaves me with just one reason you're all here...so before I say any more and see if that's the same reason I'm here, I just need to be sure which side of this you're on..."

"What are you on about, kid?" Gregor was first to speak, having gone way too long without hearing his own voice, and Tommy was every bit as eager to elaborate.

"Are you on the right side, or the wrong side? Are you with the Children of the Shadows?"

51

TOMMY GLEANED HIS ANSWER FROM THE SEA OF shocked faces staring back at him. He took an enormous leap of faith, being so direct, but he estimated they had less than a couple of hours before the moon showed up, and by then it would all be too late.

He figured if they were all part of the sinister cult his grandad stumbled upon in the seventies, then he would already be dead. Judging by their interactions so far, Tommy surmised either the short crabby guy clutching the knife was in charge, or the tall handsome fella named Peter. He hoped it was the latter, as he had an inkling what he was about to tell them next would go far smoother that way.

"No...we're not..." Surprisingly, the redhead continued as their spokesperson while the adults remained silent.

Despite her calm and mature demeanour, he could tell there was a fire in her eyes from the get-go. A fire he saw flicker the moment he mentioned the Children of the Shadows.

"You know who I'm talking about, right?" For the first

time since they bumped into each other, Tommy felt as if he had the upper hand.

"That's what the knife is for, isn't it..." He pointed at the creepy-looking dagger. "Come to kill a demon?"

"Alright kid, cut the shit...who are you and what are you really doing here?" The short guy erupted again, and Tommy noticed a few other kids in the group roll their eyes.

Perhaps he wasn't their leader after all. Ignoring his little tantrum, Tommy turned his attention back to Peter, who edged closer to the redhead.

"It's a long story, so maybe we can all walk and talk?" He pointed toward the old church tower.

"The clock's ticking and I didn't get a chance to look inside before you guys arrived...it took me bloody ages to find the place."

Before Peter replied, the redhead stepped towards him with her hand out.

"I'm Meridia..." He gently shook her hand.

"I knew you were all too polite to be in a cult." He smiled, trying to bring some levity to what he knew was a desperate situation.

"I'm Tommy...Tommy Anderson...my dad's name is Callum, and my grandad was Colin...he was a detective that worked the case of the demon in the seventies...he was also the one who stopped him."

52

Tommy's shock revelation shattered any illusion of equanimity within the group and plunged them head-long into pandemonium.

A cacophony of questions and demands lay siege on the winter air, each one pushing and shoving to be heard above the rest, but their only achievement was to turn the tiny strip of countryside into a bickering school playground.

"Guys...GUYS!" Peter bellowed above the deafening discord, which rather tellingly composed mostly of adults.

"How many times do we all need telling? We don't have time for this!" The group settled down like a rowdy classroom wrapped across the knuckles by their headteacher.

"Thank you." Peter rubbed his face in dismay. "If I'd known it was going to be like this the entire time, I'd have packed a conch..."

"Haha..." Dr Foster let out a belly laugh, then realized he was the only one in on the joke.

"It's a Lord of the Flies reference...very apt. Good book too if you've not read it..." The doctor became increasingly self-conscious with each awkward word that passed his lips as the rest of the group gawped at him bemused.

"Never mind...the point is Peter's right. Perhaps we should all take a leaf out of the kids' book and think before we speak. Empty vessels and all that...carry on Peter."

Peter nodded as he stepped alongside Tommy and ushered him toward the church tower.

"Sorry about that..." Tommy followed, as did the rest of the crowd, each faction whispering while they waited to hear more of Tommy's story.

In the distance, Peter heard a car door slam and then waited for Gregor to catch up. He had his duffel bag thrown over one shoulder, and a thin black plastic box tucked under the other arm, which he passed to Grace on his way through the pack.

"Almost forgot our Halloween costumes, Grand Master..." Peter didn't rise to the bait and instead signalled for Tommy to continue.

"So, what do you know of the demon, and what really brought you to Cold Christmas?"

"I'll keep it brief as there's a lot that's happened in the last few days..." Peter noticed he kept glancing over in Meridia's direction as he spoke, and for a moment he felt his suspicions bubble back up to the surface again, but the feeling quickly dissipated when Tommy got talking.

"I really came here to look for my dad...that's how this all started for me, at least. But I think I need to go back a couple of weeks before he disappeared for any of this to make sense. When I'm done telling you, I still wanna hear what you guys know and what that weird-looking knife's all about...there are still a few gaps in my knowledge, particularly as far as the cult is concerned. Deal?"

Peter agreed to Tommy's terms and with the wind

nipping at their backs, they trudged towards the barren woodland, snapping and cracking over brittle twigs and frozen leaves.

When they reached the edge of the clearing, they were greeted by an endless graveyard of ghostly white birch trees, their twisted limbs clawing at the sky. Here, the clouds had yet to deliver on their promise of rain, and the ground remained hard underfoot as a smattering of thorny bushes weaved their way through the tree trunks, stripped bare by the bitter unseen hand of winter.

"This place is creepy as hell, but there's no-one else here...not from what I could tell, anyway." Tommy pointed ahead. "The tower's over there, in another tiny clearing."

Peter hesitated at the first tree as thoughts of the witch came flooding back to him. He promised himself to never step foot in the woods again, yet here he was about to go steaming headfirst in search of underground tunnels and a fifty-year-old demon. He shook his head at the absurdity of it all. What he wouldn't have given to go back to his old life, spending his nights in haunted hotels and exposing fake mediums. Things were far simpler then.

"You ok?" Tommy asked, sensing his unease.

"Yes...sorry...carry on." Peter took a deep breath and reluctantly stepped over the threshold.

"So, this all started when my grandad passed a few weeks ago. My dad asked me to go with him and help sort through all his stuff...he wasn't a hoarder, but he clung on to quite a bit since moving to that house. When I went up in his loft, I found this dusty old box full of journals and case notes from his time on the force. Until then, all either of us knew was that he did a brief stint as a policeman in his twenties. He never spoke about that period of his life, not to anyone. He always said there was no point digging up old ghosts from the past. All it ever did was piss off the dead. Ha...he was funny like that...very matter of fact about stuff, you know? So, you can imagine what my dad the journo did when he found the box...he spent the rest of the day digging through it, looking for skeletons in the closet, while I did the rest of the packing. When he found all this stuff in there about the Demon of Cold Christmas and the Children of the Shadows, he became convinced there was a bigger story. One my grandad was forced to walk away from. He said it was full of conspiracy theories about this place...unsolved crimes and corruption dating back decades. I had to go back to uni that night, but whenever my dad called over the days that followed, it was all he talked about. He became obsessed, until eventually, after the funeral, he took some leave and came here to investigate..."

Tommy fell quiet for a moment to take stock of their surroundings, and Peter could tell the talk of his dad piqued his paranoia. Although gloomy, the frosty bark of the trees provided good visibility, and once satisfied they were alone, Tommy continued explaining his family's ties to the area.

"My grandad was from the city originally...London that is...turns out he was actually some hot-shot detective back in the day and solved some pretty high-profile cases...like the Shoreditch Strangler, for instance. He even got to work with Scotland Yard at one point...I mean, if that was me, I'd be telling anyone who would listen, but he never breathed a word of it. Anyway, during his time there, he built up a reputation for spotting clues no-one else noticed, but his methods were unconventional, especially back then. He had a secret weapon, you see. A consultant he would always bring in on tough cases. From what I can tell, she was some kind of clairvoyant, but he always kept her name out of any paperwork. At first, I thought it was to keep her a secret from his bosses...I mean, just imagine if they found out he was using a psychic to help solve his cases? They would have laughed him all the way out of the force. But then my dad noticed he did the same in his personal journal...he just refers to her as *'his girl with the gift'*. That got us thinking maybe he kept her name hidden to protect her...not that it did much good."

"How do you mean?" Peter probed.

"Well, I think she's the reason he eventually quit the force and moved up to Leeds. After he stopped the demon, the psychic and her niece both went missing, here in Cold Christmas, and were never seen again..."

"Her niece?" Peter quizzed, as once more, Tommy shot another sideways glance in Meridia's direction before continuing.

"Yeah, apparently, her niece was visiting when he dragged the psychic all the way to this place. Her mum was really sick, so she had nowhere else to stay. There's a picture of them in the file...at least I'm guessing it's them...there are no names on it, just a date. Fifty years ago, to the day...I think he might have let their names slip more recently, but I can't be sure...I'll come to that in a minute though..."

"Do you know how they met? Your grandad and the clairvoyant, I mean?" Peter remembered Dr Foster's theory about there being a seer born in every century and wondered if Tommy's grandfather somehow stumbled upon whoever held the mantle before Meridia.

"According to his journal, they first crossed paths on an abduction case in the early seventies...some rich kid in Kensington...anyway the psychic told my grandad exactly where the kid was being held...none of that cryptic bullshit you see on TV, she knew the full address and postcode, as if she was there when it happened. At first, he thought she was involved somehow, but when he met her, he came to thinking that wasn't the case. The way he talks about her in his journal changes after that point. He describes her as being kooky, but it sounds to me like she was a recluse... didn't enjoy being around other people much. After that they became kinda friends, although sometimes it sounds like my grandad secretly fancied her...ha...anyway he worked with her pretty regularly after that until, like I said, he brought her here to catch the demon. He used the pretence of a similar case back in London to get his bosses to sign off on being seconded here, but it didn't take long for him to become obsessed with the case. He said the local guys were either useless or hiding something, like some dark town secret. They did all they could to send him packing... complaining to his chief back in London behind his back, impeding his investigation...they even tried to intimidate him once, but my grandad wasn't having any of it. He was like a dog with a bone and once he got his teeth into something, he wouldn't let go. He ended up renting a place here for the psychic and her niece out of his own pay packet...he was so convinced there was more to it all than just a child killer. When my dad finished studying all the files, he was of the same mind and came down here snooping."

"Where are the files now?" Dr Foster asked. He quietly crept his way to the front of the crowd at the mere mention of journals.

"I have them now. My dad was staying at the Holiday Inn...he was calling five or six times a day, updating me on what he uncovered...until he stopped a few nights ago and wouldn't return any of my calls. When I called the hotel, they told me his room was empty, and his bed hadn't been slept in, so I jumped on my bike and got down here as quick as I could. He'd prepaid to the end of the week, and when I got here, it wasn't hard for me to blag my way into his room. I took the files for safekeeping. Since then, I've spent every day searching, and every night reading, looking for anything that might tell me where he might be. The last place my dad mentioned was some old church in the woods, but he couldn't find it...said the locals clammed up on him, like he rattled the wrong cage... At the time I thought he was being paranoid...god I wish I listened more...said more...maybe I could've convinced him to come home, you know..."

"Trust me, there's nothing to gain going down that road. Good or bad, your dad made his own decisions...and they were his alone to make." Peter rested his hand on Tommy's shoulder. Another young life turned upside down by this wretched town.

"What about your mum? Could he have reached out to her?"

"Nah, she left us when I was little...lives with some douche bag in Manchester now and neither of us have spoken to her in years. It's just me and my dad... and now my grandad has gone. I'm literally all he's got." Tommy's voice fractured and his head wilted beneath the weight of worry he was carrying.

Peter sensed the boy was putting on a brave front since they met him. Perhaps bolstered by a heavy dose of denial. But now, telling his story to a bunch of strangers, Tommy's darkest fears about his dad were bubbling up to the surface.

"I've read the file on the demon...and my grandad's journal...and I think my dad had it all wrong. He came here thinking he uncovered an old conspiracy that died with the demon in the seventies. Something that might shed some light on what happened to the psychic and her niece...but what I think he stumbled onto was something way worse and now he's in trouble. You see, my dad was so caught up looking at all the old case notes and journals, he missed something staring him straight in the face the entire time. My grandad carried a little notebook around with him everywhere...he said he used it to make sure he didn't forget stuff..." Tommy reached into his back pocket and pulled out a tiny black, spiral-bound notebook, then opened the first page.

"At first glance, it's just that...pint of milk, tea bags, tin of spam..." He turned to a page halfway through the book. "Arsenal, match of the day at 10pm...loads and loads of little memos to himself...that's why I think my dad just missed it."

"Missed what?" Dr Foster blurted, still hanging on Tommy's every word.

"Well, if he kept a journal in his twenties and was still taking notes in his seventies, it stood to reason he might jot down more than the odd shopping list and his favourite TV programs. So, I went through every page and sure enough, mixed in amongst the reminders, I found the odd thing about my nan...or old friends he had lunch with..." He flicked toward the back of the book and read aloud so all could hear.

Yet another victim: Helen Ashfield. I should have burned that place to the ground when I had the chance.

Peter watched the colour drain from the kids' faces the second Tommy uttered her name.

Stop hiding and do something, you silly old fart! You owe it to Julie and little Emma.

"Who are Julie and Emma?" Meridia blurted.

"I don't know. I think they could be the psychic and her niece, but there's no way to be sure. That's not all though..." He flipped past another couple of shopping lists, then continued reading.

Another night and another nightmare. No matter how far I run, I can't seem to get away from it. Maybe it's the anniversary. Julie said he would be back one day. God help the children of that town if she was right.

"Julie must be the psychic...it's the only thing that makes sense." Peter was now convinced they had uncovered another seer.

"I'm with you." Tommy nodded. "But I still have nothing other than a first name and an old picture to go on. There's one last entry, which I found odd. It says, '*DI Richards (01462 476 476). Just as shifty as his father.*' Then that's it...the pages are all blank after that."

"The phone number is local to here...he must've seen the same article about Helen that we did and called in...it was DI Richards that was asking for information, remember?" JJ shouted over Peter's shoulder.

It couldn't have been a coincidence that Colin Anderson's last entry was connected to Crooked House.

"Tommy...I'm sorry to ask this, but was your grandad ill before he passed? I mean, aside from having memory issues..."

"No...he was fit as a fiddle...that's what made it so hard on my dad. One day he was there, and the next he wasn't. I mean, I know mid-seventies is old, but it's not old-old if you know what I mean...he still went for daily walks and kept his mind in shape with crosswords and that sort of stuff..."

"So, what was the official cause of death? Again, if you don't mind me asking..."

"My dad said medical examiners don't dig too deep into a cause of death once you pass a certain age...all they told us was that he died in his sleep..."

It was as if Tommy's answer paused time. Everyone froze, caught between breaths as their eyes searched for one another in stunned silence. Again, it was far too much of a coincidence that Tommy's grandad reached out to the local police and then died shortly after. Whatever secrets were buried in those case files, Valerie's powers weren't among them. Otherwise, poor Colin would never have poked his head above the parapet.

"What is it? What did I say?" Tommy noticed the weird energy which somehow infected the trees, bringing their constant rustling to an eerie halt.

"Do you know how your grandad caught him? The demon, that is?" Meridia skilfully sidestepped Tommy's bewilderment by finally asking what was on everyone's lips.

"Er...no, that's what's so weird. He just refers to it as a 'dark secret' they swore to take to their graves. I'm guessing he means the psychic...Julie? There's no evidence of anyone else helping him. However he stopped him, it happened suddenly...like one minute he was chasing down leads, and the next it was all over. I can tell you one thing, though. The stuff he saw down here tested his faith and went way beyond the demon. Scary shit...shit he couldn't explain. His journal makes it sound like this whole town was rotten. Then the entries stop...it's as if whatever happened down here spooked him so bad he dropped everything and ran. My dad made a couple of calls to some contacts he has on the force and found he never went back to London. Instead, he moved up to Leeds and started his life over. He got a steady job in a factory and that's where he met my nan. They both kept their heads down and worked hard until they could afford to retire and that was that...never any mention of what he did or what he saw during his time in Cold Christmas." Tommy sighed and turned to Gregor.

"So, is that what your creepy knife is for? To kill the demon if he comes back? My dad found out all this stuff about ritual killings and the occult...said there was some weirdo online who knew everything about the history of this place...goes by the name of Retiarius...he reckons the demon will return on the anniversary of his reign, which is today... or at least it will be when the moon comes up. I wouldn't have believed any of it had it not been for the case file...my grandad was no mug, and neither is my dad. After a couple of days here, he was convinced it was all true...all the creepy stories about this place...the ghosts...the monsters...the devil worshippers...all of it...and now he's gone. Just like your friend...I don't know what's gonna be waiting for us inside that place, but I ain't leaving until I find my dad." Tommy came to a stop and pointed to a small clearing a few yards ahead. "The tower is just through there..."

They finally reached The Temple of Shadows.

53

As they approached the break in the trees, JJ hung back to hear what Kane thought about Tommy's story.

"How come every man and his dog found Retiarius online before we did? I feel like a complete prat..." JJ raised his eyebrows at Kane's initial takeaway but humoured him.

"Do you think it would've changed anything? If we saw all that stuff first, I mean..." It was a question JJ asked himself countless times since their first visit to Crooked House, but never asked Kane outright, until now.

"Probably not...We were so desperate for followers back then. Now look at us...we've got the whole fucking town following us."

"Careful what you wish for, I guess..." JJ trailed off as they joined the rest of the group in the clearing and came face to face with the old church tower.

Standing alone in a cathedral of trees, the Temple of Shadows appeared trapped between two worlds with its crumbling carcass reaching skyward like a withered hand, trying to claw its way free from the earth's deathly grip.

Fragments of loose rubble bled out onto the

overgrowth like a concrete waterfall, while centuries of moss and vine clung to its ramshackle walls of cracked mortar, dragging it back down towards hell where it belonged.

Shrouded in gloom beneath the sun's dying light, the tall and narrow, windowless tower echoed its nefarious flock as it cast a long dark blemish on the land, corrupting everything it touched with death and decay. Amongst the murky shadows skulking along the tangled weeds and desiccated mud, JJ spotted a handful of jagged tombstones, buried beneath a patchwork of mould and rot.

"Hey...guys...wh...what's that?" he whispered, squinting beyond the saw-toothed horizon of splintered slabs and stone memorials. The second he realized what he was staring at, JJ's blood turned to ice.

"Guys! Look..." He pointed at the slew of bodies lying face down in the dirt like scattered remnants of a ripped-up paper chain.

Before anyone could react, Gregor thrust the ceremonial knife in Tommy's direction.

"Looking for your dad, my arse...it's a trap!" Everyone instinctively closed ranks behind him as Tommy stuttered and stammered in protest.

"Wh...what? I...I swear I never saw those guys before in my life..." His eyes bounced anxiously between the savage bloodbath haemorrhaging into the earth and the dagger pointed directly at his throat.

"I never even made it this far before...Y...you guys turned up before I got the chance...I swear...whatever this is, it has nothing to do with me..."

"It's a bit convenient, isn't it..." Gregor raged. "I fucking knew you looked shifty...Grace, check his pockets. Let's find out who he really is...Fucking spies! They're everywhere..."

"Wait...just think about it..." Tommy raised both hands and pleaded his innocence.

"Why would I try to lead you here? You were coming anyway...I swear I don't know who any of those guys are... I'm just as much in the dark as you..."

"He has a point, Gregor..." Peter jumped to Tommy's defence. "This looks more like the work of Grady..."

"Wait...who's Grady?" Tommy struggled to keep up as the group turned inward to argue the toss over what to do next.

"Tie him up Grace..." Gregor barked.

"With what? Shoelaces?"

"Guys, just wait a second and think..." Peter persisted with his role as peacekeeper. "What if Tommy's telling the truth? If this is a trap, he could be caught in it with the rest of us? We need to keep our wits about us...Grady could be anywhere..."

Peter's comment sent JJ's paranoia skyrocketing, as every snap and crack of twigs underfoot took on a more sinister significance.

"Are those cars?" Zach pointed to something shimmering between the trees, beyond the litter of bodies.

"I thought you said there was only one way into this place?" Peter turned to Gregor only to find him halfway up the incline of potholed terrain where the nearest body lay sprawled.

"No, I said *we* only had one way into this place...it's all private land over that hill...a farmer's most likely..."

JJ watched as Peter hurried after him while the rest of the group remained rooted to the spot, too afraid to move.

It didn't take a genius to work out that things had gone from bad to worse ever since Gregor had rocked up at their door, and once again trust between the two groups had plummeted to an all-time low. Grady's latest killing spree was bad enough, but Gregor's slippery nature only made things worse.

It seemed any attempt to prise even a remotely straight answer from his lying lips was like trying to nail jelly to the wall, and it was clear for all to see Peter was running out of patience. As was JJ.

"I'm sorry M, but your dad is doing my head in!" He fumed.

"I mean, why can't he just be honest, for Christ's sake? Either there's one way in or there's not...nothing is ever straightforward with him and it's driving me nuts." JJ marched toward where Peter and Gregor stopped, then felt his mum tug on his sleeve.

"Don't..." she whispered, "It's not safe..."

JJ jerked free and glared at her, shaking his head.

"You're just as bad mum...you can't just show up after all the shit we've been through and expect everything to be like it was. People are dead because of you...people I cared about. How can I ever believe a word you say again?"

"Shh...he might hear..."

"Who might hear, mum? Grady? Why, cos you told him we were coming? Well, fuck him! I'm sick of this shit... we should never have left the church when we did...we were doing fine until then...now look at us! I'm going to see what's what...with my own eyes. That's the only way I can believe anything these days..." With that, he stormed off with Kane, Zach, Meridia, and Tommy in tow.

"Sorry M, I know it's not your fault about your dad...I'm just sick of all the silly little mind games he keeps playing. We ain't got time for this shit...Izzy needs us."

"I know...he's getting to me too...I think I hate him... I mean, really hate him." Meridia's gritted reply made JJ realize he may have been heavy-handed when dealing out his accusations.

"I really am sorry M...he's just getting to me, that's all...I know it's harder for you."

"Wait..." Kane chipped in before Meridia acknowledged JJ's apology.

"Before we go up there, do you really believe your dad is Retiarius? I mean, no offence, but I can't see it. All the talking in riddles and using old-school language...I thought Retiarius would be some kind of dungeons and dragons enthusiast...not a...a..."

"A gobby little knob?" Meridia finished Kane's sentence with deadpan sincerity.

"Er...well yeah. I mean, don't get me wrong, Retiarius is a bit of a knob too, but your dad is next level. I'm amazed Peter hasn't punched him."

Once again, JJ was a little miffed by Kane's timing, but the same thought crossed his mind, too. Gregor didn't seem to have it in him to be eloquent or enigmatic, although there was no disputing his knowledge of the cult's history.

"Do you think it's all another big con?" JJ asked.

"It's hard to say..." Meridia shrugged. "I don't know what to believe anymore. If you're asking me if I trust him, then the answer's no."

"So why are we all following him back to Crooked House?" Kane made a good point.

"I don't know...I just know we're on the right path...the fact that Tommy was here waiting for us proves it...doesn't it?"

They caught up with Gregor and Peter as both men finished labouring to turn the first body over. Whoever it was, he was a lump of a man, and tall, too.

"That's the guy I spoke to at the police station!" Tommy

blurted, making everyone else jump. "He was built like a brick shithouse…who the hell could've done this to him?"

The man's eyes were white like a zombie's and rolled all the way back in their sockets, while beneath his blood-streaked chin, his throat was brutally carved open and left agape, like a goofy toothless grin. Meridia and Zach were both quick to look away, while JJ and Kane both leaned in a little closer, morbidly mesmerized by the gore laid out in front of them.

JJ saw his fair share of horrors since discovering Crooked House, but now, as he soaked up the dead man's glistening wound, he came to realize this was altogether different. The sheer brutality of Grady's handiwork left him sick to his stomach, and fearing for all their lives.

"That's Richie Baker…" Gregor declared. "He's a detective…one of DI Richards' cronies…this is definitely Grady…he's almost cut the poor bastard's head off…"

Gregor surveyed the rest of the bodies scattered around them.

"They're all police…" He pointed to another. "That's Katie Rhodes…god, if you guys think I'm an arsehole, you should've seen her in action…"

JJ followed his finger to find a woman, somewhere in her mid-thirties, staring aimlessly up at the sky. Wearing a weirdly whimsical expression, her plump blue lips were upturned and ajar as if she had died daydreaming. She appeared almost serene as she lay there in a shimmering pool of her own blood. That was until JJ spotted the scarlet-speckled skull fragments and fatty brain globules on the far side of her head. Then he quickly changed his mind.

"See the tire marks in the blood there?" Gregor stepped over Katie's body and crouched down in the middle of the glossy crimson puddle.

"Their cars were moved after he killed them...the ground's too hard to leave tracks like this...see?" He pointed to a patch of parched soil that Grady's murderous rampage hadn't sullied.

"Marks like these could only have been made after her blood had softened the dirt..."

"*Squelch...*" Gregor squished a bit of Katie's brain underfoot as he straightened up, and JJ felt his stomach churn in protest.

"Oops...sorry love..." The flippancy of his admission irked JJ even more. The guy simply didn't give a damn about anyone other than himself.

"Why go to the trouble of moving the cars, only to leave the bodies out in the open?" Peter scanned the area for answers as Gregor shuffled over to the criss-cross of tread marks and peered out into the distance.

"Fuck..."

"What? What is it?" Everyone followed Gregor's gaze and froze.

The murky silhouette of an old farmhouse greeted their concern, staring down on them from its hilltop horizon like a malign watchtower.

"Grady wasn't hiding anything...he was making sure they'd be found..."

"*DONG!*"

The entire group trembled as the sonorous sound of a gong rang out from afar, rattling the birds from the trees as it rippled towards them through the roaring wind.

"Who owns that land, Gregor?" Peter snapped.

"*DONG!*"

The ominous noise reverberated again, this time reaching the rest of the group who were now congregated at the tower's cavernous mouth.

"DONG!"

Slow and methodical, it echoed once more, like a baleful alarm bell announcing their intrusion on the cult's sacred domain.

"Dammit Gregor! Who owns that land?"

"DONG!"

"I dunno...why don't you go ask whoever it is banging that gong..."

"DONG!"

Each new spine-chilling clang vibrated with a rhythmic menace, driving everyone back toward the tower in fear.

"What do we do now?" Meridia raged at her dad as they all sprinted, then stumbled downhill to join the others.

"Shit! We left our weapons in the car..." Kane cursed his own naivety as he patted his coat down. "We have to go back."

"There's no time for that now, kid. We stick to our original plan...Everyone, inside the tower now! We can lose them in the tunnels..."

"L...lose who?" Zach yelped. "There's no-one else here..."

"DONG!"

"This place will be crawling with disciples in a matter of minutes...we need to get out of sight now..."

"But what about Grady?" Tommy kept pace with Kane and JJ at the rear of the group, as they all made sure Zach and Meridia didn't trip over each other.

Even in a panic, Gregor's first thought was himself, not of his daughter. The more JJ saw of him, the more his blood boiled.

"There's no way Grady is still here. I'm even not sure we're the ones he's after anymore...Richie...Katie...they were both high-ranking disciples. The Grand Master will have his head for this…"

"*DONG!*"

"Why would he turn on his own people like that? It doesn't make any sense…what the hell's going on?" JJ was desperate for answers as they arrived at the tower's entrance.

The last thing anyone wanted was to be trapped underground with a psychotic killing machine.

"Who knows what goes on in that sicko's head…in case you haven't already noticed, he's batshit crazy. Now everyone, get inside…we don't have much time."

One by one, they piled into the jaws of the temple as the relentless ringing continued to chase them.

"*DONG!*"

Inside, the tower appeared as eerie as its unsettling exterior, but the first thing JJ noticed as he came hurtling through its entrance was the huge, stone slab table that was shunted aside to reveal a hidden stairwell. It looked as if it weighed a tonne, and he shivered at the prospect of Grady somehow moving it on his own.

The steps themselves disappeared into an inky black abyss and surrounding them, spanning the length and breadth of the room, was a pentagram carved deep into the crumbling cobbled floor. For all his smoke and mirrors, it was clear Gregor was telling the truth about this place. It hadn't been used in a very long time.

Once he was sure everyone made it inside, the next thing that struck him was the sudden change in air when he tried to catch his breath. Warm and clammy, the stench of mould lodged itself in his throat and then set about clogging up his lungs. Within seconds a chorus of coughs and splutters echoed up the tower, bouncing off the dilapidated brickwork and spiralling high above them into murky obscurity.

"C'mon guys…we need to keep going." Gregor was first to disappear down the steps, fumbling for the flashlight on his phone as he went, and as much as JJ hoped he was bravely ensuring the tunnel was safe, he knew all-too-well he was simply saving his own skin.

He watched Gregor's cronies blindly follow him below ground until all that remained was their own group, and Tommy. That was when Peter turned to face them all. He appeared unnaturally calm, given they now found themselves caught between a rock and a hard place. Over JJ's shoulder, beyond the tower's entrance, the cult's chilling alarm bell either stopped or was swallowed up by the oppressive atmosphere within, as now all he heard was the sound of Peter's voice.

"I can't see we have any other choice but to follow Gregor down those stairs… Whatever might be waiting for us down there, I know we'll find our way through it. I truly believe that. So, if you can't trust Gregor, then trust me… Now let's get going. Izzy needs us…"

Kane stepped up first, flashlight at the ready, and led Zach to the top of the stairs behind him.

"I'll go first and check it's safe. Peter, you make sure everyone else gets down after me."

Surprised by Kane's selfless reaction, JJ felt a pang of pride in his throat and suddenly teared up. Before JJ had a chance to echo his bravery, Tommy stepped forward and volunteered to escort him and Meridia down.

"You two follow me. That way, Peter can cover our backs…"

Tommy didn't have a clue where they were headed, but he rose to the challenge, like it was the easiest thing in the world. How JJ wished his mum and Gregor were more like that, instead of only thinking of themselves. As he followed Tommy towards the stairwell, he felt Meridia grab his coat tail.

"What is it?" he asked, worried if he should call down to Kane and stop him.

"This is the place..." she whispered, glancing up at the rafters. "This is the place I saw in St Peter's...the place they murdered Beth...and me."

Her words felt like an ice-cold slushy being poured straight down the back of his jumper, and he almost lost his footing as he squirmed.

"Hurry...I think I hear someone coming..." Over his shoulder, Peter nudged them along until, one by one, they descended into the belly of the beast.

54

THE NARROW SPIRAL STAIRCASE WAS STEEP AND slippery, bullying Peter into a cumbrous stoop as he made his descent. With each beleaguered step, he sensed gravity dragging him forward, threatening to topple him at any moment and wipe out everyone below like a 190lb bowling ball.

Built entirely from blue-grey limestone, its rugged walls scraped against his shoulders as he struggled to maintain balance, until finally, he reached the bottom. Opening out into a cobbled rotunda, a dozen identical stone archways leading to nothing but darkness in every direction greeted him.

The air was musty and there were no lights to lean on aside from the ethereal glow from those carrying phones, but perhaps more worryingly, there was also no sign of Gregor or his crew.

"I knew it!" JJ bleated. "Where are they?"

Peter stepped into the centre of the circle they formed and gestured for everyone to be quiet. The tunnel was eerily still, as if they travelled a hundred miles below ground, and all Peter heard was a dissonance of laboured breathing as they all came to terms with the warm muggy atmosphere now smothering them.

"C'mon then!"

They all jumped in unison as Gregor poked his head out of the pitch-black archway behind Peter and beckoned them all inside.

"I know you love to talk, pal, but there's no time for speeches now...we need to get moving." Peter grit his teeth and rose above the irony of Gregor's taunt as he ushered everyone through the murky doorway after him.

A few yards down the passageway, they rejoined the others, who anxiously huddled around the flashlight on Grace's phone. Thankfully, the ceiling was higher in this section, allowing Peter to straighten his creaking back before surveying their surroundings in more detail. The misty-white haze of Grace's flashlight rippled along the grey-bricked walls, illuminating every crack and crevice on its way to being swallowed by the inky abyss awaiting them.

As the light gently wavered in her trembling hand, Peter caught the occasional glimpse of Alice and wondered why she chose the company of Dr Foster over her only son. Despite her initial plea for forgiveness, she was quick to concede to JJ's reservations, and he couldn't help but feel there was more going on behind her stoic expression than she was letting on.

Beside her, Nadia was busy flapping at phantom spiders and their webs, as she did her utmost to contain her nerves. Out of all the people affiliated with Gregor, she seemed the most equitable, never allowing herself to get dragged into the bickering plaguing them of late.

Looking at both women side-by-side, it was difficult to believe they once shared an occupation. Nadia wore her kindness and compassion like a badge of honour, whereas Alice seemed better suited to playing professional poker. Perhaps it was a skill she cultivated during all her years craftily facilitating the end of the world.

"Did anyone see you come down here?" Gregor snapped, snatching Peter away from his thoughts.

"No. I thought I heard someone approaching in the distance, but we didn't wait around to find out."

"Ok...ok..." Gregor scrutinized both groups before continuing.

"The bodies up there should keep them busy for a bit and buy us some time...but we need to rethink our plan."

"Your plan, you mean..." Peter was quick to make the distinction.

"I think we need to split up..."

"You're joking, right?" Kane couldn't contain himself. "That's gotta be the dumbest thing you've said since you got here...and I hate to break it to you mate, you've already said some pretty dumb things..."

"Who the fu..." Gregor slapped a hand over his mouth to catch his anger, then rubbed it into his beard.

"The last thing we do now is split up. Any idiot knows that..." Kane continued to ride his luck. "We need to stick together...now more than ever. Especially if Grady's down here with us."

"He's right." Meridia leapt to Kane's defence before her dad could protest. "Besides, where else are we going to go now? We can't go back to the cars. It's too dangerous."

"Well princess, if you let me finish," Gregor glared at Kane as if the comment was intended for him.

"I was going to send you guys down a separate tunnel that took you somewhere safe. I'm not an idiot...I've seen my fair share of Michael Voorhees movies..." Kane and JJ both slouched in defeat. "Relax guys, I'm kidding..."

"We still don't know what Grady's endgame is..." Dr Foster broke away from Grace and the others to enter the discussion.

Peter knew he fancied himself as a strategist, so decided to hear him out while he gathered his own thoughts. Things were getting thick pretty fast, and aside from Gregor and perhaps Alice, none of them knew the first thing about any of the tunnels.

"We still don't know if he's cleared a path for us on purpose to reel us in, or it just so happens we've wandered into the middle of some personal vendetta. I mean, from what I've heard about him, he's not the most stable guy in the world, so who's to say he hasn't flipped his lid and gone rogue? There must be a reason he left the bunker when he did, and you can't tell me he knew this would be our play? He's a psycho, not a psychic, right?"

"What about the message he left us..." Peter knew he had put his foot in it the second the words left his lips.

"Message? What message?"

"He left me a note...back at the bunker." Gregor stepped in to diffuse the looming inquisition. "Nothing I didn't already know...but it implied he was headed to Crooked House next."

"So why come this way? Why not walk in through the front door? And why kill all those guys up top? I think Gregor's right and we get these kids to safety...they never signed up for this." The doctor had a point.

Perhaps the bloodbath above ground was the biggest sign so far that Grady was following his own agenda. Peter gazed at the youthful faces surrounding him, including their latest addition, and wasn't willing to gamble their lives away on a hunch.

Maybe Gregor was right to suggest splitting up after all. Surely there were some exceptions to the rule. Before he got the chance to air his thoughts on the matter, Kane piped up again and put everyone in their place.

"Look guys, I'm gonna spell it out to you all now. There are very specific rules we all need to follow if we wanna make it out of this alive..." He let out a deep sigh of frustration and then got to lecturing them all.

"These are all non-negotiable by the way...some of these you'll know already, but some only come into play when dealing with a slasher...and that's clearly what we're dealing with now...Grady isn't a witch or an evil spirit, he's a straight up slasher. Right, so still at number one is *'don't split up'*. Anyone who wanders off on their own should say their last goodbyes and make peace with never coming back. It's fundamental to every single horror movie ever made, no matter the sub-genre. Tell me one time everyone split up in a horror movie and they all made it to the final credits..." Kane looked at the blank faces around him.

"Exactly. Now, number two is linked to number one... *'never investigate weird noises'*. If you hear something weird, it's probably gonna be the thing that kills you, so get as far away from it as possible and don't look back. I don't care what you think it is... if it's not the killer, it's a distraction, so one way or another, it will end up getting you killed. That brings us nicely to number three. Never say *'I'll be right back'*. If you follow rules one and two, you should never need to say it anyway, but I'm telling you, nothing invites a killer to come and cut your throat like those four little words..."

"We don't have time for this...we're not in a movie, kid.

This is real life..." Peter gestured for Gregor to shut up and let Kane finish.

"Thanks. That leads me to number four, which is 'don't be a dick'. The dick always dies...period. It doesn't matter how funny or how smart the dick thinks he is, the killer always gets him." Meridia snickered over Kane's shoulder before he moved on to the next rule.

"Number five... 'always assume the killer is still alive'. I don't care if he's been stabbed twenty times and set on fire. The killer will always...always come back. Think of it like double tap multiplied by a hundred...Now I've been thinking about this one for a while and given this is England and none of us have guns...I'm thinking decapitation. It's the only way to be absolutely sure. I hope that dagger you've got is sharp, by the way...we might need to use it." Kane took a beat, lost in thought, and then concluded his crash course in survival.

"Last but not least, always listen to the kids. How many horror movies have you watched and then said to yourself at the end, if only they listened to the kid at the beginning? Let's not turn this into that kind of movie, ok? No-one wants to spend the afterlife hearing 'I told you so' for all eternity. The important thing to remember is these rules all come from somewhere...they're not just gimmicks to sell popcorn, they come from hundreds of years' worth of cautionary tales and urban legends that were originally meant to keep people safe. The rest of the slasher-specific rules aren't all that relevant to us right now. Don't watch a horror movie if you're in one...always keep your pants on...don't answer the phone..."

"Ok, ok...I get the point." Gregor relented with a wry smile.

"Well, I guess that means we're all going to Crooked

House in that case...but when we get there, you guys aren't going inside. I don't care about your golden rules...that's my non-negotiable. There's too many of us to all go steaming in at once...there's gotta be a special concession in your rules relating to rescue missions...and besides, I only packed three hoods..."

Peter noticed JJ give Kane a congratulatory nudge and watched as their little impromptu celebration spread to Meridia and Zach. What felt like a win to them sent an icy shiver scampering up Peter's spine.

Was his own unwavering belief in this group of rag-tag children still justified, or were they all about to march blindly to their deaths?

Glancing back towards the tunnel's entrance, he wondered how many of those alternate pathways might lead them out of harm's way, or better still, out of Cold Christmas altogether.

"We have to go..." He felt Meridia tap him on the back, and when he turned, the others had already disappeared halfway down the tunnel, carried away on a wave of jubilation following their small victory.

As they both scampered down the dingy passageway to catch up with them, all of Peter's doubts about Gregor came rushing back to the forefront of his mind.

Was he really a wannabe saviour, looking to make amends, or the pied piper leading them all straight to hell?

55

"ALL WE HAVE TO DO IS KEEP GOING IN A STRAIGHT line until we reach the next junction." Gregor's husky whisper rattled down the dank and dingy tunnel as Peter weaved his way through the group to join him.

Having started their journey as a tightly knit mob, glued together by fear, they had since unravelled a little and he could now hear the inaudible mutterings of secret conversations as they settled back into their silos. Still thankful he could walk upright, Peter followed the ghostly sprinkling of muted phone lights amongst the trail of gossiping silhouettes, checking in with each of the kids as he passed them by.

Tommy and Grace volunteered to relieve him from his role of bringing up the rear, and as he handed over the responsibility to them, he had a niggling feeling Kane forgot to mention one of his all-important rules.

He found Gregor walking side-by-side with Alice at the head of the human snake, and they instantly dropped their conversation the moment Peter got within earshot. Again, he couldn't fathom why Alice wasn't using this opportunity to build bridges with her son, particularly given what was now at stake.

For all they knew, Grady could be lurking around any corner, and having left the bunker in a hurry, they weren't exactly teeming with weapons to defend themselves. The light bounced off Gregor's counterfeit dagger, highlighting the curious cyphers etched into its blade, and Peter wondered how much good it would do them in a skirmish.

It resembled a sword in the diminutive Scotsman's hand. Too long and cumbersome for close quarters combat in an already cramped tunnel which now seemed as if it was only getting narrower.

"So, what's the plan?" Dr Foster snuck up behind them, giving everyone a start.

He hadn't quite got to grips with the subtlety needed for stealth, and his booming voice raced ahead of them all.

"Sorry…" He corrected himself and then tried again.

"Grace gave me this before she moved to the back…said you might want it. What is it?" He waved the black plastic box under Peter's nose so Gregor could see.

"It's a bomb." Peter felt a sudden rush of panic as Dr Foster's hand seized up and started trembling. "I'm joking. They're walkie talkies…"

"What did Kane literally just say about being a dick?" Peter shook his head in despair.

"It's a coping mechanism…" Gregor shrugged, then continued. "Although speaking of Kane, we should probably check if these violate his 'don't answer the phone' rule…psh…"

"What do we need them for? Aren't walkie talkies a little loud for where we're going?"

"They're an insurance policy…in case anything goes wrong." Gregor replied cryptically.

"The tunnel runs on a slight incline, so isn't as deep by the time we get to the house. I've already set these to a low frequency, and a low volume, which means they should still work down here over short distances. Open the box will you..."

The doctor obliged and after fumbling to find the latch in the gloom, eventually unveiled two black walkie talkies snuggly packed in grey moulded foam.

"One is for Alice, and the other one's for you Marcus..." Gregor came to a slow stop, dropped his duffle bag to the ground, and then turned to face everyone.

"For me?" Dr Foster handed one handset to Alice as instructed, then looked blankly at Peter.

"Yep. We need a lookout, and like I said, I only brought three hoods." Gregor craned his neck around the broad-shouldered doctor and whispered.

"This is the end of the road guys," then allowed the rest of the stragglers to catch up.

"But that's one each for you, me and Peter, right?" Dr Foster was confused about his role in Gregor's plan.

"Nope. There's been a slight change of plan." Alice took her handset and drifted into the shadows at the back of the crowd.

"Alice is going to wait here with Grace, Nadia, and the kids. Crooked House is only a couple hundred yards away now, so this is where their journey ends. A deal's a deal..." He glanced at Kane, then Tommy, who was standing over his shoulder.

"Tommy's coming with us now instead...you see, unlike my naïve schoolteacher here, I wasn't born yesterday, so I'm not about to let a stranger wait out here with Zach while I'm in there risking my life. I want Tommy where I can see him..."

This was the first time Gregor acknowledged the importance of Zach, and although it pained Peter to admit it, his reasoning was sound. They still didn't know nearly enough about Tommy, and although at face-value he appeared to be telling the truth, so far, they were relying a little too much on Meridia's instincts by allowing him to tag along.

"Fine by me," Tommy replied, unflinching. "What happens if this Grady fella turns up out here once all the men are gone? No offence ladies..."

"I can take care of myself, thank you!" Grace snapped back, forgetting to lower her voice.

"She can..." Gregor shrugged, "So can Alice and the boys, from what I've heard. Besides, if anything goes wrong, all they have to do is go back the way we came and take the first left. That'll take them towards the school. From there, they'll be able to get everything they need to get out of town."

"What about the cult? Won't they be looking for us?" Zach whispered timidly.

"That's the beauty of my plan, little man. They're all gonna be so preoccupied with the ritual that you should all be able to walk through the centre of town naked without anyone spotting you. In fact, in a way Grady's done us a massive favour killing all those cops, because now the only person they'll be looking for is him..." Gregor made it all sound like it was going to be plain sailing, and although he might have fooled everyone else with his box of tricks and sales patter, Peter knew all too well what dangers lurked inside Crooked House, and that was without the additional threat of a deranged killer on the rampage.

"What about the horsemen?" Peter challenged as Gregor started rifling through his duffle bag.

"Horsemen? They're the shadow monsters, right?" Tommy interrupted.

"Kane and the gang gave me a quick low-down on the way here..." Peter felt they were setting Tommy up to fail by letting him walk into Crooked House after only a 10-minute crash course in the occult, but there was nothing they could do about it now. Time was running out for all of them.

"That's right kid. They'll be weaker while the sun's up, but we won't have that advantage for long, which is why we need to get moving." Gregor tossed Tommy and Peter a hood each, then started slipping into his.

"If things go according to plan, then the only person you two are going to see is Izzy. The path we're taking leads us to a secret entrance beneath room 4, where Izzy is most likely being held. You two will get her out while I track down the real knife and swap it for this one..." He waved the giant dagger for everyone to see, then placed it on the ground.

"That's the tunnel I fell into...where we found the witch's bones..." Meridia beat Peter to the punch as they both realized the secret tunnel Gregor was alluding to.

"But...but the only way in there was via a ladder in the woods..." A dark pit opened in Peter's stomach, dragging his heart down and all his insides with it.

The last time he was in that tunnel, he was forced to confront a ghost from his past, his dead brother James. Peter fell at the first hurdle that day, and without the help of a priest, probably would have perished. The prospect of going back there with only Gregor and a complete stranger to rely on filled him with renewed dread.

"You obviously didn't look very hard when you were down there..." Gregor teased.

"I thought you were an investigator before you became a teacher. I guess it's true what they say about those who can't do in that case..." Peter wanted to knock the cocky little shit on his arse, and if it wasn't for Meridia being there, he might have.

"Don't get your knickers in a twist pal, it would be a pretty lousy secret door if just anyone could see it. It's in the middle of the old torture chamber leading up to the house... the handle looks like a rusty old shackle bolted to the wall. The cult loved their secret handles back in the day..."

Gregor fastened his cloak and scooped the dagger back up from the floor. Even with his hood down, the sight of him rendered everyone in the tunnel speechless.

Dark and mysterious, with his unkempt beard and deep-sunken eyes, he looked perfectly at home in the shadows beneath his long flowing robes. Tattered from the waist down, the thick, dark brown cloak looked like a modified monk's habit and stopped just short of Gregor's ankles. He resembled a lost knight of the realm as he held the dagger like a sword, and it brought back vivid memories of Peter's encounter at Chase Side.

For all he knew, it could have been Gregor chasing him and Izzy through the hospital that day. Then, when Tommy stepped beside him with his hood up, the memory was complete and Peter felt his paranoia shoot through the tunnel's roof. Was it just his imagination, or did Tommy's disguise fit him a little too well?

Perhaps it was a trick of the light, or just the medieval setting they found themselves in, but it seemed their newfound ally was just as comfortable as Gregor in his new garb. A cold sweat seeped through the creases in Peter's brow as his mind shifted into overdrive.

What if Gregor and Tommy were working together

from the start and set this whole thing up? Gregor's blatant mistrust of Tommy could all be for show. A ruse to throw everyone off their scent.

What if they were the ones pulling Grady's strings?

For all they knew, Gregor could be the Grand Master, or perhaps they both could. After all, Gregor was the last person to see Declan alive, and Tommy was first on the scene at the tower. Each had ample opportunity to have Grady do their dirty work so they could weasel their way into the group.

What if they carefully orchestrated this whole situation to deliver Zach to the doorstep of Crooked House?

Like a loose thread, the more 'what ifs' Peter pulled on, the more his faith in Gregor's plan unravelled. His crisis of confidence was further compounded when he realized his robes were ten inches too short and incapable of fooling anyone to think he was a member of the cult.

"Sorry pal..." Gregor chuckled. "You're a lot taller than you look on the back of your books..."

"Guys, this is just like Star Wars..." Zach was wide-eyed in wonder as he stepped out of his brother's shadow.

"Eh?" Peter was miffed by the comparison, but at least it shook him out of his downward spiral.

"You know...the bit where Luke and Han Solo dress up as storm troopers to rescue princess Leia..."

Peter was stunned by how similar both plans were in the cold light of day and, looking down at his ill-fitting disguise, he wondered if he was the Wookie in Gregor's half-baked scheme. In fact, if Peter had to put money on it, he would have said Zach just rumbled him.

"I guess that makes me R2D2 then..." Dr Foster completed their little sci-fi tribute act, and suddenly the prospect of Gregor being an evil genius became far less plausible.

"Ok gents...it's go-time." Gregor pulled his hood up and stepped aside to allow Peter, Tommy, and Dr Foster to shuffle past.

"You've got this guys...find Izzy and get the hell out of there..." JJ tried to galvanize them, while the rest of the group remained silent, gripped by pre-show jitters.

"Alice, if you don't hear us on the walkie within the next thirty minutes, then you know what to do..." Alice gave a solemn nod, switching her handset on in readiness, as Gregor ushered Peter and Tommy into the jaws of darkness.

56

Jonny Alman was traipsing underground for hours now, and during that time, the only thing he knew for certain was that his memory wasn't anywhere near as good as he hoped.

Exhausted and riddled with self-doubt, he reached the conclusion he was a useless idiot, just like his parents always told him. After being chased out of his original hiding place by a plague of angry rats, he decided it was probably best to keep moving and follow the tunnels to the edge of town.

He rather stupidly assumed if he just kept walking in the same direction, he would eventually reach the end of the line, but upon navigating T-junction after T-junction, he no longer knew where he was heading and hadn't come across an exit hatch in what felt like ages.

With nothing discernible to latch onto, the cult's underground network was a maze of identical doorways, propped up by manky wooden joists, and badly corroded limestone, dimly lit by a smattering of grimy, sallow bulbs that were on the verge of going kaput.

To add insult to injury, the last exit he stumbled upon had a legion of children laughing and gossiping on the other side of it, which meant he somehow wandered into the tunnel beneath the school. That meant he spent at least half his time underground, walking in one gigantic circle.

Jonny stopped for a second and leaned against a mould-infested wall to catch his breath. He was no stranger to cardio, but down here the air was thick and humid, like wading through warm treacle. His lungs ached as he doubled over and stared down at the murky reflection in the muddy puddle at his feet. At least he hoped it was mud. Anyone would have forgiven him for thinking he drifted into a sewage pipe. It was so disgusting.

"What a mess..." He gasped, shaking his head.

Despite his best efforts to stay clean, his face was covered in muck. Whether it was the incessant compulsion to wipe his sweaty forehead or the putrid air itself, Jonny became a dirt-magnet the second he stepped foot in this stinking cesspool.

Beneath his denim sherpa jacket, he was nothing more than a clammy cocktail of perspiration and humidity. Even his socks were sodden, painfully squelching in his worker boots, while his jeans were so heavy and damp their seams chafed his thighs with every stride.

Glancing to his right, he glimpsed yet another crossroads a few yards ahead and felt his legs wilt in dismay. The only thing keeping him going was Grady. Whilst trudging through the endless conveyor belt of filth, Jonny convinced himself that Grady spotted him cowering behind the old codger's car above ground. Over and over, he kept replaying the memory in his mind, and each time he did, he was sure they locked eyes.

For whatever reason, something else snatched the

psycho's attention, and he sped off in the opposite direction. But Jonny knew all too well Grady was like a sick and twisted elephant. He never forgot, and as soon as he had the chance, he would be back on the hunt for him.

"Scratch..."

Jonny bolted upright and winced as the drenched creases in his jeans clawed at the backs of his knees. Fumbling in his jacket pocket, he gripped his knife and held his breath.

The tunnels were a breeding ground for critters and vermin, but he couldn't afford to get complacent. Not now. Pressing his back against the wall again, he kept his head on a swivel, looking left and then right as if he was trying to cross a busy motorway.

"Scratch..."

The ominous sound echoed again, closer this time. Jonny was convinced it was somewhere to his left, in the direction he just came from. Rooted to the spot, the back of his neck tingled, and his shoulders tightened as a cold sweat leaked into the arms of the suffocating air. Someone or something was headed his way.

He skulked backwards, feeling his way down the jagged wall with one hand, his boot knife firmly gripped in the other.

"Scratch..."

The sound continued to pursue him along the grotty underpass, slow and steady, as Jonny tiptoed backwards towards the next junction. When he felt the wall's serrated edge scrape against his palm, he waited with bated breath, eyes fixed on the section of tunnel he'd left behind.

Watching and waiting, the blade trembled uncontrollably in his hand, just as it did at the hospital. He wasn't cut out to be a killer. He wasn't that day, and he wasn't now.

"*Scratch...scuff...*"

Jonny's heart leapt into his mouth as the sound crackled closer. A tall dark shadow bounced along the bumpy ground, then catapulted itself onto the wall. Jonny almost dropped his knife from fright.

If his silent stalker was Grady, then he knew he was as good as dead. Too weak and weary to put up a fight, his only chance of survival was to hide and take him by surprise.

The tunnel to his right was dark, which meant he might be close to an exit of some sort. Where to, though, he did not know. As Jonny slinked around the corner and took cover in the shadows, he grasped the knife in both hands and pulled its handle to his chest.

If, by some minor miracle, he was lucky enough to land the first blow, then he needed to make it count.

<h1 style="text-align:center">57</h1>

"How long has it been now?" Zach breathed as the group huddled anxiously in the suffocating shadows.

"About two minutes since the last time you asked…" Kane whispered back. "I doubt they've even reached Crooked House yet…"

Since Peter and the others departed, Grace had steered them all towards the wall, where they formed a human shield around Zach and Meridia. From there, they could keep a watchful eye on every direction of the dungeonesque tunnel, should Grady or anyone else decide to make a surprise appearance.

Arms locked together with Meridia, Zach felt every lump and bump of the damp limestone wall poking at his back, and it was all he could do to remain still as they waited in silence for news of Izzy's rescue attempt. The only light keeping them company came courtesy of Alice, who was standing on the other side of him. The dim green digital display of her walkie talkie bled into the gloom, just enough to give the familiar silhouettes gathered around him an eerie emerald glow.

"It's going to be ok," Meridia whispered in his ear, but once again, Zach could not tell if it was her gift speaking or just wishful thinking.

Although he was spared the sight of Declan's body, the bloody massacre in the old church grounds still haunted him every time he closed his eyes and knew their chances of surviving a similar attack were close to zero. If Grady could slay two cars-full of police officers single-handedly, then what hope would a couple of nurses, a personal trainer and a bunch of kids have of escaping him?

"M's right..." JJ added. "Peter's never let us down before...He's gonna find Izzy and bring her home."

The mere mention of 'home' stung the back of Zach's throat as a wave of sorrow swept away what remained of his composure and chased a solitary tear out of the corner of his eye. Trying his best to cuff it without Meridia noticing, he wondered if he and Kane would ever find another place they would call home. Now their parents were gone.

Of course, that all hinged on them making it through the rest of the day. As much as he wanted to share in JJ and Meridia's optimism, he couldn't help but fear the worst with a relentless, cold-blooded killer on the prowl, and the notorious demon of Cold Christmas now looming on the horizon.

Zach desperately needed to hear from Peter, even if it was only to tell them they reached the entrance to Crooked House. With each passing minute, he felt the icy grip of despair tightening around his heart and squeezing out every drop of hope he had left.

"*Chink...*" A dry, crackling staccato rattled through the darkness as a stone ricochetted across the ground. Struck by an unseen force hiding somewhere in the shadows.

"Wh...what was that?" Zach trembled, jerking Meridia's arm closer.

"Shh..." Grace took a measured step away from the pack as they all tried to place where the sound came from.

Lurking a few yards ahead of her, the pitch-black void that swallowed Peter and the others just minutes earlier seemed sentient, like a predator silently watching and waiting to devour anyone who strayed too close.

Grace took another muted step nearer, drifting away from the protection of the light and pulling Kane with her like a magnet. A gap emerged in the group as, one by one, they floated towards the darkness like moths to the flame, leaving Zach and Meridia exposed. Still, the ominous silence hung in the air, like the moment before a scream, taut and unnerving as if the tunnel took a breath it couldn't let go of.

Zach instinctively shuffled toward his brother as he threatened to wander beyond the protection of the ethereal green afterglow.

"Ow..." His muffled yelp wriggled free into the corridor as Alice snatched him back before he could go anywhere. Her nails pinching and twisting his skin as they dug into the underarm of his jacket.

"I think it came from this direction..." Grace whispered, as if to flush whoever it was out of hiding, but Zach's gut was telling him they should run. Run as far away from the all-consuming darkness as their legs would carry them.

JJ reached for his phone and directed its flashlight to the ground. The sudden shaft of dazzling white made everyone flinch before Grace backed away from the impenetrable black chasm so he could light it up. Still, the shadows held their ground, refusing to stir, as the silence sharpened, taking on an edge that was charged with menace.

To Zach's right, Nadia joined the fanning crowd of gritted teeth and clenched fists as they all waited for JJ's trembling light to brave the darkness. Cobble by cobble it crept along the ground like a sniffer dog, seeking out danger, until eventually it leapt up into the hollow and banished the blackness to reveal an empty passageway, identical to the one they were standing in. There was no sign of Grady, or anyone else, for that matter.

"Maybe it was a rat..." Kane muttered, as the entire group exhaled and their shoulders fell in unison.

"*FIZZ...CRACKLE!*"

The walkie talkie came to life in Alice's hand, setting off a domino effect of terror as everyone jerked like marionettes yanked by an invisible string. The raucous sizzle of static clattered against the walls on its way up and down the tunnel as Alice fumbled to quieten it.

"*Fizz...help...crackle...*" Dr Foster's voice sailed in and out of coherence on a sea of electrostatic, while another ominous shadow of silence crept across the group.

"*Someone...fizz...something took us by surprise...crack... I...I can't find the others...fizz...argh...*"

"Marcus? Marcus, what's going on?" Alice tried to reach him, but it was too late, the signal was dead.

"Stay here..." Kane snatched JJ's phone and darted into the tunnel.

"If I'm not back in five, then stick to the plan and get out of here. I heard something up ahead...I think they're still close..."

"Kane! No..." Zach cried out as his brother slipped through the outstretched hand of Grace and ran off in pursuit of Peter.

"Stay put spud, I'm just going to take a quick look... I'll be right back...I promise!"

<h1 style="text-align:center">58</h1>

Despite intending the pun, Kane forgot he broke another golden rule by racing off to investigate a strange noise.

He was so caught up in the moment it didn't even occur to him and the sudden realization of his mistake connected with the force of a sledgehammer, stopping him dead in his tracks. All at once, he sensed the threat of Grady pressing down on his shoulders, driving him into the ground and turning his legs to lead.

Behind him, he heard the frantic whispers of those he held dear, begging him to come back, but he was certain he caught the brittle crack of plastic hitting the ground somewhere in the gloom ahead and needed to be sure. If Peter was in trouble, he needed to at least try. They owed him that much.

Slowly sweeping the empty tunnel with JJ's flashlight, Kane resumed his advance with a healthy dollop of trepidation and an extra sprinkling of sweat on his brow. Along with Grady's suffocating presence, the air congealed as the acrid smell of limestone amalgamated with the earthy stench of wet soil.

The rank combination stuck in the pit of Kane's throat, making it all the more difficult to breathe as he continued to press on in search of Peter and the others. With each hesitant step forward, he sensed the baleful darkness at his back, patiently stalking him, having swallowed every scrap of worry his friends breathed into its bowels.

"What the…" Kane's light struck a coarse, water-stained wall in front of him as he reached a T-junction.

He was sure Gregor told everyone it was a straight line to Crooked House. Was everything that came out of that insufferable prick's mouth a twist on the truth?

It didn't take Kane long to decide which way to walk, as his flashlight skimmed the edge of a walkie talkie cast to the ground a few yards to his right. Fixating on the lifeless lump of chipped black plastic, it had all the hallmarks of a trap designed to lure him in. He needed to stay vigilant, but there was no obvious place for a killer to be hiding ahead of him.

As he surveyed the surrounding area with his light, he glimpsed a spot of crimson spattered on the ground. Then he found another, and another. The smattering of blood disappeared into the gloom beyond the reach of his beam, and although it didn't look like much, it was enough to send a wave of ice-cold prickles rushing up his spine.

"Peter?" He whispered "Dr Foster?"

Bandying his light from left to right, Kane searched for any sign of life as he edged ever closer to the scene of the crime, but the darkness seemed impenetrable. Deflecting his prying white beam as it clung onto whatever sinister secrets it held within.

Marooned and alone in a vacuum of inky nothingness,

Kane shuffled to the abandoned handheld radio. Its corner shattered on impact with the unforgiving ground, peppering the surrounding cobbles with jagged black plastic teeth. Luckily, the damage appeared superficial.

Kane slowly crouched down to pick it up. If he could get it working, he could at least check in with Alice and let her know he was ok. He didn't even make it halfway down on one knee when he was grabbed from behind.

A vice-like arm coiled around his chest, pinning his elbows to his sides, while a clammy hand clamped his mouth shut.

In a matter of seconds, Kane was hoisted into the air, then dragged, writhing and kicking, into the shadows.

59

"Shh...be quiet...it's me, Peter." He felt Kane's body go limp and cease struggling as he tried to nod his head.

Lowering him to the ground, Peter continued before removing his gag.

"There's someone else down here with us so you've got to be quiet, ok?" Again, he felt Kane nod against the palm of his hand and slowly released his grip. "You shouldn't be here...where are the others?"

"I...I left them where they were..." Kane gasped as he fought to catch his breath. His legs were still floppy like boiled spaghetti fresh from the pot.

"We heard the radio...and...and I thought I heard something drop...I thought it might be the radio, and it was...see..." Kane shone his flashlight down on the broken walkie talkie. "What happened?"

"I don't know..." Peter murmured. "Everything was fine. Marcus was behind us, watching our backs, and then something spooked him. He barged past me and knocked my phone out of my hand...we were using it as a light...I heard it smash on the ground. Then everything went dark. The next thing I heard was a scream followed by a thud... then everyone scattered in different directions. I'm not sure if I just got turned around in all the confusion or if they ran off and left me, but I can't find any of them...I was trying to follow the path when I saw your light appear behind me. That means whoever jumped Dr Foster might have seen it too. What the hell were you thinking, running in here after us?" While Peter waited for an explanation, he slipped out of his ill-fitting cloak and tossed it to the ground.

Fat lot of good it would do him now.

"Foster called on the radio asking for help, then the signal went dead. I heard him and it seemed as though the radio had a lag or something, so figured you couldn't have got far...so I came to look. I think the radio might still work, but there's blood on the ground, see..." Kane traced the blood spatter for Peter to see.

It appeared fresh as it glistened beneath the flashlight's glare, but there was nowhere near enough to be fatal, and no sign of Dr Foster. Although all signs pointed to Grady being responsible, Peter couldn't afford to rule out a potential double cross given Gregor's dubious history. He felt a fool for dragging everyone down here, but what else could he have done?

He was backed into a series of corners ever since news broke of Izzy's abduction and, in the process, became far too dependent on a bunch of relative strangers. Was this all just a series of unfortunate events, or something more devious that was meticulously planned from the get-go?

There was no way to know for sure, and that was largely because of Gregor's mercurial behaviour. The man was a walking contradiction.

Kane scooped up the walkie talkie then fumbled around

for its push-to-talk button. "Wait...Grady could be anywhere down here..." Peter blurted.

"I told the others if I wasn't back in five, they had to leave...I need to check in and tell them what's happened."

Peter conceded, half thinking the best course of action would be to send them all packing immediately. There was still a strong chance Marcus, Gregor, and Tommy had all fallen victim to Grady by now.

"You should go! Get back to them and lead them all out of here...it's not safe for any of you to be down here anymore...it never was."

"What about you?"

"I'll carry on looking for Izzy, then find another way out...I made a promise, and I intend to keep it."

"No way I'm leaving you down here on your own. I'm coming with you..."

"*Fizz...crackle...*"

Kane pushed the button on the radio and whispered into its mic.

"Hello...Alice? Can anyone hear me?"

"*Fizz...crackle...yes, we're here. What's going on?*"

Alice's voice sounded even more robotic on the walkie talkie and another alarm bell sounded in the back of Peter's mind. What if she was in on it all, too?

"I've found Peter, but we can't find the others...he thinks they all ran." Kane gave Peter a sideways glance before continuing.

"I'm gonna help him find the entrance to Crooked House...I don't think we're far and there's still a chance some of the others made it there already..."

"Wait, that's not what we agreed..." Peter's protest was drowned out by Alice.

"Crackle...ok, but you heard what Gregor said...fizz...if you're not back in 20 minutes we're leaving you..."

There was little doubt in Peter's mind that Alice would follow through on her promise; she was one cold fish.

"Is she always like that?" He asked, as Kane confirmed her terms and tucked the radio away in his back pocket. JJ always radiated warmth and optimism, yet his mum couldn't be more opposite.

"No." Kane answered without hesitation. "She's been acting weird since she got here...that's why I made sure JJ stayed back with the others. I don't trust her...and neither does he..."

Peter felt a pang of apprehension at Kane's response and immediately became fearful for JJ, Zach, and Meridia. Perhaps they were better off facing Crooked House together. Swallowing his misgivings, he rekindled the urgency of their quest.

"Let's get Izzy and get the hell out of here in that case..." Peter declared, guiding Kane down the other side of the T-junction.

"If Gregor was telling the truth, then this is the way to Crooked House. We can worry about the demon once we've regrouped..."

Kane responded, lighting up their way as they readied themselves to face the darkness once more.

"Keep your eyes peeled, Kane, and if Grady shows himself, I want you to run back the way you came and get everyone out of this godforsaken place. I'll try to buy you as much time as I can."

60

Frozen like a statue in the shadows, with his shoulders hunched around his ears, Alman clung to his knife as if his life depended on it. He sensed every taut muscle in his trembling body silently screaming at him to run, but whenever he plucked up enough courage to make a break for it, another ominous echo rippled down the tunnel in his direction.

Having waited out of sight for what felt like an eternity, the scuffs and cracks of shuffling feet turned to whispers and then screams as a sporadic stream of intruders raced past his hiding spot, poisoning the stuffy air with their panic and pricking his paranoia.

The first set of footsteps crept right by him as if they were on a covert mission, but a few moments later, things descended into chaos and the entire group scattered to the four winds. Jonny was amazed his presence went unnoticed. In all the confusion, the other party's light went out, leaving them floundering in the dark. Grady had to be the root cause, as only he could make a grown man scream.

Why did he viciously turn on his own people? Were

there really that many traitors in the Children of the Shadows? Whatever was going on, he knew Grady wasn't the only one still roaming the tunnels, but for now, at least all seemed calm and quiet.

Jonny winced at the sweet release of all the tension trapped between his shoulder blades and shakily lowered his knife. Since the commotion, he couldn't be sure exactly which direction the headless chickens fled. He knew Grady would catch them in the end. He always did.

Tired of idly waiting around for the psycho to murder him too, Jonny decided it was time he stepped back out into the open. Although he was risking detection, he needed to stick to his original plan if he was ever to find a way out of this infernal maze. Besides, with any luck, Grady spilled enough blood for one day and had already moved on.

The tunnels were vast, spanning the better part of three villages, so there was no way he could cover all that ground in a single afternoon. Deadly as he was, he was still only one man.

Jonny was about to make a break for it when he noticed movement up ahead. A series of prickly shadows scrambled along the ground like spiders as the hazy glow of a flashlight struck a smattering of loose shingles. Someone was coming.

"Scuff..."

The all-too-familiar sound of shoes scraping against the cobbles sent Jonny's pulse pounding again and his body went rigid from the jaw down. Clenching his eyes, he tried to home in on the footsteps to fathom how many he was up against, but try as he might, his thoughts raced out of sight. Chased away by images of Grady and a pack of hungry wolves in hoods, howling for his blood.

Whoever it was approaching, they were a threat to his survival. Only the disciples knew about the tunnels, and they were sure to turn him over to Grady the second they found him cowering in the shadows. Jonny tightened his grip on the blade's handle and pulled it close to chest height. It was time to make a stand.

"Strike first, make it count...strike first, make it count..." He repeated the mantra over and over in his butterfly brain as the footsteps drew nearer and the light grew brighter. "Strike first, make it count...strike first, make it count..."

"*Argh!*"

Jonny thrust his knife blindly into the light and felt the blade puncture fabric, then flesh. The handle slipped through his clammy palms as his unsuspecting victim flopped backwards onto the ground with the blade pushed down to its hilt.

Caught in a daze, Jonny stared at the crumpled heap of quilted nylon and jersey joggers to find a boy no older than his kid brother staring up at him, wide-eyed in shock. His heart shattered into a thousand pieces as the boy writhed and retched at his feet. Coughing and spluttering whilst frantically fumbling to pull the knife out of his ribs.

"Oh god...what have I done..." Time froze as the boy's anguished cries dissolved into a dull whistling hum, like the ringing silence left hanging in the air by a bomb's final roar.

In the space of a single second, every poor decision Jonny ever made in his miserable life suddenly caught up with him. All the squandered opportunities and second chances his parents gave him over the years that he churlishly tossed back in their faces.

All the lies and feeble excuses he used to convince himself that he was the victim, that he was the one the universe owed something to, when the sad and simple truth was clear for all to see. He was nothing but a worthless piece of shit, rotten to his core. A lazy, good-for-nothing scumbag, who now crossed a line there was no coming back from. A line which culminated with a frightened teenager fighting for his life as he lay in the dirt, covered in blood.

"*Crack!*"

The muffled ringing in his ears intensified to a high-pitched shrill as a thumping blow landed out of nowhere on his left temple and sent him clattering into the wall. Higginsworth again! What the hell was he doing down here?

Jonny's knees buckled and his vision blurred as the towering history teacher split into two ghostly silhouettes, both winding up to throw another punch in his direction.

"I...I didn't mean...I...I'm sorry...I thought..." Staggering back along the slimy limestone wall, Jonny fought to stay on his feet, all the while trying to avoid being clocked again.

Higginsworth took a jab step toward him, and Jonny's legs wilted. Crawling on all fours, he clambered back to his feet and then awkwardly scurried away. Tears streamed down his face, clouding his double vision as he teetered on the brink of falling face-first on the floor, but all he could think of was running away, just like he always did. Leaving his mess for some other poor schmuck to clean up.

Overwhelmed by his emotions, the murky tunnel ahead coiled and corkscrewed in front of him as he battled to keep his balance, until he went crashing to the ground like a sack of spuds.

"Oof..." Jonny felt all the air abandon his lungs as he went painfully skidding along the ground on the tip of his shoulder.

Gasping to recover his breath, he rolled onto his back and stared up at the mouldy ceiling. If Higginsworth gave chase, then Jonny was about to get the beating of his life. A beating he fully deserved.

Instead of the deceptively tough history teacher, he came face-to-face with a leering monster that was plucked from his deepest, darkest nightmares. A sight so terrifying it turned his blood to ice.

"Brother Alman! I've been looking everywhere for you..."

61

"Kane!" Having chased away the thug who attacked them, Peter turned to find Kane writhing and sobbing on the ground. His face was white with shock, and he was drunk on pain as his eyes swayed languidly back and forth beneath his drooping lids.

"Hold still...I've got you..." Peter swooped down beside him, quickly freezing the second he got close to the polished walnut knife handle sticking out of Kane's ribs.

What the hell was he meant to do now?

His mind went completely blank. Fumbling for the flashlight on the ground, he tried to get a better view of where he was stabbed without touching him, but it was too difficult to make out beneath the folds of his quilted grey puffer jacket. Blood made its way through his winter layers and was now steadily seeping into the fabric, turning the shiny charcoal nylon a deep shade of mahogany.

"Talk to me Kane...you've got to keep talking..." Peter knew that much at least, and he waited on tenterhooks for Kane to open his mouth.

"It huuurts..." He slurred. His eyes remained heavy and

lethargic, rolling around in their sockets as he searched for Peter.

"I know...I know it does...but I need you to be strong, ok? I need you to be strong for me..."

"Ok..."

Kane's head flopped backwards as he closed his eyes.

"Don't close your eyes..." Peter wasn't taking any chances and gently patted Kane's pale cheeks to rouse him.

"I need to pull the knife out...Where's the walkie talkie?" Peter rummaged around on the ground but came up empty.

If he could reach Nadia, or even Alice, then one of them could at least talk him through whatever needed to be done. Peter wore many hats of late, but until now a nurse wasn't one of them.

"Kane? Kane, wake up..." He couldn't afford to take his eyes off him for a second.

"It...it's in my back pocket..." He mumbled. "I can't reach..." A ripple of pain washed over Kane's face and slowly subsided as he tried and failed to move his arm.

"Don't move...I'll have to think of something else. I can't lift you in case I do more damage. I need a moment to think..." Peter knew by the rate the blood was expanding around his wound, he needed to think quickly.

The knife appeared lodged halfway up Kane's ribs, but he couldn't know for certain without moving him. Peter racked his brain of all its anatomical knowledge, but every image he conjured from the past painted a bleak picture. The knife could have punctured any number of vital organs, so he had no idea what to do for the best. All he knew was he couldn't sit here and do nothing while Kane bled out on the cobbles.

"Take...take it out...p...please..." Kane slurred, jarring Peter from his stupor.

"Ok...ok..." He mumbled, half to himself, then hastily slipped out of his overcoat. Peter rolled it up and placed it on the ground beside Kane's head. "Can you raise your head? I can help if not..."

Kane clenched his teeth and grimaced as he lifted his head off the ground enough for Peter to slip the makeshift pillow beneath him.

"Grr..." He helplessly watched Kane wrestle to suppress another swell of pain rising from within as his body trembled beneath the mountain of layers.

He prayed to god some of those layers helped prevent the wound from being fatal, but as his flashlight grazed the sparkling beads of sweat gathering on the poor boy's ashen face, he wasn't so sure.

"Try to relax your body, Kane...just not your mind. You have to stay lucid and keep talking. I don't care what you say...say anything...er...tell me about your favourite horror movies...I want to hear your top ten." Peter was winging it now but couldn't bear to see him in so much pain.

He pulled his sweater up over his head and carefully folded it into four to make a bandage. Once he removed the blade, he needed to dress the wound with something to stem the blood until they found help, and his sweater would be plenty long enough to tie tightly around Kane's slender midriff.

"*Argh!*"

A bloodcurdling scream erupted from the inky-black depths of the tunnel ahead and clawed its way towards them. The rushing wave of rampant terror washed over them both like nails being dragged down a chalkboard and neither could contain their fright.

"Grr...sniff..." Kane winced again, doubled up in pain at the sudden jolt, as Peter shakily shone the flashlight in search of its source. It was a man's voice, that much he was certain, and his petrified cry came from the same direction Kane's attacker fled. The same direction as Crooked House.

Allowing the blanched beam to linger as long as his nerves would allow, all Peter saw was endless mud and limestone as far as his eyes could see. There were a host of places for Grady to hide up ahead as the cobbled structure surrendered to a more crudely constructed underpass resembling an old, abandoned mineshaft, with a variety of nooks and crannies on either side of its gloomy walls.

Gregor told him the tunnel would become shallower the closer they got to Crooked House, so perhaps they weren't far from where Izzy was being held. Satisfied as he could be, there was no imminent danger. Peter dragged the light back towards Kane, but the hairs on the back of his neck refused to rest.

"We need to move quickly..." he whispered. "I don't know who or what that was, but I don't want to find out while we're exposed like this."

Peter cupped his trembling fingers around the knife's handle without touching it.

"Brace yourself, this is going to hurt. Once I pull the knife is out, I'll need to patch you up quickly so try to relax your body as best you can...the less rigid you are, the less painful this is all going to be, ok?"

"Grr...just do it..." Peter sensed the growing frustration in Kane's groans and so he gripped the handle, and in one smooth motion pulled it out, whilst trying to stay true to its original trajectory so as not to enlarge the wound.

"*Argh!*"

Kane's entire body seized up like he was plugged into

the mains as he sent a spine-tingling scream of his own tearing back down the tunnel towards Crooked House. Pushing his coat to one side, Peter's heart leapt into his throat when he saw the scarlet stain beneath it rapidly expand.

"*Argh...*"

Kane writhed again, bringing his legs up to stifle the pain, but there was no time to comfort him. He was bleeding heavily.

"*Clank!*"

Peter tossed the knife behind him and quickly set to work. Hiking Kane's sweatshirt up, he found a gaping wound steadily pumping blood down the side of his torso and onto the floor like a crimson waterfall. About an inch wide, and three deep based on the length of the blade, the gash was a little further down Kane's body than Peter expected.

He hoped by some miracle it missed his spleen and lungs. While Kane continued to groan, Peter lifted his lumber off the ground with one hand and fed the dressing through with the other. He fished the radio out of Kane's back pocket and then, making sure the bulk of the bandage was where his wound was, he pulled the ends and bound them together.

"*Argh...*"

Kane flinched under the sudden pressure, kicking his legs back out as he tried to wriggle away from the searing pain, but Peter had to stop the bleeding and so he held firm. Pressing down directly on his ribs to stem the flow of blood.

"I'm sorry...sniff...I know it hurts, but I've got to stop the bleeding...or at least slow it enough to get you out of here." Applying as much weight as Kane could stand, Peter used his free hand to feel around for the radio.

The sooner he could call for help, the greater Kane's chances of survival.

"Gotcha..." Peter held the radio under the light to find its call button but couldn't see beyond the scarlet sheen of Kane's lifeblood trickling down his palm.

"Stay with me...please..." His eyes welled up at the anguished expression etched on the boy's pallid face; his life slowly ebbing away before his eyes.

This was all Peter's fault, putting his faith in a bunch of strangers. It should've been him lying on the ground, not a fifteen-year-old boy with his whole life still ahead of him.

"Click..."

Peter pressed the call button and waited for the crackle of static to tell him he had a signal before broadcasting his last gasp plea for help.

"Alice...come in...please...we need help...Kane's hurt bad. There's so much blood, I can't stop it, and I don't know what to do...Nadia? Alice? Anyone...please come in..."

He released the button and waited for a response, but all he heard were the whispering echoes of his own voice forsaking him as it scurried away down the desolate tunnel.

Peter stared at the radio, willing it to beep, but nothing happened. There was no-one coming to save them. They were on their own.

62

"What are you waiting for? Why don't you answer them?" Zach was frantic at the news of his brother, but Alice stared into the darkness, lost in a daze.

Grace and Nadia took a step toward her in unison, sharing a sideways glance of bewilderment.

"Alice? Alice...what's wrong?"

Still clasping Zach's arm, Alice tucked the walkie talkie into the pocket of her raincoat.

"Let me go! Kane needs me..." Zach tried to wriggle free, but Alice held fast and Meridia's stomach churned as though a dark storm was brewing in its depths. Something was horribly wrong.

"Mum? What are you doing? Let him go..." JJ completed the semi-circle of suspicion, closing in around her as she refused to react to Peter's SOS.

Stone-faced, she opened her mouth to speak and pulled Zach closer.

"Fate has marked your card, child..."

"And now your time is up..." Meridia blurted out the rest of the ominous sentence that haunted her dreams as

Alice pulled the knife from her pocket and held it to Zach's throat.

The entire group froze in a moment of panic, and Meridia sensed someone walk over her grave as she realized her fatal mistake. Damn her infuriating gift. How could she have been so blind?

All this time, she thought the demon would be the one to utter those words, only to find it was a monster of a different kind. One they welcomed in with open arms.

"What are you doing?!" JJ's exasperation reverberated around them as Zach squirmed in Alice's arms, doing all he could to shrink away from the blade prickling his windpipe.

"This is the only way..." Alice blustered. "If the boy dies now, then the prophecy can never be fulfilled...you all heard the radio. They never even made it to Crooked House. It's over...we've lost."

JJ and Grace inched closer, but Alice was quick to shut them down. "Stay where you are!"

"Ow..."

She pressed the knife tighter to Zach's throat and nicked his skin. A thin trail of blood snaked down his neck and disappeared into the shadows beneath his sweater. The callous show of intent was enough to stop everyone in their tracks and force them into submission.

"Please, mum...don't do this...I'm begging you." JJ's voice fractured as he pleaded for Zach's life.

"Don't you see? I'm doing this for you...I'm trying to save all of you...one boy's life to prevent the death of millions. We don't have a choice anymore..." For the first time since revealing her hand, Alice showed some semblance of emotion. Her bottom lip quivering as she continued to lament.

"All I ever wanted was you...sniff...the lengths I went

to...just to hold you in my arms...you have no idea. This is the only way I can protect you...I have no choice..."

"There's always a choice..." Meridia snapped defiantly.

She had enough of listening to morally bankrupt adults trying to justify their short-sighted, selfish decisions as being noble. Everyone attached to the cult was rotten to their core, her dad included, and the fact he and Alice colluded to murder her best friend, an innocent in all this, only proved what she knew all along. They were better off without them.

"What do you think we've been doing this entire time? The first time I found out I had this bloody curse, I stopped the prophecy...it was meant to happen that same day. I saw it! I saw all of it..." She glanced at JJ and felt her temper tighten its grip on the wheel.

"I watched your son die...along with everyone I care about...but I stopped it. Not you with all your spying...or my dad with all his bullshit. *I* stopped it. Then, when all the monsters in that evil house tried again and sent a witch after us, we stopped her too..."

"M?" JJ tried to calm her, but Meridia was having none of it.

"I'm sorry, JJ, but I'm sick of this shit." She glared at Alice.

"We even stopped Valerie. The biggest killer since smallpox...whatever that is...I even stopped my own mother..." Meridia teetered on the brink of tears, but dug in deep and continued through gritted teeth.

"I saw her...the real her, back in the bunker. She was insane. There was nothing I could do to save her. I know that now... But I can save us. I can stop the demon. I know I can...that's why I'm here..." Zach was sobbing now as he cowered in Alice's grip, and amid her fiery outburst, all Meridia wanted to do was hug him.

The sudden downpour of affection reminded her that beneath all that rage she remained so afraid of, something soft and enduring was keeping her from losing herself: love.

"I refuse to let another person I love die...so let Zach go now...let us end this once and for all...please."

Meridia held her breath as the blade trembled in Alice's hand. Perhaps, for the first time, she saw a glimmer of hope they could avert the latest in a long line of tragedies that dogged them ever since the day began.

"Please, mum..." JJ doubled down on Meridia's appeal and risked shuffling closer. "Put down the knife. You're not a killer. You don't have to do this..."

Alice's hand wavered a little as JJ took another step closer, giving Zach breathing space between him and the knife's razor-sharp edge. But even Meridia, with her all-seeing eye, couldn't have predicted what followed. It all happened so fast.

"I'm sorry...I can't..." Alice wept. "Please forgive me..."

As her knuckles whitened around the knife handle, Zach took his chance and drove his heel down hard on the tip of her toes. Seizing his opportunity, JJ closed in and grappled for control of the knife. Frantically writhing and wriggling out of his coat, Zach broke free and lunged out of harm's way, leaving Alice clinging onto an empty sleeve.

"Please...stop..." JJ begged, as they cancelled each other out in the scuffle and ended up driving the blade down between them.

Alice used the wall at her back to launch forward and barge JJ out of the way, but her foot got tangled up with the hood of Zach's jacket and both mother and son clattered to the ground with a sickening thud.

"Oof..." JJ took the full brunt of the fall, trapped at the bottom of the tussle.

His head bounced back off the stony ground with a sickening '*crack*', and his body instantly fell limp. The force of the impact plunged the tunnel into an ominous silence as time turned to quicksand, dragging every second into a sticky, suffocating slowness.

Meridia's stomach turned to lead as she watched Alice's eyes widen with horror, and then she saw why. A dark, crimson lake seeped outward beneath them, creeping across the cobbles and staining everything in its path like ink spilled on paper.

Within a matter of seconds, JJ was swimming in a shimmering pool of blood as he lay lifeless on the ground.

63

Despite the tunnel's natural humidity, an icy numbness seeped its way into Kane's bones as he hobbled along the dingy passageway, using his mentor as a crutch.

Although Peter did his best to patch him up, his makeshift dressing was already drenched, and Kane felt the soggy warmth of blood-soaked cashmere clinging to his skin. The knife was thrust in so deep; he felt it scrape against the underside of his rib.

It was a miracle to be back on his feet, but at what cost? With each laboured step, his body grew weaker. He was slowing Peter down. As the deathly anaesthesia coursed through his depleted veins, all he thought of was Izzy and how he didn't want to be the reason she died today.

"I...I don't think...kaff... I don't think I can make it...kaff kaff..." he gasped. "You...you need to leave me here. Otherwise, we won't make it..."

Peter shone his torch down at Kane's wound, unable to mask his grave expression. He already knew it was bad, but seeing Peter's unfiltered reaction left him in little doubt it was time to throw in the towel. Dropping to his knees, Kane coughed and spluttered his morbid conclusion.

"I mean it Peter...kaff...I can b...barely walk now. You need to go..." The acrid taste of copper slithered its way up the back of his throat as he spoke, tainting his tongue and making him even more queasy.

Suddenly surrender didn't seem all that bad. If he closed his eyes for a moment and melted away into the empty nothingness of sleep's embrace, then he might finally be free of all the pain and heartbreak he was carrying. He would no longer be a burden to Peter, or anyone, ever again.

As he silently succumbed to the cosy blanket of tranquillity he languidly knitted in his mind, he felt a warm soothing hand cup his forehead, then Peter drew him in for a hug.

"I'm not going anywhere without you ok...sniff...keep talking while I figure something out...Kane...Kane!" Peter's voice washed over him like the lapping waves on a distant shore, fading out of his awareness before he could grasp the words.

"S...sorry...I'm just so tired..." With every breath, his chest gurgled and burbled as if he guzzled a bottle of glue.

"Kane?" He felt a gentle nudge on his shoulder.

"Kaff...kaff...I'm still here...but you need to go...kaff... there's not enough time..." Somewhere in the daydream haze of Kane's waning consciousness was the muffled and monotonous sound of a ticking clock. Both he and Izzy were running out of time, and without help, there was only one person Peter could save.

"C'mon Kane, stay with me... I'm getting you out of here."

Kane was certain he heard a renewed purpose somewhere in the static of Peter's voice, and the next thing he knew, he was being hoisted into the air and carried along the corridor. Perhaps help had finally arrived and they would both be saved.

"Wait here while I go check it out." Peter whispered, gently setting him back down against a wall.

Check what out? Kane watched the bleary torchlight slowly fade into the gloom until only darkness remained.

All alone, he rested his weary bones and pulled the shutters down on the rest of the world, not noticing the seamless handover between black and black.

As he emptied his spent lungs, the icy shivers rattling his every limb finally subsided, and his body fell limp.

64

"JJ! Noooo..." Meridia's cry was enough to wake the dead as it reverberated down the tunnel and snapped the hands of time back into motion.

Everyone flocked to JJ's aid as Grace and Nadia dragged Alice up off him by her elbows. Claret covered his chest, but as Meridia searched for the cause of the bloodbath, she found no mark on him.

Glancing up at Alice, she was greeted by the same horrified expression she saw when they both hit the ground, and then she saw the knife handle sticking out of her chest. Nadia and Grace were a split-second behind Meridia's shock discovery. When they realized what happened, they lowered Alice to the ground, but it didn't take a doctor to tell she was already dead.

"She's gone," Nadia declared, checking for a pulse. "She's been stabbed through the heart...there's nothing I can do..."

"What the fuck was she thinking?" Grace was trembling from the sudden turn of events.

"You mean what was Gregor thinking?!" Nadia fumed.

"He put her up to this...maybe Peter was right about him after all..."

She glanced at Meridia and Zach, who were both crouched at JJ's side, and then knelt between them.

"I need to check the back of his head...he hit the ground pretty hard..." She checked his pulse and studied the base of his skull from the side.

"I can't see any sign of blood, and his pulse is normal. He's just unconscious. Who knows? Maybe that's the best place for him at the moment..." Nadia studied Alice's lifeless body, and her eyes glazed over. "What the hell do we tell him when he wakes up?"

Before anyone answered, Zach cut across them in a state of panic.

"Kane...w...we need to find him..."

"I'm on it..." Quick to volunteer, Nadia rose to her feet and swung her first aid kid back over her shoulder. "There isn't much more I can do here, and he couldn't have gone very far..."

"I'm coming..." Zach scooped his coat up from the ground and was tying it around his waist.

"Er..." Nadia and Grace both looked at one another, unsure what to say. "I don't think that's such a good idea... you guys should wait here with Grace. We still don't know what happened...it might not be safe."

"Call him back...the radio..." Zach marched towards Alice's body and slammed on the brakes when he saw the haunting, wide-eyed expression still etched on her face.

Meridia placed a tender hand on JJ's shoulder, the only part of him that wasn't covered in blood, before leaving his side to usher Zach away from the scene. Her mind was completely at sea, awash with anger and guilt. Why did her gift keep leading her astray? First her own mother, and now JJ's.

It seemed the more she tried to control it, the more cryptic and dangerous it became. She could have avoided all this if she only realized who was invading her nightmares all this time. She heard the words countless times, but not once did she think it might be Alice. Maybe she was too focused on the shadow of the demon looming over them.

If that was the case, then what else had she missed? Was Kane the next in line to fall foul of her ineptitude? How many more people she loved was she destined to let down?

"Grr..." Her rage boiled over as Grace felt around inside Alice's pockets for the walkie talkie.

"I'll come..." she finally declared.

"I know Kane told us not to split up, but surely we're better in pairs, right? Plus, I'm the only one who's been in that section of the tunnel before..." She felt Zach grip her hand, and so she gave him a firm squeeze back.

"You stay here and look after JJ..." she whispered. "He's going to need you when he wakes up. I promise I'll be right...humph..." Meridia corrected herself just in time.

"I'll be right around the corner..." She pointed into the gloom just in time to catch Grace pull the knife from Alice's chest.

Slathered in claret, the blade dripped viscous blood like a broken pipette from one of her science lessons. Unaware she was being watched, Grace wiped the blade clean on Alice's coat and tucked it into her back pocket. She was already holding the radio in her other hand and set about locating the call button. There was something mercenary about the way Grace was so quick to take the knife.

Although Alice betrayed them, her body was still warm.

Perhaps it was her survivalist nature, but having already missed one assassin, Meridia worried she was about to let another slip through the net. Would Zach be safe alone with her, or should she stay with him after all?

How she wished she could turn her gift on whenever it suited, but like all things in her life, nothing came easy.

"*Crackle...buzz...*"

Meridia's ballooning indecision was burst by the sound of static on the radio as Grace found the right button. Bound in a single, shallow breath, Zach and Meridia clung to each other as they waited on the brink of despair for the latest on Kane's condition.

The blood-soaked air was thick with unsaid words. A shared, silent prayer that whatever update crackled through would not carry in its jaws the venomous bite of bad news.

"Peter...are you there? Come in Peter..."

65

Torch in hand, Peter tiptoed toward the intersection he spotted in the wall, not wishing to disturb any rats that might lurk in the shadows.

The last time he was this close to Crooked House, the tunnel was crawling alive, and he would have no way of protecting Kane should another plague suddenly materialize. Creeping closer to the opening, he heard a strange rhythmic pulsating which sounded like a cat purring.

Hesitating, he searched for a better angle to shine a light inside, but whatever was making the unsettling noise lay hidden around a blind corner. If he was to have any chance of saving Kane, he needed to push on, so Peter edged a little closer, taking the corner as wide as possible.

"*Squelch.*"

As he reached the alcove's entrance, Peter felt something sticky underfoot, so adjusted his torch to see what it was. He gasped in horror to find the ground thick with glistening yellow mucus and caught a mouthful of a vile, sulphurous stench leaking from the shadows.

Peter had made a terrible mistake, but it was too late now. The moment his torchlight struck the back wall and illuminated the source of the ominous sound, he felt his legs seize up and a prickly cold sweat broke beneath his shirt. Trembling in petrified silence, his shaky spotlight surveyed the rest of the recess to see the full extent of the nightmare he stumbled into.

A cluster of crusty, slime-infested eggs, the size of giant pumpkins, lay scattered across the ground, twitching and throbbing like ticking time bombs of terror. Weavers, dozens of them, waiting to hatch.

The Children of the Shadows were secretly harvesting an arachnid army, and Peter knew if just one of these monsters got loose, the war would be lost, demon or not. He glanced over his shoulder at Kane, who was bloodied and barely breathing in the corridor outside.

Turning his attention back to the menacing brood, he knew what he needed to do. There was no way he could allow a single egg to survive, no matter the cost. But where was the mother?

Standing at the foot of the weaver's nest, Peter's blood suddenly ran cold as he realized he was yet to look up. With so many eggs, it stood to reason their mother would be somewhere nearby, and if these terrifying creatures were anything like any other spider he encountered, they probably preferred to skulk around ceiling corners.

Peter took in a huge lungful of sticky, sulphurous air and forced his trembling hand skyward. The frail, ghostly beam painted jittery patches of light across the jagged limestone ceiling, casting erratic shadows that danced and flickered like petrified insects seeking refuge from an unseen predator hiding in the darkness. The alcove was high. Far higher than the rest of the tunnel and offered ample crawlspace for a weaver on the prowl.

Scrutinizing every angle of the room, Peter guided the quivering light across the rocky terrain like a reluctant lighthouse, too afraid to confront the impending catastrophe that might lurk around the next corner. With no sign of the weaver anywhere, there was only one more section of the ceiling to lay bare, and that was directly above his head.

Dry mouthed, Peter braved glancing up, then shakily moved the pale torchlight overhead. Inching closer, the light banished the shadows away, all but one, which clung doggedly to the rocky ceiling at the room's narrow entrance. Quivering, he pushed on, determined to face whatever loomed above.

"*Crackle...*"

The radio cracked through the silence like a live wire, jolting Peter's spine and jerked the flashlight onto the ominous shadow looking down on him.

"Phew..." Swallowing his heart back into his chest, he hunched on his knees in relief having found nothing more than a huge water stain above him. It was a surefire sign they were close to ground.

"*Buzz... Peter...are you there? Come in, Peter...*" The beleaguered voice belonged to Grace.

Perhaps help was on its way after all. Retreating from the alcove, he fumbled for the walkie talkie before it buzzed again. He had no idea if even the slightest sound could stir any of the pulsating eggs to life, or worse, attract their ferocious mother.

"Grace...thank god." He whispered, "I need help now... Kane's hurt bad and...and..." He trailed off when he couldn't tell if Kane was breathing.

"Kane? Kane!"

In a moment of panic, Peter shook him by the shoulder.

"Ow...kaff...kaff..." Kane winced at the sudden intrusion, then slumped back against the wall as if still in a deep sleep.

"You need to come quickly...he's bleeding heavily again, and I can't stop it."

"Buzz...Peter, this is Nadia...you need to tell me exactly what happened. I can talk you through what you need to do until I get there, ok?"

"He was stabbed...in the ribs, about halfway up his left side. The knife went all the way in. I didn't know what else to do, so I took it out...I couldn't move him otherwise. I've wrapped a jumper around the wound and tied it as tight as I could, but the bleeding...it's getting worse again..." Peter glanced down at the dark crimson patch forming on the ground and his heart sunk. He was only gone for a matter of minutes.

"Crackle...Is he on his back? You need to make sure he's lying flat on his back...that will slow the bleeding."

"Shit!" Peter didn't think of that when he propped him up. It was his stupid fault the bleeding got worse. He quickly laid Kane down as Nadia chimed in again.

"Buzz... I need you to put pressure on the wound until I get there. Do you know how long the blade was?"

"Ok..." Peter pressed down firm on Kane's ribs and stirred him again. His painful grimace was a welcome relief, as at least proved he was still alive.

"Crackle...the blade Peter, how long was it?"

"Er...I'm not sure...maybe 3 inches...I didn't know what to do...he came out of nowhere and then ran...I should've been more careful..." Peter's voice cracked under the mountain of guilt and worry on his shoulders.

"Buzz...It's ok Peter...you did what you had to do. Now

keep the pressure on until I get there...you need to act as a plug to keep the blood from escaping...can you do that?"

"Yes...yes, I can do that. Just hurry...please."

"Crackle...you have to tell me where you are, Peter...we're all still where you left us..."

Peter wracked his brain to retrace his steps, but after the incident with Marcus, they were all turned around. Kane found him, which meant he must have taken a straight route. Since then, he was sure they only took the one left.

"Buzz...Peter? Are you still there?"

"Yes...sorry...you need to follow the tunnel and take the first left. Keep walking until you see more mud than cobbles. I'll leave the light on for as long as I can so you can find me, but you need to be careful. I think Grady might be the least of our worries down here..."

66

"What do you think he meant?" Nadia trembled.

Peter's cryptic warning took some of the shine off her valour.

"I guess we won't know until we find them. If it was something really bad, Peter would have told us." Despite her brave face, Meridia shared Nadia's apprehension.

Deep down, she knew the closer they got to Crooked House, the more dangers they would face, which meant there would be plenty more to be afraid of than Grady. Ever since the horsemen announced their return, things had spiralled out of control, including Meridia's gift. It couldn't be a coincidence.

Perhaps there was a shift in the balance of power, and now all they were doing was treading water in Dr Foster's goldfish bowl. Whatever the reason, and regardless of the odds they now faced, Kane needed them, so it was time to go.

"Look after JJ..." she whispered as she gave Zach an enormous hug. She felt him breath it all in as his nose tickled the side of her neck.

"We'll be right behind you as soon as we can..." He assured, glancing at JJ, who was still out cold on the cobbles.

There was a steel in his eyes Meridia hadn't seen before and she wondered what was going on behind that brown floppy fringe of his.

"You can't go anywhere near that place...you know that. You need to wait here and stick to the plan."

"We'll see..." Zach dug his heels in as Meridia grabbed him by the shoulders.

"Promise me...promise me you'll stay well away from that house...I can't lose you. Not after everything we've been through. Promise me..." She held Zach's gaze for as long as she could until Nadia signalled she was ready.

"I promise..." He said reluctantly. "But if you don't come back, then all bets are off and I'm coming to rescue you...I'm sick of running and hiding all the time. Everyone else has stepped up except me...you must think I'm a total coward..."

"You're the bravest of all of us," Meridia asserted. "You have the biggest heart." With that, she gave him on last squeeze and joined Nadia at the edge of darkness.

"Light?" she said, and Meridia fished her phone out and switched the flashlight on.

"Here, sounds like you might need this more than us..." Grace handed her the knife from her back pocket and Meridia took a peculiar degree of comfort from the feel of its warm polished handle in her palm.

"I don't know if we can trust what Gregor said earlier about the way out of here, so we'll stay put until we hear from you. This place is like a maze, and it won't be safe to go back the way we came, so let's hope you pass another exit on your travels. I'd hate to think our only way out now is through Crooked House..." The harrowing prospect chilled the marrow of Meridia's bones.

"Good luck..." Grace finished on a token positive that was swallowed by the whirling storm of worry now brewing behind Meridia's eyes. The last place any of them wanted to be today of all days was trapped in the forsaken halls of Crooked House.

67

"SHH..." NADIA CAME TO A SUDDEN HALT. "DID YOU just hear something?"

Peter's last word of warning obviously rattled her, and Meridia was seeing why Grace handed her the knife and not Nadia. She was so jumpy and on edge, Meridia fully expected her to clobber the first person to cross her path with her first aid bag. Either that or run screaming for the hills.

"It's probably rats...there were loads down here last time..." The moment the words left her mouth, Meridia realized she poured gasoline onto the debilitating flames of Nadia's imagination.

"R...rats?!" Nadia's voice echoed ahead of them into the gloomy unknown and Meridia seized her opportunity to set a faster pace.

"Yeah, but they only come out if you stand still for too long. That's why we need to keep moving..." As much as she preferred Nadia above all the other residents of Drayton Hollow, her constant hesitation was already grating.

Marching ahead, Meridia almost heard the cogs turning in Nadia's mind as she weighed up the pitfalls of dillydallying in a rat's nest.

"Wait for me..." she whispered, scurrying to escape the trail of darkness Meridia was leaving in her wake.

As they both nervously pressed on, Meridia sensed the tunnel tighten around them, as if somewhere along the line they wandered into the oesophagus of a slimy cobbled snake that was stealthily swallowing them whole. A patchwork of greens and browns paved the way into its belly, like a vomit-stained carpet that felt damp and slippery underfoot. At times, Meridia almost felt as if she was walking on ice.

Meanwhile, with each new stride, the sticky air grew thicker, and the stench of mould and decay clung to the back of her throat like unwanted phlegm from a chesty cough. They had to be getting close to the mud Peter mentioned.

What other explanation could there be for the sudden change in smell?

Then they saw it, a festering T-junction of earth and stone where the cobbles bled out into the sodden dirt just the way Peter described.

"Look..." To their left they saw a fragile ember in the distance, barely holding back the murky void of the tunnel as it flickered like a whisper of hope in the darkness.

"It has to be them..." Meridia declared, racing off down the winding passageway with Nadia in tow.

Puffing and panting their way through the clammy air, they arrived to find Peter in pieces and Kane at death's door. Dark crimson rivulets weaved their way between a bed of mouldy cobbles, sinking into the surrounding dirt. He looked like a castaway, pale and lifeless, washed-up ashore on a tiny island of red and grey pebbles.

His sweater was at half-mast, revealing a blood-soaked cashmere bandage flowing seamlessly from cherry-red to charcoal-grey as it stretched away from where Peter's quivering hands were pressed. He, too, looked pale and panicked in the gloomy recess of the tunnel branching off towards another dark and mysterious alcove in the distance.

His hands were tightly knit together like he was performing some botched attempt at CPR, missing his patient's heart by a mile. They were covered with blood. Some of which already dried in the tiny ravines of his whitened knuckles.

"Nadia..." He gasped, "Thank god..."

Peter's eyes were bloodshot and brimming with tears as Nadia swooped in and set her first aid kit down beside them. Now it was Meridia's turn to falter, standing listlessly in the passageway. It was all she could do to stay upright. The shock of seeing Kane so pale and drenched in blood transported her back to Drayton Hollow and her breakfast with the demon. Her gift deceived her once again.

"Wh...who did this?" She mumbled, bewildered by her own narrow-mindedness.

Ever since their encounter with Valerie, she was fooled into thinking she turned a corner. That she somehow gained more control over her gift, and as such, slipped into a dangerous pattern of taking all her visions literally. A pattern which already cost JJ and now Kane.

"I...I don't know..." Peter stuttered as he made room for Nadia to take over.

"It all happened so quickly...but I've never seen him before. He was young...no older than Tommy. I hit him, instinctively...and then he ran. I think it was an accident...a tragic accident. He looked just as scared as we were...like he was running from someone...or something..."

"Peter..." Nadia interrupted, "I need your help..." Unlike her reluctant journey through the tunnels, here she was in her element.

Having wasted no time cutting Kane free from his bandage, she was already examining the gaping wound halfway up his ribcage. Still leaking blood, but not gushing, Kane winced as she delicately cleaned his gash with a sterile wipe. It was the first sign of life since their arrival and proved enough to heave Meridia from the dark doldrums of her haunting prophecy and drag her back to the present.

"I need you to pinch here...like this..." Nadia pressed Kane's wound together with both thumbs.

"Argh..." He twitched and writhed in agony, hammering the ground with his heel in protest.

"I know dear...I'm sorry, but I need to seal the wound." Nadia released her grip, then nodded to Peter. "When I say go, I need you to hold the skin together as tight as you can, but don't get your fingers too close...do it exactly the way I showed you." She placed a soothing hand on Kane's forehead.

"Kane, when I say go, it's going to hurt again, but I promise it won't be for long, ok? You're being so brave...I just need you to be brave a little longer so I can fix you up..."

Kane was breathing heavily and wheezing now. That was when Nadia noticed the dried blood in the corner of his mouth.

"Did he cough this up?" She pointed so Peter could see, and then hurriedly opened his mouth to look inside.

"I...I'm not sure..." Peter stammered.

"Give me the light..." Nadia shone Peter's torch inside Kane's mouth and down his throat. "I need to know where this blood came from...without an MRI, I can't tell what internal damage there is...I need to make sure the blade didn't hit any organs..."

Although Meridia was no nurse, she recognized the worry in Nadia's voice, and it spread like wildfire to her and Peter.

"What is it? Is he ok?" Peter's nerves were shredded as he tried to peer over Nadia's shoulder into Kane's mouth. "Nadia? Say something, please..."

"It's ok..." she declared after what seemed like an eternity on tenterhooks.

"He must've bitten his tongue at some point...there's no sign of anything sinister..." She gave the wound another wipe, and then nodded at Peter again as she pulled a small white pointed tube from her bag.

"Is that superglue?" He asked.

"Uh huh...it's the quickest way to seal the wound and the best I can do for now. When I say go, you do just like I showed you. Meridia, you might wanna hold Kane's hand for this...it'll help with the pain." Meridia did as instructed and tentatively slipped her hand inside Kane's.

His skin was icy-cold and clammy in her palm, but her growing sense of dread subsided when she felt him instinctively cling onto her like a newborn. Taking a deep breath, she glanced up at Nadia and gave her the green light.

"Go..."

"Ow..." Meridia and Kane winced in unison as Peter squeezed the tear in his ribs together, and Kane paid the favour forward by crushing Meridia's hand.

"Just a second more..." Nadia mumbled as she delicately traced the fold in Kane's flesh, sealing the join like she was repairing a cracked porcelain doll.

Once done, she leaned in and blew on the silvery trail,

bonding Kane's skin together and signalled for Peter to let go. Although there was a discernible lag between Peter relinquishing his grip and Kane relinquishing his, Meridia couldn't tear her eyes away from the pleat in his skin as they all anxiously waited to find out if the glue would hold firm against the natural elasticity of youth.

"It worked..." Nadia concluded, as Meridia's hand slithered free of Kane's greasy cocktail of sweat and exhaustion.

"I need to give it one more coat to be sure..." As she leant in and traced the line again, it was clear to see she stemmed the flow of blood, for now at least, and the tunnel breathed a collective sigh of relief.

"He's not out of the woods yet...Although that'll stop the bleeding, I still need to take a better look at him. I'm not a surgeon and there could still be a second bleed we don't know about. He also needs meds to minimize the chance of infection...meds I don't have here." She whacked her first aid bag in frustration, then continued with a more heavy-handed bedside manner, as if Kane was shrouded in ignorance by a hospital curtain.

"We need to get him back above ground right away...if he stays down here too long, he might die."

68

"How?" Meridia asked. "Where?" Still reeling from Kane's ominous prognosis.

"What's through there?" Nadia pointed at the alcove over Peter's shoulder and the colour instantly drained from his chiselled cheeks.

"That leads us to our next problem..." He trailed off as Meridia wandered towards the opening with her torch.

Upon her approach, she heard a soft purring sound oscillating from the gloom as if Peter stumbled upon a secret cat café. She was amazed she didn't notice it when she first arrived, but she was so focussed on Kane the peculiar hum must have sailed right by her. Now she could almost feel it vibrating her bones and pulling her closer with its magnetic pulse.

"Wait!" Peter called after her, springing to his feet and turning Meridia's legs to jelly. "It's not safe..."

He shielded her from the entrance, then exposed the terrifying source of the mesmeric drone with his torch.

"What the..." Meridia's heart galloped into her throat as the gilded glow of Peter's flashlight stretched out across the miniature rocky mountaintops like the early morning sun, illuminating row upon row of scabby, egg-shaped globs dripping with glistening mucus.

Like a pulsating pumpkin patch slavered in slime, they looked primed and ready to hatch as their thick crusty shells cracked and creaked with each revolting throb.

"W...weavers..." she stuttered and was instantly transported back to her mother's gruesome death. Could this be the same brood responsible?

"We must stop them from hatching..." Peter whispered, scared the slightest sound might disturb their embryonic slumber.

"I've seen the damage just one of these things can do... an army of them doesn't even bear thinking about." Meridia scanned the nest with her own torch.

There had to be at least thirty eggs scattered across the gunk-smothered shingles of the alcove. Each ominous pulse of their mottled grey surface secreted a vile yellow pus that oozed down their jagged husks and dripped onto the ground, adding a foul sulphurous stink to the already suffocating air.

"But how do we kill them? Fire?" She asked.

"That's the best I could come up with, but we have nothing we can use. Also, we still don't know where the mother is..." Peter's jarring comment snatched at Meridia's strings like she was a dancing marionette, jerking her into action as she scrutinized the rest of the room.

"What's that..." She hovered her light over the gargantuan chunk of limestone jutting out at the far end of the alcove.

"What?" Peter probed, bolstering her spotlight with his own.

"There...see?" As his flashlight overlay hers, she glimpsed a shadow within the rock.

It was almost invisible at first, hidden within the misty layers of grime and mould.

"Move your light away from mine a sec..." she whispered impatiently. Then, with a vacillating hand, as if she was hosing down a muddy patio, she showered the stone in light.

"It's a secret door..." she declared triumphantly. "Look... I bet that's the handle..."

She lingered on a peculiar-looking cleft halfway up, curving like a crescent moon. Tracing the door's outline to the ground, she found a series of scuff marks in the dirt. A whispering trail where the earth was smudged and smoothed over time.

"Guys?" Nadia called out from the tunnel, startling them both. Meridia watched Peter's emerald eyes weave an imaginary route across the eggs before he answered.

"Bear with me...we might have the way out you wanted..." Craning his neck, he sized up the distance between each egg and searched along the ground for anything else untoward, as if weavers weren't enough.

"What are you doing?" Meridia tugged at his sleeve in the doorway as he shuffled further inside.

"We need to get Kane out of here...and you, for that matter. You were never meant to be down here..." He wriggled free of Meridia's grip, then took another slow, deliberate step towards the first row of eggs.

"If that door leads to an exit, then it could be Kane's only way out. I can carry him across, then come back for Izzy. We still have time, but only if I move quickly."

"But..."

"We can't risk going any deeper into the tunnels...who

knows where the next exit might be? For all we know, the only other way out might be through Crooked House, and I don't think any of us want that now do we..." He glanced nervously at the floor and Meridia saw his hands were really shaking now. His torchlight bouncing erratically between each disgusting egg like a pinball.

"Please be careful..." she pleaded from the sidelines, a jittery spectator feeling every strenuous step as if it was her own.

Peter's long legs bounded up and then down as if he was traversing a minefield of warm sticky toffee. Around halfway across, he covered his mouth and nose, then wobbled precariously on one leg as he skidded on the oozing blanket of slime beneath him.

Meridia could barely watch as he rediscovered his footing and then awkwardly plodded on toward the door. They had no idea if it would even open, let alone what might be waiting for them on the other side, but Peter was right. They needed to at least try for Kane's sake.

The further he ventured into the unknown, the more Meridia's nerves jangled, as thoughts and fears of the weaver crawling back to check on her young scurried up and down her spine.

Twitching and fidgeting on the spot, her level of discomfort was excruciating until, for some inexplicable reason, she was reminded of the story of *"Goldilocks and the Three Bears."*

'Who's been sneaking in my crib?' she thought. A nervous laugh leaked out from under her breath, and she wondered if the humidity had sent her barmy.

By the time Peter made it all the way through the slime-infested jungle of rancid, oversized eggs, Meridia was seriously questioning her own sanity. Had she finally lost the plot? Was that why she let so many crucial visions slip through her fingers of late?

She figured it was probably inevitable given everything she'd been through, and now she came to think about it, she was amazed she made it this far. Perhaps the thought of being devoured by a giant mutant spider was simply the straw that broke the camel's back.

"*Creeeeak...*"

Peter wasted no time in trying the door, gently nudging Meridia free from the clutch of her babbling brain. A narrow band of sallow light cracked into the alcove, fracturing the gloom, and carrying with it the distant hum of high-speed traffic.

"It's another passage..." he declared, forcing the door wider.

It opened far easier than either of them expected as Peter established the heavy limestone exterior was nothing more than a paper-thin façade, mounted on old and decayed wood.

"Can you hear that?" He whispered. "Cars...lots of them. We must be close to the dual carriageway." He poked his head inquisitively through the gap and then pulled back to face Meridia.

"I think there's a door at the other end...I'm going to see where it leads..." Before she could object, he slipped out of sight, leaving behind a wedge of flickering light that sliced through the viscid air and struck a gaggle of bloated, mutant eggs. A queasy shiver raced down her spine, as if cold slimy tendrils were slowly slivering across skin, one vertebra at a time.

Arching her back to get away from the gruesome sight, Meridia checked on Nadia, who was quiet since Peter's somewhat hasty act of bravery. Crouched with her back towards her, she was still busy fussing over Kane on the tunnel floor and had now emptied half the contents of her first aid bag beside her.

A pile of ripped green and white paper sachets littered the ground along with a ragged roll of gauze and what resembled an unopened syringe. Her phone completed the haphazard ensemble, serving as an improvised bedside light, and its lambent beam bounced off the surrounding cobbles and flickered in the crinkles of a crushed plastic water bottle lying next to Kane's hand. Although she couldn't quite see his face from where she was standing, she clung onto the thin thread of hope that maybe he was strong enough to drink it unaided.

"Bang!"

Meridia flinched, then reeled back around to face the grisly alcove. It sounded like a door slamming shut.

"P...Peter? Is that you?" She stuttered, but there was no answer.

The mysterious door was still ajar, just as he left it, but the light leaking through was no longer a flicker. She had no idea how long the passage was, or where it went, but she recognized the afterglow of florescent bulbs when she saw it. Having spent most of her life couped up like a battery hen at St Swithun's, she would have recognized it anywhere.

"Peter?" she whispered again, shuffling further into the room.

If she could get a better look beyond the door, it would help her understand what was going on, but the fact Peter wasn't answering filled her full of dread. Hugging the wall, Meridia sidestepped her way along until the secret passageway came into view. It was a drab concrete walkway, much like any underpass you would stumble upon along a main road, and just as she thought, it was illuminated by strip lighting. The same cheap council issue fare that lit the bunker's kitchen.

The distant drone of whistling traffic distracted her from the steaming piles of pus under her nose and reminded her that somewhere beyond the confines of her latest nightmare, the rest of civilization continued on with its daily business, even if it was still rotten to its core.

"Peter..." she called once more, louder this time, all the while shuffling to see more of the secret passage.

Almost perfectly square and smooth, the stone-cold grey walls composed of enormous slabs, seamlessly sewn together, which bore a subtle sheen shimmering beneath the incandescent light. More factory-made than handcrafted, this was clearly a contemporary extension to the cult's original network. Its path curving out of sight like the inside of a giant concrete worm.

There was no sign of Peter, or the door she thought she heard banging shut. Inching further to her left, Meridia tried her best to see deeper into the belly of the worm, and then she saw it. A long dark shadow skulking around its bend. Someone was coming.

"*Screeeeeeech*"

A grating sound, like nails down a chalkboard, echoed along the sterile-looking corridor, drowning out the whirring traffic as it seeped its way into Meridia's gums, rattling her teeth and juddering her bones.

Within a matter of seconds, she saw a dazzling flash of light as the luminous bulbs bounced off the blood-stained blade of a hunting knife. Slow and steady, its razor-sharp tip scraped against the concrete, leaving a dusty trail in its wake, as its owner gradually crept ever closer. Gripped by a glistening crimson hand that was basted in blood, the knife sprinkled the lustrous grey surface with ruby-red speckles as it came around the corner.

Meridia's body locked up like a statue, eyes unblinking, as wraithlike, coffee-coloured robes ebbed and flowed like ragged drapes billowing in the breeze and Silas Grady sauntered into view. Hood down and bunched around his shoulders, his ashen face was a living mask of terror, smeared with scarlet streaks around his eyes and mouth to form a wide, jagged smile that stretched from ear to ear.

Dripping red, he resembled a twisted jester from the depths of hell with deep-sunken eyes, blackened by blood, that bore the hollow stare of a demon.

Twinkling sapphire orbs flickered from the depth of his skull as he paused beneath the overhead lights and sneered, stretching his creepy clown-mouth to its limits and turning the air around Meridia to ice.

He slowly held aloft his trailing hand for her to see. There, dangling from a tuft of silken hair, hung the severed head of Peter Higginsworth.

69

"Ahh!"

JJ sat bolt upright with a start, nearly head-butting Zach in the face, who was caught unawares whilst keeping vigil.

No sooner he sat up, did he wearily slump back down onto his elbows as a kaleidoscope of cobbles swirled around him at break-neck speed. The back of his head was throbbing like a toothache, and when he reached up, he felt a bump the size of a golf ball at the base of his closely cropped fade. A nauseating stink clung to his airways like rusty puddles, and his chest was warm and soaking wet.

"Easy...you banged your head pretty bad." Both Zachs whispered in dissonance while they weaved in and out of one another like they were dancing a ceroc.

"Wh...what happened?" JJ mumbled, his own voice reverberating between his ears like a deafening bell ring.

He swallowed down the sudden urge to vomit and closed his eyes to steady the room, but his brain continued to somersault in harmony with his stomach. The woozy feeling reminded him of a trip to the dentist one time when he was young. He needed four extractions because of overcrowding and his dentist, a mild-mannered Indian man whose name now escaped him, used a general anaesthetic.

JJ went out like a light before the count of five, but when he came to again, the world was a giddying blur, just as it was now. He threw up that day, peppering the concrete steps of the dentist as he staggered out with his dad in his hurry to return home. Coco pops and orange juice. He could taste it even now.

Looking within, he searched the blackness behind his eyes for the threads of what left him feeling this way. It was like wading through a fog made of treacle when all the while his memory flashed by at light speeds like a library microfiche reader on steroids. The endless conveyor belt of images made him even queasier, so he focused on his breathing instead.

In and out to the rhythm of the soothing beat pulsating somewhere toward the back of his throat, and then he remembered. A scuffle with his mum. JJ's eyes sprung open to find a woman looming over him. Her elfin features and blonde pixie cut reminded him of Link from Legend of Zelda, and for an instant he imagined he was in the princess's castle. Truth be told, he would rather be anywhere than here. Anywhere than the real world.

"JJ...can you hear me?" Link asked, or was it Grace? His mind was a muddle and the voices underwater, as he languidly searched the room for the one person he wanted to see. The one who was missing: his mum.

Glancing down at his chest in panic, his fears were confirmed. The vivid crimson ruffles of his blood-soaked sweater rippled towards him like turbulent waves on a stormy red sea. Each one drowning him as it chased away the fog and swept JJ back to shore. Back to face the bludgeoning reality of what he had done.

"Mum!" He tried to sit up again.

This time forcing his befuddled body to see it through. Beyond the worried faces crowding over him, he saw her. Or what remained of her. A lifeless husk, half-hidden under a grubby beige raincoat smeared with blood. How demeaning. His mother's life, spanning over fifty years, was now reduced to a homogeneous lump of crumpled nylon with only a manicured hand to tell her apart from a pile of dirty laundry. JJ scrutinized the delicate digits laying palm-up on the pebbles and wished he was caught in a concussion-fuelled fantasy. Alas, it wasn't the case.

A cyclone of inaudible whispers swirled around him, bouncing off the stony walls and showering him with sympathy. Every well-intended word sailed by the by, as all he could do was stare at the purple painted nails on his mother's lifeless hand. A hand that tucked him in at night, tended to him when he was sick, fed him, clothed him, and then ultimately betrayed him.

The puddle blossoming beneath it looked like spilled wine, thick and clinging to the cobbles, filling their trenches, as if reaching for something from beyond the grave. Maybe she was reaching out to him. A last gasp, sorry for all the hurt and pain she caused. The lives she ruined. Or was it a more haunting indictment? A glossy red finger of blame, seeking him out along the tunnel's tiny canals.

"JJ..." Zach's voice whipped into his awareness with a little more vigour, this time snapping through the static. "We've got to go...someone's coming..."

Even the threat of Grady didn't stir him. He felt both lost and at a loss. Although he knew he should try to muster a reaction, he couldn't. He knew he should cry, but he couldn't. Try as he might, the tears would not come. He already grieved once for his mum, but this was different.

This time he felt the knife go in, saw the whites of her eyes. In that split second before he hit the ground, he felt the tiny pop of her flesh and then the rest was written on his shirt and all over the ground.

Was it an accident? Was it what she deserved?

A spiralling vortex of anguish clawed at his insides, hollowing out every ounce of his tortured soul, but no matter how much it hurt. No matter how desperately he wanted to scream, still he refused to cry.

"Please...it's not safe..." He felt Zach tugging at his arm to get up. "We can't stay here..."

Why would anyone want to stay here? Trapped in this putrid underbelly of an unspeakable evil, poisoning every poor bastard foolish enough to enter its bowels. His mum, his dad. In fact, all their parents.

"I'm sorry JJ...we have to go now..."

JJ lumbered to his feet like a zombie, still in a daze. The only frailty in his eyes stemming from the searing headache banging his brain like a gong. In the distance, he heard footsteps echoing towards them, just as Zach warned. It was time to go.

"Bye mum..." He whispered, then promised himself there would be time to grieve later.

70

Meridia felt the rutted limestone poke the small of her back as she recoiled at the heartbreaking sight emerging from the secret passage.

Glassy-eyed and slack-jawed, Peter's chiselled features wilted like the waxy remnants of a candle burned down to the wick. All the warmth and light that once defined him was cruelly snuffed out, leaving behind a cold, hollow shell of a man she considered a surrogate father.

Swaying from side to side like a gruesome jack-o'-lantern, his saw-toothed gullet left a mottled trail of gore glistening on the ground. Meridia stood paralyzed, as if her feet were fused to the floor, unable to wrench her bleary eyes away from the blood-curdling horror show floating toward her.

Somewhere above the sound of a madman's rasping blade and the pounding of her own heart, she heard Peter's flaccid tongue lapping against the inner lining of his cheeks. A haunting synthesis of pain and sorrow. The sickening sound echoed from his gaping mouth until she could no longer contain the vomit bubbling up in her throat.

"Kaff...splat..." Meridia peppered her shoes with slimy chunks of beans and carrots as she coughed her guts up onto the cobbles.

Her eyes were streaming now, and although the threat of Grady loomed near, the shackles of such tragic loss proved far too gruelling to escape from, and so she emptied her soul onto the ground, all the while battling to breathe through the bitter taste of bile.

"Crunch...crack..."

The sudden sound cut through her misery like a knife and Meridia's head snapped up as if waking from a terrible dream. She expected to find Grady standing over her. His demented, blood-smeared grin leering like a twisted cheshire cat as he posed with his stomach-churning trophy. What she found was far worse.

"Crunch...crack..."

The closest calcified egg to where she was standing fractured, splintering in two like the serrated jaws of a fossilized Venus flytrap. Its cavernous mouth oozed thick yellow mucus from each corner that sizzled as it seeped onto the stony ground. The crumbling carcass of its brittle shell then collapsed into the smouldering cesspool of slime below. A landslide of sulphurous stink and foreboding, as elongated legs, like long bony fingers, snapped and cracked free from their fetid cocoon.

"Crack...crunch..."

Another ruptured, then another, and another, as one by one each insidious egg combined to form a sickening crescendo of clicking and slurping. Thorny malformed spider legs filled the alcove, twisting at unnatural angles and decorating its walls with their barbed silhouettes.

"Click clack...click clack..."

The brood of weavers closed in around her. Mutant

spiders with black bulbous bodies the size of basketballs, skittering across the stones and blocking her only exit in their thirst for blood. The sight of them made her flesh crawl, maybe more than the full-sized weaver she encountered in the depths of hell.

Row upon row of razor-sharp teeth on prickly legs, like crawling piranhas, licked their lips in unison at the prospect of devouring her bones and all.

"N...Nadia..." Meridia squeaked, her vocal cords garrotted by fear, as a sea of fiery orbs glared up at her from the broken ruins of their decomposed chrysalides.

"No-one can help you now, seer..." Grady sneered from the doorway, eyes ablaze.

"The game is up...and I've won. There's nothing you can do to stop me now...just ask poor Peter..." He held Peter's head out in front of him triumphantly, like a slain medusa, and sure enough, its haunting gaze turned Meridia to stone.

Through the misty haze of defeat, she saw Peter's lips quiver. The sudden, inexplicable motion shook her from her trance, and the faintest flutter of his eyes swiftly followed it. Within a matter of seconds, his entire face jerked back to life. Back from the dead.

Muscular spasms and erratic convulsions followed a flurry of ticks and twitches as he wrestled to regain control of his faculties, like an awakening zombie coming to terms with rigor mortis of the mouth.

His emerald eyes greyed over like milky white marbles seething with storm clouds, then retreated deep into their sockets as if all the air was sucked right out of his face. His cheeks drew thin and gaunt to reveal the bony outline of his skull, whilst what remained of his earthly complexion withered to a deathly shade of blue.

Confounding every remaining law of nature, he opened his mouth to speak. His rasping zombie voice was barely audible over the relentlessly clacking arachnids and the bustling traffic, but with a little concentration, she tuned into his supernatural frequency.

"One musssst sssstay..." He hissed, drooling thick black tar from his emaciated lips. *"Only you can ssssstop him ..."* Meridia clenched her eyes, desperate to escape from her waking nightmare.

"Count to ten..." she muttered, "Count to ten and it'll all be over..."

She tried to focus on the humming traffic, anything to block out the noise of the nefarious spirit currently hounding her.

Was this really a glimpse of things to come? Had Grady been waiting for Peter at the end of that long, winding passage all along?

"One..." She clung to the belief her gift could no longer be trusted. That it was back to its old, cryptic ways.

"Two..." That every cue she received of late sent her hurtling headfirst in the wrong direction.

"Three..." Did this mean Kane and Nadia were the ones in danger? Or Zach? Please, not Zach.

"Four..." She wrestled with the temptation to peek. To run, screaming out of the tunnel and as far away from this godforsaken place as her wobbly legs would carry her.

"Five..." Maybe it was safe now? She could no longer hear the clicking of creatures baying for her blood, or the rasping breath of a beheaded spectre.

"Six..." Just a glimpse, just to be sure. It would all be ok now, it had to be. Peter would be back safe and sound, and it would all be ok.

"Seven..." With a huff, Meridia broke her count and

risked one eye. "Ahh!" She flinched, now nose-to-nose with Peter's ghoulish head.

She felt his cold, rancid breath on her lips and smelt the blood on Grady's knife as he stood over her, gleefully spectating.

"One musssst ssssstay, the other musssst go..." Peter howled, louder this time. Loud enough to wake the dead. His voice was suddenly sonorous and coherent. "It's the only way to save Zach's soul..."

"Argh!"

A bristly swarm of spider legs, twisted and barbed, skittered up Meridia's trembling body as the horde of hungry weavers made their ascent. She felt each spine-tingling tap of their thorny limbs pricking her skin as they scampered their way up, all to a chorus of ravenous, razor-sharp teeth chomping together in unison, hungry for their first taste of human flesh.

Meridia screamed again, ear-splittingly shrill, as she writhed and wriggled in a last ditched dance to shake them all off. But the weavers held onto her fast, pinching her skin and nipping at her neck as they continued to climb.

Within seconds, she was drowning in a sea of inky black atrocities, tugging at her greasy hair and tickling the crevasses of her ears with their acrid breath as they bundled her to the ground; all to the tune of Grady's maniacal laugh echoing through the alcove.

"Stop!" Her desperate plea reverberated around the empty room as Peter reappeared from behind its secret door.

Meridia was curled in a ball on the ground, her back wedged up against the coarse and clammy wall as she cowered at the foot of a weaver egg. There was no sign of the evil arachnid spawn or their malevolent master. There was only her and Peter.

"I've found a way out..." he trailed off when he locked eyes with hers. "What happened?"

Peter hopped and skipped his way through the tangle of cystic eggs, but by the time he reached her, Meridia was already back on her feet. Twitching erratically as if her spine was made of elastic, she frantically flapped at her hair and brushed her shoulders as the whispering footprints of a two-dozen weavers continued to crawl all over her from the great beyond.

"What is it?" Peter pressed, checking her for any obvious signs of injury. "Where did you go?"

"I...d...didn't g...go anywhere..." She squirmed. "I was right here...I saw the weavers...and Grady..." she contemplated, telling him more, then thought better of it. Such was her disillusionment with her so-called gift.

"I'm...I'm fine...it only lasted a moment, and then it was gone..." she lied, unable to look Peter in the eye for fear his head might cave in again.

"Where does it lead?" She changed the topic, knowing time was running out for Kane and Izzy.

"It's an underpass. It runs below the main road and pops up just outside of Cold Christmas...we need to call the others. This is your ticket out of here..."

71

"Where are they?" Peter was spooked by Meridia's caginess and convinced himself something bad befell the others.

As they reached Nadia, he swooped down by Kane's side to check on him.

Some of his colour had returned to his cheeks, and he seemed lucid. A massive improvement from when he last saw him.

"How is he?" He looked to Nadia for a more informed update, knowing all too well appearances could be deceiving.

"He's still pretty weak, but stable. He's a fighter..." She half-smiled the way doctors often do when trying to feign positivity, and he sensed their predicament remained unchanged. They needed to get Kane to safety.

"Can we move him? I've found a way out, but it's... complicated..." Peter was confident he could carry Kane across the obstacle course of dormant weavers, but they still needed to move quick as their mother could return at any moment.

Where the hell were the others?

"He's ok to move. He might even be able to walk a short distance, with help. I have a shot of adrenalin we can use, but I'd sooner hang onto it in case we find ourselves in trouble..."

"Trouble? You mean this isn't enough trouble, Nad?" Grace came creeping around the corner with Zach and JJ in tow. JJ was covered in blood.

"Oh my god, what happened?!" Peter was first to react to the sight of him as he waited for Alice to emerge.

Before anyone answered, Zach broke away from the pack and ran to his brother in floods of tears..

"My mum..." JJ mumbled, glassy-eyed and staring at the floor. "It...it was an accident...she tried to hurt Zach...it was their plan all along..."

"We have to go..." Grace cut across him. "Someone is coming up the tunnel behind us. We need to keep moving... we need to get out of here..."

Peter felt the muscles in his neck tighten. He was sick of running.

"Disciples...from the temple..." He whispered. "Gregor said it wouldn't take them long to follow us down here."

He glanced again at JJ, who was still yet to react to Kane's condition, and was obviously suffering from shock. There would be time to address that later. Right now, Peter needed to get them all out of here, but first he needed to break the bad news.

"We need to move quickly...I've found a tunnel leading out to the dual carriageway...a secret underpass. I've checked, and it's clear, but in order to get to it you'll need to pass...er..."

"Weaver eggs..." Meridia ended his hesitation.

He could tell she was growing impatient and wondered what it was she wasn't telling him.

"There's a whole nest of them next door, but if we're careful, we can get out. Peter did, and he's just fine." Meridia's bluntness buried everyone beneath a blanket of hush, but still JJ seemed unphased as if the entire conversation sailed over his head.

"M's right...but we need to get moving. It's only a short way across them, then it's onto a concrete passage. I can carry Kane, but I want the rest of you out of here, too. Nadia and Grace can get you all to safety above ground while I go back for Izzy."

"Bu..." Peter shut down Grace's protest.

"No buts I'm afraid. These guys need protecting while I'm gone. From the exit, you should be able to get back to the cars without being spotted. Especially if the Children of the Shadows are busy down here looking for us...c'mon, let's get to it."

"*Clank...*"

"What was that?" Meridia trembled as the sound of a shingle being kicked across the cobbles rippled its way toward them.

"They've found us..." Grace whispered. "We need to go..."

"There isn't time. Kane can barely move, and we still have the weavers to consider." The echo of footsteps rang out from the blackened void they left behind.

Someone was definitely coming, but as Peter listened carefully, he was convinced the person was alone.

"Get behind me..." He stepped into the space between them and the unknown, clenching his fists in anticipation of a fight.

There was no time to run to the exit now, and the only other direction available would lead them straight to Crooked House. It was time to make a stand.

Grace brushed his arm as she stepped into the breach beside him, fists raised and ready for a scrap. It was the final confirmation she could be trusted. Somewhere in the darkness up ahead, they heard the clip-clop-scuff of footsteps ease up on their approach. The flashlights dotted around clearly gave their pursuer cause for consideration, but Peter wasn't sure if that was a good or bad thing.

With Grady on the loose, along with an unknown thug and an expectant weaver, they already had their hands full. Who knew what other monsters wandered these dank and dismal tunnels? Particularly so close to the epicentre of evil: Crooked House.

"Look..." Grace whispered, gesturing toward a shadow skulking within the gloom, beyond the reach of their flashlight.

It was definitely human, and Peter breathed a silent sigh of relief he wouldn't need to square up to a giant, acid-spitting arachnid. Not for now, at least.

"Show yourself...whoever you are..." Peter was tired of playing games and was ready for whatever the tunnel of horrors threw at him next. Then he whispered under his breath to Grace.

"If it's Grady, then I'll buy you all as much time as I can. Just get as many of the kids out of here as possible..."

"Wait...*gasp*...it's me..." Dr Foster staggered out of the shadows, wheezing and puffing like he'd just run a marathon. Blood caked his forehead, and his legs wobbled like jelly.

"Why the fuck do y'all keep running away from me..." He huffed. "I'm too old for this shit..."

"What the hell happened, Marcus? We thought you were dead..." Grace waded straight in, bypassing any show of concern for the sizable gash congealing along the top of his hairline. She sounded annoyed, if anything, like it was all she could do not to slap him.

"What happened to the others?" Peter jumped on the bandwagon.

"After you barged past, I got turned around in the dark and lost everyone." He was still secretly holding onto his conspiracy theory about Gregor and Tommy engineering this whole scenario, and hoped Dr Foster's shock return might offer some answers.

"I...I..." The doctor hung his head, and beneath the hazy flashlight glow, Peter noticed swelling around the open wound, as if struck by a blunt object..

"I felt something at my back I swear...like someone breathing down the back of my neck...I...I just panicked and ran...I thought it was Grady...or worse. This whole place had me spooked from the get-go. All that talk of shadow creatures and demons..." He shook his head, abashed.

"I just kept running like a goddam idiot...ran headlong straight into a wall...I ...I ...got my bell rung so hard I dropped the radio and didn't know where I was...I woke up down a tunnel somewhere and I've being trying to find my way back ever since. This place is like a goddam maze...I think maybe I took a right when I shoulda gone left...ended up going in one big loop until I found all those arches we saw back at the start...I'm sorry guys...I really screwed up..."

"Let me take a look Marcus..." Nadia stepped across, but the doctor was quick to wave her away.

"I'll live...think I damaged my ego more than my head. I'm really sorry Peter...I didn't see no one until...until..." He glanced over at JJ, who was still in a world of his own, staring at the floor.

"What happened?" His shame gave way to sorrow, and as Peter contemplated addressing the elephant in the room, Nadia stepped in again.

"We need to get Kane out of here now, guys. The longer he spends down here, the more he's at risk of infection. Have you seen this place? Do you know how many millions of different bacteria there probably are just in this section alone? It's like a breeding ground for disease."

"You're right." Peter concurred. "We can all swap stories later when we're out of this hellhole."

He turned to Zach, who was still hunkered next to his brother, holding his hand and whispering words of reassurance.

"Zach...I need you to be brave for me, ok? I need you to take Kane and JJ out through the tunnel next door and help Nadia look after them. Do you think you can do that?" Being the youngest of the group, Peter was worried how Zach would cope with his brother so badly injured and a weaver's nest to contend with, particularly given his fear of spiders.

"What about Izzy?" He sobbed.

"I'm going to go get her and then I'll meet you all someplace else that's safe. Marcus, you're with me. That is, if you're up for some redemption? The rest of you will go with Grace and Nadia. Once you reach the dual carriageway, you can follow the road back to where the cars are parked and get the hell out of here."

"I've got to stay..." Meridia blurted somewhat cryptically.

"The vision I had...I think it makes sense now..." She

paced between them all. The cogs of her mind setting her in motion as she pieced the latest puzzled together on the fly.

"One must stay and the other must go..." she mumbled. "Zach has to go, and I have to stay. I'm the only one who can stop the demon...it said there's no other way. I need to stay and see this through. I need to go back to Crooked House..."

<h1 style="text-align:center">72</h1>

After a few minutes of heated whispers, toing and froing with the volume turned down, Meridia eventually got her way under the strict condition she would wait outside the jaws of hell with Dr Foster while Peter ventured inside in search of Izzy.

Considering the doctor's embarrassing confession, there was still an outside chance her dad and Tommy made it to Crooked House ahead of them. If they did, and her dad stole the ceremonial knife, they might never need to face the demon at all. She prayed that was the case and for once, Gregor was here to do the right thing. However, given the actions of Alice, it was looking increasingly unlikely.

Whether it was the demon stalking her from the fiery depths of hell, or her gift conjuring up her worst nightmare to labour a point, she didn't want to encounter the evil child murderer on his own turf. She was half-bluffing with her bold claim that she alone could stop him, but it was the only thing that made any sense following the visit from Peter's talking head.

The only two people inextricably tied to the cult's

prophecy were her and Zach. If one of them needed to go, then Zach was the obvious choice. In fact, he was the only choice.

Unsurprisingly, out of everyone, it was Zach who had the biggest problem with their new arrangement, repeatedly reminding her of Kane's rule about splitting up. When Meridia pointed out Izzy's absence meant they were already technically split up, Zach finally conceded and agreed to follow the others above ground. It was a decision Kane was in tacit agreement with.

Although he somehow scraped himself up off the floor, it was clear every step he took was agony. By the time Peter guided him to the alcove's entrance, he was dripping with sweat from exertion and totally spent. JJ was equally dependant, being shepherded around like a lost lamb by Grace as they shuffled their way to the weaver's lair.

Meridia felt the hairs on the back of her neck stand to attention the moment she clapped eyes on the vile pulsating eggs, and a gaggle of goosebumps bristled up her arms beneath her jumper. The feeling was infectious, and a debilitating sensation of dread soon swept its way around the group, stopping each of them in their tracks the second they collided with the alcove's acrid odour.

Without a second to spare, Peter wasted no time scooping Kane up and navigating his way across the deadly assault course of dormant acid-spewing abominations.

One by one they followed their newly appointed leader to the concrete safety of the secret passage, and when it came to Zach's turn, he gently brushed shoulder to shoulder with her, the way a cat does when looking for attention.

"Please promise me you won't go inside unless you have no choice..." He mumbled. His voice splintering as each ominous word stuck in his throat like a jagged shard of glass.

"I'm scared M...Kane...JJ...we almost lost them both today. What if we never see each other again? What if this is the end? I...I can't lose you...if I do, then what's the point?" His voice shattered into a thousand tiny pieces, so she squeezed his hand and then reached into her pocket.

"Remember this?" Meridia whispered, pulling out the tiny Lego figurine he gave her. She clenched it tight in her hand.

"I'll always find you...no matter what...I promise..." She placed the toy back in her pocket, then cuffed the tears rolling down her cheeks.

The thought of losing anyone else was too much to bear, but deep down, Meridia knew losing Zach would break her. She battled so hard to overcome such devastating loss and crippling grief, to brave horrors beyond her darkest nightmares, but in that moment, she realized it was all for him.

Ever since learning what was at stake, the thought of losing him, the thought of never seeing her best friend in the entire world, chilled Meridia to the bone. It was the one thing keeping her going after everything she went through, and now, one way or another, it was all coming to a head.

Zach was right. They might not see each other again. This might be the end of everything.

"It's time, Zach." Grace put her arm on Zach's shoulder. It was his turn. This was it.

Meridia felt the delicate thread holding her heart together unravel as all the pain and angst she so tightly clung to finally came undone and bled out into her chest. The searing sensation stung like liquid nitrogen, freezing her lungs until she could no longer breathe, and all the words she longed to say, but didn't know how, knotted together to form a lump in her throat.

"Be brave..." Meridia mumbled, for her own benefit, more than Zach's. "I'll find you...I promise."

She gave his hand one last squeeze, then watched as he tiptoed through the tangled web of weaver eggs and disappeared with Grace into the hazy fluorescent glow of the tunnel.

Although Peter and Dr Foster were quick to console her, all she felt was alone.

'*One must stay, and the other must go.*' The baleful words echoed in her mind. It was all on her now.

The fate of the world and her best friend's soul.

73

"It's all gonna be ok, you know..." Dr Foster stuck close to Meridia's side while Peter lit the way with JJ's phone.

They were approaching the last stretch of their journey as they searched for the secret passage that would lead them to Crooked House.

The uneven ground underfoot was more mud than stone, with damp, mouldy brickwork on either side giving the impression they wandered into the depths of an old castle dungeon. It felt cooler here too, which meant they were close.

"Your friends are in safe hands..." He continued.

The timbre of his voice was soothing, even as a whisper, like some of the old seventies soul singers her parents used to listen to on Sunday mornings, back when life was good.

"Nadia is gonna get Kane patched up, and Grace will keep them safe...she's much tougher than she looks." He dabbed at the cut on his head. A nervous tick he developed since leaving the others.

"You know what, though? I'd say you're the toughest of us all...maybe the toughest I've ever met, in fact."

"I don't feel tough right now...I feel useless. This power I have, that everyone keeps calling a gift, used to feel like a curse. Now I'm thinking maybe I'm the curse. All I do is put everyone around me in danger...it's like...it's like I'm a magnet. Just when I think I understand things...when I think I can even control it a little, it all changes again." Meridia shook her head and let out a deep sigh. "It's all so confusing...so...so..."

"Cryptic?"

"Yes...cryptic. That's the word. I wish I knew how to understand better so I could do something. Kane...JJ...Izzy... I can't seem to protect them...not like I did at the start. It's so frustrating. I keep worrying that I'm missing something... Just look at Tommy...I saw him in the future...not even that far in the future, but now he's gone. I mean, where is he? How can he save me in the future if Grady gets him in the present? Does it mean he's gonna be ok no matter what, or has the future already changed? And if the future has changed, then what happens to my...my mum?" The more she talked, the more her brain twisted like a pretzel.

"For what it's worth, I don't believe any of that negative crap you're filling your head with. You're not cursed...I think you're working through some kinks in your gift. My best guess is it's because you've not come of age yet. Those books I gave you back at the bunker...they're written by people just like you, and in every one of their stories they never saw so much as a sniff of a vision until they turned thirteen. Unlucky for some, eh?" He gave her a playful nudge to lift her from the doldrums.

"So that's why you asked back at the bunker...but what's so special about thirteen? Why am I seeing things early?"

"I don't know M...can I call you M?"

"Of course..."

"Well M, my best guess is that you're stronger than those who came before you..."

"Wait... when I saw another seer in the past...Beth...she told me I was the best of them...do you think that's what she meant? I'm sure she said I was the last too...but what if we can't wait till I'm thirteen? I don't even know if we're gonna make it through the next hour...I can't see anything right now but mould and rot..."

"Woah...easy. Instead of thinking about what you can't do, try thinking about everything you've already done...all the lives you've saved, over and over. For most people, this world is like granite. No matter what they do, they never quite leave the mark on it, they hoped. Or the one they were capable of. In fact, many struggle to leave any kind of mark at all. It all feels so rigid...rigged even. But for you, it's like wet clay...you can mould it and shape it into whatever you want it to be. That right there is a gift in my book. Don't underestimate all you've done. Now, as for the future, none of us truly know the mysteries of time, but for what it's worth, I think what you're seeing in your visions are ripples in time. I believe they're coming from the waves you and your friend have been making as you try to change things for the better. Sometimes to see more clearly, the only thing you can do is let the waters settle..."

"This must be it." Peter came to a sudden halt and traced the shabby wall to their right with his flashlight until it reached a narrow opening between the bricks.

"Looks like someone beat us here...the door's already open."

"Gregor?"

"Who knows...could've been Grady...or maybe whoever

attacked Kane...I heard a scream in the tunnel earlier and it came from this direction." He shone his torch at the doorway and watched the impenetrable darkness devour its beam whole.

"Only one way to find out..." He shrugged, edging closer, and Meridia felt the icy fingers of dread creep up her spine and grip the back of her neck.

She was enjoying her exchange with the doctor until that point, and even though his comment about ripples and water settling sailed over her head, it gave her something else to think about beyond Zach.

Maybe one day they would get the chance to continue the conversation under better circumstances, but for now, all eyes were on the ominous void waiting in front of them.

"Wait!" Dr Foster grabbed Peter's arm; his nerves were getting the better of him again. "Wh...what if Grady's in there...or worse?"

"It doesn't really matter who's in there...I've still got to go through that door to get to Izzy." As Peter ventured nearer, he saw the door to the secret entrance was ajar, obstructing his view inside.

"I think you should both wait here now to be safe. If what Gregor told us is true, then the chamber on the other side of this door sits underneath Crooked House, so if I'm not back within the hour, then you need to leave me and go. Understand?" Peter gave them both a stern look.

"I don't want any last ditched heroics. Just cut and run. M, if you are the only one who can stop the demon, then you can do it from elsewhere...that was the deal."

Meridia nodded reluctantly, and Peter placed a hand on the open door then planted his feet.

"Wait..." Again, Dr Foster stalled.

"What now?" Peter rasped.

"What happened to your disguise? You can't go in like that. They'll see you coming from a mile away..."

"I think that plan went out the window the second we all got separated, so now I'm hoping there's still time to get in and out with no one seeing me. The trapdoor leads directly to where Izzy's being held, and Gregor didn't seem to think anyone else would be in that room until the ceremony. So, if there's nothing else you want to chat about, I'm going to get going now, ok?"

"Sorry..." Dr Foster waved his hands in surrender.

"Er...go get 'em?" Meridia cringed as he shook a fist in the air as a show of support.

He was a weird fish. One minute full of poise and self-assurance, the next riddled with crippling awkwardness. She was slowly warming to him, though, and in some strange way, his failed pep talk took the sting out of the tension brewing since they waved goodbye to the others.

Peter nodded, stifling a cringe of his own, and then disappeared into the murky catacombs beneath Crooked House.

<h1 style="text-align:center">74</h1>

Peter didn't make it more than a few tentative steps inside the murky torture chamber when his flashlight clipped the edge of a solitary crimson spot on the ground about the size of a penny.

It appeared fresh as it shimmered in the shadows, patiently waiting for the desiccated earth beneath to lay claim to it. The instant his brain registered the blood spatter, the world around him fell deathly silent and all Peter heard was his heartbeat pounding in his ears like the drums of war.

Every fibre of his being was screaming for him to bolt, but his legs remained frozen, fixed to the spot by an invisible force. Peter guided the quivering torchlight deeper into the darkness, remembering his last visit to this part of the tunnel. His brother's burnt-out car and grisly charred remains greeted him that day.

What horrors lurked in the shadows this time?

The stony walls beneath Crooked House were reminiscent of a castle dungeon. Composed of oversized and crudely cut bricks that came in a hotchpotch of shapes and shades ranging from insipid taupe to putrid green.

To his left was the busted remains of an old wooden door. Its jagged splinters littered across the ground like forgotten firewood left to rot. Peter knew somewhere beyond the battered doorway was the dreaded crypt beneath room 4.

Rotting corpses filled the room floor to ceiling the last time he was here. Nameless victims of an ancient evil, fused together by rancid decay. Then, shortly after, the tunnel was teeming with hooded maniacs like a pack of rabid guard dogs ready to chase away any unwanted trespassers.

Peter knew he needed to keep moving, but the single speck of blood wouldn't leave him alone. Calling to him from within the darkness and dragging his flashlight back toward its thick, glossy sheen. In his bid to rediscover it, his light found the foreboding flicker of another, and then another.

A trail of bloody breadcrumbs, each speck larger than the last, leading to the furthest corner of the dungeon, until eventually his curiosity turned to regret, and he almost dropped his phone in horror.

"Dear god..." he muttered, clamping his mouth shut in disgust.

A grotesque, tangled mess of flaccid organs and twisted entrails lay gathered in the corner, glistening red in the dim light. Coiled intestines sprawled across the ground like a string of splattered sausages, leaving a gory trail of congealed claret clinging to the dirt.

Edging closer, Peter hit an invisible wall of metallic stench as it overpowered the stink of mildew and brought him to a halt. Beyond the hideous pile of innards, the corner of the dungeon was bare apart from a brown worker boot streaked with blood.

Was this the work of a weaver?

"Drip...drop..."

Startled by what sounded like a leaky tap, Peter jerked his flashlight skyward and felt the warm and slushy contents of his stomach erupt from the pit of his throat.

"Kaff...splat..." He peppered the ground with puke as he reeled away from the grisly sight shackled to the ceiling.

The boy who stabbed Kane was now hanging high above him. Chained by his wrists and ankles, then hoisted into the rafters. With arms spread out like wings, he resembled a fallen angel, plucked of all his feathers and dangling on display. His ribcage was cracked wide open like a piñata, spilling his shiny guts onto the ground below, while jagged splinters of blood-streaked bone, like ivory fingers, reached out from the gory depths of his hollow chest.

Staring down glassy-eyed at the twisted bouquet of viscera, his face, bruised and bloodied, was aghast with fear, frozen in the last moments of a brutal and sadistic death.

It had to be the work of Grady. Another barbarous show of strength, left out like a gruesome scarecrow to frighten away anyone foolish enough to follow him.

As Peter backed away from the macabre spectacle, his thoughts turned to Izzy and the chilling message Grady carved into Declan's corpse. Both he and Gregor interpreted it as a sickening reminder of the approaching sacrifice, but now Peter wasn't so sure.

With all signs pointing to Grady going rogue and turning against his master, there was no telling if it was already too late to save Izzy.

Regardless of what might be waiting for him inside

room 4, he needed to stay focused and prepare for the worst. Peter fumbled around in the doorway for a splinter of wood he could use as a weapon and settled on a sharpened stake fit for a vampire.

Holding it aloft to get a feel for its weight, he found its underbelly was crawling alive with termites. Dozens of tiny, almond-shelled parasites tickled the hairs on his hand and arm as they abandoned their home and burrowed up his shirt sleeve.

"*Clatter!*"

Peter launched the lump of wood at the nearest wall, then set about brushing and shaking off the skittering crustaceans. Even though he knew they weren't dangerous, he could already feel them halfway up his arm. Skin crawling and spine tingling, he danced a mini jig trying to rid himself of the horde of prickly legs running amok beneath his clothes, frantically slapping and squishing them under the folds of his shirt.

"Ahh!"

Blindly backing out of the dungeon in a tizzy, he turned and collided with a hooded figure lurking in the doorway behind him.

The man, shrouded in tattered robes, stood his ground and watched Peter from beneath the shadow of his cowl. There was only one way he could get to Izzy now, and that was through the menacing disciple blocking his path.

75

"Peter...thank god! It's me, Tommy..." Tommy lowered his hood and let out a tremendous sigh as he hunched over on his knees in relief. "I...I thought Grady got you..."

"Where's Gregor?" Peter got straight to the point, refusing to unclench his fists.

He had lingering doubts about Tommy, so he wasn't about to let his guard down now.

"Where the hell have you been, pal?" Gregor peered around the corner behind Tommy. "I was just about to go in without you..."

"*Whack!*"

Peter marched over and punched the diminutive Scotsman square on the jaw, knocking him to the ground and sending his ceremonial dagger clattering against the shingly earth.

"That's for Zach!" Peter fumed, standing over him whilst gearing up to take another swing.

"Woah woah woah...what's going on?" Tommy stepped

in between them as Gregor scraped himself back up off the floor, clutching his chin.

"Stay out of this Tommy, it doesn't concern you...or perhaps is does. Perhaps you've both been in on this from the start..." Peter took a step back to create some space between them and tried to gauge Tommy's reaction.

"In on what?" His bewilderment seemed genuine as his eyes bounced blankly between both men.

"It's my bad..." Gregor snickered.

His flush cheeks belied his flippant tone, and it was easy for Peter to see where Meridia got her temper from. Unlike his daughter, though, Gregor exercised some restraint.

"I probably had that coming...but you won't get another one on the house, pal. You try that shit again and, giant or not, I'll hit you back."

"You've had more than that coming, you slippery little shit...conspiring to kill a twelve-year-old boy? You're lucky I don't knock you into next week..."

"Wait...what?" Tommy was out of the loop or an Oscar worthy actor, as he immediately sided with Peter and scowled at Gregor.

"C'mon...you mean to tell me that thought never crossed your mind? No, Zach equals no prophecy..."

"You sick fuck..." Peter took another step towards him in anger.

"Bring it on beanpole...you don't scare me." Gregor was all bark and no bite, sidestepping behind Tommy whilst pretending to square up to Peter, the way squabbling school children try to save face whilst avoiding a beating.

"It was just an insurance policy...in case the plan failed... I guess Alice got a bit trigger-happy. Can't say I blame her, given the circumstances. I mean, put yourself in our shoes...

we both have kids whose lives are on the line every second that Jackson boy is still breathing. What would you do? How far would you go to protect your own? It's the only guaranteed way to stop the prophecy from happening..."

"Well, it backfired and now JJ is without a mother and her blood is on your hands!" Peter growled.

All he wanted to do was knock seven bells out of Gregor, but there was no time. He needed to get back on track, with or without the conniving scumbag's help. He shoved past him and made his way out into the corridor.

Five shattered doors on either side and a brick wall up ahead were waiting for him. To his mild surprised, Tommy was quick to follow.

"Wait...Alice is...dead? How?" Peter ignored Gregor and instead focused on getting his bearings.

"What the hell have you both been doing all this time?" Peter fizzed.

"Hiding..." Tommy confessed.

"When we came under attack, we heard someone ahead of us ...Gregor snatched me away, down a side tunnel...we waited there until things settled. It was a good thing too... the guy in that room...I...I heard his screams as Grady did that to him...*sniff*...It could've been me..." Tommy's voice fractured like it was made of silica glass.

"We only ventured out when you showed up behind us...we...we heard a door slam and Gregor thinks he's moved on now, but we don't know where..." Tommy trailed off as Peter gestured to another dungeon on the opposite side of the passageway.

"Room 4 is that way..." As his flashlight skimmed the rusted brass number nailed above the forbidding doorway, he felt a shiver scuttle up his spine abruptly, followed by a wave of nausea, and he fleetingly wondered if it was a runaway woodlouse.

There was every chance now Grady was waiting for them inside Crooked House. He only hoped he didn't already follow through on his earlier promise and Izzy was still alive. He glanced at his watch.

"We have less than an hour now before sunset, so we need to get moving."

"You can't get up there without me..." Gregor boasted. "Only I know where the ladder is."

"Up where?" Tommy asked naively, and then gasped as Peter illuminated the dungeon for all to see.

The cell beneath room 4 changed considerably since Peter's last visit, and he breathed a sigh of relief when he found the putrid pile of bodies was no longer there. All that remained were a smattering of sludgy puddles where the decomposed corpses once oozed into the earth, along with the lingering stench of sulphur and rotting flesh.

Their absence cleared a path for Peter to see the pentagram in all its glory, carved deep into the muddy ground. Its slop-filled trenches were now bone dry. Licked clean by a hungry weaver, if Zach's terrifying dream was to be believed.

As he continued to scan the room, Peter's torch ricochetted off shards of broken mirror that lay scattered on the ground, throwing jagged echoes of light into the gloom. This was where the weaver was summoned.

Perhaps this was the final confirmation that whatever visions Valerie subjected Zach to that night were rooted in reality. To think Meridia endured such horrors on a daily basis was too much for Peter to comprehend. Marcus was right. She was the bravest of them all.

"You mean that ladder?" Tommy pointed up towards

the ceiling and Peter followed with his flashlight, catching the rungs of a rope ladder dangling beneath a square wooden hatch.

Its shadow sprawled down the stony wall like an ominous spider's web, each rung a harsh reminder of their impending ascent into hell. There was little doubt now that Grady passed through the tunnel before them, and as the ladder hung like a twisted spine, Peter knew its crooked vertebrae would lead them straight to him.

"Grady's up there...waiting. We need to find another way inside..." Gregor trembled.

"It's too late for that...I made a promise and I'm going to stick to it." Peter snapped, gripping the nearest rung and steadying the ropes.

"Don't you see? He already has the higher ground... we're on a hiding to nothing. It's suicide..."

"I'm going up to get Izzy, and I'm going to get her out of here. We don't have time to find another way inside. Not now. You can do whatever you want with your toy knife... I'll take my chances with the demon." Peter began climbing.

"Hold it still for me will you..." He gestured to Tommy below as the ladder corkscrewed with every step.

"Hold it will you..." Tommy delegated to Gregor and stepped onto the ladder behind Peter. "If my dad's up there, then I need to find him...Grady can't take us both on at once..."

Peter felt another tug on the ladder beneath and saw Gregor joined them on their ascent. The ceiling was close to thirty feet high, but despite the ladder's twisting and writhing, it didn't take long to reach its summit. Peter pressed his palm against the cold wooden struts of the trapdoor and gave it a gentle nudge.

"*Creeeeak...*"

Surprisingly, the hatch offered little resistance and so, accepting the element of surprise had long since deserted them, he gave the door a firm shove and flipped it open.

"*Bang!*"

The trapdoor opened unhindered, slamming against the floor on the other side, and Peter wasted no time hoisting himself up through the opening. He was halfway through wriggling out of the hatch onto his belly when he heard a familiar smarmy voice ring out over his shoulder.

"How nice of you to drop in, Peter...we've been waiting for you..."

76

"I feel useless just waiting here," Meridia huffed. "What if they need me?"

"Shh...we don't know who or what else might be roaming these tunnels..." Dr Foster was twitchier than ever.

Having coxed her a few yards away from the secret door, he was now nervously glancing at either end of the tunnel as his eyes chased phantom noises in the dark.

"You heard the voices too...I think one of them might have been my dad." Meridia shuffled away from the wall they were both hugging.

"He can't be trusted...not after what he tried to do to Zach..." Her father's latest stunt was unforgivable, crossing a line there was no coming back from.

Although she loathed to say it, as far as she was concerned, Gregor might as well be dead to her now. The thought he might now be alone with Peter tightened the knot of dread that now permanently lived in the pit of her stomach.

"*Bang...*"

"Did you hear that?" Meridia pleaded. "Peter could be in trouble."

The muffled sound of a door slamming only added to the growing tension in the otherwise eerily quiet tunnel.

"We need to go look...he'd do it for us, and you know he would."

"He told me I have to keep you safe, and that's what I'm doing..." Dr Foster tried to shepherd Meridia back to the safety of the wall as if they were both standing on the ledge of a skyscraper.

She saw his fear got the better of him again, and even if they needed to flee back down the tunnel, she doubted his congealed legs would allow him. Maybe she should make a run for it, force the issue. The doctor would either follow her or not, and despite her fondness of him as a person, she knew she couldn't depend on his heroics in a time of crisis.

In fact, watching him squirm in the shadows, he reminded her of the cowardly lion in The Wizard of Oz and she could just picture him anxiously petting his own tail to soothe his jittery nerves.

Meridia needed to do something. In the seconds that elapsed since the sudden door slam, the tunnel was quick to resume its unnatural stillness. But the silence wasn't empty. It carried a weight with it.

An oppressive heaviness grew thicker and colder. With each passing minute, she was forced to fidget impatiently with her back to the cobbles, hamstrung by a giant scaredy-cat.

She thought about faking a vision, concocting a reason for them to go in after Peter; one that was more convincing than a 12-year-old's instincts. Then she heard it.

A whispery voice weaving its way out of the darkness,

and her conscience reminded her to be careful of what she wished for.

"*Meridiaaa...*"

77

As Peter scrambled to his feet, the ghoulish and unsettling face of Grady greeted him.

A far cry from the oily tick he encountered at Chase Side. He was now the stuff of nightmares. His homemade makeup was a crimson mess smeared into a bloody smile that was far too wide for his narrow face, and far too vivid to be anything but deranged. The same glistening cherry-red circled his deep-set eyes, giving him the hollow, sunken look of a skull, with only the occasion glint of sapphire to suggest he had any eyes at all.

Cowering in front of him was Izzy, his serrated knife pressed to her throat. Her appearance was every bit as shocking as Grady's, almost reducing Peter to tears the moment he locked eyes with her.

Dishevelled and in distress, she looked a pale, emaciated shadow of her former self. With lank hair matted to her grubby face, and tattered clothes swamping her scrawny frame, Izzy's bloodshot eyes looked empty behind her grimy glasses and her spirit broken.

"Izzy!" She flinched as her name erupted from Peter's mouth, a mix of anger and sorrow, while Grady held onto her firm. His demented smile spread wider across his smug face like a slithering snake.

"Ah, you've brought some friends...who do we have here then?" Over his shoulder, Peter heard Tommy clamber up through the trapdoor, followed by Gregor. "Well, well, well...the prodigal troll returns...you shouldn't have dressed up on my account, brother...and you've brought a toy knife with you. How sweet!"

"Let the girl go, Grady!" Peter regained some of his composure as he carefully surveyed their surroundings.

The room was stripped of all its furniture, aside from a red rug tossed into its corner, and a heavy chest of drawers with a macabre iron bust on top of it. He came across the creepy sculpture before, on his first visit to Crooked House, and was instantly reminded why it made its owner's skin crawl.

Staring out from beneath a thorny veil of barbed wire, the statuette's haunting gaze watched over them all from the middle of the room like a nefarious arbiter overseeing a deadly game of chess.

In the farthest corner, Grady stood with his back pressed against a door. Their only other means of escape from a concrete prison where the day's dying light waned through the heavy wooden slats of its barricaded windows.

"Ha! Is this it?" Grady glanced down at the trapdoor, expecting more to join them.

"Where's the rest of the gang? Where's the seer and that snivelling little shit Zach that everyone's so obsessed with?"

For the first time since Peter met him, Gregor held his tongue. Tommy also remained silent but circled around to

Peter's left in a show of support, even if he was now clearly way out of his depth.

"Zach is dead..." Peter bluffed. "Murdered by one of yours..."

He watched the news shatter Izzy like a porcelain doll, but Grady remained poker-faced, his beady blue eyes narrowing in contemplation.

"It's over, Grady...your master's precious prophecy is ruined. Let the girl go..."

"Can't you tell? I am my own master now..." Grady sneered, gesturing at his bloodstained face. "I am here to fulfill my own prophecy..."

Izzy winced as he pulled the blade closer to her throat.

"Wait!" Peter exclaimed. "Let her go and take me instead..." He shuffled a step closer with both hands raised in submission.

"Ha ha...you can't bargain here teacher...you have nothing to bargain with. You see, when I kill this whining little bitch, I'm going to kill all of you anyway...ha ha...you really think you're something, don't you? A knight in shining armour, swooping in to save the day. I watched you in the hospital carpark, rescuing this one..." He pulled Izzy's head up by her hair, stretching her slender neck to its limit.

"You think you stand a chance against me? Do you think any of you do? Don't let a lucky punch go to your head teacher...so you bopped a frightened kid on the nose, big deal. Brother Alman was punished for his incompetence. In fact, you might have bumped into him on your way in here...I had his guts for garters...ha ha..."

It was clear Grady was a different animal to the smarmy nurse Peter bumped into at the hospital. The man they were at the mercy of now was a monster in every sense of the word. Wildly unpredictable and thirsty for blood, regardless of who it belonged to.

There would be no reasoning with him, and with the knife so close to Izzy's jugular, he could slit her throat in a heartbeat.

"We saw the bloodbath at the temple..." Gregor joined the fray.

"What's the Grand Master gonna do when he finds out what you've done? You reckon he'll think twice about killing a basket case like you? Fuck me, you have gone mad brother...and what's your handler gonna say too when she finds out? Tut tut..." Shaking his head condescendingly, he stepped shoulder to shoulder with Peter and slipped something into his back pocket without Grady noticing.

Peter checked to see what he was given and felt the smooth plastic of a car key fob between his fingers. What was Gregor up to?

"She already knows..." Grady shrugged. "I drove my knife right through her miserable face, then left her to rot in my van. I did it before I butchered your chubby little friend. Ha ha...he begged, you know...he got down on his knees and begged me to spare him. I never spare anyone...not anymore..."

Peter saw Grady's knuckles whiten as he tightened his grip on the knife and so took another tentative step closer.

"Not anymore...ha ha..." The killer's eyes glazed over, and for a moment the only sound in the room was Izzy's whimpering.

"*I've got no strings to hold me down... to make me fret, or make me frown...*" Grady's head seesawed from side to side to a silent melody as he mumbled his way through the song from Pinocchio.

"*I've got no strings, so I have fun...I'm not tied up to*

anyone. They've got strings, but you can see...there are no strings on me..."

Grady was a ticking time bomb of unspeakable violence and right now he held Izzy's life in the palm of his bloody hand.

"What about the moon?" Peter blurted.

He was desperate now, sensing Grady was on the verge of doing something drastic.

"Killing her now won't bring back the demon..."

"Ha, that's it!" Gregor scoffed. "You want to summon him, don't you...You want to be the one that resurrects him so you can control him...ha ha...what is this amateur hour? They're never going to let a nut job like you get away with that...besides you don't even have the right knife dipshit..." Gregor waved the replica to make his point.

Peter had no clue what reckless game Gregor was playing, but if the success of his plan hinged on getting under Grady's skin, then so far, he was failing miserably.

"Oh, you mean this old thing?" Grady reached behind him and revealed the real ceremonial dagger in all its handcrafted, cypher-engraved glory.

The sight of it sucked the air out of the room and sent Izzy into a tailspin.

"What's the matter, brother? Cat got your tongue? I know what you're doing by the way...goading me...trying to rattle my cage in the hope I lose my head...make a mistake. I know all the tricks, brother...just like I know you're all creeping that little bit closer. Must we go through these tired old motions? Come as close as you want. It won't change anything. You're about to discover the stories about me are all true. None of you will leave here alive..." Grady grinned, but his pristine teeth looked lost in the expanse of his chainsaw smile.

"How about you put the knife away and let's see just how true those stories are..." Gregor continued to poke and prod, looking for a chink in Grady's armour.

All Peter saw was the blade inching ever closer to Izzy's throat.

"*I know something you don't know. I know something you don't know...*" He descended into a playground chant as once again the pendulum of his splintered personality swung from calculated killer to petulant child.

Maybe Gregor was slowly wearing him down after all, but at what cost?

"C'mon then...why don't you put your money where your stupid looking mouth is and let's see what you're made of mummy's boy." Gregor was like a dog with a bone, refusing to let up.

"C'mon, what are you waiting for? Put the knife down and give me your best shot...I dare you..." Grady ignored the bate and spoke with disconcerting calmness.

"You can't provoke me...any more than you can reason with me or appeal to some deep-rooted sensibility. You're all so hung up on your tedious little rules that you've forgotten what you are... as if any of your pathetic games really matter... Do you honestly think a fair fight means anything to me? Look at me! Look at my face! Do you think I do what I do for status? For childish bragging rights? You all stand there judging me by your own petty values...like my urge to rip your spines out with my bare hands is somehow tempered by a burning desire for parity... as if I care."

"Deep down you're all the same...you, the Grand Master...this entire worthless town. You all like to pretend you're better than everyone else...perpetually reinventing right and wrong just so you can condemn others to make yourselves feel better about your worthless, miserable lives...

but it's all a sham. You're all slaves to a concept...you're handcuffed to it. Humanity is a label concocted to control you, a lie you've been sold to keep you in your place. You're all conditioned to do exactly as you're told...and if you break the rules, then you're conditioned to carry the burden of your sins for the rest of your lives. You wear them like a ridiculous badge of honour. It's all designed that way...to keep you fluctuating between fear and regret...denying you of your urges so you stay inside the lines. I know...I spent most of my childhood that way...bullied, picked on... tormented for being different...but the truth was, they were all jealous." Grady's sinister smile slivered further across his face as he continued.

"You're all jealous...you secretly envy me because I'm free. I can see that now. It was the demon who showed me all those years ago. I watched him kill my brother in front of me...not for favour, but for joy...because he wanted to. Because he had an itch, and he chose to scratch it. In that moment, he showed me the way, and I was free. Free from years of abuse. Years of suffocation. He saw it as I crushed my brother's eyeball to mush in the palm of my chubby little hand. He saw it and he let me live. But the truth is, I haven't lived...not really. I stumbled out of the frying pan and into the fire...became a prisoner to another set of stupid rules. A slave to another false promise. Don't do this Silas...don't do that..."

"You're the boy, aren't you..." Gregor was quick to pounce. "The little boy in the woods that was so pathetic even the demon took pity on him...ha! You're the snivelling bedwetter...it all makes sense now. Your mummy and daddy issues...rebelling against your master..."

Grady's smile abruptly dropped, and he lowered his ghoulish gaze toward Izzy.

"You don't know what you're talking about. None of you do! The Grand Master is a liar, like all the rest of you. The demon deserves better...I can see that now, so I'm here to set him free...repay the debt I owe. That's why I took the master's precious knife...but it's not why I killed all those pitiful police officers who were tasked with protecting it...I did that because I wanted to. It brought me joy. Just as it will when I slit this girl's throat and watch her bleed out all over the floor..."

Peter heard the knife handle creak in Grady's palm and felt a heavy sinking sensation in the pit of his stomach that dragged all hope down with it.

"Killing her now won't bring the demon back..." Despite everything he heard, Peter persisted in trying to force the irrational psychopath to see reason. 'Going through the motions' as Grady called it. Not because he expected a different outcome or for the killer to come to his senses, but because when push came to shove, reason and logic were the only weapons Peter had in his arsenal.

"See, there you go again..." Grady snorted.

"Tied to those silly little rules and traditions...they blind you all to the truth. I'm not such a stickler, you see...not anymore. I'm evolving...changing...from a caterpillar to a butterfly. That's why I'm here and the Grand Master isn't..." Grady swapped his hunting knife out in favour of the dagger and Gregor's foot tremored, scuffing the stone tile he was rooted to as he sensed the briefest of openings.

But the slightest sniff of any advantage was instantly snuffed out by Grady's speed, and they returned to their high-stakes standoff. The sands of time were slipping away from them, and the serrated ceremonial blade glimmered ominously beneath the embers of light still seeping through the room's boarded windows as Grady pressed it tight to Izzy's neck.

"You all think the moon only rears its head at night, but a free man like me can already see it poking through the clouds. You mindless puppets think it's me that's too early, when really it's you who are all too late. Look outside if you don't believe me. The blood moon has already ascended and the dawn of the demon is upon us..."

<h1 style="text-align:center">78</h1>

"*Meridiaaa...*"

The ghostly whisper grew louder, a child's voice.

Meridia glanced up at Dr Foster to find him standing stock-still like a waxwork. His eyes were glazed and his face wrought with worry as he stared into the gloomy distance of the tunnel. A nanosecond of pensive dread expanded in perpetuity, while Meridia remained free to roam beyond the confines of space and time.

Even the air felt cold and still, holding the rancid stench of decay at bay, while dozens of dust particles dithered beneath the opaque glow of Dr Foster's frozen flashlight, like tiny helicopters searching for a landing spot.

"Granite vs clay..." she mumbled. The doctor's baffling comparison made a little more sense as she straddled both worlds simultaneously.

"*Meridiaaa...hehe...*"

The voice grew louder still, now less of a whisper and more of a playground taunt. Nasal and playful. With her only source of light pointed firmly at the ground, she gazed deeper into the black abyss, beyond the threshold of the secret door, and waited.

If her gift had a message to deliver, it could damn well come to her this time. She had more than her fill of wandering off in search of phantom apparitions bearing bad news.

"Who's there..." she called, then rolled her eyes. Even with time frozen still, she lacked the patience to wait.

"What do you want?" She doubled down, straining to see through the murk.

The door was ajar, just as Peter left it, but the narrow opening gave her nothing to go on and was too far away for her to see into clearly. Perhaps if she shuffled just a little closer?

Meridia skirted sideways along the tunnel like a nervous crab, scraping the back of her coat along the icy limestone with each angst-ridden step. The more cobbles she covered, the more the temperature plummeted, until she saw each breath linger in front of her, then slowly evaporate upward toward the tunnel's ceiling.

Whoever was calling her name remained silent in the shadows, reeling her in on their line like a prize catch. A prize idiot, Meridia thought, as she continued on. Her curiosity and impatience conspiring against her as they so often did.

"*Hehehe...*"

A blackness, deeper than the surrounding gloom, flashed past at supernatural speed beyond the door's entrance, and Meridia froze mid-step. She saw nothing more than a glimpse. A shifting ripple of shadows vanished into the void as quickly as it appeared, but that was all it took to deter her from venturing any further.

"J...Jessica?" Meridia stammered in hope, but her legs

knew otherwise, turning to lead and keeping her anchored where she was.

The wall's arctic chill seeped through her winter coat and into her bones, tickling her spine as she stood with her back pressed against it, paralyzed by fear.

"Sh...show yourself..." Her runaway mouth struck again, calling out whatever baleful spectre was lurking up ahead.

'Careful what you wish for,' her whispering conscience retorted.

"Crack! Clatter!"

Suddenly, the wall behind her fractured and a legion of rotten, maggot-riddled hands with splintered nails and shrivelled skin, clawed their way through the cracks and crumbling stone, latching onto Meridia's limbs and pinning her to the cobbles with their icy grip.

"Argh..."

A fetid hand quickly snuffed her screams out, clamping across her mouth. The festering stink of decay seared her nostrils and clung to the back of her throat as she writhed in vain to break free from their slimy skeletal fingers.

Alone and trapped between two worlds, Meridia's eyes dilated in horror beneath their unyielding grasp as a scrawny, child-like figure slinked towards her from the shadows.

Crawling on all fours, it twitched and jerked like a juddering bag of bones, scraping the ground with a lank mop of scraggly hair that in life might have been blonde, but in death was a mouldy shade of green.

The feral zombie's bony carcass was a flurry of scabby knees and jagged elbows as it scuttled closer like a stop-motion spider, and as it reached the threshold of the light,

Meridia saw its cadaverous skin was a mottled melange of decomposed flesh, caked in congealed blood.

Approaching the tangled vines of undead hands holding Meridia prisoner, her spine-chilling stalker stopped and looked up from under her musty mane. Soulless, milky-white orbs scowled at her from the depths of their scaly sockets.

"Our blood is on your hands..." the child rasped.

Its withered face was so hideously decomposed it was impossible for Meridia to tell if it was a girl or a boy. Then she saw the tattered necktie dangling beneath its sallow jowl. Soiled with blood, the red and black stripes of St Swithun's were unmistakable, and the sight of them made Meridia's blood run cold.

"Scrape-slap...scrape-slap..."

The door behind her gruesome schoolmate violently erupted and a stampede of skittering corpses, like the one crouched at Meridia's feet, poured into the tunnel, scurrying straight for her.

Clambering up the walls and scampering across the ceiling, the infestation of twisted and tormented souls looked like they clawed their way out from the bottom of a malignant well, but amongst the patchwork quilt of putrid flesh and protruding bones, they all had one thing in common: the red and black of St Swithun's. From manky blazers to ragged ties, each wore the shabby remnants of Meridia's school uniform.

Streaming into the corridor like a burst water main, the sea of twitching and creaking cadavers stopped in unison and stared at Meridia with alabaster disdain, as another silhouette slowly emerged from the shadows behind them.

"You're too late..." Meridia instantly recognized the whispery, wraithlike voice as Izzy staggered into the light.

Scuffing and dragging her lumbering feet along the ground, her head was slumped onto her scrawny shoulder, held on by a sliver of serrated skin like stretched elastic. Her throat was brutally slashed to the bone from ear to ear and bleeding out into her grubby, threadbare sweater.

"This isn't real... This isn't real..." Meridia clenched her eyes shut, unable to stomach the sight of her mutilated friend.

"*I waited for you...*" she wheezed and gurgled, "*...but you never came. Now look at what you've done...*"

Did this mean Peter failed? Was Izzy already dead? With gritted teeth, Meridia prised her weeping eyes open. What use was a vision of the future if she couldn't alter its course?

Her world was meant to be wet clay, not dried cement, and so she forced herself to heed Izzy's ominous message.

"*I belong to him now...*" Izzy rasped. "*Beware the lost souls Meridia...We are the eyes and ears of the beast...*"

Blinking away her tears, she found her cadaverous peers stacked on top of one another in a pyramid of unnatural angles. Their scraggy arms and legs twisted like broken mannequins, whilst their gaunt faces hung agape in a chorus of silent screams.

No longer the living dead, they were just dead. Their pale, waxy flesh glistening in the dim afterglow of Dr Foster's flashlight. Atop the pile of bloodless bodies lay Izzy, her neck still ajar as she gazed up at the ceiling. Her expression was one of release, not suffering, and from her gory wound a crimson stream trickled down into the crevasses of her fallen schoolmates like water down a mountain.

Suddenly, the horde of decomposed hands holding her hostage crumbled and turned to dust, releasing Meridia from their rancid embrace. Darting clear of the wall, she felt her knees give way at the gory spectacle sprawled out before her. She needed to get out of here and find Peter. Izzy's message was loud and clear. Meridia wasted too much time on the sidelines.

"Time to wake up M..." she growled, clenching her fists as she tried to wrestle back the wheel from her wretched gift.

"*Wheeze...*"

Izzy's gaping mouth released a gush of air, as if she were winded, and it dragged Meridia back, kicking and screaming, to the confines of her grisly vision. Perhaps there was more to her heartbreaking premonition.

"Izzy?" Meridia whispered, shuffling closer to the putrefied pile of human remains.

"Izzy!" She flinched as Izzy arched her back to form a bridge. Her spine crackled with rigor mortis, and then she fell limp again.

"Izzy?" Meridia mumbled, then baulked when Izzy's back arched again, this time to the point of breaking, as she folded herself completely in half.

"*Crack!*"

Her spine finally snapped. A stomach-turning crunch, rattling even Meridia's bones, then Izzy's body fell limp, and her arms flopped back to her side like a rag doll.

"*Crack...splat!*"

A humongous, brawny hand swathed in blood violently punched a hole through Izzy's ribcage, erupting from inside her chest like a volcano. Veins pulsing, it clawed toward the ceiling with sinewy fingers, curled with murderous intent as it heralded the demon's resurrection.

"Ahh!" Meridia's scream shook the tunnel, as a hand clamped down on her shoulder.

"Meridia, you need to stay away from the door..." Dr Foster wore feigned disapproval as he tried to usher her back towards the safety of the wall. The same wall was just pinned to by an army of the undead.

She turned back to find her harrowing vision had delivered its final punchline and exited the stage, leaving the path clear for Meridia to make her escape.

"I'm sorry doctor..." she mumbled before wriggling free of his grip and bolting through the open door.

Fumbling for her phone to light the way, she charged through the secret dungeon without looking back until she stumbled out into the tunnel beneath Crooked House. She heard Dr Foster hot on her heels, so without a moment's hesitation, she found her bearings and raced toward the chamber that would take her to room 4. Enough was enough.

The time for creeping around in the shadows was over. Piece by painful piece, this vile and despicable house was relentlessly taking everything from her, stripping her bare.

Meridia would be damned if she was going to let it take Izzy. She needed to find her before it was too late.

79

"CREAK..."

Inside the pressure cooker of room 4, Peter heard the rope creak over his shoulder and then felt the blood drain from his face. Someone else was on their way up the ladder, and he had a terrible feeling it was Meridia.

"What's this I hear? More visitors?" Grady beamed like a dog with two tails and granted Izzy a temporary stay of execution.

Regardless of his scathing lecture on the shortcomings of humanity, it was clear Grady's ego was still at play and Peter was certain he'd noticed a twitch in the corner of the killer's mouth during Gregor's last tirade of abuse. His air of self-control was the biggest sham, and beneath his disturbing war paint, it was clear to see he remained highly unstable.

Perhaps if they all chipped in to undermine him, they would fluster him long enough to get to Izzy. As he glanced at the dagger's razor-sharp teeth digging into her quivering flesh, he thought better of it. Besides, even if Gregor struck a raw nerve, there was nothing to suggest Grady wouldn't follow through on his threat to Izzy before turning his attention to the rest of them.

"*Huff...*"

Just as Peter feared, a wavy red mop of hair poked up through the trapdoor as Meridia puffed and panted her way into the room. What on earth was she thinking, blundering into Crooked House with no thought to her own safety? Where the hell was Dr Foster?

"Wow...I am honoured..." Grady mocked. "The infamous seer, gracing me with her presence..."

Meridia got to her feet and immediately baulked at the disturbing sight of their demented host. Before she uttered a word, Grady cut across her with another sardonic jibe.

"And who's this I hear bringing up the rear? Could it be your evil bitch of a mother, or is it one of the Jackson boys looking to avenge their poor mummy and daddy?"

The rope stopped creaking for a moment and Peter could almost hear the cogs turning in Marcus' brain as he no doubt contemplated running away with his tail between his legs.

"Hurry up...we haven't got all day." Grady bleated, and for a moment he relaxed his hold on Izzy to tap an imaginary watch with the tip of his blade.

Again, Gregor held off from making a move as the rope resumed its creaking, and Dr Foster clumsily clambered through the trapdoor to join them.

"Oh...who are you?" Grady looked bemused beneath his maniacal mask as the doctor scrambled to his feet and then flinched at the lunatic's disturbing appearance.

"Another vagrant from Drayton Hollow, I presume...I planned to butcher you all when I did your muffin-top friend, but I had more pressing matters to attend to." He twisted the knife in his hand and painted the ceiling with fractured reflections of illegible glyphs.

"Still, it was extremely thoughtful of you all to come to me...saves me hunting you down later. It's been a very taxing afternoon in case you hadn't noticed..."

Grady feigned a toothy grin that had now lost some of its malevolent polish, and if Peter didn't know better, he would have said he was stalling. Maybe it was the surprise arrival of Meridia, or the line he was about to cross. Even if all the stories were true, surely, he was no match for the horsemen or their master. He was only human, after all, wasn't he?

"Enough of the small talk fuckwit..." Gregor rounded on him again and Peter heard Meridia and Marcus gasp in unison.

"You might wanna change your trousers before you off the girl...you don't want the demon to think you're still pissing your pants, do you?"

Everyone glanced down at the floor where Grady was standing and saw the dark yellow puddle expanding around his feet. Clearly Izzy's, the sight of it flustered him and Peter noticed the knife tremble in his hand.

"Hahahahaha..." Gregor forced a loud belly laugh, then cemented Grady's humiliation with a juvenile chant. "Pissy pants...pissy pants..."

Tommy joined in to form a two-man choir as they both belted out the crippling chorus, and Peter saw the cracks show in Grady's facade as he twitched and blinked his way to a full-blown fit.

Meridia was next to lend her voice, elevating the tone from a football chant to one fit for a playground. They delivered each spiteful verse vehemently, hitting their warped target with the force of a devastating body blow.

Grady's shoulders rose to the ceiling as he tried to quell his temper, but the chant kept coming, like a pit of poisonous snakes, poking and prodding at him as they tried to sink their teeth into his flesh. They were dicing with death now in every sense of the word, as Grady continued to tick his way closer to exploding.

Sensing the tables might turn, Peter joined in the aural assault, as did Marcus. Then, against all odds, Izzy summoned the strength and courage to accompany them, and that was the straw that broke the camel's back.

"Enough!" Grady screamed, pushing Izzy to the floor and launching himself at Gregor.

With lightning speed, Grady brutally lanced Gregor through the heart with the ceremonial dagger and then hoisted him into the air with one hand. Growling like a wild animal, he triumphantly shook Gregor by the knife's hilt, spattering the floor with flecks of claret.

The blood-streaked tip of the dagger glimmered as it jutted out between Gregor's shoulder blades, while his face, wide-eyed and aghast, fell limp towards his chest.

"You, brother Wilson...you can be the sacrifice now..." Grady hissed, and then tossed his body to the ground with the blade still in him.

"Noooooo!" Meridia screamed and made a lunge toward her dad, but Dr Foster was quick to restrain her as Peter scrambled to get Izzy behind him.

Poor Gregor didn't stand a chance. There was no way Grady was human, not with such devastating speed and strength on tap. Peter put as much distance between them as possible, backing everyone into the furthest corner of the room while Gregor's lifeless body slowly bled out onto the stony floor.

Grady's face lit up like a Christmas tree, his jagged and maniacal grin stretching beyond the bony confines of his jaw. His eyes were ablaze with a maddened fervour as he raised both bloody hands skyward like an evangelist of unadulterated evil.

"Now you'll see..." he bellowed. "You'll see, and then you will die at the hands of the demon...you will *all* be my offering, and there will be no escaping his wrath..."

His words were like venom, dripping into the ears of his imprisoned flock as he painted the air with foamed words and wild gestures like a crazed preacher. Gone was all trace of Grady's fleeting fragility and hesitation. He had crossed a line. There was no way back, not for any of them. As Peter stared at the locked door beyond the superhuman psycho, gone too was any hope of escape.

"Behold!" Grady cried, pointing to the floor. "Behold and bear witness...to the dawn of the demon..."

Between Peter and their chilling tormentor, Gregor lay curled in a crumpled heap. The only movement came from beneath him as his shimmering blood spread across the floor like satin, rich and smooth as it slowly seeped into the cracks and crevasses of the mottled stone tiles.

A stunned silence swept through the group as Grady ceased his ominous sermon, and they all stared with bated breath as the crimson pool soaked into the grey sandstone slabs of room 4 like they were cut from sponge. Crooked House was sucking every drop of blood from Grady's sacrificial offering, and Peter saw Gregor's flaccid hand grow whiter with each passing second.

As the ground continued to gorge, every cleft and

contour of Gregor's bones were laid bare as tissue and muscle disintegrated beneath his desiccated skin. The folds and furrows of his robes deflated like a burst balloon until all that remained was an emaciated husk shrouded in tragedy.

All signs pointed to defeat, but Peter refused to stand and wait to die at the hands of the demon. So, whilst all those around him lost their heads, he wracked his brain for another way out. The trapdoor was the only other option, but with a thirty-foot drop and only a solitary rope ladder to make their descent, there was no way he could get more than a couple to safety before Grady either cut the rope or sent the demon down after them. Not unless, that was, Peter could buy them more time.

Wild-eyed and revelling in his victory, Grady remained mesmerized by the grisly spectacle unfolding at the room's centre. Gregor's robes hardened like crystallized ginger, and the once flowing brown fabric now looked sallow and brittle, as if it were about to crumble. The creased edges, sucked dry of all their colour, were a powdery shade of silver and showed signs of cracking as the ground continued to devour the last vestiges of Meridia's father.

To Peter's left, Tommy remained frozen in a slack-jawed stupor and hadn't moved a muscle since Grady ruthlessly silenced their playground chant. Behind him, Marcus wrestled to contain Meridia, and now Izzy, who were both hysterical, following Gregor's shock demise.

The entire room was a raging storm of chaos and confusion, yet Peter had to find a way to sail through it if any of them were to survive. He grabbed Tommy's arm and pulled him tight to his side, forming a two-man wall as if they were lining up to defend a free-kick in a football match.

"Stay close..." he whispered.

His eyes never deviating from Grady and Gregor's carcass. Deeply immersed in his idol's impending return, the deranged killer didn't bat an eyelid at their sudden movement, so Peter moved onto the next phase of his tenuous plan.

Pointing vigorously at the trapdoor behind his back, he fought to get Marcus' attention over the pandemonium encircling him. It didn't take long for the doctor to get the message, and within a matter of seconds, he was crouched behind the human shield and trying his best to persuade both girls to retreat into the tunnels.

"Smash!"

A violent, icy gale burst into the room, shattering the windows behind their boarded barricades and showering everyone in prickly glass particles that nicked and nipped at their faces like a swarm of angry mosquitoes.

Shielding his eyes, Peter battled to see through the cutting wind as it continued to whip up into a wicked tornado, hellbent on ripping everything to shreds with its razor-tipped shrapnel. Scratching and clawing every corner of the room as if searching for a way out, the whistling rampage provided all the convincing Meridia and Izzy needed, and Peter saw Marcus guide them both down the trapdoor.

In the storm's eye, Grady seemed oblivious to the fact two of his hostages were about to slip through his bloodstained fingers as he danced and twirled in the savage tempest, impervious to its relentless barrage.

"Go..." Peter growled, yanking Tommy by the elbow and forcibly steering him toward Marcus, who was already halfway down the hatch.

Tommy bounced back in protest, so Peter gave him a

firmer shove, pushing him to the ground, bullying him into submission to join the others in their descent.

There was no telling if Grady knew what they were doing or even cared, such was his giddy jubilation, but if Peter had to die so Meridia and Zach might live to fight another day, then it was a price he was willing to pay. He made his peace with the decision long before today, but there was no way he would go down without a fight.

Torn between following Tommy underground or tackling Grady head-on, Peter felt the cyclone of splintered glass change its direction and whiz past him. Now he could see it, circling the room like a malevolent spirit.

The sparkling slipstream of swirling dust and broken glass snaked from pillar to post like an angry sea serpent, and in that moment, Peter realized it wasn't the wind battering the room. It was the demon's life-force, and it was looking for a new place to call its home.

In his heart, he knew there was no stopping the resurrection now as the shimmering apparition hovered above Grady's head. An ominous storm cloud fixing to unleash hell. Peter locked eyes with his newfound nemesis and the air fell unnaturally still as the walls of Crooked House buzzed with a foreboding hum.

Every hair on Peter's body tingled as an icy, static electricity charged the room. It was as if the house itself was suppressing a scream. A terrifying secret. Just seconds away from manifesting into a malevolent form.

Where were the horsemen and the Grand Master in all this? Surely they weren't about to let a deranged lunatic seize control of their prized asset?

Snapping free of Grady's beady gaze, Peter glanced at the trapdoor over his shoulder. There was no shame in running.

"Go ahead and run, teacher..." Grady sneered. "You won't get far. There will be no escape..."

Almost on cue, the ghostly spectre coiled around its new master and rained down over Gregor's body on a malevolent helter-skelter. Shards of glass bounced and ricochetted off the floor, forcing Peter to shield his eyes once more, and then all was calm, bar the erratic breathing of Grady.

High on adrenalin, his robes heaved up and down as he stared at the crumpled, colourless carcass by his feet. Gregor's withered remains resembled an unfinished ice-sculpture, scuffed and chipped, without so much as a trace of the scarlet lake that spread so eagerly across the cobbles to satisfy the demon's bloodlust.

Peter staggered backwards on rigid legs, held captive by his own curiosity, as a series of lightning cracks emerged in the frosty husk, splintering its brittle shell and causing it to crumble.

A pale, monstrous hand burst up through the chalky rubble and snatched at the air as if rising from its grave. Thorny obsidian nails scraped at the stone-tiles, setting Peter's teeth on edge, as it heaved the rest of its body from the dusty remnants of Gregor Wilson. Its ashen skin was rough and rugged, like an elephant's hide, tattooed in the same mysterious glyphs as the ceremonial dagger.

Each intricate symbol was etched into the demon's skin and Peter could see their jagged trenches expand and contract with every pulsing muscle as the colossal beast scratched and clawed its way into the room. Whatever abomination was rising from the ashes, it wasn't the infamous child killer from the seventies he expected, not in the same guise at least.

This was something raw and beyond terrifying. A

physical presence like the terminator, dominating the room. Stripped of all its hair, the same creepy cryptograms that were carved into its gargantuan body covered every inch of its skeletal face.

Oversized raven orbs glared at Peter from their cavernous sockets, too broad and bulbous for the rest of its gaunt features, as if it bore the eyes of a demonic alligator. With a chipped cavity for a nose, the upper half of the creature's head resembled the skull of a primeval alien. Bony and angular in a way that twisted all the hallmarks of humanity into a terrifying atrocity.

Beneath its scowl was less like a mouth and a more violent tear in its malformed face, teeming with thorny teeth that shimmered silver in the remnants of daylight bleeding in from outside. It was as if the ritual distilled the demon down to its nefarious core, and all that remained was the evil within.

The spine-chilling sight turned Peter's veins to ice and spurred him into action. He darted towards the hatch, still unable to tear his eyes from the rising demon as it continued to thrash its way closer to freedom.

"Hahahahaha…"

Grady's unhinged laughter echoed around the room as he stood behind the towering abomination like a mad scientist welcoming his diabolical creation into the world. Peter had seen enough. He sat on the edge of the trapdoor and fumbled to find the furthest rung he could reach with his foot.

As he scrambled down through the hatch, a bloodcurdling roar exploded above him, shaking the very foundations of Crooked House and almost rattled Peter off the rope ladder. The demon was reborn.

Tangled and twisted in the rigging of his only escape, he

used all his upper body strength to force the rungs straight again, frantically continuing his descent whilst skipping as many rungs as his long legs would allow.

Still trembling, he dropped the final six feet and then stumbled his way towards the dungeon's exit. As he reached the jaws of the tunnel, he heard Grady's chilling kill command bellow out behind him.

"Kill them...kill them all..."

80

Swept along in a tidal wave of panic, Izzy couldn't muster the emotions, or the energy needed to move her legs fast enough.

Her sodden thighs were chafing from the clingy warmth of her accident, and her joints were an incumbering contradiction–both rigid and weary in equal measure, as if they belonged to a pensioner. A cacophony of heavy breathing and the occasional nudge pushed her along the dingy tunnel as the broad-beam glow of a flashlight bounced between the cobbled walls like a fluorescent pinball.

Lethargically staggering and fumbling her way through the dark, she felt as if she was tangled up in the folds of a suffocating curtain and unable to break free. Her senses were muted and the strangers' voices behind her muffled as they barked instructions in which direction she should run. She felt Meridia's hand in hers. Warm and clammy, pulling her onward, and somewhere in the thick of the chaos, she thought she heard her sobbing.

"Argh!"

Meridia's bloodcurdling scream sliced through the

static in Izzy's mind as the flashlight struck a mutilated corpse chained to the rafters of a dungeon. With arms outstretched like an ungainly bird, his ribs were brutally ripped apart to reveal a hollow cavity where his insides once were.

Beneath him, a disgusting pile of entrails lay slopped on the floor as if they wandered into a depraved butcher's shop. The stranger's light lingered morbidly on the grisly atrocity just long enough for Izzy to see movement among the sticky slew of congealed intestines.

A swarm of roaches were feasting on his entrails, skittering all over his glistening guts and viscid organs. It was the most vile and grotesque sight Izzy had ever seen, but her body lacked the strength to retch. She was beat.

"It's Alman's brother..." Meridia gasped. "We need another way out..."

"The ladder..." Izzy slurred, punch-drunk on lethargy. "The one that leads to the woods..."

Despite her somnolent limbs, her faculties were slowly stirring, kick-started only out of her devotion to Meridia. Her own miserable life meant nothing anymore.

Meridia dragged Izzy back out through the dungeon's busted doorway and into the wider tunnel. There they clattered into Peter, his face riddled with fear as if he saw something even more terrifying than the Alman boy.

"W...we can't go that way..." Meridia stammered. "We need to go out through the woods...remember?"

"Go...quickly..." He urged them all to the opposite end of the tunnel, a secret passageway Meridia fell into once when fleeing the witch.

If they continued the path they were now on, they could be above ground and clear of Crooked House, instead of bouncing blindly from one horror to the next like a bunch of hapless lab rats trapped in the cult's underground catacombs.

"*Roar!*"

A primal howl erupted from deep within the darkness, rattling Izzy's bones and turning her weary legs to jelly. The demon was coming.

"Go!" Peter cried, scooping Izzy up and bounding after Meridia down the tunnel.

On they raced for what felt like forever, blundering their way over the bumpy terrain, all the while being stalked by the unholy roar of a monster hungry for their blood.

"What the fuck is that?" She heard one stranger gasp over Peter's shoulder, but her galloping carriage stayed silent as he focused on the task in hand, being careful not to fall.

Up ahead, Izzy spotted a narrow shaft of light coming into view. Its pale glow leaking in from the dwindling daylight above ground. They were close to the tunnel's exit now, and she felt Peter accelerate in response.

The cool rush of air carried with it the earthy aroma of trees in winter as it washed over her and helped dilute the embarrassing smell of ammonia she was carrying since escaping Grady's clutches.

When they arrived at the foot of the ladder, Peter swung her onto his back.

"Hold on..." He puffed, urging Meridia up the splintered rungs ahead of him.

Izzy felt her grip around Peter's neck, slipping with each step as he ascended the makeshift ladder, so she clung onto his waist with her knees just to stay on. Despite everything she had been through and all the terrible things she had done, there was some sliver of her that still wanted to live.

To redeem herself, perhaps. Glancing up, she watched Meridia's legs disappear over the lip of the opening, then felt the icy assault of the evening air on her cheeks. The jagged circle of dusky light had an ethereal glow, framed by rippling tufts of grass and tangled branches swaying from side to side like her own private welcoming committee.

As Izzy's head poked above the parapet, Meridia was quick to help haul her up so Peter could climb out. The two strangers followed. A late teen with a penchant for denim, and a stocky middle-aged black man dressed as a college professor. As they scrambled to their feet, the demon's roar rang out beneath them, shaking the ground and scaring the birds from their trees. It was gaining ground.

"This way..." Peter hoisted her up over his shoulder in a fireman's carry, her head languishing around his lumber, and then set off into the woods.

"If I'm right, then the tower should be this way, and so should the car." He reached into his pocket then dangled a car key for everyone's benefit and that was all the convincing they needed to follow him.

Overhead, the descending twilight unfurled its heavy velvet curtain, smothering the woods in murk as they fumbled their way from bark to bark. In a matter of minutes, it would be fully dark, and then all the horrors inside Crooked House would be free to roam and join in the hunt.

They only hoped Peter was right, and they could get to the car in time, but as another guttural roar bellowed through the trees, Izzy saw the hulking silhouette of the demon emerge from the shadows behind them.

It was catching up, and it was catching up fast.

81

"*Crunch...*"

Grady crushed a chunk of Gregor's husk underfoot and dragged its chalky residue along the floor with the sole of his boot. He stared down and smiled at the curious white scuff it left behind.

A pseudo-snow angel made from the scrapings of a crumpled human carcass. Although it lacked the allure of blood, it was another first for him in his growing thirst to experience new things. It was a day of many firsts, in fact.

"Fascinating..." he murmured, his mind aflutter with a million different questions relating to the animalistic evil he just unleashed on the hapless residents of Cold Christmas.

Beyond his rudimental understanding of the ritual, he did not know what to expect from the demon and wasn't entirely sure if the order he barked in his moment of triumph was specific enough for the creature to grasp. Would it return to him once it killed the teacher and his adolescent groupies, like some kind of loyal bloodhound fetching a stick for its master, or would it keep killing indiscriminately until Grady told it to stop?

Either way, it seemed to get the gist of what he wanted as it galloped down the trapdoor after them all. Perhaps he would delay his decision to free the monster from his sacred obligations and see how it fared against the horsemen.

Grady was less concerned about the Grand Master, but the horsemen remained an unknown quantity. Perhaps they would be open to switching allegiances once he did away with their dawdling leader?

If it were up to Grady, the prophecy would've been put to bed ages ago. The day he butchered the Jacksons, Zach was cowering under his bed like a snivelling little chicken-shit. He could've easily snatched him and then rounded up the seer on his way back to Crooked House.

Zach would have gladly followed her inside like a lovesick puppy and met his rightful end in room 10, as the prophecy required. But no, we needed to go the scenic route. The Grand Master's methods were so convoluted and tiresome. All so he could recruit an angry pre-teen and her magical crystal ball.

Instead, in the space of a few weeks, he lost their priestess and the night walker to a bunch of kids, and now, to add insult to injury, he let the infamous demon slip through his fingers, too.

"Imbecile..." he muttered, snatching up the ceremonial knife from the floor.

The time came for Grady to disappear and lie low while he contemplated his next move. He expected the Grand Master would return to Crooked House any moment now, and he didn't want to face the horsemen on their home turf, particularly so close to nightfall.

His time now would be better spent watching his new toy in action and perhaps joining in the fun. He was revelling in his newfound freedom and couldn't wait to experiment again. If he was quick enough, he might even have time to wipe the smug grin off that upstart Higginsworth's face.

Of course, by wipe he meant hack, and by smile he meant his whole infuriating face, scalp and all. There was something about his entire middle-class privilege aura that irked Grady, and the longer he went unchecked, the more insufferable he seemed to become.

As he stepped towards the trapdoor to leave Crooked House, the winter breeze stirred once more and wasted no time whipping up into a gale, howling through the barricaded windows and slamming the hatch shut with a bang. He sensed the vigour of the arctic blast, trying to peg him back as he battled against its current. This was no ordinary wind.

Many of his former brethren believed the house itself to be evil, and that its nefarious inhabitants were simply drawn to it, the way sharks are drawn to the smell of blood. That somewhere deep beneath its stone and timber façade were the blackened roots of a festering evil, choking the foundations and corrupting the land. An evil that now perhaps didn't want him to leave.

Pausing in the room's centre, the whistling wind continued to circle him like a wake of buzzards, ruffling their feathers and pecking at his face with their icy beaks. Grady didn't believe every tall story he heard about Crooked House, and he didn't have time for this.

Whatever this was, there was something more than mother nature at play here. Perhaps he awoke more than the demon with his one-man rebellion, and the house was limbering up to voice its disapproval.

"Creeeak..."

He turned to the wall on his left. Its dingy cream

wallpaper delineating the dusty outline of where an enormous wardrobe once stood, preserving the room's original banal colour. Within the insipid hues made hazy by the dwindling light, he saw movement, as if someone or something on the other side was trying to force its way in.

Shadows rippled across the undulating wall to a rhythmic chorus of creaks and cracks, each growing louder as if competing with the wind, and Grady saw a series of hairline fractures spider across the patternless surface. The ruptures in the room's masonry continued to spread as paper and plaster flaked to the ground like dead skin to reveal an unearthly blackness beneath.

Staring into the abyss, Grady realized this wasn't the work of the house at all, for deep within the murk he saw the spectral silhouette of a horseman. Its translucent robes ebbing and flowing like vaporous tendrils tearing open a dark gaping wound in the fabric of reality.

"Busted..." he smirked to himself like a shifty shop worker caught with his hand in the till.

Still clutching the ceremonial dagger, he gave its blade a quick glance, then decided against swapping it out for his favoured hunting knife. If he was to fight his way out of here, then it was only fitting he would slay them all with their own precious dagger.

Outside, it was close to dusk, and as the inky portal continued to expand, it swallowed all the remaining light from the room. As it teetered on the brink of full dark, another ethereal glow emerged in the depths of the gloom, as if someone opened a window into another world.

It was a blur at first. A foggy assortment of shadows seen through frosted glass. As the pallid pastiche of colours swirled into focus, they revealed an all too familiar figure.

One that was the bane of his existence of late. Even more so than the intolerable teacher.

"*What have you done?!*" The Grand Master bellowed as he stepped beyond the veil of empty nothingness and entered the room.

The folds and creases of his fiendish mask rippled like mercury amongst the shadows as he circled the ashes of Grady's sacrifice. Over his shoulder, lurking in the depths of the liquid void, the horseman hissed and growled. Its hypnotic glare tearing through the gloom like frozen stars.

The creature was alone, or it was so far as Grady could tell, but for some unknown reason, it remained in the wings, watching from afar. He wondered where the other two horsemen were and gave the rest of the room a quick glance. Nothing. It was just him and the Grand Master. Maybe now was the time to put his new dagger to use?

As they sized each other up from across the room, the wind settled to an inaudible murmur, and the only discernible sound Grady heard was the raspy breath of the Grand Master as he seethed beneath his metal veneer.

"The demon belongs to me now..." Grady sliced through the growing tension with his signature disdain.

"I grew tired of waiting for you to give me what was rightfully mine...what was promised...and so I took matters into my own hands. Then I took your precious demon while I was at it!" Grady sneered.

A condescending sneer that stretched his macabre crimson smile up towards his hairline.

"The shackles are off old man, and I am the monster now...can't you tell?" He performed a mock curtsy, but beneath his playful contempt, he was secretly battling with the urge to lunge at his former master and hack his shiny head off.

"You fool...you think playing dress-up and betraying the temple makes you a monster?"

"My ascension was prophesied...It was promised!" Grady snapped back.

"I've waited long enough in your shadow while you play god with all these pathetic weaklings...chasing after children. Children I could have delivered to you long ago if you let me! It's time you step aside slowpoke...hang up your tin mask and get out of my way...or else you'll find out which of us is playing dress-up..."

Grady took a tentative sidestep to gage his rival's reaction, and the Grand Master mirrored his move in the opposite direction, maintaining the distance between them. Grady continued to push the matter, taking another sidestep, and then another, as both men circled Gregor's disintegrated remains, like two wrestlers psyching themselves up to grapple with one another.

"The priestess gave you but a taste of your future, but like all men, that power has corrupted you and now you crave more. You are the one who's weak brother...far weaker than you realize." The Grand Master stopped circling.

He was unarmed and there was still no sign of the horsemen rushing to his aid, yet he remained calm and composed.

"Let me show you a real monster..." He snarled, then gestured towards the mysterious portal that was still bleeding darkness into the room.

Grady stared down at the wraithlike creature lurking within the swell of shadows and readied himself for a fight. Whatever happened next would be the ultimate proof he was ready to fulfil his destiny.

To become the monster he was born to be. He squeezed the knife in his hand and felt it creak against the congealed blood caking his palm, but the horseman remained still. Its rumblings all but subsided. Then he heard it.

A noise he didn't consider in his perfidious deliberations. A noise that might have struck fear into his heart, if, of course, he had one.

"Click-clack...click-clack..."

82

Meridia stumbled her way through the tangle of towering trees, gasping and wheezing as she pushed herself from one moss-mottled bark to the next.

Laced with the early onset of evening frost, the air was like barbed wire, clawing at her face and scratching at her lungs as she tried not to trip on the thorny bushes and shrubs nipping at her ankles. The last dregs of daylight were fading fast and the wall of oak and silver birch ahead blurred seamlessly into one.

An impenetrable cul-de-sac, stitched together by gnarled and twisted branches hellbent on hindering their escape. Alongside her, Peter and Tommy kept pace, never drifting further than a tree's width away from each other, while Dr Foster lagged wearily behind.

Izzy remained flung over Peter's shoulder like a rolled-up rug. Neck craned and head bouncing up and down with each desperate stride, she kept watch behind as the demon continued to bear down on them all.

The creature's bloodcurdling roars abated as it silently

stalked them through its old hunting ground. A discord of snapping twigs and scrunching leaves echoed underfoot, holding the creeping quiet at bay and keeping everyone on edge as they second-guessed every sound, never knowing if the next breath they felt might be the demon's down their neck.

"I...*gasp*...I can't keep up..." Dr Foster's rasping voice rattled behind her, but she daren't look back for fear of slamming face-first into a tree.

If Peter was right, then they should have seen the tower by now, but all she saw ahead of them was endless woodland, and even Meridia knew they couldn't keep this pace up forever.

"Where is it?" She grunted. "We should be there by now..."

Risking a quick glance to her right, she found Izzy aghast with terror, arm outstretched and pointing behind them. Meridia's legs wobbled beneath her as if her joints turned to liquid, and she staggered onto her hands and knees in the dirt.

"Argh..." Izzy's hoarse scream crackled in Peter's slipstream and forced everyone to slam on the brakes.

Trembling on all fours, Meridia looked over her shoulder as she scrambled back to her feet. Dr Foster was gone.

"W...where'd he go?" She whispered, backing up to where the others had come to a stop.

The trees all stood in breathless silence, like tall, twisted chess pieces, watching and waiting for one of them to make the next move.

"It...it took him..." Izzy stuttered.

Despite the alarming nature of her shellshocked announcement, they all took up root on the spot, like the cold-hearted woods keeping them prisoner. There was no sign of the doctor or the demon anywhere, and although the trees were dense and tainted by the imminent arrival of nightfall, there was no way such a hulking monster could hide in plain sight.

"What do we do?" Tommy asked, as Peter fumbled for the flashlight on his hand-me-down phone. Its quivering beam was pitiful in the vastness of the great outdoors and barely made it two trees deep into the woodland.

"We have to keep moving..." he breathed. "This is the demon's home turf...we can't just stand around waiting to be..."

He trailed off and Meridia followed his gaze toward the purple infused sky. A globular shadow was looping through the air like a cannonball, clearing the tops of the highest branches, before dive-bombing right in front of them.

"*Clatter...*"

It landed on a pile of mulched leaves a few yards from where they were standing and rolled the rest of the way to Peter's feet, peppering him from the waist down with dark crimson freckles.

"Argh!"

Meridia's primal scream tore through the trees, drenched in panic and disbelief, as she locked eyes with Dr Foster's decapitated head. Missing his lower jaw and wearing a serrated half-smile, his face came to a stop sunny side up and lay there staring at them all dead-eyed, in grotesque silence.

The doctor's tortured expression was savagely pulled apart. Torn from the corners of his mouth to the tips of his earlobes, as if the demon thrust its hand down his throat and ripped his head clean off by his front teeth.

In the jagged void beneath his skull, Peter's light

skimmed the sinewy remnants of snapped tendons and shredded ligaments bleeding out into the dirt. Meridia screamed again, screaming as if her life depended on it.

The demon emerged from the twisted shadows of the trees, and it was marching straight towards them.

83

"Run!"

Peter shoved Meridia and Tommy behind him and cracked the whip to get them moving again. Not that either of them needed any encouragement. They both bolted away through the trees.

Meridia was still screaming as she lithely ducked and darted between the barbed branches of silver birch, while Tommy battled to keep up.

Peter faltered, staggering backwards after them, wrapped in the advancing abomination and unable to drag his eyes away from its formidable form.

Overhead, the pale moon bled into the melancholy sky, bathing the twisted treetops in an eerie silver sheen as the day surrendered the sun's muted rays to the night's cold dominion.

The demon's colourless skin shimmered beneath the pastel glow, like a ghost gliding effortlessly through the woods, and as it marched ever closer. Peter saw its raven orbs, like bottomless pits of ink, swirling in the cavernous hollows of a tattooed skull thirsty for more bloodshed.

He turned and galloped after the others, frantically wracking his brain for a new plan. Or even some way to slow the demon down that wouldn't amount to suicide.

With Izzy still dangling helplessly over his shoulder, he couldn't afford to do anything stupid. She could barely walk, let-alone run, so the only logical thing he could do right now was keep everyone moving. The woods couldn't go on forever.

"What's it doing, Izz…" He gasped, doing his best to navigate the prickly sideswipes from low-hanging branches.

She felt ridiculously light as he zig-zagged through the thorny obstacle course, and her knobbly knees dug into his chest as he clung onto her legs to stop her from slipping.

"It's…still walking…" she juddered back. "But…I think… I think we're losing it…"

Peter slowed down and glanced over his spare shoulder to find Izzy was right. They put some distance between themselves and the demon, but it remained unperturbed, which made the creature all the more menacing, like it knew something Peter didn't.

Now, instead of galloping after them like a ferocious animal, it relentlessly marched over its old stomping ground like a cliché serial killer from an 80s slasher movie. Peter wished Kane were here. He would know exactly what to do. He would pluck some obscure scenario from an even more obscure horror movie like he always did, and it would spark an idea. He could almost hear his buoyant voice bouncing along on top of the breeze.

'In the movie *Camp Slaughter 6: The Marshmallow Massacre, they escape the killer by…*'

What Peter wouldn't give to hear the rest of that sentence right now. What he wouldn't give to see Kane's bubbling enthusiasm as he waxed lyrical about the hidden depth of horror movies and the subtle social subtext disguised within them.

"Look!" Tommy's voice snapped Peter out of his wistful tangent.

Up ahead, a thin pale beacon of hope crept over the horizon and weaved its hazy white web between the trees. Car headlights perhaps, or a powerful torch.

"Go..." Peter urged them forward, then checked on the demon's progress.

The creature either dropped too far behind or was now using the shadows as cover, but the fact its ghoulish face was no longer staring straight back at him through the murk allowed Peter to relax his shoulders for a second and think. They still had no idea what the source of the light was, or if they were approaching the tower as he'd first intended.

They would need to proceed with a little more caution. There was no telling what might wait to greet them, and it was highly likely the Children of the Shadows were still combing the area in search of whoever killed their brethren. A sudden pang of worry gripped his chest and knocked him off his stride.

"Wait!" he whispered, rushing to draw level with them.

Meridia and Tommy slowed to a halt and caught their breath. Gasping and wheezing, they propped themselves against the nearest bark while Peter tiptoed between them.

"Did we lose it?" Tommy puffed.

He was hunched over, hands resting on his knees as he squinted back at the distance they covered. Peter double checked and there was still no trace of the demon behind them. Was that a good sign or a bad one?

If Peter didn't know better, he could've sworn he saw the demon crack a leering smile as he stomped towards them.

"I...I'm not sure..." he whispered, distracted. "I think so."

Aside from the anxious chorus of suppressed inhales and exhales, all was eerily still in the woods, just as it was in the moments leading up to Dr Foster's brutal beheading. A gnawing sensation of dread clawed its way out from the pit of Peter's stomach and coiled itself around his larynx, trapping his breath somewhere between lungs and throat.

Not only did they have a bloodthirsty killing machine hunting them down, but now a knife wielding fanatic could lurk behind any tree ahead of them, waiting to avenge their slain brothers and sisters. Perhaps it was a mistake to come this way, but with their only other choice leading back towards Crooked House, Peter did the best he could with the shitty hand they were dealt.

"I think I can see the tower." Meridia interrupted his temporary paralysis, wearily pointing at the caged ball of light in the distance. She was right.

Its fractured beam shaved the ragged edge of something man-made, casting a tall silhouette amongst the reedy barks of silver birch and skeletal shrubs. Peter's initial sense of dread barely subsided before a darker, deeper tremor reverberated through his body, triggered by the shadowy structure in the distance.

What if Grace and the others never made it out of here? His mouth went dry at the thought, but there was no time to languish in a mire of what ifs. They needed to keep going.

"That light could be the cult...looking for us." He cleared his throat. "We need to move quickly, but quietly. I'll lead the way...we don't know who or what else might be out here with us."

He switched his torch off to avoid any unwanted attention. It took a second or two for his eyes to adjust to the indigo haze, with the only light to guide them coming from the ominous blood moon overhead and the enigmatic glow of an unknown horizon.

"Izzy, do you think you're strong enough to walk?"

"It's ok, I'll carry her on my back," Tommy quickly volunteered.

His eagerness to get everyone moving again was palpable. Peter gently planted Izzy back down on her feet and felt her wobble in the middle of the three-person circle. Each one of its members twitching and cocking their heads around them like anxious sparrows on the lookout for a marauding cat.

"Just stay close and stay behind me." Peter continued.

"*Crack...*"

The delicate snap reverberated through the woods like a warning shot and triggered an alarm bell in Peter's head that rattled him to his boots. Trembling in a nerve-jangling combination of fear and fatigue, he felt the temperature plummet to mark the arrival of an unseen predator. They had company.

Tommy quietly crouched so Izzy could scrabble onto his back, then hoisted her up high to stop her from strangling him as they readied themselves to run again. Seconds felt like hours as they watched and waited. Their feet fused to the ground like it was quicksand.

"What the f..." Tommy gasped, as a shadow flashed beyond the tangle of knotted prison bars, its murky contrast of black on black barely visible beneath the desolate sky.

"We need to get moving..." Peter stammered, shepherding everyone behind him again as he stared eagle-eyed at the unflinching expanse of gnarled sentinels.

Clenching both fists, he tried to quell the irrepressible

tremors threatening to topple his composure, but it only made matters worse.

"Nice and steady…" he whispered, almost to himself as he backed up towards Tommy and Meridia to usher them along.

"*Crack…*"

Another brittle twig crackled like a bone snapping in the aubergine expanse. This time echoing somewhere to their left. Whatever was out there skulking in the shadows, it was circling them.

Between two barks, Peter glimpsed a wispy silhouette that didn't belong to the trees, but it wasn't the demon. Gawky and graceless, it twitched and jerked its way through the undergrowth towards them like a stumbling marionette with broken strings.

"Are you all seeing this?" Meridia whispered, shuffling forward a little.

"Uh huh…" Tommy breathed in disbelief.

They were all hypnotized by the scrawny, wraithlike figure as it lurched closer, each rickety motion like a video skipping frames.

"It can't be…I…I've seen this before…" Meridia stuttered.

"If…if this is real, then it knows where we are…we need to get moving. We need to get out of here now!"

84

The faceless shape grew sharper as it lumbered out of the shadows. It was small. Smaller than Meridia, and as the moonlight brushed against the bony angles of its withered face, Peter's mind momentarily disconnected from reality. Unable to grasp what he was seeing.

A shambling husk of a young girl, held together by a patchwork of rotting flesh and shrivelled tendons, tottered towards them as if she clawed her way out of a shallow grave. The bulk of her skull was bare, corroded and cracked from decades of decay, whilst wispy strands of lank, sallow hair clung to the scabby remnants of her scalp.

Amidst the layers of muck and grime smothering her sodden clothes, Peter recognized the colours of the manky school tie dangling around her scrawny neck. St Swithun's. Her shoulder grazed a tree trunk, and the undead corpse juddered to a halt as if she ran out of steam, like a town drunk taking a breather whilst staggering home in the dark.

"It's one of its victims...if it can see us, then so can the demon. They're its eyes and ears...We need to go..." Meridia insisted, but still nobody moved.

Peter and Tommy were both held hostage by grim fascination as the walking cadaver raised its head and broke free from the shadows shrouding its face.

Hollow-eyed and emaciated, the girl resembled a shrivelled peach. Her features all but nibbled away by gluttonous insects and the onset of rot.

Then she opened her mouth as if to speak. A toothless mouth oozing black treacle, a coagulated casserole of decomposed organs left to fester inside her scraggy body, and that was when Peter saw it. A glimmer of the demon in her twisted expression, as her cavernous eye sockets expanded, and a wicked sneer flashed across her face.

"I see you teacher..." The rasping voice was not a child's nor a man's.

It was something cold and corrupt, worming its way inside Peter's brain and contaminating his mind. He felt this way before. A foreign presence in his thoughts. Insidious. Nefarious. A door the witch once opened, that now refused to close.

Leaning in a little, he waited on tenterhooks for the demon's next ominous message, like an addict desperate for their next hit. He knew they should run, but his will remained clouded by a thick and poisonous fog descending on his mind. Wrestling his resolve for control.

"Rooaaar!"

They all flinched in unison, yanked upright by invisible strings, as an unearthly growl erupted from the zombie's mouth. A terrifying discord of tormented souls howling from the depths of hell. It charged, sprinting and screaming; a dead-eyed replica of the demon fashioned from the putrefied remains of one of its adolescent victims.

A macabre spying satellite sent to flush them out of hiding, mindlessly thundering through the woods to a chorus of stomach-turning crackles and pops as it battled against the shackles of rigor mortis.

"RUN!" Peter bellowed over the tumult of rage as he sidestepped the oncoming zombie and grabbed whatever flailing limbs he could latch onto.

In one fell swoop, he doubled down on his grip, snatching hold of a trailing leg, and flung the reanimated carcass deep into the woods like an Olympic hammer thrower.

"Snap"

The undead child clattered into a tree somewhere in the gloom, while Peter was left holding her twitching forearm. Its grimy skeletal hand was still scratching and clawing at the air as it tried to wriggle free from his grip, and so he tossed that into the woods, too. When he turned to catch up with the others, he found them all still facing him, slack-jawed from his gutsy quick-thinking.

"Go!" He shouted again, shaking them from their stupor, and this time they complied, scattering like the wind.

They deftly traversed the rutted terrain as if the trees carved paths just for them, seamlessly following the natural contours of the woodland as they crisscrossed and zigzagged their way toward the light. That was, until a tiny lapse of concentration turned their elegantly orchestrated escape into a chaotic tumble.

"Thud!"

Tripped by a shrub, or something similar, Peter went crashing to the ground. Arms flung out in front of him, he landed heavily on his wrist and felt a sickening pop. Not a break, but enough of a crick to make him wince. A cold sweat broke from the pain the moment he put weight on it and Peter slumped face-first onto the mulch.

"Keep going..." He whimpered, but his muted call came too late as both Tommy and Meridia were already doubling back.

"My foot's caught..." He groaned, flopping onto his back like a beached whale as he cradled his injured wrist.

Staring down at his feet, he saw the decomposing hand of a child clasped around the heel of his boot, the rest of its body buried somewhere beneath him. Peter jolted to life like he was struck by lightning, writhing and kicking at the grisly hand as its crooked fingers skittered halfway up his ankle.

"*Crunch!*"

Meridia was the first to react, slamming her foot down on the zombie's hand and sending its gnarled digits splintering in every direction. As Peter tried to scramble to his feet, another mouldy hand burst out from the soil to his left and latched onto his elbow, pinning him back down to the ground.

"Ahh!"

Tommy was next to be accosted as yet another withered mitt sprouted behind him and clamped down on his calf. The shock attack sent Izzy tumbling to the dirt, and within a matter of seconds, they were under siege from a sea of insidious hands snatching and grasping at their legs and feet.

Each pint-sized paw belonged to one of the demon's victims. Once someone's son or daughter, but now only a mindless minion. A legion of undead watchers in the woods.

"It's the lost souls..." Meridia exclaimed.

The only person to have stayed on her feet. She was now playing a ghoulish game of whack-a-mole, stomping on parched limbs and skeletal fingers, snapping them like dusty dried out twigs to save her friends.

"Foster was right...this must be where they're buried." As Peter kicked his way free, he clambered to his feet and surveyed the surrounding ground.

After fifty years of slumber, the lost souls of St Swithun's were rising from the dead to a cacophony of crackling and twitching bones. As each grotesquely decomposed face broke free from the desecrated ground, it swiftly mimicked the demon's malformed appearance and began howling like a banshee.

Slowly drowning in a malodorous mire of ravenous corpses, Peter and Meridia did all they could to free Tommy and Izzy. Snapping and stamping on desiccated limbs as they battled to break free from the clutches of the screaming dead, but they were vastly outnumbered.

No sooner had they dismembered one frenzied cadaver, did another three claw their way out of the earth and bundle on top of them.

In a matter of minutes, they found themselves on the losing end of a deadly game of twister, buried deep beneath a twitching and convulsing horde of undead school children, each one beckoning for their master to come and join in the fun.

85

GRADY SEETHED AS HE WATCHED THE GRAND MASTER trade places with the weaver and retreat to the safety of his portal. Coward.

"Little miss Muffet sat on her tuffet, eating her curds and whey. When along came a spider who sat down beside her, and frightened miss Muffet away...but then came the monster, who wanted to kill her...haha... so now the spider must pay..." Grady forced a toothy grin, stretching his reedy lips as far as his bony face would allow.

"Going so soon?" He goaded the Grand Master. "Is it not enough to hide behind that silly mask you have to cower behind your pet spider too? Not to worry...I'll be coming for you next."

"You are a fool, brother. Your actions change nothing. I have already given the order...the Omega Council are readying themselves for war. If the demon has killed the boy and the seer, then we must eradicate humanity without the last harbinger. As for you...you will meet the same fate as any other traitor..."

With another flick of his wrist, both the Grand Master

and his ghoulish henchman were slowly absorbed by the shadows as the liquid darkness surrounding them collapsed inward, folding and curling like burnt paper to reveal the tired insipid wallpaper of room 4 beneath.

Now it was just Grady and the weaver. Monster vs monster.

The sun's absence turned the room into a cavernous void, with the only light now coming from the muted beams of the blood moon as they crept through the boarded windows and coalesced with the creature's blazing eyes.

Grady stared intently at the unblinking orbs of rage as they flickered gold and amber in the gloom. Despite the lack of visibility, all he needed to do was keep track of the weaver's head in the dark, and thankfully, the creature's own defective DNA served that information up to him on a plate.

"Click-clack...click-clack..."

The enormous arachnid scuttled to Grady's left, and as it did, its eyes weaved intricate webs of fire in the abyss. Within the trail of orange afterglow, Grady glimpsed the creature's bulbous body oscillating as it purred like a gruesome black cat. Its coarse, matted hair gently lapping back and forth like an ocean of oil in the inky expanse.

"Hisssss..."

The weaver bared its teeth. Row upon row of serrated fangs glistened in the gloom as if the creature were chewing on a mouthful of broken glass. It might as well have slapped a glow-in-the-dark sticker on its forehead as Grady cemented his grip on the ceremonial dagger and hissed back.

"Haha..." he jeered, blowing back the rancid stench of sulphur and decay wafting from the arachnid's jagged maws.

Having seen the creature in combat, he knew exactly what to expect. Yet another faux pas by the dithering tin man. Oh, how he would make him pay when he was done with this giant fur ball of thorny legs and pointy teeth.

Grady waited for the weaver to start proceedings with its all-too predictable heaving and retching, but it click-clacked around him, continuing the pointless merry-go-round of posturing, right where its pathetic master had left off.

Perhaps even the weaver in all its savage ferocity could tell he was not to be trifled with. The thought gave him pause, and he felt an unexpected pang of sympathy within, followed by an overwhelming urge to pet the creature's head. It seemed a waste to slay the beast, and in another life, maybe he could have made room for it by his side. But it was too late now.

Grady already had a lethal creature of his own at his beck and call, which meant there was no room for a third wheeling weaver, particularly one so loyal to his sworn enemy. Besides, he never spilled a monster's blood before, so perhaps he wasn't quite done with breaking new ground today after all.

A sneer slithered across his face at the prospect of seeing the weaver's insides, so he escalated things. He made a sudden jab-step in the creature's direction to flush out its first move. To Grady's surprise, it reared up onto its hind legs like an irate horse and let out a deafening hiss.

Looming high above him, the hulking mass silhouetted against the gloom like an eight-legged executioner preparing to swing his axe, and Grady lost all sight of the monster's fiery eyes to the rafters of room 4.

Time froze for a moment as the arachnid hung in the pitch-black air for what felt like an eternity. Poised like a prickly guillotine, waiting to rain down chitin tusks and razor-sharp fangs on its disoriented prey.

Not for the first time that day, Grady was forced to improvise and the instant he heard the staccato chink of the weaver's legs scrape against the stone tiles in the darkness, he rolled onto his back and thrust the knife high into the air.

"*Yelp...*"

The weaver let out a guttural whimper as the dagger skewered its head like a shish kebab. Its barbed legs came crashing down around him in a clattering crescendo of clicking joints and fractured limestone until they fell limp.

Grady felt the full weight of the beast on his outstretched arms. It was heavy, even for him, and as he strained to push the creature off, he heard a rasping hum rumble in the depths of the creature's belly like an ominous death knell.

A wave of panic washed over him as he lay sandwiched between an immovable stone and the hefty corpse of his latest kill. The feeling was a peculiar one, alien, yet painfully familiar as it harked back to his excruciating childhood before the demon rescued him.

The immense load of the weaver's bloated carcass tremored, pressing down further on his pelvis and stubbornly pinning him to the floor. The sudden increase in pressure was enough to snatch Grady back from his whimsical detour down memory lane.

Unable to see in the pitch-black room, all he could do was try to wriggle free of the wreckage before the creature regurgitated its deadly mucus and melted his face to mush. Although the priestess bestowed him with supernatural strength and guile, he was still just flesh and bone, like any other man.

"*Gurgle...*"

The unearthly stomach-growl rattled his legs as the weaver spontaneously coughed up its guts. He felt the sudden warmth of the slimy green phlegm through his robes as it trundled up the creature's gullet and into its throat.

Almost free, he writhed and twisted out from underneath but didn't bank on the sulphurous acid leaking from the weaver's wound.

"Argh!"

It trickled down like a leaky faucet, peppering Grady's face with corrosive gunk. The agony was instant as the viscous goo tore through flesh and tissue like molten lava. Wildy shaking his head from side to side. He tried to stem the flow of acid searing his nose and mouth, but it clung to him like glue, hissing and bubbling as it devoured his face to the bone.

His harrowing screams continued, echoing throughout Crooked House, as his nose slowly disintegrated, leaving nothing but a charred, hollow cavity in its wake. Finally squirming the rest of the way free from the weaver's deadly grip, Grady's screams turned to hysterical, unhinged laughter as he snaked his way toward the trapdoor.

A smouldering mess dripping liquified sinew and toxic residue across the stony ground as half his features dissolved into a steaming, rancid puddle.

Writhing in agony, he flopped through the hatch and plummeted into the dank and dreary depths of the dungeon below with one final bloodcurdling scream.

86

"Gasp! Kaff...kaff..."

Coughing and wheezing, Meridia battled to catch her breath as she came to.

She found herself being dragged backwards along a path of crusty mulch with thorny twigs tugging at her hair and clawing at her lumber. Twisted silhouettes of barren branches danced and swayed above her, basking in the hazy glow of the blood moon, before sailing out of sight on an endless conveyor belt of thickets.

Somewhere in the distance, she could still hear the terrifying roar of the lost souls as they howled for their master to join them. They sounded more like an air-raid siren shrieking in some war-torn jungle, not the backwoods of a sleepy ghost town like Cold Christmas.

Craning her neck, she found Tommy was doing the dragging. Her shoulders pressed against her ears as he hauled her along by her wrists. Her hands were numb, as if she were standing out in the cold for too long, and her cheeks were stinging like they were covered in paper cuts.

Tommy glanced down at her, fraught with fear, his

youthful face covered in scratches dished out by the demon's legion of undead spies.

"She's ok..." He gasped, glancing nervously behind them before scooping her back onto her feet.

"We need to keep moving..." Grabbing her by the elbow, he yanked her along with him, fighting his way through any undergrowth that stood in their way.

Glancing over her shoulder, she saw the plague of feral cadavers crouched in the shadows of the trees like a pack of hungry wolves waiting to pounce. A sea of obsidian eyes glimmering with malice.

However, they didn't take up chase. Instead, they pointed at her with barbed fingers and bared their rotten teeth like the savage flesh-eating zombies she saw on TV. Why weren't they moving?

A sudden jolt of panic rippled through her chest like a bird flapping its wings beneath her ribs and she frantically searched for the others in the misty gloom. She found Peter a few yards away. He was breathing heavily and clutching his wrist as he dashed through the woods on high alert.

Izzy was limping beside him, struggling to keep pace. She had her fair share of cuts and grazes too, particularly on her arm that was missing a sleeve. She must've been freezing. Meridia couldn't believe how frail she looked, as she trembled from one tree to the next. She was a fighter, though, that much was for sure.

Dog tired, she felt as if she was running in a bouncy castle. Her knees were like rubber, and everything underfoot felt shaky and unsure. The last thing she remembered was being smothered by a swarm of scampering carcasses.

"Wh...what happened...*kaff*..." she mumbled, still

gagging on the putrid stench of mould and decay lodged in her throat.

"It was all Peter..." Tommy explained. "He went full-on berserker mode and kicked the living crap out of those... those..."

"Zombies?" Meridia nudged him over his mental speed bump.

"This is all so insane..." Tommy shook his head as a look of bewilderment washed across his bloodied face. "He's pretty banged up now, though. Don't think he'll be stepping in the ring again anytime soon..."

"Eh?" The analogy went straight over her head as she glanced back toward the lost souls. "Why aren't they following?"

"They just stopped...Peter reckons they can't cross the threshold of where they were buried. That's why I dragged you out...they stopped the second we got clear...it was as if they hit an invisible wall or something. This is all so insane..."

"B...but what if it's the demon!" Meridia momentarily seized up as she rediscovered control of her limbs. "Wh... what if it found us?"

"That was his other theory..." Tommy tried to placate her whilst gently steering her back on course.

"That's why we're making a run for the car...we'll just have to take our chances when we get there. We don't have much choice now. We're all running on empty." He pointed up ahead, and Meridia saw the hazy glow getting closer with every hurried step.

There was no telling how close the demon might be now following their run-in with its ferocious acolytes. She wondered what other monsters might be lurking in the woods.

Was Grady out here somewhere in this murky expanse?

On the prowl for any scraps, the demon might leave. Or perhaps the horsemen joined the hunt now they were free from the shackles of daylight.

Whatever horrors waited in store for them, they were about to discover if the mysterious light was among them as Peter took cover behind a dense cluster of silver birch and signalled for them all to fan out.

Ducking behind the thorny skeleton of a hawthorn, Meridia peered over Tommy's shoulder to see what brought them to a sudden halt. Up close, it was clear to see they were car headlights puncturing the tangle of knotted trunks and twisted branches.

Static and unblinking, their pale beams stretched into the darkness, clipping the tops of cracked gravestones on their way to silhouetting the tower's crumbling veneer. At a guess, she would have said the car was parked in the small clearing between the cult's sacred temple and the creepy farmhouse on the hill. It had to be the Children of the Shadows.

"Crack!"

Her heart plummeted to the icy depths of her stomach as she glimpsed a flicker of movement up ahead. A hooded figure slipped between the beams. The light barely catching its edges before it disappeared out of sight, and then she heard a man's bellowing voice shatter the ominous silence and turned her legs to jelly.

"I've found them...quick, they're over here!"

<h1 style="text-align:center">87</h1>

Peter heard the rustling of bushes and snapping of twigs to his left and instinctively put himself between Izzy and the approaching disciples.

The vibrant glare of the car headlights made it almost impossible to see anything up-close as it augmented the shadows of the trees, blurring everything around them into a murky purple abyss.

"Run" He barked to anyone who would listen in the hope at least one of them might escape the marauding mob of hooded maniacs.

Unable to use his dominant hand he took a wild swing with his left at an approaching silhouette and felt it clatter against fabric and bone, but it wasn't clean enough, and before he knew it, he was wrestled to the dirt by a man half his size but twice as heavy. Peter brought his knee up hard between the man's legs and heard him whimper as he tried to roll him off.

Clamped together at the elbows, both men tumbled through the undergrowth, exchanging places until Peter gained the advantage of being on top. With their legs in a tangle, he tried smashing the man's head on the ground like it was a coconut.

"Oof"

Again, the disciple yelped, but the ground was too soft to do any meaningful damage.

"*Ahh!*"

A scream reverberated over his shoulder, sending shockwaves through the woods. One of the girls was in trouble. Peter tried to break from the man's grip, but he clung to him like a dog with a bone.

He threw another stilted punch with his left but missed his mark and felt his knuckles scuff the man's sweaty brow. The wild swing knocked him off balance, and the disciple rolled back on top of him. Peter tried the same move as before, but the man's bulky thigh blocked his knee this time.

Still weary from their encounter with the souls of St Swithun's, Peter lacked the strength to throw the man off and could feel the fight slowly ebbing away from him.

"*Crack!*"

The disciple's head came down like a jackhammer, clattering against Peter's forehead and ringing his skull like a church bell. A high-pitched dog whistle only he could hear swallowed all the surrounding sounds as his eyes misted over like frosted glass.

Somewhere beyond his comprehension, the angst-ridden cries of all his friends floated overhead like driftwood while Peter languished, punch-drunk on concussion, at the bottom of a murky, cataleptic ocean.

"*Crack!*"

Another ferocious head butt connected with his eye socket and rattled his brain, turning down the dimmer switch on all his senses until everything faded to black and remained that way.

88

When Peter came to, the blinding glare of a 55-watt headlight and a banging headache greeted him.

Trying to shield his eyes, he discovered both wrists were bound tightly behind his back. He winced, first from the pain of his injury, and then from the unexpected chafe of nylon as it sliced through his skin like cheese wire.

"Looks like sleeping beauty's awake..."

The man's voice drifted in and then out of his consciousness like a train rumbling through a derelict station. Squinting, Peter searched for its owner, but the dazzling light was too intense for his fragile state and easily forced his eyes back behind their weary lids.

The last thing he saw before pulling the shutters down on his open air prison cell were a handful of hazy silhouettes, slumped on their knees in the dirt in front of him.

"Where is she?" The same voice boomed, this time right by his ear.

"We know she's out here with you..." He tasted the stale

coffee on his breath as it wafted over his lips on the wintry breeze.

Peter's thoughts gravitated to Meridia. Did she give them the slip? He prayed to god she did, but then who were the other shadows? He thought he glimpsed at least four, but judging by the amount his head was spinning, it could have just as easily been one.

"*Crack!*"

Completely blindsided, Peter was socked hard in the jaw and sent crashing to the ground as a chorus of muffled gasps and screams erupted around him. A searing pain lit up the nerve endings in his face like a Christmas tree and tingled the synapses between tooth and cheekbone.

Tears streamed from the corners of his clenched eyes as he emptied his mouth of the warm coppery spittle pooling beneath his tongue. He tried to haul himself back up, but with his ankles tightly bound, he flopped onto his back like a trussed-up turkey.

"I don't know what you're talking about..." he rasped, pleading ignorance whilst still spitting blood.

"I suppose you don't know who slaughtered our brothers and sisters either do you...cop killer!"

Manhandled by his cowardly assailant, Peter was yanked back up onto his knees. He gasped as he licked his split lip. The sharp twinge of pain prickled his gums and made his teeth tingle as if they were floating inside his mouth. He was just about to open his eyes again and brave the light when he heard the shuffling of feet beside him.

"*Crack!*"

No sooner did he find his balance was he brutally beaten back down to the ground. This time, the crushing blow landed flush with his temple, ringing his bell and leaving him floundering in the dirt.

"Tell us where the seer is...we know she's with you." The man raged.

"Leave him alone...she's not here!" Zach's voice sliced through the static in Peter's head and ripped his heart out. Grace and the others never made it out of Cold Christmas.

"Nooo!" Peter burst to life, writhing and wrestling against his restraints in a fit of temper, but there was just no budging them.

Blinking away the blood, sweat and tears, he forced his eyes open. The bleary silhouettes in front of him flickered like distant memories before hardening into familiar faces as the harsh glow of the headlights slowly gave way to clarity.

For a split-second, Peter wished he never opened them. Such was the harrowing sight waiting for him. Grace was the first person he locked eyes with. Her pixy nose was broken and bloodied like a crooked ski slope framed by nicotine bruises on each side.

A jagged crimson canyon carved its way across the bridge of her nose and was steadily oozing claret into the gully of her swollen mouth.

It glistened vividly beneath the harsh white headlights; a sickening spectacle of technicolour torture. Slumped beside her, JJ took a similar beating. His left eye was closed, sealed shut by a pinkish-purple welt resembling a second pair of lips sprouting from his socket. It took a real monster to beat a child, and the sight of him poured gasoline on Peter's blistering rage.

"Grr..." He took another shot at snapping his restraints, but once again, it was in vain.

Searching for the others, he quickly found Kane curled up on his side between Grace and Nadia. Hair matted to his forehead, he was gleaming with sweat and white as a ghost. As Peter was hauled back up onto his knees for the second time, his eyes remained fixed on Kane's chest, watching him like a hawk for any sign of life.

A shallow breath rippled beneath the bloodstained creases of his sweatshirt, and Peter let go of the gasp that was stuck in his throat. That was when he noticed Nadia. Hunched forward unmoving, her glossy black bob dangled like a morose veil covering her face, and at first glance, it appeared as if she succumbed to a lazy late afternoon nap.

However, below her slouched chin, the state of her clothes painted a different picture. Drenched in blood from the neck down, it was clear she received a battering too, perhaps even more severe than Grace and JJ.

But why? Was this all just to get to Meridia, or had they simply cross paths with a bunch of cold-blooded sadists out looking for kicks? The wrong place at the wrong time.

As Peter braced himself for his next pasting, he finally found Zach and Izzy to his right. Shaken up and bordering on hysterical, they were separated slightly from the rest of the group and seemed physically unhurt.

Perhaps even the Children of the Shadows had their limits, although the emotional scars of seeing their friends beaten half to death would take far longer to heal than any cuts and bruises. The only silver lining to the thick black cloud hanging over them all was that Meridia wasn't among them, and neither was Tommy.

"You fucking cowards!" Peter spat, looking up at his tormentors.

The three disciples towered over him. Their identities shrouded in shadow beneath their cowls as their hooded peaks disappeared into the night sky like a mysterious mountain range rising above the mist. They were all men, that much Peter was sure. Each of them were thick set beneath the folds of their cloaks. A gang of cartoon heavies, recruited for one sole purpose: violence.

"You're going to get us all killed!" Peter fumed. "The demon is out here and he's coming..."

"Ha! Why else do you think we're here?" The shorter of the three goons gloated.

"We're just softening you up for when he arrives... maybe then you'll tell us where the girl is." He reached into his robes and pulled out a thick, gold-plated knuckleduster, then slipped it over his bloodied fingers.

Peter's legs wilted. He knew a well-aimed blow with that wrapped around the thug's fist could crack his skull open.

"You don't understand..." Peter pleaded, "He's under the control of someone else...the same psycho who butchered your people...the demon answers to Grady now, not your master... You're in just as much danger as we are... Maybe more given Grady let us go."

His minor embellishment was meant to unsettle, and it's exactly what it did.

A perturbed hush befell the disciples, as if Peter's words sucked all the wind from their sails. As the deafening vacuum of silence continued to expand around them, the cold winter air grew heavy as the trees held their breath in anticipation of the disciples' next move.

"He's lying..." One of them bellowed, but Peter could tell from his tone his conviction was wavering.

"Grady would never betray us..." His feeble attempt to double down was even less convincing as it was swallowed by the vast expanse of their underlying fears.

"It's true...sniff..." Izzy sobbed. "I was there...I saw it..."

"They're bluffing brothers..." The third tried to rally them.

"They're looking to buy more time..." He separated from the pack and snatched Kane by his ankle, then dragged him across the ground towards Peter.

"Let him go!" Peter growled defiantly amidst a discord of wails and whimpers coming from Zach and Izzy.

Although he wasn't shackled like the rest of them, Kane was in no position to fight back. His lifeless body carved a shallow trench in the dry earth as the disciple belligerently tossed him around like a rag doll.

"Leave him alone! He's just a kid..." Peter begged, his voice on the brink of collapse.

"Can you hear me, seer?" The disciple's voice crackled through the trees as he brought his boot down on Kane's wound.

"If you can, then this is on you..." He put some of his weight on Kane's ribs and he instantly awoke from his semi-coma with an agonizing scream.

"Argh!"

"Stop! You're killing him..." Peter broke down as Kane squirmed in slow-motion beneath the disciple's boot. His listless limbs flailing sluggishly as whatever shred of strength he had left slowly ebbed away.

"Give yourself up now or else I'll crush him like a bug..." His voice was swallowed by the oppressive stillness of the woods, where even the breeze now feared to tread.

Peter knew Meridia wouldn't refuse the call. She couldn't possibly after hearing Kane's bloodcurdling cries.

"Have it your way..." He hollered after only a moment's pause, and then pressed down heavily on Kane's midriff, using his considerable weight to crush his ribs.

"Argh..." Kane screamed again, but this time with weary resignation. His hands made a weak attempt at flapping, like a wounded bird in the final throes of death, gripped by delirium.

"*Crack!*"

Peter heard the sickening sound of a rib snapping under the disciple's foot, and Zach promptly peppered the dirt with the contents of his stomach. Kane's arms flopped down beside him at the same time his head fell limp, as if to shun them all.

"Nooo!" Peter shrieked until he was red in the face, his heart irrevocably broken. He had failed all of them.

"I'm going to fucking kill you for what you've done!" He screeched, punching a hole through the foreboding silence now emanating from where Kane lay lifeless.

Behind his back, he felt the nylon restraints finally give under the weight of his grief and then ping apart.

"*Snap...*"

A brickly twig breaking to his left masked the sound of his sudden breakthrough and was swiftly followed by the sound of leaves and mulch crunching underfoot.

"Look..." A disciple pointed at the gloom.

"I think I can see her...see there, the shadow between the trees? Go fetch her brother Smith, while we get rid of the others. They've outlived their use to us now..."

Through tears of rage, Peter saw a flash of light twinkle in the disciple's hand as he pulled a knife from his robe and marched toward Nadia.

"Wait!" the disciple creeping towards the shadow in the woods suddenly called back to his accomplices. "Kill the kids first...leave the women for me..."

The chilling command folded Peter into the dirt. A sickening gut-punch that left him scrambling for air. In a state of blind panic, he fumbled frantically behind his back to free his ankles, wrestling to get a decent grip on his restraint.

Even if he could somehow snap its ironclad hold, there was no way he would ever reach Zach and Izzy in time.

89

Meridia writhed and wriggled as she struggled to break free of Tommy's vice-like grip, but no matter how much she kicked his shins and stamped on his feet, he continued to hold on with the strength of a boa constrictor.

With one hand clamping her mouth shut, his other arm was coiled around her torso, pinning her elbows to her ribs and leaving her powerless to watch as the disciple tortured Kane in her name.

"You can't go..." He breathed into her ear. "It's suicide..."

The whole situation smacked of her mother's gruesome death and made her sick to her stomach. Deep down she knew he was right, just as he was then, but if she could save even one of her friends, then surely it would be worth the sacrifice. There was no way she could cope with losing anyone else. The cult had already taken so much.

Brimming with despair, she could hardly see now. Her long eyelashes could not keep up with the torrent of tears as she tried in vain to blink free from their bleary embrace.

Kane looked like the victim of a stampede, his body

reduced to a crumpled pile of crimson and grey beneath the glare of the unforgiving car headlights. How could this be happening?

They should have been long gone since finding the secret passage in the weaver's lair. No matter what they did to break free from their deadly clutches, the cult always seemed to be one step ahead of them.

She watched the ruthless disciple call out to someone on the opposite side of the trees, but his voice was lost amongst the thumping of her heart as it threatened to burst her eardrums. She was finding it hard to breathe now, with Tommy's hand sliding too close to her nose as she continued to squirm.

"He thinks it's you..." Tommy whispered, relaxing his grip just enough for Meridia to seize her opportunity. She opened her mouth and sank her teeth into his fingers.

"Ow..." Clamping down as hard as she could, Meridia clung on as if her life depended on it, until he had no choice but to let her go.

She tasted the warm metal of his blood as he skinned his knuckles against the tiny serrations of her teeth in his efforts to break free.

"Ow..." He yelped again, before finally prising his fingers out then shaking them in the winter chill.

The momentary respite was all Meridia needed to make her presence felt and put an end to anymore suffering.

As she opened her mouth to scream, all that escaped her lips was a sharp, choked gasp as she saw another shadow stomping through the trees, leaving her trembling like a leaf.

The demon of Cold Christmas had arrived, and it was heading straight towards her friends.

90

"WAIT!"

The disciple known only as Smith called out again to his deputized executioner, stopping him just short of where Zach and Izzy were cowering.

"What now?" He bleated back at him, clearly eager to get on with the killing.

When he didn't get an immediate answer, he threw both hands at the ground like a petulant child and turned to see what the holdup was.

Zach remained oblivious, gripped by the icy numbness of his trance, like he was sitting at the bottom of a swimming pool, waiting to drown. Crushed by the suffocating loss of his brother and traumatized by the brutal beating of his friends, he stared blankly at his steaming pile of vomit as it glistened in the dirt.

He vaguely sensed Izzy beside him, nudging and prodding with her knobbly elbow to stir him from his lethargy, but all he wanted was for the parched ground beneath him to open its dusty jaws and swallow him whole. Anything to quell the nauseating crack of Kane's rib reverberating over and over again in his grief-stricken mind. Anything to make the pain go away.

All other sounds beyond that were simply washed away in a wave of misery. Reduced to inaudible undertones, he could barely hear from the depths of his own private lido.

"Flop!"

A dismembered arm slapped to the ground, dive-bombing his puke and peppering him with blood and bile.

Savagely ripped from its socket, the gory limb was flaccid bar the tips of the forefinger and thumb which twitched momentarily before accepting their fate. The lower half of its fingers were bound by a shiny gold knuckleduster, and its grand entrance proved enough to wake Zach from his apathetic slumber. He languidly traced the limb's trajectory back to its source and found a one-armed disciple. The one who had beaten everyone so savagely was standing at the cusp of the car headlights, wearing an expression of utter dismay.

Karma was indeed a bitch, as Kane always said it was. Towering behind the disjointed disciple was a barbaric creature the likes of which Zach had never seen. The demon of Cold Christmas. More terrifying than any monster he ever encountered in the forsaken halls of Crooked House, its grey leathery skin was a grisly work of art.

Every inch was covered in cryptic symbols carved into its skeletal face and hulking body. Beyond black, its eyes verged on reptilian, catching the moonlight from the depths of their craterous sockets and glistening with malicious intent as it gripped the man's head with both its brawny hands and twisted it clean off.

"Crunch!"

Zach flinched at the gut-wrenching sound of flesh and

bone being brutally torn in two as the man's body collapsed to the ground like a sack of spuds and pumped its glistening crimson wares into the dried-out dirt.

"Ahh!"

Izzy screamed as the demon turned the decapitated head around for all to see and sneered. Its mouth was a thorny crown of shattered glass jutting out in every direction. The mutilated disciple still had the same slack-jawed expression on his face, as the creature released its grip and callously crushed the man's skull underfoot.

"*Crack-splat!*"

Splinters of bone and sinew erupted from either side of the demon's protruding heel, splattering the ground like a Jackson Pollock as the creature relentlessly marched on.

The two remaining disciples turned to stone in the car's headlights as Peter's chilling premonition violently bled into reality. Their unholy idol was evil incarnate, and on nobody's side other than its own, but instead of wildly ripping its worshipers limb from limb, it stood before them like a nefarious preacher primed to deliver a sermon.

Once again, a barbed sneer slivered across its emaciated face, but it made no sound. At least not that Zach heard above Izzy's hysterical screams as she bum-shuffled away from him like a hamstrung caterpillar. She was the only one able to move aside from Peter, who was down on his side again and wrestling to break free.

His eye was swollen and bloodied, enough to knock the stuffing out of most men, but still he battled on, doing all he could to save them while the others remained cataleptic. Punched into oblivion by a bunch of bullies who, with any luck, were about to be mauled by one of their false gods.

Meanwhile, Zach remained inert. Paralyzed by a different pain. A pain that crushed his spirit in one fell swoop. Although the demon's ruthless brutality would be enough to send anyone in their right mind running, it had yet to scrape the surface of Zach's doleful detachment.

If anything, he would welcome the demon with open arms. At least in death he could be with his brother again.

So, he sat there, watching and waiting for the end of the world to unfold in front of him, just as he told himself it would on that ill-fated day, when five friends uncovered an ancient curse in a place called Crooked House.

91

"*Snap*."

Exhausted and mildly concussed, Peter clawed free of the nylon leash, cutting into his ankles and then scrambled to his feet.

A sudden rush of blood to the head stopped him in his tracks. Overshadowing his vision with a white-stippled haze that slowly bled into one. Clinging to the insoles of his boots with his toes, he spent a moment teetering on the brink of collapse while he waited for the sensation to subside.

Even if he could break free of the residual brain fog, he knew it would be futile to tackle the demon head on, so the only thing left for him to do was free as many hostages as possible in the hope some of them might make it out alive.

Surveying the sea of bruised and battered faces, the only people even remotely alert were Izzy and Zach. The former crawled around the edge of the car that was lighting up death row, whilst the latter remained motionless, locked in a severe state of shock. From the corner of his eye, he saw the sole of Kane's shoe and wrestled to resist its magnetic pull. Heartbreaking as it was, he had no choice but to focus on those he could still save.

Rushing towards Zach, Peter was quickly intercepted by the taller of the two remaining disciples. He appeared unarmed and, based on his body language, seemed torn between instigating another fight and running for his life. His cruel accomplice, the overzealous brute with the knife, remained embroiled in a peculiar death-stare with the demon a few yards behind him.

"They're just kids, for God's sake..." Peter growled, clenching his fists. "Just let me get them out of here while I still can..."

The disciple hesitated for a moment, glancing back toward his brother, then at the mutilated corpse on the ground.

"I...I..." He stuttered, turning back towards Peter before lowering his hood.

He was young. Somewhere in his mid-twenties, with a mousy buzz-cut and matching stubble. Completely aghast, he rubbed the top of his head as his beady brown eyes surveyed the battered bodies littered around them.

"I..." He tried to speak again, but his indecision was brought to a brutal end by a three-inch steel blade being slammed into his temple.

Peter recoiled as the blade disappeared all the way to its hilt inside the man's skull, while his white-knuckled executioner used the handle like a corn holder to keep his victim upright and on his feet.

"I...I was...eating the sky...the blue part..." The man mumbled as his left eye wandered off in search of the blade bayonetting his brain, while his right remained glued to Peter, dilated in shock.

"Do you taste it too?" He asked. "Too loud...the clouds are scratching my teeth..."

A deep sigh followed the stuttering string of gobbledegook. The kind reserved for fresh bedsheets or an open fire on a cold winter's night. Then the man's shoulders dropped in tandem with his jaw as he succumbed to his grisly fate.

Clutching the knife, fresh from his parley with the demon, the last remaining disciple reared his head over his victim's shoulder and grinned at Peter from beneath his cowl.

"*Squelch!*"

He ruthlessly yanked the knife out of his brethren's head, then pushed his flaccid corpse aside and squared up to Peter.

Wearing the same unhinged expression as the lost souls of St Swithun's, the disciple was a grotesque parody of jubilation. Pencil-thin lips pulled back so far, they looked as if they might split his face in two. His eyes were swirling black holes of infinite darkness, voraciously devouring all light, and Peter sensed himself being drawn towards them as he gazed into their hollow depths.

The demon was now nowhere to be seen. A phantom slipping in and out of the shadows at will. All that remained was his murderous puppet, clutching a razor-sharp knife that was dripping with gore and pointed at Peter.

"There's no escape teacher..." A twisted mouthpiece for his new master.

The disciple's voice was a guttural snarl, sailing on a torrent of tormented souls, each murmuring secrets that ebbed and flowed with the winter breeze.

"You think you can save your friends? Their souls

belong to me...as does yours. Look at me teacher...watch as I tear your world apart..."

Eyes glued to the shimmering blade, Peter hardened himself for a fight. Instead of lunging with his knife, as he looked set to do, the demonic disciple held the blade up to his own throat and in one swift motion, without a moment's hesitation, carved a crimson ravine from ear to ear, passing right through the centre of his Adam's apple.

Still grinning like a madman, his black eyes widened with demented glee as the gash erupted into a coughing and spluttering deluge of blood. Rooted to the spot, Peter watched in horror as each pulse of the disciple's dwindling heart sent another scarlet surge gushing down his gaping neck, filling his jugular notch and soaking the creases of his robes.

"Thud!"

Peter flinched as the disciple dropped to his knees and fell face down in the dirt. His blood blossomed outwards, filling the cracks in the desecrated ground. A terrifying demonstration of the demon's preternatural power, and one that made vanquishing the creature all the more impossible.

Staggering back on leaden legs, Peter collided with an immovable object and felt his veins instantly run cold. He shivered as an icy burst of rancid breath chilled the nape of his neck, then turned to face his destiny.

Standing right behind him was the demon of Cold Christmas.

92

Meridia made it a few yards closer to her friends when Tommy rugby tackled her from behind and brought her crashing face-first down to the ground.

"We can't help them..." He gasped. "We need to get out of here."

His instinct to cut and run was at odds with the courage he showed when facing Grady, but as she watched Peter stand nose-to-nose with the demon through the undergrowth, the hopelessness of their situation finally sunk in.

Maybe Tommy was right. Maybe her father was right too, and they all were riding their luck up to this point. The demon wasn't a frail old woman lying comatose in a hospital bed, or the 300-year-old remains of a witch. It was a colossal monster that could not only rip through flesh and bone like it was butter, but now it seemed it could also possess a person's soul.

What chance did a 12-year-old girl with anger issues and a university drop-out have of stopping it?

Still, Meridia refused to quit. She didn't know how. It

was as if that strand of her DNA was stripped from her when this nightmare began. Now, as she watched Peter backing away from a hulking monster that made him look like a puny teenager, all she wanted to do was leap onto the creature's back and scratch its eyes out.

"Get off me..." she growled, but Tommy had her legs pinned now. His entire weight was on the small of her back as he jostled to restrain her arms.

"He's going to kill him..." She pleaded, but Tommy refused to relent, and so she was forced to watch beneath the cover of thickets as the demon gripped Peter by the face, hoisted him into the air, and then launched him ferociously at the car like it was throwing a shot put.

"*Smash!*"

Peter shattered the windscreen with his back, peppering Zach with glittery glass fragments as he sat agog by the car's wheel arch.

"Noooo!" Meridia screamed as Peter lay sprawled across the car bonnet, a grandstand view of the main event.

Her cry snatched Zach's attention, and for a split-second she saw his bloodshot eyes flit in her direction, but even her voice wasn't enough to rouse him. He was lost again in the unfolding chaos as the demon made a beeline for Nadia.

93

Zach saw Peter's hand flop over the edge of the car bonnet and couldn't tell if he was dead or alive.

Either way, it didn't matter much, as it would all be over soon. Somewhere amongst the carnage, he thought he heard Meridia cry out from the woods. He prayed to God, she had the sense to leave them all behind this time and run.

Gregor was right. The demon was unlike anything else they ever encountered. Perhaps he was right to tell Alice to kill him, too. Maybe none of this would be happening now if JJ didn't stop her. If he didn't accidentally stab her. Another death on Zach's hands.

This was all because of him. He knew that now. All his friends, putting their lives on the line to save his, and for what? His brother was dead, stabbed and tortured, with the rest of them not far behind.

Even Izzy had only shuffled a measly car's length away before running out of steam. In that time, the demon had butchered three disciples and thrown Peter through a car windscreen. There was no point in running now, or shuffling, for that matter.

What good would it do? It was over.

Just a bunch of dumb kids tied up and waiting in line to meet their maker. Not that he cared about that anymore, either. What kind of God turned his back on his children? Left them to die like this? No God Zach would ever entertain again, that was for sure, not that he ever did to begin with.

Gazing out across a desolate sea of red-tinted mud and severed limbs, he washed up on the shores of his brother's body. Kane cast a long dark shadow on the horizon that crept as far as Nadia. Still hunched unconscious, she had no idea of the approaching demon. Nor did Grace or JJ, as all three of them lurched in a line, oblivious.

Three wise monkeys, each of them choosing to see no evil. Well, evil saw the three of them, and now it was coming to collect their souls. Somewhere above him, Zach heard a faint groan of protest as Peter pleaded for the monster to stop, or perhaps he was pleading for mercy from above.

Either way, the answer remained the same as the demon swooped down, clamped Nadia's head between both palms, and then snatched her up into the air. As she instinctively kicked with both feet, Zach saw her blackened eyes flicker back to life and dart around in search of a saviour. As was the case ever since they stepped foot in this wretched place, no-one was coming to rescue her.

Held aloft by her head alone, Nadia's neck stretched unnaturally as if her spine might snap at a moment's notice whilst she wriggled helplessly on the demon's hook. Its thorny nails curled around her crown like a nutcracker fixing to shell her skull.

It seemed to revel in the fear it inflicted, and Zach wondered if that was where it gleaned its sustenance from.

Well, it wouldn't feed on his fear. He was too far gone for that. All he felt was a surreal detachment now, as if his brain somehow escaped and left his body alone to face the unfurling horror show.

He watched Nadia's beleaguered body continue to resist the imminent approach of what was sure to be a gruesome and painful death. The sight made him sad, more than afraid or repulsed. *Just put her out of her misery, why don't you,* he thought. Put us all out of our misery while you're at it. We get it, you've won.

His torpid attention wavered, half-drifting back towards the island of Kane, just as Nadia ceased struggling and opened her mouth as if to release a scream that was stuck in her elongated throat.

"*Crack!*"

The sickening, hollow sound of bones fracturing was all that escaped her plump lips as the demon gleefully caved her head in with its bare hands.

"*Crack-crunch-crack...*"

A cacophony of snaps and pops reverberated in Zach's private theatre of despair as the demon continued to crush Nadia's head into a bloody pulp. Ruptured bone and glistening sinew slopped to the floor, oozing out from between the creature's calloused fingertips. Her semi-decapitated body soon followed as gravity laid claim to it, stretching the last remaining tendons and ligaments of her pulverized flesh beyond the breaking point.

"*Thud!*"

The demon sneered, satisfied with its grisly handiwork as it shook the sloppy remnants of Nadia's face from between its fingers. A mushy eyeball, a smattering of teeth, and gooey morsels of blood-streaked brain tissue all spattered over her twitching body as flailing limbs searched for severed signals from her smashed cerebellum.

"Ahh!"

Grace unexpectedly snapped to with a chesty gasp and started screaming at the mutilation and mayhem surrounding her. Everywhere she looked, she was greeted by something altogether horrifying, and her desperate cries went up by another decibel.

First Nadia's headless corpse, then the disciple's dismembered body, until finally she locked eyes with the demon and her tonsils gave out. A patchwork of pain, her bruised and bloodied mouth remained stretched to its limit, silently shrieking, as she wrestled to break free of her nylon restraints.

"Thud!"

Peter rolled off the car bonnet and almost flattened Zach as he fell flat on his face beside him. The sudden start gave him a faint flicker of hope, but it was quickly snuffed out as he watched his mentor flounder in the dirt like a well-beaten boxer, still trying to beat the ten-count long after his corner had thrown in the towel.

Searching within, Zach tried once more to galvanize himself, to swim free of his debilitating nihilism. He thought maybe if he pictured Meridia, she might save him from wherever she was, but still, he couldn't see beyond the crumpled body of his beloved brother. Everything else was just black on black. A swirling vortex of pain and misery, hellbent on pulling him under.

"Grr..." Zach was so resigned to his fate, he almost missed Grace's second wind.

Shakily rising to her feet, she somehow snapped her wrist restraints, just as Peter had, and was now wrestling to keep her balance as she stood at the starting line of an invisible sack race. The unexpected act of defiance buoyed Zach, keeping him afloat just long enough to take a gasping breath.

"Run Grace!" He shouted, his voice not quite his own.

Before his words registered, the demon was upon her. It appeared twice her size from where Zach was kneeling, but that didn't stop Grace from taking a swing at it.

Dr Foster was right. She was tougher than she looked, and even though she hit nothing but the bitter evening air, she gave Zach something to root for. The demon, however, was less impressed as it stretched its mouth from ear to ear to form a contemptuous smirk. A gauntlet of razor-sharp spikes glistened beneath the glare of the car headlights, ready to tear Grace apart.

Whether she was unperturbed or simply at the end of her rope, Grace wasted no time taking another wild swing, and as the creature easily grabbed a hold of her forearm, Zach felt his ribs tighten.

"*Crack!*"

The savage blow echoed like a gunshot in the night as the demon snapped Grace's arm at the elbow then, in one swift motion, wrenched her splintered limb free and thrust the jagged shard of bone up under her chin, spearing her windpipe, and reducing her final scream to a gory gurgle.

Hoisting her aloft, the demon dangled Grace like a broken doll, savouring every twitch and spasm as the life drained from her body and her bloody stump fell limp at her side.

"Please god...*sniff*..."

As the creature tossed Grace's mutilated carcass to the ground and cast its ominous shadow over JJ, Zach could hear Peter's cracked-rib gasps. He barely moved since rolling onto the ground, and given his run-in with the demon was akin to losing a game of chicken with a freight train, it was little wonder.

Even now, he still tried to find his footing amongst the loose dirt and mulch, dragging the sole of his boot along the ground to get back up, despite his body's refusal to cooperate.

Whether it was sheer stubbornness, or a parent's instinct to protect their young, the man simply didn't know how to quit.

When the demon snatched JJ up off the ground and clamped its hands around his skull, as it did Nadia, Peter's foot ground to a halt, and his shoulders slumped in resignation.

Zach's throat tightened, tingling his tear ducts, as he glanced from Peter's surrender to JJ's. Suspended in the air, his unimpaired eye was open.

Perhaps it was that way the entire time. There was no kicking or struggling, only stillness as the demon sneered, then readied itself to squeeze.

94

THIS COULDN'T BE THE END. NOT AFTER ALL THEY HAD been through together. Not after all her harrowing visions and brushes with death.

There was no way Meridia was going to let her friends go out with a whimper at the hands of a savage monster, while she lay squashed beneath a well-intentioned outsider who didn't have the first fucking clue who or what he was dealing with. Entangled in a heated game of twister, her face and neck were flush with rage as her left arm continued to evade Tommy's clutches.

She felt his sweaty palm threatening to lose its grip on her other wrist. Reaching out as far as she could, she stopped struggling and baited him into making a last-ditched lunge.

As she felt his weight ease a little off her right shoulder, she twisted back to life and yanked her right hand free.

"Crack!"

The bony bump of Meridia's elbow connected hard with Tommy's cheek and turned his own momentum against him, sending him sprawling, whilst she corkscrewed her body to roll him off.

Wriggling free, she was back on her feet and running before he even knew what had hit him. Leaping over thorny shrubs and thickets, she charged towards the light with gritted teeth. JJ was up in the air now and about to meet the same grisly end as Nadia.

Meridia's blood was like acid coursing through her veins as she homed in on her target. She had to stop him. She was the only one who could. '*One must stay and the other must go...*' She repeated the message like a mantra, using it to psych herself up.

Once again, she got it all backwards before, but she was determined to make it right now. She knew what she needed to do. Her ears were pounding and her heart pumping wildly as she heard Tommy take up chase over her shoulder, but she was already too far ahead.

Despite his puffing and panting, and rustling of bushes, he would never catch her now. All she had to do was reach JJ in time.

Taking aim at the demon's back, the dazzling spotlight punching a hole in the gloom flickered around its edges. Or at least, that's what Meridia thought. As she drew closer, the flicker grew more intense, bleeding beyond the confines of the car's broad-beamed glare and lighting up her path.

Now everything around her was breathing light. A shimmering silvery veneer, as if the fabric of reality was secretly made up of stars.

Behind her, Tommy's traipsing turned to a whistling hum, which then escalated to an ear-splitting screech. Still, she galloped on, furiously pounding the dirt and mulch with her feet until she was almost within reach.

Half blinded by the alabaster glow and burning up beneath its blistering heat, Meridia planted both feet and threw herself at the shrinking triangular back of the beast just as the world, and everyone she cared about, was swallowed whole by a brilliant white light.

95

Zach melted into the dirt as his limbs turned to liquid. He was down and out again, having lost the last grain of hope Grace tossed in his direction during her final moments of defiance.

Now all he saw was a gruesome death waiting for him and the other transient survivors of Crooked House. God, he hated every putrid brick of that place.

A few yards in front of him, Peter creaked like an old wooden staircase as he found one final half-push and then collapsed in a rasping, wheezing heap. Beyond him, in the demon's deadly grip, was JJ. Still refusing to fight.

He just dangled languidly from his brawny hanging tree, waiting for the demon to kick the stool out from under him. Three generations of men, savagely beaten into submission by the nefarious cult and their deadly Demogorgon. It was over. For real this time.

The invisible war: a concept so abstract and alien to Zach when he first heard it uttered by his 'other self' finally reached its harrowing conclusion, just as he prophesied all those months ago.

"I love you guys..." he blurted.

The words gauchely leaking out of his gummy mouth. It was meant for all of them, his brother included. How he wished he could tell him to his face one last time. Not his lifeless husk lying in the dirt, but his actual brother, Kane, the hero. Kane his universe.

"I love you." He said again, glancing at JJ, and his voice fractured this time but sounded less abashed.

There was a flicker of acknowledgement in JJ's tearful eye that blossomed into a weak smile. Even in their darkest hour, his infectious light somehow found its way through the gloom.

Although it was barely there, and may well have been a trick of the light, his smile made it all the way to Zach's lips, like an unsaid secret shared between two brothers across a crowded room. JJ's muted smile turned to a grimace as the demon pressed his palms together, and Zach felt every major organ inside him turn into a fist.

Unable to watch, he held his breath and stared out into the murky undergrowth, all the while shaking his head in dismay.

Then, for a moment, he thought he heard JJ's bones creak. With tears rolling down his cheeks, he covered his ears to spare himself the sickening crack of his adoptive brother's skull splitting. That was when he saw her. Meridia, tearing through the trees towards them, blazing a trail of blinding white light in the darkness. Not just a hero in Zach's eyes, but a superhero.

Her vibrant auburn waves were flowing wildly behind her as she charged, screaming like a girl possessed. Not a scream born out of fear, but a battle cry. A raging declaration of war that rattled the woods like a roaring thunderstorm and shook the ground beneath Zach's feet.

Hissing and crackling like a lit fuse, she raced headlong at the demon, illuminating the indigo sky in her wake and sending a shockwave of raw electricity rippling through the atmosphere. Zach felt its current coursing through his weary body, galvanizing him. Raising him from the dead. The closer Meridia got, the more powerful her beacon of hope became, until she arrived at the edge of the clearing and threw herself at the demon.

Squinting through the glare as it singed his retinas, Zach saw her fearlessly clamber halfway up the creature's burly back. Clinging to its waist, Meridia turned feral, relentlessly gouging and clawing at the demon's eyes with every ounce of strength she could muster until it released JJ from its grip and dropped him face-first at its feet.

"*Roaaaaar!*"

The demon let out a guttural howl as it tried to shake Meridia off like a barbarous bucking bronco, but still she clung on, scratching and tearing at its face like a wild animal while Zach was forced to watch helplessly from the sidelines.

As she continued to rain down blow upon blow, Meridia's scream morphed into a shrill whistling sound that ricocheted from tree to tree. Nails down a chalkboard, circling the clearing and slicing through Zach's brain. Around and around, the sound shrieked; faster and faster. A dizzying auditory onslaught, winding itself up towards an ear-splitting crescendo as the battling forms melted into one.

Straining to see beyond the glare, he baulked when he found them twitching and writhing beneath the white-hot glow; a grotesque amalgam of tangled flesh and twisted limbs, corkscrewing towards the heavens as the dazzling light reached breaking point and then,

"Boom!"

Meridia and the demon were swallowed whole by the searing white light, their hazy silhouettes dissolving like shadows in a sunset. Bleary-eyed, Zach searched the wide-open clearing in front of him; his ears still ringing from the aftershock of Meridia's disappearance.

"M..." He called blindly, still adjusting to the more tolerable glare of the car headlights.

"M?!" His voice broke beneath the weight of worry bearing down on his mind, as he realized there was no sign of Meridia anywhere. She was gone.

A chilly breeze washed over him, pricking his tear-stained cheeks, and for a second he caught a waft of lemon and mint; Meridia's signature scent. The cool and zesty smell floated all the way to the back of his throat, so Zach rested his eyes and breathed in the saccharine nostalgia. Summer barbeques and water fights, bike rides in the park and Fortnite marathons. It was amazing how a single smell could be so transportive. A sensory time machine.

For a fleeting moment, it felt like she was standing right there beside him, until it drifted away again on the wind and melted into the evening air.

As his feet gently touched back down on earth, he heard footsteps crunching towards him as a mysterious shadow stomped through the blanket of dead leaves and twigs littering the woods. In a matter of seconds, Tommy came bounding into the clearing from the same direction Meridia did.

Wide-eyed and covered in scratches, he didn't notice JJ lying on the floor until it was almost too late. He nimbly leapt over him only to clip Kane's shoulder with his trailing foot and then trip onto all fours.

"Uugh...kaff...kaff..."

Kane groaned wearily, as if Tommy had just disturbed him from a drowsy slumber on a lazy Sunday morning. Groaning once more, he arched his back and rolled onto his side, then was still again.

"Kane!" Zach burst into life, sobbing and slinking his way over to him in a frenzy. "Help...please..."

He cried out to Tommy as he shuffled past Peter and saw his eyes were open, brimming with tears from a crippling cocktail of suffering and release. Kane was alive. Kane was alive.

"Wh...where did she go?" Tommy asked, surveying the bomb site, not knowing who to help first.

"Please...just untie me...Kane...Kane!" Zach slithered all the way past Peter now and had reached his brother's feet.

"Izzy's back there too..." He glanced over his shoulder and found her rocking back and forth by the car boot, silently staring into the distance as she bordered on catatonic. She looked so thin and pale, like a skeleton in the shadows, oblivious to everything that was going on around her.

As Tommy feverishly worked on breaking the abrasive ties, keeping him from hugging his brother, Zach scanned the wreckage of their lives, still hoping to find Meridia standing there in the clearing, smiling at him. Once again, she found a way to rescue him. All of them.

As he soaked in the scarlet sea of splintered bones and shredded limbs littering the entrance to the Temple of Shadows, he wondered if any of them could ever recover from today's devastation. Over the course of a week, the toll of their first credulous trip to Crooked House became unbearable, and their loss was unimaginable.

Snapped free of his shackles, Zach dived onto the dirt beside his brother and found him too, staring glassy eyed into the distance. The ruffles of his coat hid his breathing, but he was alive; barely.

"Kane..." Zach sobbed, clasping his cold, trembling hand. "Kane please...blink if you can hear me..."

Kane blinked, a slow and sluggish blink that allowed Zach to let go of the breath he'd been holding in.

"We're gonna get you out of here...you're going to be ok..."

96

By the time Tommy pulled up outside the Shawbrook Holiday Inn, it was a little after 10pm.

Peter sat hunched in the passenger seat, nursing his broken ribs and what felt like a cracked coccyx, whilst Zach doted on Kane at the very back of the midnight-blue seven-seater. Between them, Izzy and JJ sat in shock-silence.

JJ remained in a stupor, listlessly holding an icepack to his welted eye they salvaged from Nadia's first-aid kit, whereas Izzy spent the entire journey staring down at her hands as they lay palm-up on her lap.

Having waited as long as they could for Meridia to return, Tommy convinced them to come back to the Inn, where he believed he might have some answers, crazy as it sounded. In all honesty, nothing sounded crazy anymore, and as Peter tried to keep his breathing shallow to stem the intense stabbing pain shooting up the left side of his torso, he attempted to make sense of all that had happened that night.

Thoughts of Meridia, the demon and Grady twisted his brain into a pretzel, and although he knew it would be better to rest his addled mind, his curiosity kept prodding and probing for answers.

From experience, he knew there were no guarantees Meridia would reappear in the same spot she vanished from, but this was already by far the longest she had ever been gone. Just as concerning was the murderous cargo she took with her. With infinite possibilities around where she may have travelled to, there were also an infinite number of threads for Peter to pull on to tie himself in even more knots.

As inappropriate as it sounded, he contemplated switching the radio on just to distract him from his thoughts. *'In order to see more clearly, the only thing you can do is let the waters settle.'*

Dr Foster's tiny pearl of wisdom floated into his awareness, and Peter let out a melancholy sigh as Tommy unclipped his seatbelt and turned to face everyone.

"I'll be back in a sec..." He mumbled wearily, practically out on his feet.

"I'll leave the ignition on and the keys with you, Peter." Tommy placed the fob down on the driver's seat and left.

Without the engine's purr, the only sound in the car was Zach, whispering words of comfort to his brother. Although stamped on, it seemed Kane's dressing held under the pressure and whilst he remained incredibly weak. He was at least stable. Unable to get any of them the proper medical attention they needed, Peter had no idea where they would go from here.

Homeless and on the run, his best bet was to seek other members of Gregor's resistance movement in the hope they might find someone else they could trust. That would require a trip back to Drayton Hollow to recover Dr Foster's directory. Going back there would be risky, but with no-one else to turn to, that book might be their only shot at survival.

Outside, the roads were quiet, as they often were at this time of night, and so Peter rested his pounding head against the slat in the window and breathed in the cool night air. He craved a little more respite from the pungent stench of sweat and urine choking the car since it had come to a stop. He also craved a break from his bemused brain.

"Click."

He finally succumbed and switched the car radio on, then searched through the channels for Hert FM to catch the nightly news. For a while he was a regular listener, often tuning in for some company whilst marking school papers on long, lonely evenings. Now what he wanted was a sliver of normalcy. He wanted, no, he needed, to know there was still a world somewhere outside of Cold Christmas.

"...came after an emergency session in Brussels this evening, where Article 5 of the NATO Charter was invoked. This comes after growing tensions and reported attacks on alliance territory."

"Joining us live from London is our senior political correspondent, Sarah Connell. Sarah, what can you tell us?"

"Well Jay, the news is still sinking in here, but needless to say, this is a historic and deeply sobering time. Although many commentators have said the writing has been on the wall for a while now, in his address to the nation just moments ago, the Prime Minister stated that this decision was not taken lightly but was a necessary measure to ensure the security and sovereignty of NATO member states. Citing clear and irrefutable evidence of unprovoked Russian aggression, including targeted strikes in Poland and the Baltic, NATO has been left with no choice but to deem them acts of war under international law."

Peter's blood turned to brittle ice at the news, wincing as he leaned in closer to the car's speakers, not quite believing what he was hearing.

"Sarah, what's been the response from other NATO states so far?"

"Well, there's already concern this will escalate to a far wider global war. Parliament will be convening overnight to discuss further measures, including conscription and increased defence spending. Germany and the US have already echoed Britain's sentiments and pledged their support, with troops and equipment being deployed to reinforce eastern front lines. Meanwhile, humanitarian organizations are now warning of a refugee crisis, as families flee affected conflict zones."

"And finally, what's the government's advice to all our listeners?"

"For now, Parliament is urging calm. People should stay informed from trusted sources and be prepared for potential disruptions, but we're also hearing rumours there are plans to raise the national threat level to 'substantial' which means an attack is likely. Security is being raised across the UK with an increased military presence in key areas across the country. The Prime Minister has assured the public that contingencies are in place to safeguard against an attack, but acknowledges that these are uncertain times for everyone."

"It's them isn't it..." JJ interrupted the anchor as he thanked their London correspondent for their report. It was the first time he spoke since getting in the car. "It's the cult. They're behind all this, aren't they..."

Peter nodded solemnly as he turned his attention back to the radio.

"Stay tuned to Hert FM as we bring you regular updates on this global crisis. Now in local news, the police are

currently conducting a county-wide manhunt for a suspect wanted in connection with the brutal murder of nine highly decorated police officers earlier this evening, along with the suspected kidnapping of five local children. Police have identified the suspect as Peter Higginsworth, famed author and now lecturer at St Swithun's School in Shawbrook. Considered armed and extremely dangerous, the public is being urged not to approach him but to call 999 immediately if they see anything suspici..."

"*Click!*"

Peter turned the radio off, gingerly eased back into his chair, and then let out a deep sigh.

"Well, I guess there's your answer..." He wheezed, trailing off when he noticed Tommy hurrying back to the car. He had a black Nike sports bag thrown over his shoulder and was hugging a big brown cardboard box.

"What are we gonna do now?" JJ whispered, almost to himself. "What are we gonna do without M?"

"She's coming back." Zach answered doggedly from the backseat as Tommy opened the boot and dumped his stuff.

"She's gonna find us like she always does. She has something... of mine... Something that she can use. She'll find us, I know she will..."

"But how's she gonna find us if we're on the run? How's she gonna know where to go?" This was now the most JJ had spoken since his mother died and his voice sounded fragile, as if it might shatter in a heartbeat. "Where are we gonna go?"

"We need to go back to the bunker..." Peter declared. There was no point beating about the bush anymore.

"Wait, what?" JJ's voice hardened as Peter's bombshell jarred him from his lethargy. "We can't go back there...that's suicide."

"We have no other choice. We won't last long like this out in the open, so we need somewhere to lie low while we heal..."

"But what about the cult?"

"It's a risk, but a calculated one..." Peter presented his case to anyone who was listening.

"Since Grady has now gone rogue, I think it's safe to assume he hasn't told anyone else about the bunker. If he did, the place would've been crawling alive with disciples when we left. Now I'm not suggesting we stay there. Dr Foster had a book; a directory of others like us. I say we reach out to the people in that book and see who'll take us in, at least until we can get back on our feet. Kane needs proper medical attention, as do I. There's nowhere else to run to, and with me now wanted for murder, I can't so much as buy a chocolate bar without giving away our location... that's if they haven't already frozen all my assets. I just can't see any other way..."

"What's wrong?"

Tommy slipped back inside the car and immediately picked up on the weird energy.

"Nothing...we can talk about it later. You don't have a hat in that bag, do you?" Peter couldn't afford to be spotted as they drove through town to get to Drayton.

"No, but I have something else..." Tommy was holding a shiny green plastic folder with a handful of papers inside.

He rifled through its contents and then pulled an old polaroid picture out; its edges curling with age. He held it face down on his thigh and turned to Peter in earnest.

"This might sound crazy..." he trembled, "But then again, after what I've seen tonight, maybe it won't." He nervously played with the corner of the picture in search of his next words.

"I found this in my grandad's files...it's a photograph, taken in 1974 in a restaurant not far from here...my grandad's in the picture, but the other two people with him have remained a mystery...until today that is..."

Tommy turned the picture over like a magician pulling an ace from the pack, then handed it over. The hairs on the back of Peter's neck gave a standing ovation and sent an ice-cold shiver scuttling down to his aching tailbone.

Feeling heavier than it had any right to in his trembling hand, he stared at the sepia toned photo in total disbelief.

There, in the middle of its sun-blanched ivory frame, smiling between two strangers and not a day older than the last time he saw her, was Meridia.

97

Venules of putrid water snaked down the cracks in the limestone wall, pooling into stagnant puddles that shimmered taupe beneath the solitary shaft of light.

Thick with the acrid stink of mould and rot, the abandoned tunnel was a labyrinth of decay, caked in decades of filth and muck. Its only inhabitant, the occasional cockroach, skittering in and out of hidden crevasses in search of its next meal. Its only inhabitant that was until now...

"Kaff...kaff..."

Coughing and spluttering, the scraggy shadow clawed its way across the rust-coloured cobbles like a wounded animal until it reached the murky water's edge.

"Drip...drop...drip...drop..."

Staring down into the puddle of filth, Silas Grady watched with gruesome fascination as each drip-drop ripple distorted his malformed grin into something even more hideous.

His skin was a montage of charbroiled flesh and craggy,

555

marbleized bone. With a gaping hole where his nose once was and half his mouth melted into a permanent skeletal sneer, he was the stuff of every child's nightmare.

Was this what the witch prophesied all along?

Not a mythical monster plucked from the pages of a grim fairy-tale as he'd been told, but a brutally burned and disgustingly disfigured one now forced to walk the earth in limbo. He would have the Grand Master's skull as an ashtray for what he did and burn the town of Shawbrook down to the ground.

"Drip...drop...drip...drop..."

A blistering rage swelled within as a string of drool leaked from the congealed blood clinging to his nasal cavity and wrinkled his reflection further, turning his sneer into a scowl. He welcomed the fury in with open arms, embracing the flames as they boiled his blood and poisoned his mind.

All-consumed, his body tingled with a voracious wrath. A power beyond anything he ever felt before. Then he saw it, burning in the depths of his vile reflection, blazing red orbs where ocean blue once was, and his metamorphosis was finally complete.

Somewhere in the dank and dismal catacombs beneath Cold Christmas, another monster was forged from darkness.

EPILOGUE

It's been 18 months and 12 days since you disappeared M, and so much has changed. We thought things were bad before, but nothing could've prepared us for what we face now. The sky is literally on fire, just like you said it would be.

When the war broke, all the major capitals around the world fell to the cult within a matter of weeks and our entire civilization went to shit. We blamed the Russians. The Russians blamed the US. The US blamed China. Every country pointed their finger, and their missiles, at someone different and now all that's left is a smouldering pile of rubble.

Peter called it the greatest magic trick of all time. Er... 'A carefully orchestrated act of annihilation, centuries in the making, that no-one saw coming. Except for a few.' He still loves his dramatic speeches.

The directory saved us. The day we lost you, we were down and out with no place to go. But that list; it gave us hope. Pretty soon we found others, just like us...and although there weren't as many as we'd hoped for; we survived. Now that's all we do. Survive. Barely.

We live mostly in the shadows, drifting from town to town, but never straying far from Cold Christmas. Crooked House is still at the centre of everything, but don't worry, I'm never allowed to wander too close.

I'm on the move most of the time; moving from the burnt-out ruins of one street to the next. Keeping me moving keeps me safe; at least that's what everyone tells me. I still can't believe how many people are putting their lives on the line; just for me. I just can't wrap my head around it.

It's lonely out on the road, but I can feel you checking in on me from time to time. Sometimes it's like you're right here with me. It's as if you know when I'm at my lowest, when I'm missing Kane and the others. You always find a way to lift me up, and give me hope. Even now when you're so far away.

While I lie low and stay out of sight, Kane and Peter are out there in the warzone, looking for the one thing that could help end this nightmare: for good. Dr Foster was onto something with his research, so now that's what they spend all their time working on. The Eye of Corvus. It's here somewhere; they just need to find it, but it's so hard.

Nowhere is safe anymore. The Children of the Shadows control everything. They have an entire army of disciples and weavers scouring the streets, looking for me and anyone else who might stand in their way. There's so much death and destruction, M, everywhere I look. I feel almost numb to it, like it's become normal.

You wouldn't believe some of the things I've seen on the road. Terrible things. Sometimes I wonder if we're even worth saving. That maybe this is just the end we deserve.

It's not like we didn't have a couple of million years to get our shit together.

Sorry. Kane keeps telling me to stay positive, but it's just so hard at the moment. Never knowing where I'm going to be one day to the next. Never knowing if today is the day I'm gonna get caught.

The house we're staying in tonight had a family already in it when we got here. All of them murdered in their beds. Their brains bashed in, including their kids, while they slept. Toddlers M. All for some stale bread and a few tins of beans. It's not just the cult killing people now, there are others. Vultures, we call them. Not on anyone's side, but their own. Prowling the streets, raiding houses and killing anything that breathes like a bunch of savages. And then there's Grady. We still don't know where he is or what he's up to. He keeps leaving messages. Scrawled in blood. Most of them are for the Grand Master and his minions, but some are for us, too. He's even more insane than he was before, and twice as deadly, but no-one has seen him since that day in room 4. No-one that's lived to tell the tale.

Sorry, Kane's right: I must stay positive. Peter says if we can cut off the head of the serpent, then maybe we can rebuild. Forge a new path. That's what keeps me going most days. That and you, of course.

JJ and Izzy are still doing what they can, but neither are the same people they were when you left. That day broke them in a million different ways. JJ's mostly quiet now and Izzy is scared of her own shadow.

We have a base that the cult doesn't know about, and they spend most of their time there, doing what they can to help. Behind the scenes. I miss them too. I miss us. The five of us, together. Back when we were fighting witches and monsters, at least we always had each other. The day you went missing took all that away from us. Sometimes it feels like the cult won that day without even knowing it. They took away our biggest advantage, our sacred bond. I know that sounds corny, but I don't know how else to explain it. That was always our superpower.

But while JJ and Izzy have taken a step back, others have stepped forward.

Alman is with us. The cult butchered his family, too. Turns out he's not such a dick after all. We picked him up on your old road. He was running from a weaver patrol. Said he thought he saw you in the rubble of your old house, but then you vanished like a ghost. Said you looked younger, like you did back when we were all at school. When there was a school. It's nothing but a graveyard these days; crawling with weavers, so we stay well clear.

None of us understand how time works, or what version of you will come back to us when you're ready, but I know you'll be home soon.

Tommy figured it all out. You were right about him. He's saved our skins plenty of times since the day we lost you, and if he's right about this, then I'll be seeing you again any day now. He showed us an old photo of you from the seventies. You're with his grandad and his psychic friend. We think she's the other seer and taking care of you while you're there. Once we figured that part, Tommy used his grandad's old journal and case notes to work out roughly how long you were stuck in the past for. It looks like you were there the entire time the demon was active, which must be ending soon, given how long you've been gone.

What?

Ok... I'm coming.

I have to go. Weavers have been spotted a couple of streets away, so this place isn't safe.

I'll keep sending these voice notes when I can, hoping I'll see two blue ticks one day. Then I'll know that you're back. Until then M...see you soon.

"AH, YOUNG LOVE..." GRADY ALLOWED ZACH'S MESSAGE to play out, then turned to face Meridia.

Quivering and covered in blood, her face was a picture of torment as she sat gagged and shackled to the mottled wall of his underground lair. Seeing his face for the first time, she flinched, as everyone did, then scampered backwards like a crab until the rusty chain around her neck clinked to full stretch.

Wincing from the pain, she tried to scream again, but the sound was quickly swallowed by the musty rag he shoved down her throat. He watched her for a moment, puffing and panting on all fours as she tried not to choke on her tears. How could such a pathetic little brat take the demon down twice?

"You were a fool to come back, seer..." he hissed. "You should've stayed in the past. But seeing as you are here now, it would be a shame not to get the band back together, don't you think..."

Grady pulled his knife out from beneath his cloak and squeezed its handle with blanched knuckles. He inhaled a long, deep lungful of mould and mildew as the warm burnished wood creaked in his palm and sent its sinister vibration crawling up his skin. The prickly tingle of goosebumps was electric. Each tiny spark feeding the growing sneer curling at the edges of his seared lips.

"I wonder how much persuading it'll take for young lover boy to come rescue you? I've been wanting to add his skull to my collection for some time now...and yours, of course."

"*Click-click*"

The camera flash erupted like a lightning strike, freezing the terror in Meridia's ocean-blue stare, and Grady watched with glee as they widened at the whooshing sound of him sending the picture to her precious Zach.

"*Grrmph!*" She tried to scream again, this time in rage, and he saw a flicker of raw energy flash across her eyes, like the promise of a storm on the horizon.

There she was.

The famous demon killer.

He couldn't wait to peel her pasty skin back whilst she lay kicking and screaming on his table.

Oh, what fun they were going to have together!

AUTHOR'S NOTE

Dawn of the Demon was always destined to be my ode to the slasher genre, but when it came to deciding on which type of killer I wanted to run with I was surprisingly torn.

Like a lot of horror fans born in the 70s, I spent most of my teenage years on a steady diet of slasher movies. Just old enough to experience the golden age of horror as it unfolded, I worked my way through the major franchises of the time and found myself inexplicably drawn to killers who led with their personality, versus those who hid behind a mask.

Wes Craven's Freddy Krueger and his criminally underrated Horace Pinker were among my favourites growing up. With razor-sharp wit, their quips were every bit as cutting as their blades. There was something about their levity that appealed to my own dark sense of humour, and although Pinker never got the franchise he deserved, and Freddy eventually descended into self-parody, Craven set a new standard for the anti-hero which has often been imitated but never matched.

That's not to say the silent stalkers didn't have their own

unique appeal, and John Carpenter's Halloween still holds a special place in my heart due to The Shape's primal nature. There is something deeply unsettling about a relentless killer who commits acts of sheer brutality without reason or conscience. An unstoppable force of evil, Michael Myers has an intimidating presence like no other, so when it came to writing this book, I felt I couldn't do the slasher genre justice without capturing some of those more primordial qualities.

As a result, Dawn of the Demon features two distinctly different killers who combine to create the darkest instalment of the series so far, and one with the biggest body count.

I hope you have as much fun navigating the twists and turns as I did concocting them.

ACKNOWLEDGMENTS

As always, I'd like to thank Raymond and Adam at Wicked Ink for their continued support and encouragement. Your insight and guidance have helped me improve with each book and I wouldn't be doing this without you.

I'd like to thank my son for being a crash test dummy for some of the most gruesome kills I've ever created. I hope when you come to read this finished version it doesn't give you too many nightmares.

I'd like to thank my wife for putting up with my constant ramblings about complex plot details and character arcs. You have the patience of a saint.

I'd like to thank fellow author Holly Knightley for being a sounding board and constant cheerleader for the series. Your continued support means the world to me.

Finally, I'd like to thank my good friend Lance. Despite your fear of spiders, when I mentioned the concept of weavers, you leapt at the chance to appear in this book. I'm sure you had no idea what you were getting yourself into at the time, so I hope you enjoy your contribution to the Crooked Tales cannon. That said, if you think this book is going to help you overcome your phobia, you've got another think coming.

ABOUT THE AUTHOR

© Chris Harrison

Chris Harrison, born in North London, is not just a writer, producer, and author of the *Crooked Tales Series*; he's a storyteller on a mission. Graduating from Middlesex University with a degree in Film, Chris turned his fascination with the art of storytelling into a lifelong exploration of literary and cinematic horror. Having previously written for film and education, he's now dedicated to realizing a dream—crafting immersive worlds filled with spine-tingling terror for a young adult audience.

Chris's creations fuse classic supernatural themes with contemporary urban mythology, re-imagining our deepest fears for a new generation of horror enthusiasts.

www.chris-harrison.com

instagram.com/chrisharrison1975
threads.com/@chrisharrison1975
tiktok.com/@chris.harrison75
x.com/CHarrison22975